The Carob Tree

Ron Benjamin

ISBN : 1-4196-5210-9

To order additional copies, please contact us.
BookSurge, LLC
www.booksurge.com
1-866-308-6235
orders@booksurge.com

The Carob Tree

DEDICATION

Yeshua (Jesus), Sovereign Lord. Words on paper are inadequate to express what you wrote in blood at Calvary.

My precious wife Suzi: without her belief in me, this novel would still be on the shelf in our closet.

Bea Carlton, an outstanding editor, novelist and a great encouragement.

"It was difficult for Sarah to grasp that all this had happened in the space of a few minutes or that it had happened at all. But she quickly realized that her life had just been miraculously spared. While attempting to relax and breathe normally again, Sarah's body convulsed in grateful sobs.

Oblivious to her own bleeding and physical pain, she turned her head and stared incredulously at the most baffling sight she'd ever seen. Surely her eyes were deceiving her. "

FOREWORD

By February 7, 1921, when Sarah Anna Rubenstein was born, storm clouds were looming large and dark for Jewish people. Her first seven years were lived in one of the last remaining *shtetls* of Eastern Europe, the little town of Tishevits, Lublin province, in Southeast Poland. *Shtetls* were Jewish farming communities that existed mainly between the years of 1800-1914. The towns served to keep the more pious Jews separate from non-Jews. The Jews preferred it that way. It wasn't so much that they feared the Christians themselves, but rather they feared the Christian religion.

For the people of the *Diaspora*, *shtetls* were, in a real sense, a home away from home. In *shtetls*, Jews learned ethics and values by immersing themselves in their religious heritage. Dependence on one another as well as diligent study of the Torah-Talmud were main ingredients. Charity was also stressed. The small towns became self maintained with their own set of laws and court systems. They were like mystical havens and, though void of luxuries and conveniences, they brought people of like mind together in a shared common experience. In *shtetls*, Jews could maintain their integrity as a people chosen to deliver the laws of God, and to celebrate their passion for life.

Tishevits—with all its unique and colorful characters, its six wooden bridges leading across the Hutshve River which surrounded the town, and its many abandoned churchyards and cemeteries—was an agricultural settlement that could arouse any child's imagination.

The most exciting days Sarah could remember were the Wednesday afternoons when the unpaved market area, empty six days a week, suddenly exploded with teeming crowds of people hawking every possible type of merchandise. Shops of every description encircled the town; shops dealing in textiles, leather goods, shoes and hats, fruit and meat, furs and pelts. Some stores were even turned into granaries. Pharmacies offered varieties of mysterious concoctions and elixirs.

On market day, pungent aromas permeated the town. Peasant wagons loaded with produce and livestock, arrived early and set up shop. The animals to be sold were frequently horses, cows and chickens.

Sarah delighted in the festival of haggling, curious as to what new addition would become a fixture in the Rubenstein household, and fascinated and intrigued by the bartering procedures. Every sale concluded with the clap of hands. Living in Tishevits until 1928 were some of the happiest years of Sarah's life.

For almost twenty centuries, since their Temple was destroyed in 70 A.D., the Jewish people survived in spite of themselves, often living in contained environments like *shtetls* or ghettos. Persecutions should have destroyed them. History recorded that most civilizations once scattered, such as the Assyrians and Chaldeans, were assimilated into other cultures within the space of fifty years.

Yet, miraculously, the Jews had survived almost 2,000 years as a distinct race. They survived because their spirit never left them, partly due to their strict adherence to their faith and partly because the rabbis and teachers refused to let it happen. Consequently, the rabbis and teachers always held the positions of highest esteem.

But when she was seven, the economy became very weak in Tishevits. Thievery and violence increased and the use of brass knuckles became more prevalent. For this reason, Sarah's parents decided to leave and emigrate to Frankfurt am Main in Germany. There, Avron and Leah opened a small watch repair shop, with Avron doing carpentry work on the side.

At first, young Sarah was saddened by moving to such a large city with over a half million people. But once settled, she, like her parents, was surprised at how easily Jews had integrated into German society. In fact, most Jews living there considered themselves Germans first, Jews second.

But the seeds of anti-Semitism had already been planted through the preaching of German oriental scholar Paul de Lagarde, the neo-Darwinist philosopher Eugene Duhring, and racist journalist, William Marr. All of them exploited the myth of Aryan supremacy and reminded the German people of their heritage of Teutonic glory founded on the principles of worshipping false gods.

To be sure, there were other purveyors of the cult of racism who were attracted to German philosophy and militarism. Chief among them was Englishman Houston Stewart Chamberlain who maintained that the German people were indeed the "master race" and, by contrast the Jews were an inferior "bastard" race. But in 1928, when the

Rubensteins arrived in Frankfurt am Main, the seeds had not yet taken root. The so-called illegitimate race of people had instead distinguished themselves.

Though the Jews were less than one percent of the total German population, their numbers included businessmen, lawyers, writers, professors, physicians, scientists and composers. In fact, several among them had won Nobel Prizes. In large measure, pre-Hitler Germany reflected so many of the ideals similar to the precepts of Judaism that it caused many Jews to neglect their faith entirely. They not only assimilated into the German culture and lifestyle, their accomplishments as a minority became a source of pride for German leaders.

As in Judaism, German writers and philosophers, for the most part, believed and emphasized tolerance and respect for others. They also placed an emphasis on love and justice. But Germany had a thorn in her flesh that rubbed her skin raw and was growing into a festering open wound. She had suffered a humiliating defeat in World War I and her economy was in shambles. The American depression in 1929 spilled over into Europe and only served to worsen Germany's financial woes.

When the nation's unemployment rate climbed to a staggering six million people by 1932, the seeds of acrimony finally rooted and there began an increased stirring of hatred and discontent. Something—or someone—was to blame! An often ridiculed and fringe group, the German Workers' Party, offered up a culprit—"the Jew!" Seizing the opportunity, they changed their name to the more encompassing National Socialist German Workers' Party, and contended for the hearts and minds of growing numbers of dispirited and disenfranchised people. The party soon became more commonly known by its acronym: NAZI. Its spell-binding orator and leader proclaimed, "By defending myself against the Jews, I am doing the work of the Lord." He told the lie long enough and loud enough that many in Germany finally believed it!

AND THE PRINCE OF DARKNESS GOT A FOOTHOLD—On January 30, 1933, the Nazi Party took control and Adolph Hitler was appointed Chancellor of Germany. The dark side of the soul of man soon emerged. Fueled by haranguing, hate-filled speeches and a poisoned spirit, with the Fuhrer himself taking the lead, Germany turned within and began to gorge itself with a cannibalistic bloodthirsty rage.

The jackbooted, goose-stepping, brown-shirted *Sturmabteilungen* (storm troopers) soon began their funeral march across the German cities and hinterlands. Their dirges were played for communists, gypsies, homosexuals, Serbs, cripples, Jehovah's Witnesses, the mentally ill and street beggars. Their real hatred, however, was reserved for the "People of the Devil," the Jews.

The storm troopers spewed forth a whole new set of ideals, all emanating from the mouth of the bone-chilling, messianic-like dragon named Hitler. Almost immediately, kiosks all over Germany were plastered with notices to boycott Jewish businesses. Leaflets and placards depicted Jews as having rat-like faces with exaggerated noses and fangs of dripping blood. The two great contradictions were, one: that the so-called "racially inferior" and "bastardized" people were condemned for being just the opposite—an obviously "cultured and distinct race"; and, two: that the inferior race of Jews, that flawed, defective lineage of Abraham, was responsible for Germany's failures because they had become too prominent and successful in a nation of allegedly superior Aryan people.

But hate overcame logic and the then-possessed dragon-Fuhrer appealed to man's worst sin—the sin of pride. Influenced by yet another of the coterie of racial mythologists, the demented Lanz von Liebenfels and his visions for a blond master race, Hitler held out to willing Germans the chance to participate in Liebenfels' delusion. They could put the stamp of approval on the Teutonic people as being the only ones truly created in God's image.

. . . AND THE PRINCE OF DARKNESS TOLD EVE TO . . . EAT OF THE FRUIT, THAT YOU WILL NOT SURELY DIE, BUT YOUR EYES WILL BE OPENED AND YOU WILL BE LIKE GOD . . .

. . . and the German people became like Eve and ate of the fruit yet a second time. And they knew good and evil . . . and they chose evil.

Soon the whole nation was inflamed with hatred for God's chosen. They sung frightful songs with blood-curdling refrains, "Oh what a glorious day it will be [Wenn Judenblut Von Messer Spritzt] when Jewish blood spurts from the knife." They renamed all the streets that had Jewish names and burned all the books written by Jews, or books by anyone which did not suit their taste. And, more incredulously, they rewrote some of the fairy tales. In the Nazi version, Sleeping Beauty was now the German nation. The handsome prince who kissed her and woke her was, of course, Adolph Hitler.

Their hatred spilled over into other nations as well. Anti-Semitism was on the rise in Austria, Greece, Yugoslavia, Italy and France...and in the United States. One ship, the St. Louis, with more than 900 Jewish refugees aboard, was turned away from Cuba although the refugees had landing certificates. On its way back to Europe, the St. Louis passed very close to Florida's shores but the U.S. Coast Guard was under government instructions not to let even one refugee jump ship. So the passengers returned to Europe, to Hungary, Belgium and France, and within a year, those countries fell to the Germans. Many of those passengers would die in the death vans, the ovens and the gas chambers of Auschwitz, Dachau, Buchenwald, Bergen-Belsen, Treblinka and others.

Another refugee ship left the country where hatred of Jews rivaled that of Germany. The SS Struma left Romania with 769 refugees aboard. They were first refused entrance into Turkey and later into British-owned Palestine. The passengers displayed a large sign, "Save Us," but no country would take them. After two months, a tugboat eventually took them out to icy waters where, on the following day, the ship sank. Seventy children were among the 768 who perished. Only one person survived.

So when the world went mad, Sarah's father, once a carpenter and now a watchmaker from the little *shtetl* of Tishevits, retreated back into the temple of his faith. In Avron Rubenstein's temple there were always saviors—a Moses confronting a Pharaoh, a Samson bringing down the temple of Dagon, a David taking on the giant of Gath. And "One day," Avron Rubenstein kept reminding his daughter, pointing to the heavens, "He will come—the Meshiach! He will put an end to all this madness!" And Sarah would pray with her beloved father that "one day" would come very soon. Or one day, there might be no more Jews.

. . . *AND THE PRINCE OF DARKNESS CONCLUDED HIS SUCCESSFUL MISSION. HE HAD INTOXICATED HIS PREY WITH A THIRST FOR POWER AND A DESIRE FOR IMMORTALITY. THEN HE ABANDONED HIS PREY IN THEIR DRUNKEN STUPOR TO FACE THEIR OWN RUINATION. EVEN THE DRAGON FUHRER WOULD EVENTUALLY TAKE HIS OWN LIFE. THE PRINCE OF DARKNESS THEN SLITHERED BACK INTO THE CATACOMBS OF HELL...CONTENT FOR A SEASON.*

Chapter 1

On Kristallnacht, later known among Jewish people as the Night of Broken Glass, seventeen year old Sarah Anna Rubenstein looked anxiously out the window of her home. "Why don't they come home?" she worried aloud. Her parents usually were home before dark, especially since all the disturbing talk against Jewish people had begun.

Suddenly she became aware of a strange, foreign sound, almost like a rumbling but quickly it became more pronounced. Her heart lurched with fear. Faraway shouts, crashing sounds and crackling that sounded like breaking glass filled the night air. A mob?

Terror threatened to engulf her but she fought it down. "I must warn Papa and Mama!" Fear beat in her throat as she flung open the door and raced down the street. Thankfully their small watch repair shop was not far!

Until this moment, despite the rising tide of anti-Semitism, despite the fact that hatred of Jews had become more virulent, she still had hope that everything would turn out all right, her hope centered in her belief in the goodness, intelligence and the reason of man.

Sarah had read of many great cities but she couldn't imagine that any were finer than the one she lived in, Frankfurt am Main. Hers was a historic city which boasted a great seaport, allowing it to be a transportation hub for much of Germany. It was a city of tremendous culture and diversity, a major publishing center and a place where many writers and philosophers congregated. Many trade-fairs were held there. In some ways, it was Germany's renaissance city. It was also a financial center, where the famous Rothchilds had grown to prominence.

When many of the smaller cities started deporting Jews, pronouncing themselves to be "friends of the Nazis" and "*Judenrein*" (free of Jews), Frankfurt am Main was where many Jews chose to come. *Certainly, if anywhere*, Sarah thought, *Frankfurt am Main would be the most logical place a civilized people would come back to their senses and cast away their hate and resentment against other humans.*

For seventeen years her world had been wrapped in a tight, neat little bundle. Now abruptly it was crashing in on her. The mercy she so earnestly petitioned God for, the prayers she so diligently prayed along with her father, had apparently fallen on deaf ears.

Sarah turned the corner and her horrified eyes took in the devastation on the usually peaceful and busy street. All up and down the street, shop windows were shattered, the sidewalks covered in glass and debris. Panic-stricken, she stumbled the few remaining doors to her parent's shop, slipping and skidding on broken glass and mortar, and panting for breath. She could scarcely take in what her eyes told her. The door hung drunkenly on one hinge and only jagged pieces of glass clung to the window frames. Her trembling hands pressed against her pounding heart, she felt that her heart would burst from her body. Where were her parents...oh, dear God...they had to be all right!

A strangled sob rose up from deep inside, as she crunched over the broken glass into the shop. Even before she saw the twisted, blood-drenched forms of her parents crumpled on the floor, she knew in her heart she was too late. Her kindly parents who would never have harmed a living soul, lay on the floor in a pool of blood, in the wreckage of their neat shop, bludgeoned to death.

Sudden blackness and faintness swept over her and she turned quickly away. Steadying herself with a hand on a counter she retched until she was exhausted. Then straightening she began to scream and wail at the top of her lungs. Clenching her fists, Sarah shook them at the heavens, yelling, "Where were you, God? Where were you!?"

Finally she quieted and tried to pull herself together. Dazed and overwrought by emotion, she peered about the shop and saw that most of the merchandise had been smashed or looted. Debris was strewn everywhere. All the windows had been smashed. From the street lamp outside, thousands of shards of broken glass from inside the shop cast off and reflected brilliant and eerie luminescent flashes of light.

In the distance, she could still hear the crazed and riotous crowds voicing invectives towards Jewish shop owners. With the multitudes cheering them on, the tumult seemed to be growing louder. "I must get out of here and find a place to hide," she said in a shaking voice "but first..." Sarah found an old pea-green colored blanket and placed it over her parents' bodies, lying next to each other.

She was suddenly startled by the gravely sound of glass being crunched beneath someone's footsteps. Were they going to get her too? Terror again gripped her heart as she turned to find two large German youths stepping through the doorway, both with insidious and malevolent grins on their faces. One of the young men, lantern-jawed, with powerful looking arms, was slapping a huge stick in the palm of his hand. He taunted, "The bloodsucking pigs deserved to die, you Juden-bitch!"

In her fury and wrath, Sarah flew at him, flailing her fists, kicking and clawing, and screaming at the top of her voice. She managed to draw blood from his face, but then he drew the stick back and brought it down against the back of her head. Stunned by the blow, a swirl of lights spiraled before her eyes as she fell.

Still dazed, their vile epithets ringing in her ears, Sarah strove to rise when she was felled a second time by a large boot slamming against her forehead. With the room spinning, she felt as though she were in a vortex, and attempted to focus her eyes, all the while realizing the futility of trying to get back up. Each time one of the young men stepped closer, she inched backwards. While still scooting on the floor, she gulped hard as she watched the muscular youth toss his stick aside and take a large switchblade from his back pocket.

Both her attackers had deranged looks about them, their eyes wide and bulging. Petrified with fear, Sarah continued moving backward on her haunches, her heart in her throat. Then to her surprise, her right hand touched something hard and metal. She cautiously wrapped her fingers around the object which turned out to be a tire iron someone had apparently thrown through a window. Gripping it firmly in her hand, she brought it quickly forward, and in rapid motion brandished it back and forth across her body as she slowly staggered to her feet.

The surprised youths stepped back a few feet and spread apart to come back at her from different angles. Sarah held the tire iron at waist level and with both hands continued to wave it menacingly in a frantic attempt to discourage them. They stalked her as she tried to keep both in sight. The knife-wielder then boldly stepped forward and stood but a few feet away. He again taunted her.

"Come on, Juden slut! We just want to have a little fun and then we'll let you go."

In a state of panic, Sarah realized she had lost sight of the second youth who had skulked behind her. Before she could turn around, she felt the upper portion of her arms grabbed and held in a vise-like grip. "I got her! I got the *kike*," he screamed.

In her struggle to break free, Sarah felt a sharp pain ripping across her left shoulder and noticed that part of her blouse had been cut away. Blood was flowing from where the knife had penetrated her skin. In total desperation, her arms being securely held from in back with the tire iron still clasped in her hands, Sarah turned, twisted and kicked out with her legs with all the strength she had within her. Noticing that the arms of the youth grappling her had slid slightly upwards, she lowered her chin and was able to lock her teeth on his right hand. She bit deeply into his flesh. Cursing savagely, he cried out and sprang backwards.

Her arms finally free, an enraged and hysterical Sarah instinctively whirled about, whipping the tire iron furiously in every direction. Each powerful thrust of the unwieldy heavy weapon wrenching an exhausted grunt from her, until shockingly it struck solid with a tremendous *CLAP*!

The peculiar, discordant sound sent shivers down her spine. Unwittingly, she lowered her weapon as she beheld the youth who had grabbed her. His own expression took on one of horror as he instantaneously brought both hands up to cover his now bleeding, gaping eye-socket. Seeming to be in deep shock, with blood spurting between his fingers, the youth ran, screaming hysterically into the darkened streets. Sickened and stunned by what happened, Sarah allowed the tire iron to slip from her grasp and onto the floor, making a loud clanging sound.

Feeling lightheaded and weak, Sarah turned ever so slowly and brought her hands to the side of her face. Her principal attacker, his friend injured, now appeared more wild-eyed and vengeful than before! Brandishing the knife, the muscular youth swiped purposefully and viciously at Sarah's face. Each time, she jerked her head backwards, and each time the pointed edge of the blade missed her face by inches!

She was totally defenseless, stepping precipitously and blindly backwards over piles of debris. Her assailant sneered at her while making sport of her predicament. Her foot became tangled in a loose cord and while frantically trying to extricate it, she lost her balance and cried out as she fell backwards to the floor!

Removing her foot from the cord, Sarah scurried back on all fours like a trapped animal, but succeeded only in maneuvering herself into a corner. Weak and paralyzed with fright, she trembled in dreaded anticipation of what was about to happen. Moaning, she curled up in a fetal position by raising her knees up and covering her face with her arms.

She knew she was about to be slashed or killed, possibly both, and her heart beat so loud she thought it would burst. (She hoped it would, so her terrible ordeal would be over.) She closed her eyes, allowing herself only to see the ominous shadow of her attacker as he lowered himself to one knee and lurched forward over her body. He grabbed her left arm and pulled her closer.

"Come to Klaus, Judenschwein. You should not have to suffer long. But unfortunately, Jew-pig, because of my friend, I will now have to fix your face permanently."

He rested the cold-bladed, razor-sharp edge of the knife on Sarah's upper cheekbone, and scraped it down the side of her face in deliberate fashion. She was jolted by the sharp, stinging pain on the lower side of her left jaw. She instinctively slapped a hand to her face, feeling the stream of blood there.

With one of her legs, she feebly attempted to kick her attacker away and again he derisively mocked her. He was the most cruel, diabolical and sadistic human being she had ever encountered. Again, she wished she were already dead. Despairingly, she wondered why she had to be put through this endless nightmare and torture.

Suddenly, and without warning, there came an explosive rushing sound, followed by a wicked and powerful <u>CRACK</u> of something being struck by tremendous force. Still too fearful to look, she then heard a sickening, guttural moan. Even with her eyes shut, she sensed that now two shadows stood over her. Had the other man returned?

Mustering the courage to open her eyes, Sarah was astonished to see her despised antagonist laboring to stand up. His previously, square-jawed and unblemished face had become strangely distorted and his legs were wobbly and unsteady as he barely managed to stagger to his feet. Then she saw that the entire left side of his face was split from mouth to ear and was turning into a reddish-purplish ooze! He stumbled sideways as he started turning around, the switchblade still in his hand. Before he could completely turn, however, the large thick wooden weapon again came whistling through the air. Again it struck viciously against his face, snapping his head sharply back and causing him to spew forth blood and teeth. The magnitude of the blow split the heavy and honed-handled board in half and part of it went zooming across the room.

Sarah kept her eyes trained on the malignant, black-hearted creature, who only a moment ago had tried to maim her. His now grotesquely misshapened face revealed a missing upper lip along with several broken and dangling teeth. His nose pressed upwards and sideways against his cheekbone. All the bones on the left side of his skull were so badly pulverized that he appeared to have only half of a face. In stunned silence and disbelief, she watched intently as his eyes rolled back in his head and the wounded and disfigured human being then fell face first into a bloody heap on the floor.

It was difficult for Sarah to grasp that all this had happened in the space of a few minutes or that it happened at all. But she quickly realized that her life had just been miraculously spared. While attempting to relax and breathe normally again, Sarah's body convulsed in grateful sobs.

Oblivious to her own bleeding and physical pain, she turned her head and stared incredulously at the most baffling sight she'd ever seen. Surely her eyes were deceiving her. Then the shadow stepped out of the darkness, into the light, and there was no longer any doubt. Her deliverer was a young, blond German soldier!

"My God!" her intercessor exclaimed. "What have we done?"

Sarah attempted to respond. "Who are you? Why . . .?"

"Sweet Jesus! You're bleeding badly," he exclaimed.

Like a newborn colt on gimpy legs, Sarah tried to get up, but fell. On her second try, she stood long enough to edge herself closer to her dead parents. Numbed, and in a state of shock, she held on to the counter with one hand while extending the other. She reached for the blanket she had earlier placed over her parents' bodies thinking in her irrational state of mind that perhaps they weren't really dead. Her knees then buckled and her legs gave way as she fell across the part of the blanket covering her mother.

Clutching the lifeless form, Sarah again gave way to a torrent of emotional grief. "Mama-a-a-a! Papa-a-a-a!"

She lay there for several seconds, sobbing uncontrollably until she felt two strong but gentle hands pulling her up by the shoulders. "No," the voice said. "Looking at them that way is not the way you should remember them."

Sarah's body still heaved with incessant sobs as her rescuer, after helping her to her feet, turned her around to face him. With tear-stained eyes, she looked up at him, and he returned her gaze with a look of compassion. "They're in God's hands now. They'll be okay."

"What God?" Sarah shouted back angrily.

"Come," was his soft reply. "We must not be found here with your attacker. We must go quickly." He stepped closer. "Let me see if I can do something to stop the blood on your cut face. He dabbed at the blood with a clean handkerchief, then spoke regretfully," I cannot stop the bleeding," he said. "It will have to be stitched." He then pulled off his necktie and pressed it tightly beneath the gash on her chin, then wrapped it around her head and knotted it on top. He secured it so tightly that it caused her to grimace, but he cautioned her against removing it.

"There," he said. "Now it looks like you have a bad toothache." He smiled, then glanced quickly toward the doorway. Immediately, she sensed why. It would have been very difficult for him to explain to his superiors, how he, a member of the German *Sturmabteilungen*, a corporal in the SA, avowed enemies of the Jews, who were known for their attacks on Jews in restaurants and synagogues, was instead saving the life of a Jew.

She could see a look of concern on his face. *My slashed chin must be pretty bad*, she thought, then repeated her question. "You didn't answer me. I am a Jew. Why are you helping me?"

Again the soldier avoided her question, but turned and walked a short distance away to pick up something from the floor. Shaking off the broken glass from the blue woolen coat that had belonged to Sarah's mother, he draped it over Sarah's partially bare shoulders. For some reason, she felt a tremendous calm in his presence.

"You didn't answer me," Sarah repeated. Still the young blond-haired soldier ignored her query. He just looked back at her, extended his arm and motioned her forward.

"Come now, we must hurry. It is dangerous here for both of us. This one, and the injured boy I saw running and screaming, were attempting to prove their worthiness to become members of Himmler's notorious Death Head Units."

"What do you mean?" Sarah asked.

"The Death Head Units are the ones in control of the concentration camps that have been set up. Tonight they are rounding up many Jews to fill the camps. These two were being recruited as guards, provided they could demonstrate the required brutality."

"He was going to kill me, wasn't he?"

"Yes, but only after he made you suffer."

Sarah's voice quivered, "Corporal, he *did* make me suffer. Why are people so cruel?"

"I'm sorry," he answered. "I don't have time to explain my theories and there are others nearby equally as cruel. We must go quickly now. We are both in much danger if we are found."

Sarah cautiously stepped across the debris and took the soldier's extended hand and he led her out the back door into the alley. The smoke still lingered in the air and cast a heavy pall over the entire city, carrying with it the unmistakable smell of death. Sarah almost gagged, the pungent odor was so strong. The young German soldier, who appeared to be in his early twenties, shook his head. "They loot, burn and destroy not only the shops," he said, "but all the synagogues as well."

As they hurried along the alley, the soldier—alert and watchful, asked "What is your name?"

"Sarah."

"Sarah, I will try to explain, but there is little time to waste. First I want you to know that I am not like the rest. My own parents convinced me that Hitler would be Germany's savior. So, like my father, I joined the SA. My father was an engineer and joined as an officer. He had been with the Kaiser's Army in the last war and losing that war was difficult for him to live with. He was a very proud man and saw in the Fuhrer a chance for redemption. He also felt that Hitler would bring about great social and economic changes.

"In June of 1934, my father, along with other high-ranking SA officers, were murdered by members of Himmler's and Goering's Schutzstaffel. To make matters worse, many—including my father— were then branded as traitors and as soldiers who had no morals. Nothing could have been further from the truth. But then what does the Fuhrer and his henchmen know about truth? It opened my eyes. Since then I have done much soul searching. I have been reading the writings of a man named Dietrich Bonhoeffer. He is a German theologian. Have you heard of him?"

"No," Sarah replied curiously.

The young man continued. "I heard him speak once when he was directing a training college at Finkenwalde near Stettin. He has long spoken out against the Fuhrer, yet he is but 34 years old. Bonhoeffer believes the Christian church is here to serve the world, not to make laws against the Jews. He regards morality as centered within the individual. Morality, according to Bonhoeffer, is based on love, not law, and it cannot be legislated. It is also his belief that Hitler is evil and will lead Germany to its destruction.

"I believe, Sarah, as Bonhoeffer believes. So I do what I can, when I can. In the meantime, because of my father, I know I am being watched, and I am careful to act as the model soldier."

Sarah stood in total amazement, too shocked to speak. Perhaps her prayers for restored reason among those who hated her people weren't totally non-effectual. To hear this tall, handsome, very Aryan German soldier speak in this manner made the night even that much more unreal. All she could think was, *What a shocking contradiction to those who hate and promote it.*

The young soldier stopped suddenly. The terrible sounds of the mob could no longer be heard. Drawing her into the shadows of a gutted building, he pulled a pad from his pocket on which he scribbled some words. Tearing the paper from his pad, he pressed it into the palm of her hand. Looking anxiously in each direction, he instructed, "Sarah, you are not far from your destination now and I must leave you. Take this paper and go to the docks by the river front. There you will find a tavern called 'The Schooner' owned by a Frenchwoman named Forguet.

"Be very careful you are not seen. Many German soldiers and seamen frequent the tavern. Most of the time they are loud, obnoxious and drunk. Go to the back door, knock twice, wait ten seconds, then knock three more times. Someone will answer and ask who you are. Slip this note under the door and they will let you in."

"Who will let me in?"

He spoke swiftly now, "Mrs. Forguet is usually in the front watching over her girls, making sure everyone is having a good time without anyone busting up the place. In the rear, there are sleeping quarters and a kitchen. One of two people will let you in. Either Ernest, a stalwart but slow-witted man, frightening to look at, but gentle as a lamb. He does many menial tasks about the loading docks but he also helps Mrs. Forguet. She was the first person to ever treat him like a human being and he worships her.

"The second person is Katalin Zichy, a girl younger than yourself. Although she is young, she is street-wise and very brave. Her parents, too, were killed and she was forced to live as a waif in the parks and the sewers for almost two years."

"Her parents were Jews?"

"No, they were Hungarian Orthodox Christians living in Weisbaden. Katalin's father was the priest of a small congregation of Hungarian émigrés, and he dared to speak out against the Fuhrer. It's not just the Jews, Sarah. Now it is anyone who disagrees. But go now. In that back room I spoke of is a concealed trap door and stairs that lead to a cellar. You will be hidden there until it is safe, then they will likely attempt to smuggle you into France as they have others. Go Sarah." He gave her a gentle push, then added, "And Sarah, you have neither seen me nor do you know me."

Sarah started to walk away but then did something that surprised even her. She rushed back, craned her neck and kissed the soldier on the cheek. She then drew her fingers over the name patch stitched above his brown shirt pocket. "But I do know you, Corporal Grauer," she spoke gratefully. "And I shall never forget you. You can be sure, though, that if I don't make it, I will choose to die before I reveal your name. My parents, Corporal, will you make sure they have a proper burial?"

"I will try."

"Will you find someone who can say Kaddish, the Jewish prayers for the dead?"

"I cannot promise but will try. Go now!" A trace of a smile crossed his lips and Sarah thought she saw his eyes grow moist. When they were a few steps apart, the German soldier called back to her, "Sarah?"

Sarah turned. "Yes, Corporal Grauer!"

For the space of several seconds they stared at each other. Then he finally broke the silence. "Shalom, Sarah."

Sarah bit down hard as the tears again began to flow. In a choked voice, she said goodbye to the only friend she had left in the world, a friend she felt she would never see again. "Shalom, my good friend."

Chapter 2

Exhausted, terrified and near collapse from pain and fear, Sarah eventually reached the tavern and gave the signal as Corporal Grauer had instructed her. He was right about Ernest. He had to be six foot six or seven and at least 300 pounds. He was almost totally bald except for some short curly strands of hair on the back part of his pate. Half of his teeth were missing and those that remained were either silver-capped or rotted. He was indeed very frightening to look at as well as slow of speech.

After Ernest opened the door to let her in, Sarah spotted a teen-age girl standing close by, to the side and slightly to the rear. She had an astonished look about her. *This must be Katalin*, Sarah thought.

"Oh my," the girl exclaimed as she rushed toward Sarah and patted the bloodied necktie with her hand.

"Ernest!" she shouted. "Hurry, get me some hot water, some bandages and stitching. We'll bring her downstairs to the cellar. Then go to the trunk where Mrs. Forguet keeps her extra dresses."

Ernest grunted obligingly, as if excited to be involved in a mission of such urgency.

"Don't be scared of Ernest. He's got a heart of gold and if asked, he would die to protect you. What is your name?"

"I am Sarah."

"Sarah, I am Katalin Zichy. I hope we will become friends."

Sarah was sure they would.

Ernest soon returned with all the medical gear. He then scooted aside a large wooden table and pulled back an oblong, red and brown braided rug. Beneath the rug was the concealed trap door that Corporal Grauer had mentioned. Sarah was then led down the stairwell into the darkened cellar, the only lighting provided by a drop cord from the ceiling with an attached light bulb.

Ernest was the last one down. He carried the bandages and then returned topside to again camouflage the trap door. He would remain upstairs and at first opportunity inform Mrs. Forguet of the new arrival.

Once in the cellar, seeing only one chair and table in the middle of the room, Sarah chose to sit on a concealed wooden bench bolted into the wall. Katalin asked for her coat and when she saw Sarah's shoulder, she shook her head in disbelief, now understanding fully the pure hell Sarah had been put through. Moved to compassion, she gripped Sarah's hands tightly in her own and squeezed them. After cleaning and wrapping the shoulder wound, she did what she could to clean and bandage the slashed chin. She would await Mrs. Forguet for assistance in the stitching.

Sarah was impressed by Katalin's striking beauty. Her hair was cut short and she had a smooth dark complexion and dark eyebrows. Her high cheekbones seemed perfectly sculpted to accentuate her radiant and deep blue eyes. She had a sharp upturned nose and her smile revealed gleaming even, white teeth. Sarah guessed her to be only about five foot, two inches, but the pixyish child-woman seemed younger than her fifteen years. Despite her attractiveness, Sarah was even more impressed by Katalin's remarkable maturity.

After Mrs. Forguet had come in and helped stitch up her chin, Sarah and Katalin talked well into the night. As Sarah came to know her better, she would learn of a young girl, extraordinary in every sense of the word. Not only was she bright and non-assuming, Katalin had purposely deflected any questions concerning her own personal tragedy. What Sarah learned later was that Katalin had also lost a younger brother to pneumonia, but after sharing that fact, Katalin reminded Sarah that, "God has dealt with my pain by giving me an extra measure of His love."

It was obvious to Sarah that Katalin's indomitable faith was at the very core of her being. Katalin's only failing that first night was her inability to convince a tragically despondent Sarah that God still indeed had a plan for her life. After the events of *Kristallnacht*, Sarah's entire outlook about life had taken an abrupt turn towards cynicism. "Well, I just don't agree with God anymore," she told Katalin. "And what's more," she added, "after what happened tonight, seeing my parents just lying there dead like that, I don't think I shall ever trust God again."

During her conversation that night, Katalin mentioned that she had twice seen the German soldier Sarah spoke of. He had followed the same procedure, knocking, then slipping the code-note under the door. Katalin had on each occasion let him in.

Although smiling politely, the soldier was resolute in manner, refusing to engage in conversation and demanding instead to speak with Mrs. Forguet quickly and in private. On the one occasion Katalin asked Mrs. Forguet about the soldier, her curt response was, "It's better you do not worry yourself about him," adding that the German soldier had his own reasons for despising the Fuhrer.

Sarah then shared with Katalin what she thought those reasons were. When she mentioned that the soldier was an admirer of a man named Bonhoeffer, Katalin's eyes lit up. "I should have known," she exulted.

The concrete floor and walls of the cellar were cold, dark and depressing with the dim lighting adding to the gloomy atmosphere. Whenever someone moved a finger or a hand, it emerged as enlarged black shadows, hovering over the walls like phantoms on a chalky gray canvas. Blankets stacked in a corner were the only concession made to providing comfort or warmth. A paint-chipped and splintered white door served as an entrance to the smallest of facilities, containing a cracked sink and barely usable commode.

When Sarah first entered the cellar and reached the bottom of the stairs, she noticed two adolescents sleeping next to the blanket pile. They were using some of the blankets as a mattress cushion and cover. When she asked Katalin who they were, she was taken aback by the answer.

Apparently there was no end to the debilitating mind set that had gripped Germany like a plague. They were children of gypsies, a ten-year-old boy and his eight-year-old sister. On the night of the heavy rains the previous week, they were found hiding as stowaways on one of the merchant vessels in dock.

The children were fortunate in not being turned over to the authorities who were looking for them. Their parents, like a growing number of others in the gypsy community, had sold them to the SS for use in medical experiments by the infamous Nazi doctor, Joseph Mengele. The siblings overheard their parents bartering them away in exchange for cash and guaranteed safety. Terrified at the prospect of being used as human guinea pigs, and equally fearful of being at the mercy of the heinous Dr. Mengele, the children ran off.

The French sea captain, Captain Demoucelle—who discovered the children during the downpour, hiding under one of the tarpaulins—was a long-time friend of Mrs. Forguet and he knew that she was harboring individuals at the Schooner and spiriting them out of Germany. He imposed on her to provide them food and shelter.

His motives weren't entirely pure but certainly couldn't be faulted. After eight years, he and his wife were still childless. He felt that perhaps fate had intervened. In two days the captain's ship was leaving port and, with the children's permission, he was taking them with him. What nobody including the captain knew at the time was that Sarah and Katalin would be on that same ship.

Finally the day came for the escape. The evening's adventure started about seven o'clock. Sarah and Katalin were busily knitting stocking caps for the children when they heard clamoring from upstairs. Suddenly, and with a loud noise, the trap door crashed open and Mrs. Forguet and Ernest quickly descended the stairs. Mrs. Forguet was breathing hard and appeared extremely nervous.

Ernest, meanwhile, made a beeline towards the bench. With his massive arms, he lifted it from one end, tilted it, then ripped it from the wall, leaving several gaping holes. The bench that had been boarded and shielded from the outside was hollowed out from the inside. That Ernest didn't take the time to unscrew the bolts indicated to Sarah that something was very wrong. The bench had served as a secret compartment.

Ernest grabbed at some clothing—nun's habits—and tossed them hastily across the floor. Stuffing a German Luger inside his belt, he then found a ledger which he quickly gave to Mrs. Forguet.

Last, but most important, Ernest cautiously removed a beige cloth suitcase with orange stripes running vertically down the middle. No sooner had he handed the suitcase to Mrs. Forguet than she laid it on the table in the middle of the room and unsnapped it, revealing inside the suitcase a radio transmitter and receiver, a telegraph key and antenna coil.

There was also a headphone which she immediately placed over her ears and, within moments, she was beating out a message on the telephone keys. While anxiously awaiting a reply to her message, she told everyone to get ready to leave. She had gotten wind that certain German soldiers had become suspicious and there was a strong possibility of a raid on the Schooner. At best, she felt that they had about thirty minutes to get out.

Sarah was given one of the nun's habits to put over her clothes and it fit almost perfectly, the collar covering the deep red swelling and stitches on her chin. Injecting some levity into their desperate situation, Mrs. Forguet commented, "Think of it, Sarah, you'll be the first Jewish nun in history."

With Ernest leading the way, Sarah, Katalin and the two children left the cellar. They headed over to the Frankfurt Cathedral to meet Captain Demoucelle who was surprised to find out that his eight o'clock rendezvous with the two children now included the two teenagers. But he didn't complain. "If Jeanne Forguet wishes I take forty children, I take them," he said. "There is no more courageous lady in all of France."

Before Sarah left the cellar, Mrs. Forguet had slipped her the ledger taken from behind the bench and told her to guard it with her life. When Sarah asked why it was so important, the mysterious and middle-aged Frenchwoman confided that the ledger contained elicited remarks from German sailors and soldiers, obtained while they looked up the bottom of an empty whiskey bottle.

Companionship had its price, and information—according to Mrs. Forguet—was far more valuable these days than the German mark. The information being extracted, though in bits and pieces, was a consistent pattern of an aggressive buildup of military forces and weaponry.

Thus, in a matter of a few days, Sarah went from being a naive but relatively optimistic teenager, the daughter of a Jewish watchmaker and his wife, to being an orphan, a survivor of a brutal knife attack, a hardened cynic and a courier for a French spy. Sarah's one last retreat into susceptibility was the fatuous remark she posed to Mrs. Forguet upon receiving the ledger, "Do you really think Germany plans to invade other nations?"

"My dear," Mrs. Forguet replied, "German children have been doing the *Sieg Heil's* since 1933. And now, at the ripe age of six years, they are being forced into military training. It doesn't appear that they are planning for future massive bake-sales." It would be the last question an embarrassed Sarah would ever ask of Mrs. Forguet. The Frenchwoman's prediction that Poland would likely be the first to fall eventually proved correct.

The captain's ship took them down the Rhine as far as Mainze. At that point Katalin and Sarah, alias "Sister Aleen," disembarked. There, as Mrs. Forguet had planned, they were met by a young French couple to whom Sarah gave the ledger.

They spent the next three and a half hours in the rear seat of a black Renault riding over serpentine roads throughout the still dark, early morning hours. It was not only deathly quiet, Sarah didn't remember their passing even one vehicle coming the other way. Katalin was seated next to her and for much of the trip her head was rested on Sarah's shoulder.

Tired herself, but unable to sleep, Sarah stared out the window at the shadowy undulating hills, looking more like cardboard cut-outs pasted against a blue-black sky. The full moon seemed to drift and tag along as it cast a thinly veiled beam through a net of dawdling dark, gray clouds.

It was almost too serene given the circumstances. Sarah wondered if it was God's answer to her raging demand of, "Where were you?" Perhaps He was telling her that He was where He always was, and nothing had changed and nothing surprised Him. Was He reminding her that once before, the world had become so wicked that He had to destroy it in order to save it—leaving, in fact, only eight people on the earth to replenish it? *Perhaps he would have to do it again*! she thought. And if the pressures got too much for her to bear, if her world got too hectic or confusing, then all the more reason to seek His sanctuary.

Having convinced herself, she again made peace with her God. She didn't want the world to be destroyed again, not while there were certain people still in it. She didn't want God's wrath to fall on her new and precious friend of the heart, Katalin Zichy. Or on the compassionate Captain Demoucelle. Or on the two frightened and innocent gypsy children. Or on an obedient Ernest, or on a courageous and determined Mrs. Forguet. Most of all, she didn't want God's wrath to fall on her brave and larger-than-life German soldier, Corporal Grauer.

What she still had difficulty reconciling was that she got to know these people only because of the tragic loss of her parents. Perhaps Katalin was right when she tried to convince Sarah that God had a plan for her, that "God never promised to deliver us from our trials, but to join us in them." And she wondered if these people were indeed part of God's blueprint.

At the border crossing stood a guard shack manned and patrolled by two black-shirted SS. About a mile from the crossing, the small Renault came to a stop and everyone got out. Once outside the car and after stretching, Sarah discarded her nun's habit. The young Frenchman put on a fancy white shirt and undid the top three buttons, then mussed up his hair, while his female companion changed into a shorter and sexier skirt which rode high on her thighs. She then re-applied her lipstick and purposely smeared it.

Katalin watched with wide-eyed curiosity as the young man removed three bottles of expensive French Bordeaux from underneath the front seat. The couple then took a swig from one of the bottles they opened and dabbed some of the wine on their clothing.

With a loud shout of *"c'est la vie!"* the young lady took the nape of the bottle and turned it upside down, spilling its contents on the ground. The empty bottle was then intentionally placed next to the unopened ones in the rear seat of the car.

Part of the pair's role as French Resistance fighters would now include being actors. The two would pretend to be lovers out celebrating their engagement who, in their exuberance, managed to over-indulge. They anticipated that the German SS guards would hassle them while carefully checking their *carte d'identite'*. There was also the likelihood that they would confiscate their Bordeaux—as a matter of principle, of course, since the young French couple might eventually get too drunk to manage the road safely. And as the two "lovers" then explained, "While we are busy distracting them, our *Compagnons de voyage*—Mademoiselles Rubenstein and Zichy—will be 200 yards away climbing the eight foot high wire fence."

Before they executed their plan, the French girl asked Sarah about the wound on her chin, now apparent since removing her collar. Sarah briefly told her what happened. Moved to compassion, the French girl embraced her.

Once over the fence and on French soil, Sarah never looked back. She and Katalin would spend the next year in France, working and learning English. When Mrs. Forguet's prophecy that Poland would fall came true, the two friends used all their money to book passage to America, fearing the second part of Mrs. Forguet's prophecy—that France would also be invaded.

Whenever possible, Sarah tried to disconnect. She had become an American citizen. Her life had new meaning and whatever was in her past should remain in her past, even her German soldier. But sometimes, like now, eleven years later, her memories came boldly searching for her. It still felt as though everything had happened just yesterday.

Chapter 3

1949, Eleven Years Later

Sarah Katz brimmed with anticipation as she and her husband Ira circulated among the crowd. Only Rabbi Kramer couldn't make the *bris,* the circumcision ceremony for Sarah and Ira's second son. That led to Dr. Sidney Shwartz becoming the *Mohel* (surgeon).

Sarah smiled fondly as she sighted her six-year-old son David-Jacob sitting at the top of the tall winding stairway. She thought him a uniquely handsome child with his high forehead, a shock of wavy black hair and his deep blue eyes. Countless freckles dotted the upper part of his cheeks and short pug nose.

Born in January of 1943, he was unusually strong for his age. In fact, some relatives and family friends dubbed him "Little Samson. Others were not so favorably inclined, she knew. Often Marvin Katz, Ira's older brother, lost patience with David-Jacob. As far as Marvin was concerned, his young nephew was some form of God's retribution against him for forsaking his rabbinical studies sixteen years ago.

Not that Marvin didn't care about his nephew. After all, he was his brother's son. But, Sarah had overheard him referring to David-Jacob as "the kid from hell." Although they were a close family Marvin seemed to dread the sight of David-Jacob in his home, and with good reason. Invariably, Marvin could count on a broken mirror, a busted chair, a smashed vase or even a door coming off its hinges after being used as a swinging vine.

She thought back. Last month had been the proverbial straw that broke the camel's back. It happened just two days after Passover. Marvin and his wife, Ruth, along with Ira and Sarah, were playing bridge in the dining area opposite the kitchen. The women had already baked *Kichelach,* the puffed-up doughy cookies made with eggs and a sprinkling of sugar, and the foursome were enjoying it with wine. Marvin's eight-year-old daughter, Rachel, and David-Jacob were in Rachel's playroom listening to Orson Welles' narration of Dr. Jekyll and Mr. Hyde on the radio.

After Jekyll-and-Hyde was over, David-Jacob suddenly got it into his mind that he had drunk the wrong potion and had been transformed into the meanest dog in all the world, "Killer-dog Kilroy." Killer-dog then began chasing the Katz's prize-winning Siamese cat, Cleopatra, through every room and under every bed, chair and table in the house.

When Marvin finally stepped out of the dining room into the living room to shout, "Why all the commotion?", an exhausted and frantic Cleo, hissing and squealing, her fur flying, bolted through the air like scattered buckshot, spread-eagled herself and imbedded her claws in Marvin's chest. No sooner than a startled and in pain Marvin muttered, *"oy vay iz meer!"* (oh, woe is me) when a still yelping and rampaging Killer-dog Kilroy came hook-sliding across the floor to take him out at the knees. What Marvin then muttered, nobody dared repeat.

It was three days before Marvin could walk without crutches and he swore that no amount of coercion would ever convince him to once again admit the "monster child" into his house. Anxious and concerned over Marvin's proclamation, Ira and Sarah finally managed to diffuse the situation by designating Marvin as the *Sandek* or godfather to their newborn child, should it be a boy. As *Sandek*, Marvin would assist the *Mohel* in the Jewish rite of circumcision, known ceremonially as a *Brith Milah*.

Marvin, a barrel-chested bear of a man with a salt-and-pepper beard, was generally considered to be as stubborn as a mongrel dog but he was humbled by the honor being bestowed upon him. Participating in what was generally referred to as a *bris* had served to mollify his anger.

"He's all bluff," Sarah would comment to Ira. "The grizzly, at heart, is really just a teddy."

As one who had considered the rabbinate, Marvin Katz knew it was considered a *mitzvah* (good deed) to participate in the fulfillment of a tradition or commandment—in this case, a *bris*. Historically, circumcision had been practiced by the Jews for 3500 years, although other civilizations had preceded them in the custom. The rite took on special significance for the Jews when it became for them an injunction by God, marking the sealing of the covenant between God and Abraham written of in the Torah (Genesis 17).

Sarah remembered Marvin tried to explain all this to David-Jacob, who had become dispirited an hour earlier upon learning he was to be exiled to the top of the stairwell during the ceremony, because it was decided things might go smoother without the child downstairs.

"You see, *boychik*," Uncle Marvin said, "God was rewarding Abraham for his faith. First God changed his name from Abram to Abraham and, at the same time, he gave Abraham the rite of circumcison to seal the covenant between God and his people, the Jews. And so, this morning we are going to circumcise your baby brother because it is the eighth day, which is when God commanded us to do so. The *bris* is a reminder to us as parents, and as aunts and uncles, to teach good things to our children. And, most of all, to teach God's laws."

"Uncle Marvin?" David-Jacob asked.

"What?"

"If I sit at the top of the staircase, then God will see me better, won't He?"

"Trust me, David-Jacob. God already knows all about you. In my conversations with Him, I have discussed you many times."

In addition to him being the *Sandek*, when it was first suggested that the *bris* be held at his house, Marvin literally beamed. Ira and Sarah were well aware of how proud Marvin was of his new two-story status symbol in Jamaica Heights, only an hour's drive from Brooklyn. In honor of the occasion, Marvin had purchased an expensive Persian rug, thinking it was certain to draw favorable comments from the guests in attendance.

Along with all the plans that had to be made and deciding which people to invite, a solution needed to be worked out concerning David-Jacob. The family realized that although he was rambunctious and loved to roughhouse, he wasn't purposely malicious. His apologies were genuine, as was his remorse. They concluded that he was just a very active child who never thought through the consequences of his actions. Spanking didn't help. Neither did cajoling or verbal tongue lashings. The parents even resorted to bribery by offering him extra portions of his favorite dessert—strawberry blintzes. Although the rolled pancake was normally stuffed with cottage cheese, for David-Jacob they would make an exception, but even that didn't work.

Obviously, the only thing that was going to work was patience and forbearance. In the meantime, the two families' combined intelligence hit upon an idea to lasso him in. Henceforward, David-Jacob would only be allowed in certain areas of the Melvin Katz house. In addition, he would be instructed as to what the penalties would be should he disobey. Last, but not least, he was to be in an area where he could always be observed and far removed from anything fragile. At this morning's *bris*, that meant sitting at the top of the staircase.

Sarah felt sympathy for David-Jacob, and knew he couldn't understand why they made him sit at the top of the staircase. He had complained to her minutes ago, *"Fatso Rachel is downstairs stealing all the food off the table, while I have to sit away up here."*

Sarah wondered if David-Jacob was also starting to feel a sense of loss. His baby brother had arrived eight days ago and since then, things weren't the same. His yet unnamed brother was suddenly center stage; his parent's love now had to be shared.

Twenty-four folding chairs had already been set up facing the area where the *Sandek* and *Mohel* would perform the ceremony. Two rows of six chairs each were placed on either side with a small aisle in between. So far, of the twenty-three guests present, all but three were over the age of thirteen, the age required for the *Minyan*. Orthodox Judaism maintained that there must be ten males of at least that age to form the communal prayer group.

Three days earlier, Marvin—Ira's elder brother and employer—and Sarah had had a heated discussion concerning the makeup of the *Minyan*. As the argument flashed back in her mind, Sarah felt lightheaded and excused herself to go to the kitchen and sit down. It was still nearly an hour before the actual ceremony would begin. Ira meanwhile offered to bring her some cold seltzer water.

Once seated in the kitchen, Sarah replayed in her mind the confrontation with Marvin that had begun in the hospital. She had been sitting on the edge of her hospital bed, dressed and waiting for the nurse to bring her baby. Ira was seated in a chair next to the bed when Marvin lumbered in, slapping his huge bear-like palms together like a pair of clapping cymbals.

"Nu! Sarah. We're ready! The car is outside running. Where's the little bed wetter?"

"The doctor is giving him a final check-up. So, tell me, who's watching the store?"

"Goldblum, the *k'nocker* [big-shot braggart]."

Sarah frowned slightly. "Irv Goldblum? Why do you still keep him? Doesn't he upset your customers?"

Marvin threw up his hands. "What! It isn't so easy to get good help. Half the ex-servicemen are still happy to go to Times Square and loaf. For the price of a quarter, they can get into Loews State and watch Porky Pig all day. Why should they work? Hey look, at least Goldblum's not a *shlep* [an unkempt person]. He gives me a day's work for a day's wages. Besides, he used to lay linoleum so he knows the business." Marvin impatiently looked at his watch. "Nu., the nurse, where is she? We'll be here 'til the Messiah comes."

"I'll go get her," Ira volunteered. He rose and left the room.

Marvin then turned to Sarah. "Everything's ready, Sarah," he said. "Ruth took care of calling the bakery and the delicatessen. Oh, and Rabbi Kramer has to be out of town so Dr. Shwartz will do the cutting. Also, I made sure there were enough men arriving to do the <u>Minyan</u>. So just show up with a kid and we'll have a <u>bris</u>."

Sarah looked timidly back at Marvin and gritted her teeth. She had to tell him. . . .

"Marvin, I meant to tell you. I know we haven't talked about this. . . ." She purposely let her statement dangle in the air to see Marvin's reaction.

"Talk about what?" He arched his eyebrows.

"About the *Minyan*. I . . . ah . . . want women to be part of the *Minyan*."

Stunned, Marvin bellowed, "What! You want women, what?"

"To be part of the *Minyan*," she repeated.

"Over my dead body!"

"It's my baby!" Sarah shrieked.

"It's my house!" The shouting match began in earnest.   Sarah's blood began to rise. She shot to her feet, squared her shoulders and placed her fisted hands on her hips. "Oh! And I suppose you don't think women are capable of praying, let alone be part of a *Minyan*!"

"I think if you want to become a lousy Reform Jew, you may as well become a Protestant or a Catholic! Maybe we should invite the Pope to the *bris*!"

"If he'd like to come, he's welcome!"

"Ha!"

"Ha back! And I am not Reform, I am Conservative. I still believe in the Torah, the Talmud and tradition . . . sometimes."

"Tradition? What do you know about tradition? I suppose you even want to be present at the circumcision?"

"I most certainly do."

Marvin threw up his hands in resignation. "So much for tradition. My brother married a meshuggeneh [crazy woman]!" Marvin then turned his back on Sarah.

During the argument, Ira had returned, holding their infant. He had witnessed Marvin and Sarah's confrontations before and he wanted no part of it. Gingerly stepping past the two combatants, he seated himself in the chair by the side of the bed.

"Man's tradition, Marvin! And I resent being called a *meshuggeneh*."

Marvin turned again to face Sarah. "Man's tradition is Jewish tradition, Sarah. They were all men: Hillel, Rabbi Judah, Solomon ben Isaac, Akiva, Maimonides. And if they were alive today, they would all *plotz* because Mrs. Sarah Katz, Mrs. Madame Moses here, is going to rewrite a whole new Torah."

"The Torah, Marvin, says nothing about a *Minyan*."

"The Talmud does."

"The Talmud? Written by men?"

"Oh, God forbid!"

"May I remind you, Mr. Smartmouth, that the Talmud is only a man's interpretation of the Torah."

"Well, after listening to you I sure would hate to see a woman's interpretation. And the *Mishnah*, I suppose you have something also against the *Mishnah*?"

"The *Mishnah* is the code of rules for discussing the Talmud, again, written by men."

"Good, Sarah. I need a Hebrew lesson."

"I am only stating fact, Marvin. It's not like I'm opposing the Ten Commandments."

"Bet you would if you could, 'cause God gave it to a man. Oy oy oy, that God would do such a thing." Marvin laid the palm of his hand against the side of his face for emphasis.

"Oh grow up, Marvin."

"Look, Sarah, Jews have had their traditions for thousands of years. Why do you want to change them?"

"Marvin, if you were told you could not pray because you were a man, would that not bother you? Would it not upset you if you were told you could not have an opinion?"

"Ha! Since when have you not had an opinion?"

"Since when have you ever listened to one?"

"Like I have a choice? Sarah, God put man in charge to make the rules. One of the rules is that women are to be a helpmate and otherwise be quiet." His voice rose again. "It's always been that way. It's tradition!" He waved his hands in the air.

"Oh!" Sarah retorted, "and does tradition say that women can't pray?"

"Of course they can pray."

"Good! We finally agree."

"Agree on what?" Marvin sensed he'd been had.

"Agree that women can pray. And since they can pray, they will be part of the *Minyan* at my son's *bris*—at which, I remind you, *I* will be watching!" Sarah stood, smug-faced and arms folded.

"I give up!" Marvin noticed Ira sitting in the chair and screamed at him for his lack of help. "Ira! A *shaynim donk in pupik*! [a pretty thanks in the navel—thanks for nothing]."

Ira stood and placed his still sleeping child on the hospital bed. Walking over to Marvin, he laid a hand on his shoulder, whispering, "go," and motioning with his head the direction of the door. Exasperated and resigned, Marvin obediently left the room. Ira then turned and stared at his wife who stood but a few feet away.

Thinking back, Sarah remembered feeling embarrassed as she sheepishly looked back at her husband. All Ira had to do was tilt his head slightly and stare at her with a blank expression and she knew she was being mildly rebuked. He was as much as saying, "Sarah, I love you, but you were out of line." Sarah's disconnected thoughts then strayed and merged into images of her husband.

Ira had recently turned thirty-two years old. They would celebrate his birthday and that of his new son on consecutive days, Ira's birthday coming the day after Sarah gave birth. Four years Marvin's junior, Ira weighed in at 170 pounds, about sixty pounds lighter than his brother. At six feet, two inches and with a straight frame, he gave the appearance of being thin.

Sarah often marveled at the dissimilarity of the two brothers, both in personality and the way they presented themselves. Marvin Katz was very gregarious and informal. Because of his size he found it more practical to wear his shirttail out. Seldom did he wear a belt and he swore he would not be caught dead in suspenders. Possessing a ruddy complexion, he was bearded, with a heavy thatch of badly receding hair. Although stubborn and temperamental he was generous to a fault.

Ira, on the other hand, was clean shaven with an occasional shadow of a mustache. Always impeccably dressed, he preferred neatly pressed white shirts which he often ironed himself and, unlike Marvin, he had no problems feeling comfortable in suspenders. His complexion was smooth, his skin tanned, a small mole showed above his right upper lip. Because of farsightedness he wore glasses. He had his hair cut every two weeks—short-cropped, almost a military style.

The opposite of his older brother's personality, Ira was often more subdued and reclusive, but not shy. A confident man, he didn't suffer fools gladly. If really provoked, he had a volatile temper. Despite that one major flaw, Sarah felt fortunate to have fallen in love with such a decent and honest man. Extremely considerate and attentive to her needs, he made a wonderful husband and father.

Sarah recalled Ira's last fit of rage. It had occurred about three months ago when he was returning from the Bronx Zoo with David-Jacob. As he related to his wife, the two of them were walking by a small outdoor fruit stand when their son accidentally brushed against an pyramid of several dozen apples. A dozen or so of them had rolled into the street and they quickly retrieved them. Ira reached into his pocket to pay the merchant for the bruised fruit and after he did so, the fruit vendor made an anti-Semitic remark. When Sarah heard from David-Jacob about the incident, she confronted her husband.

"Ira! What's this that happened that David-Jacob was telling me about?"

"You mean about the fruit stand?"

"Is there another incident?"

"Of course not. DeeJay wasn't looking where he was going and he accidentally knocked some apples into the street."

"How many apples?"

"Maybe twelve or thirteen. But we paid the man and I apologized, then he made a snide remark about Jews. How he knows we're Jews I have no idea."

"Perhaps Ira, it is because you wear the map of Israel on your face."

"You think so?"

"I think so. But is that any excuse to hit the poor man?"

"What? Hit? DeeJay is telling you stories. I gave the man a little shove."

"I know about your little shoves, Ira. You shove a man in New York, he ends up in Michigan."

"The man upset me, Sarah. He was a big man, like Marvin, and I'm sure he is used to intimidating people."

"What kind of snide remark did he make, Ira?"

"I gave him first a dollar to pay for the apples. They are six cents an apple or, according to his sign, fifty cents a dozen. So I gave him twice that. Then he says to me, 'Next time, tell your little Jew-boy to watch where he's walking.' Outside, Sarah, I am calm, but inside I'm seething. I want to kill the man."

"Oh well, then he's dead. It's perfectly fine and a great example for David-Jacob!"

"To be honest, Sarah, it occurred to me."

"So when did the fight start?"

"Sarah, there was no fight! I am angry, sure. Am I supposed to stand there and let him insult my child? What would DeeJay then think of me?"

"Okay, enough with the big *megillah* [boring-extended details]. Then what happened?"

"The man insulted me. All right? So I said to him, 'Look, I don't think I paid you enough,' and I reached into my wallet, took out three more dollars and handed them to him."

"After he insults you? You hand him three more dollars?"

"It's something my father taught me. I did it to distract him. He takes the three dollars, folds them and puts them in his back pocket. Then he says to me, 'Well, at least you're not like the other Jew-chiselers I've met.' So I grabbed him with both hands underneath his collar and I give him a little shove, that's all. It just so happens that he lands in his *farshtinkener* [stinking] fruit stand. So maybe a hundred apples go rolling in the street."

"A hundred apples!"

"The *gonif* [crook] had it coming, Sarah."

"Oh, and who made you a judge? And what about the man?"

"I don't think he converted to Judaism. How should I know? We didn't stay long enough to find out."

"Ira . . ."

"No, Sarah!" He abruptly cut her off. "Sarah, I understand why you feel the way you do. I know and appreciate what you've been through. But Sarah, it's time we defended ourselves against ignorant people who denigrate us and attempt to make us feel less than human. I will not, mind you, will not have DeeJay growing up that way."

"And the biblical injunction, Ira, 'He who lives by the sword will die by the sword.' What about that, Ira?"

"Better to die with a sword in our hand than a yellow streak down our back." Sarah knew that her protestations were futile and she wasn't entirely sure that her husband wasn't right.

Chapter 4

Other than her father, Ira Katz was the only man Sarah ever truly loved. They had met at a skating rink in Central Park in January of 1942 and were married in March of the same year, just two months before Corporal Katz was shipped overseas. Sarah had confided, however, and Ira was keenly aware, that another man would always share her life, if only as a memory.

Although the young German soldier was but a hazy remembrance and Sarah only knew him for the space of about twenty minutes, he periodically occupied her thoughts. He existed in the deep, scarred wells of her mind as a beam of light during a night of unspeakable horror. That soldier became the most unlikely of heroes and an angel of mercy on November 9, 1938 [the Night of Broken Glass]. It was to Ira's credit that he wasn't the least bit jealous of the memory. In fact, he just wished he could meet the soldier to whom he was eternally grateful.

Regathering her rambling thoughts, Sarah's mind centered again on the aftermath of her argument with Marvin at the hospital three days ago. After Marvin had left the room, mumbling and disgruntled over Sarah's wanting women to be part of the *Minyan*, Ira walked over to his wife and gently placed his hands on her shoulders. He drew her close to him, looked directly into her eyes and pecked her on her forehead. Sarah felt somewhat embarrassed and shyly lowered her chin. Ira then tenderly tucked his index finger beneath her chin and again raised it to eye level.

"Sarah, Sarah, Sarah. Whatever am I going to do with you? Not only does Marvin give me a job at his store, he trains me and makes me a manager. Now he even talks of making me a partner. Should we decide to move to another state, like we are thinking of doing, it will break my heart to tell him. I feel very close to my brother. I mean, DeeJay almost breaks his leg and practically destroys everything in his house, and still Marvin refuses to allow me to pay for anything. And you know how much he and Ruth love and admire you. So why do you cause him so much *tsouris* [trouble]?"

Sarah was about to reply but Ira gently placed the tip of his finger over her lips. "Don't answer, Sarah. I'll tell you why. It is because you are both very strong-willed people and you both care too deeply. I think that Marvin sometimes overcompensates because he feels guilty about dropping out of rabbinical studies at Yeshiva. Though he is a successful businessman he feels that he has cheated God in some way.

"You, on the other hand, feel that we as Jews, the people of the *Diaspora*, of countless persecutions, contradict ourselves by not allowing women to participate fully in our traditions. Am I right?"

"Do you remember why I told you that, Ira?"

"Yes, because having seen so much suffering yourself firsthand, you are no longer satisfied for the rabbis and teachers to tell us what to do and make decisions for us."

Sarah felt a rush of emotion. "It isn't that I don't respect our rabbis and teachers, but God forbid another holocaust, Ira. We won't survive another one! And all the tradition in the world won't save us. We can become a more vibrant, effective and stronger people if we weren't so strict with ourselves. Ira . . ."

Ira cut her off. "Sarah, that may all be true. And in good time. But now is not the time for radical changes. Tradition still binds us together as a people. And now we have Israel to help serve as our voice."

"But Ira . . ."

"No, Sarah. Please listen. If we don't have tradition to hold us together as a people, and if we all go our own separate ways, all of us with our own ideas, then we are too few. We have to speak with one voice and let change come gradually."

"You believe that Marvin is right then? Women should stay silent and pray only when instructed? That we are less important than men. Don't we reduce our numbers that way as well?"

"No, Sarah, I don't believe that. Please don't put words into my mouth. I believe that Jewish men and women exist or perish together. But we cannot exist by being insensitive to each other. Traditions die hard. In time, Sarah, I believe it will become commonplace for women to be part of the *Minyan*. But to thrust it on Marvin at this time, at his house, in front of his many friends—many of them still Orthodox— would be for him a humiliation. Sarah, instead it would be for you a *mitzvah* if you just let it go. Let the *Minyan* remain as it is, for men only, and don't cause any more trouble."

"And Ira, do you believe also that I should adhere to the custom of the mother of the child about to be circumcised, not to be present to watch?"

"I believe that is your prerogative as a mother. How can a man know of a mother's love or concern for her newborn child? For Marvin to understand that, then that for him should be a *mitzvah*."

Sarah smiled at Ira and then buried her head in his chest. Looking back up, she kissed him on the cheek and gently removed his glasses. "Do you know, with your glasses off you look like Clark Gable?"

"You think so, Sarah?"

"I think so, Ira. Of course, when I once mentioned that to Marvin, he didn't agree."

"Oh, and who does Marvin think I look like?"

"He thinks, my darling, that you look like *Chaim Yankel* [a nobody, non-entity]. Sarah delighted to see Ira's broad smile.

"You feeling okay, Sarah? You look a little down."

Sarah's remembrances of three days ago were suddenly interrupted when Ira walked into the kitchen with a cold glass of seltzer water.

"I feel fine, Ira. Thanks for the seltzer. I'm just tired, a lot has happened in the last few days."

"You should have stayed in the hospital longer as the doctor suggested."

"You're right. I shouldn't have insisted. I just wanted to be sure that everything went okay. You go back to our guests. Go, so they shouldn't ask questions."

"You sure?"

"I'm sure, I'm sure. I think I will look in on the baby. Maybe give Katalin a break. What time is it?"

"We have a half hour before Katalin should give the baby to the godmother. Tomorrow, Sarah, promise me you will rest."

"I will, Katalin has already promised to stay over while you are at work. Go now."

Sarah rose from her chair and kissed Ira on the cheek. Once he left the kitchen, she drank a sip of seltzer water and then also left the room. She had mixed emotions. Her strong desire to be with her child conflicted somewhat with her exceedingly strong desire to be alone with her thoughts. The teak-floored hallway led past two bedrooms, a bath, and finally to a small guest room. She cracked open the door, ever so slightly, in case her baby was still sleeping.

Upon entering the guest room, Katalin Zichy, Sarah's dearest and closest friend, crossed her lips with her index finger. "Sh-h-h. The baby's still sleeping, Sarah."

The maternal scene served to momentarily uplift Sarah's spirits. She walked toward the bed where Katalin sat, and peeked into the bassinet. Her tiny newborn had his fingers curled together in a fist with the thumbs of each hand pointing up towards the sky. Sarah bit her lip as tears welled up in her eyes. "My, what innocence."

Katalin rose from her seat on the bed and she and Sarah embraced. "Sarah, my precious friend. The Lord is restoring to you the years the locusts have eaten."

"I'm almost afraid to be happy, Katalin. Once before I was happy and . . ."

Katalin stopped her in mid-sentence. "Quit torturing yourself, Sarah. It's in the past. You can't change what happened and you have a right to be happy."

"Katalin, the last two days, I can think of nothing else but my parents. If they could have only known their grandchildren. Life is not fair."

"It often isn't. But Sarah, somehow I think your parents know of your feelings for them. They only want your happiness."

"Does your Christian Bible really teach that, Katalin? Does it speak of loved ones knowing how much they are missed?"

"It speaks, Sarah, that the Lord will someday dry all our tears, and there will be no more pain or suffering. How God brings that about is up to Him. Dear Sarah, rejoice that we both now live in a free country. Fix your thoughts on your children and take delight in their lives. Teach them and dream with them. Be happy that you have a good husband. They are not always easy to find, you know."

Sarah forced a smile and nodded. She wondered if anybody on earth was allowed dark thoughts while in the presence of Katalin Zichy. Her radiant countenance, her general good cheer and optimism were too overpowering.

Katalin, at twenty-six years old, was two years younger than Sarah. But she was more than Sarah's friend, she was her soul mate. They had both lost their parents under tragic circumstances while living in Nazi Germany, albeit for different reasons. Katalin's parents dared speak out against Hitler and in defense of the Jews. Sarah's parents were killed simply because they were Jews. Before they met, Katalin had already lived as a street waif in the parks and sewers in Germany for two years. Then, eleven years ago, they found themselves hiding out together in the tavern cellar of a French woman spy.

That's where their similarities ended, however. Whereas Sarah felt trapped by her torturous past, Katalin, to Sarah's thinking, was almost dispassionate about her own searing memories. It was the only thing that ever bothered Sarah about her Christian friend. Only once did Katalin ever attempt to proselytize her, but her deep quiet faith appeared to Sarah as pollyannaish in light of her circumstances. Certainly they were in direct contrast to the sometimes anger and victimization that resided in her own troubled spirit.

After silently observing Sarah's baby, Katalin posed a question to Sarah that went unanswered. She then realized that although Sarah was staring at her child, she wasn't really looking at him. After eleven years Katalin had become used to Sarah's sometimes glazed over look and sudden change in disposition. She sensed that the same melancholy that set in six years ago when David-Jacob was born was manifesting itself again. On other occasions, Katalin was aware of Sarah's trance-like stares where she became oblivious to the world. Once commenting to Sarah about her vacuous expressions, Sarah replied, "Katalin, sometimes I feel trapped by this world and I feel the desperate need to step out of it—if only for a moment."

Now Katalin gave Sarah a hug and brushed back a loose strand of hair that had fallen over Sarah's forehead. She started to leave the room when Sarah called out to her. "Katalin!"

Sarah extended her hand and Katalin clasped it tightly in hers and then slowly withdrew it. She knew Sarah wanted to be alone and was at least encouraged that Sarah, with a tender touch and a smile, had acknowledged her leaving.

Sarah sat on the bed where Katalin was sitting previously. Alone, while watching her still sleeping infant, she again let her memories consume her.

Just outside the room, Katalin leaned against the wall of the corridor. She breathed a heavy sigh while closing her eyes in prayer.

"Blessed Lord Jesus, I ask not for myself but for the friend you have chosen to grace my life with these last eleven years. Her memories, O Lord, are as painful and sharp as the scorpion's sting.

I have neither the words nor the wisdom to give her. If it be Thy will I would choose to be Thy instrument. Put the thoughts in my mind and the words on my tongue, O Lord, to speak to her.

And Lord, may the dedication of her child this day be to your everlasting glory. I remain your humble servant. Amen.

And immediately, God placed in her mind the memory of a long ago conversation with her father. A Hungarian Orthodox priest with a love for the Jews, her father had said, "Despite all the pogroms and inquisitions that have tragically reduced their numbers, despite all the venal and pejorative remarks aimed at them like poisoned arrows, despite their being scattered for almost two thousand years, the Jew still exists. For God has inured them with a remarkable propensity, that being an incredible resilience, marked by their ability to laugh through their tears.—"

And Katalin thought, 'If only father could see Sarah now. Despite her present despondency, he would see just how correct his observation was.

Opening her eyes, Katalin observed Marvin's wife Ruth smiling at her. "Blessed Katalin, may your prayers reach heaven's doorstep. Tell Sarah it is time for the bris."

Chapter 5

David-Jacob had had just about all he could take of his cousin Rachel's teasing. Twice now she had deliberately stomped up the stairs just to provoke him. Both times, her hands were wrapped around his favorite delicacy—strawberry blintzes. On each occasion, she would lick her lips before consuming them. The strawberry filling would ooze out the center, trickle down the corners of her mouth and down her chin. She would then dab the sweet sticky confection with her index finger and wipe her finger on her tongue.

Each time, it had caused David-Jacob to drool and now he was angry. *She better not come up here again*, he thought.

He was still sitting precariously between the ornate wooden rails with only space in front and a steep drop below him. Both hands gripped the rails behind him as he watched his Uncle Marvin rise from the "Chair of Elijah" to receive his baby brother from Aunt Ruth. The <u>Minyan</u> stood and uttered a blessing in unison, "Blessed be he that cometh . . . " The ten men began rocking back and forth while chanting in Hebrew.

Then suddenly, David-Jacob heard once more the dreaded sound of Rachel Katz clomping up the stairs. Peering between the rails he saw her climbing the stairs, only this time balancing three blintzes. He thought to himself that she was obviously going to give him one of them. While rising to his feet and holding on to the rail with his right hand, he extended his left hand over the top to receive one, but Rachel Katz just smirked at him. "No, get your own. These are mine."

David-Jacob became livid. "Then go ahead and eat them, you fat ol' blintz blimp!"

"Shut-up you little pisher boy [bed wetter]."

"If you don't give me one, I'm gonna jump all the way down an' tell 'em you pushed me."

Rachel knew it was an idle threat. "Oh sure, you dumb dope. You'd break your head open."

"Okay, here goes."

David-Jacob continued to hold on with one hand while precipitously leaning out at a 45-degree angle. Below him were the two oblong food tables that had been shoved together. Placed atop the tables were four very expensive and elegant silver lame' tablecloths.

While in his perilous stance, he observed the cornucopia of food that had been set out. On one end sat a huge silver punch bowl with engraved Hebrew lettering, filled to the brim with red punch. Across the tables were similar colored trays loaded with condiments. Then came two plates, stacked high with corned beef and pastrami and a huge plate of liverwurst. The long buffet included sliced rye bread and pumpernickel, four loaves of challah twist and the inevitable staple of several dozen bagels arrayed in a large mound. On the opposite end of the punch bowl were jars of pickled herring, borscht, kosher dills and gefilte fish.

David-Jacob thought to himself that it would take all of Bensonhurst to eat all that food. *Except*, he mused, *if fat ol' Rachel started eating it.* Then like a lightning bolt it struck him: There were no more blintzes! With a scowl on his face he shot a quick angry glance at Rachel.

Rachel's expression was one of alarm. "David-Jacob! Quit leaning over like that. You could fall. I'll give you a stupid blintz."

As she held out the blintz, David-Jacob felt both triumphant and relieved. He realized how far he could fall if he lost his grip and was only too happy to pull himself upright. Only he couldn't!

He started grunting until his face was beet red . . . but something was wrong! Instead of being able to pull himself back to the stairs, too much of his weight was pulling him forwards. His fingers begin to uncouple. His palms were moist with sweat and his grip loosened. He barely managed to hold on with his fingertips.

He heard his heart pounding inside his head as a cold sweat beaded on his brow. He then heard Rachel gasping in the background and charging down the stairs. The teakwood floor began to swirl beneath him and he froze in dizzying terror at what he knew was about to happen.

His hawk-like eyes trained themselves on the table below and on the challah and huge mound of bagels. He knew it was his only hope as one last guttural moan crossed his lips and he tasted air.

"Uh! Oh-h-h-h-h!"

Just as Marvin Katz was about to hand the yet uncircumcised baby to the <u>Mohel</u>, Rachel Katz's shrill and piercing scream filled the air. Those who turned in time gasped and shrieked in horror to see David-Jacob tumbling head-over-heels as he plummeted through space. The six-year-old human missile crashed through the seam of the two tables and through the platters of challah and bagels.

Immediately platters of food catapulted high into the air, overturning and spraying food in every direction. A deluge of meats, condiments and globs of liverwurst rained from the ceiling. Jars of pickled herring, borscht, kosher dills and gefilte fish propelled across the room as the guests dove for cover.

The elaborate silver embossed punch bowl—containing a mixture of Kool Aid, ginger ale and sparking water—slid slowly down one of the broken legged tables. When it reached floor level, it overturned, spilling its contents. The red and sticky liquid divided into rivulets, the largest of them seeping towards the new Persian Rug Uncle Marvin purchased specifically for the occasion. Within moments, the carpet had become as worthless as the punch that flowed over it.

In the crowd of guests, Fern Liebowicz, a distant cousin of the Katz's, attempted to be the first to reach an obviously injured, perhaps dead, David-Jacob. But the buxomly woman lost her balance in her heels and fell face first, with a loud grunt, into the quagmire. As her shorter and thinner husband attempted to lift her back up, he stepped on the string of pearls about her neck, causing them to roll loose across the floor. This created more havoc, some of those in the Minyan taking clownish pratfalls as they stepped on the translucent beads, their Yarmulkes and tallisses becoming part of the mire.

Ira, Katalin and Dr. Shwartz were best at negotiating the food and punch bog, finally managing to reach David-Jacob. Meanwhile, Ruth had raced down the hall to inform Sarah. For several anxious moments a quiet hush hung like a pall over the concerned guests. Then, very slowly, a four foot mound of tablecloth began to rise. Only David-Jacob's protruding nose and eyeballs prevented him from being confused with a diminutive ghost.

A stunned and surprised Sarah broke through the gathered crowd and, in a rush of emotion, clutched her child to her breast as Ira jerked the tablecloth off his head and shoulders. There were choir sounds of sighing relief and expressions of thanks to God, even some hand clapping among the guests.

A dazed David-Jacob, with noticeable bleeding from the corner of his lip, struggled poutfully to speak. "I-I- don't fe-e-el good!" He pointed his finger to his limp left arm.

Dr. Shwartz held the boy's left hand and gently touched the deep swelling occurring about his elbow. He then nodded to Ira. "It's broken. We'll put it in a sling and take him to the hospital."

"I wanna stay!" David-Jacob screamed.

"DeeJay, your arm's broken, son," Ira remonstrated.

"I wanna watch the *bris* first."

"Ira? Perhaps if he feels okay?" Sarah asked her husband.

They both looked at the doctor. "Well," he reluctantly agreed, "we'd better put an ice bag over the swelling. I'll set the sling."

In quick order, a mop and bucket brigade started stirring and only then did it occur to Ira, Sarah, Katalin and Ruth that Marvin had been totally ignored during the whole, almost tragic event. Simultaneously they all looked in his direction, where he sat motionless wearing the numbed expression of a man in a catatonic state. He was still sitting in the Chair of Elijah and the only thing that had changed since before David-Jacob's plunge was that the infant he cradled had turned face downward.

Katalin was helping the doctor set a sling about the neck and arm of David-Jacob who, meanwhile, was accepting congratulations of a relieved contingent of witnesses to his miraculous achievement. "Certainly," they muttered among themselves, "he must be blessed of God." David-Jacob's chest so swelled with pride that he barely sensed the persistent throbbing pain about the elbow area.

No sooner had Ira, Sarah and Ruth approached the still stupefied Marvin Katz than Sarah's baby decided to empty his bladder. The hot stream went down Marvin's pant leg and formed a puddle on the floor. Sarah bit hard to keep from laughing as the look on her brother-in-law's face indicated that he had indeed been pushed over the brink. His clenched teeth now formed a gap at the corner as Ruth quickly took the baby from Marvin and handed the child to Sarah. She whispered a note of caution, "I think Mt. Vesuvius is about ready to blow."

David-Jacob, his arm now in a sling, rushed over towards his uncle. "Uncle Marvin, look! I got a broken arm! Now I get to sit in the front and watch the *bris*."

Marvin only mumbled a few incoherent words then, moving cautiously backwards, he quickly turned and scurried out of the living room.

"Marvin! The *bris*!" Ruth screamed.

"I'll be back," he yelled as he exited.

A moment later, there was heard throughout the house a loud, wall-shaking bellowing cry. The wailing was so loud it stopped everyone in their tracks.

"Wow!" David-Jacob exclaimed. "Uncle Marvin's even louder than Tarzan!"

And that's what happened on the morning of May 11, 1949. It was a day of great importance and one that none in attendance would ever forget. A day of chaos and a day of remembrance of past and tragic memories. The only one who would have no recollection of the event was the one in whose honor the day was planned—eight-day old Joshua-Caleb Katz.

Chapter 6

Katalin couldn't remember the last time she was alone with Ira, if ever?
Asked by her church to select some new carpet and tile, she instinctively
chose to purchase at Marvin and Ira's floor covering store. While there,
Ira unexpectedly invited her to the next door delicatessen, telling her
he had an important matter he had been wanting to speak to her about.
Ira's tone was disconcerting. Ever since Ira had been discharged from
the Army in late 1945, their once strong bond of friendship was never
the same. Sarah was also aware that Ira's once easy going nature had
become far more intense after the war. He was more somber now, often
less approachable, less affable and communicative. However, Sarah
was more dismissive of Ira's change in personality than she was. Sarah
attributing Ira's modest change in personality to what often happens
to soldiers back from war. But intuitively, Katalin sensed in her spirit
that something far deeper was troubling Ira and whatever it was, it now
included her.

Katalin couldn't understand why but nothing she ever said or did of
late, seemed to change Ira's attitude towards her? Ira returned from the
deli counter with both their sandwiches and while setting their plates
down, icily addressed her.

"Katalin, I'm having a real hard time with your and Sarah's close
relationship. I do have enormous respect for you and what you've been
through and what you and Sarah have gone through together but when
I married Sarah I didn't know you were going to be so much a part of
the package. Right now Sarah is fighting me on our possible move to
Arizona, possibly opening our own store there and I really think it has
a lot to do with not wanting to abandon you. Also, I feel my family's
Jewish identity is being compromised by your influence. DeeJay loves
you a great deal and I constantly see him wanting to know more about
your Christian beliefs.

Faced with the prospect of losing the relationship most important
and dear to her, feeling as if she'd just been ambushed, Katalin's eyes
teared as she struggled for the right words with which to respond...

"Ira...my dear soul...what have I ever...ever done to make you dislike me so!!? I would never, not in my wildest imagination, knowingly cause you and Sarah trouble. And besides, she loves you more than life itself. I am merely a very close friend. I would also never proselytize DeeJay and if you are talking about when I took him to the zoo last week and I talked to him about Jesus, it was only in response to questions he asked me? I only shared of what I believe, not how your family should believe. That is not my place. I so respect how you and Sarah believe so why would you think that of me? You have me all wrong Ira..." Ira shot back..

"No...too many times I have heard DeeJay speak about Jesus and what Aunt Katalin believes and it is always Jesus this and Jesus that!"

"Ira...if DeeJay speaks that strongly about Jesus and I am the one responsible, despite how I truly believe, then I most certainly apologize and I will promise to be more careful but for you to think I would do that purposely is wrong. Is that why you asked me to lunch, Ira!? To wrongly accuse me of proselytizing DeeJay!?"

"Katalin...the last thing I wish to do is offend or hurt you. That is not my intent. I'm not sure what I'm saying is coming out the way I want it to. I don't mind your friendship with Sarah and I know you love the kids and I appreciate that but I'm very leery of your Christian beliefs because of all the harm it has brought to our people over the centuries and even all the anti-semitism that exists in the world today, I think, in large part is due to Christian attitudes towards Jews. You have too much influence in the life of my family and you need to start backing off. You and Sarah have the ability to overlook your religious and cultural differences but now that it is affecting my son I just can't pretend any longer that it isn't there. I don't want your Christian God influencing our lives anymore like it has..."

Katalin looked quizzically at Ira, 'What happened to you, Ira!?"

"What do you mean?"

"Before, when I knew you, when Sarah and I first met you, you were different. You always appeared so happy and carefree. Granted, you were always a quiet type person, but you smiled a lot and you seemed to always be at peace with yourself, not anxious and certainly not suspicious of me. I always looked up to you as a big brother, always so kind and supportive and now...now I don't know what I think? I mean, I prayed so hard, so diligently for your and Sarah's love to grow and I was so thrilled when it did. But even then I thought the three of us were so close that nothing would ever come between any of us. I have always greatly admired you. I guess I still do which is why your speaking to me now as some kind of interloper, an outsider, just hurts me so much. Especially, for reasons I feel you have mostly manufactured on your own. You not only don't like me, now you don't even want me around? You disparage my beliefs and you think things of me that just are not true. You were not like this before!?"

Ira responded rhetorically. "I suppose you are speaking about before the war?"

"Yes...and I know I don't have the right to ask you, Ira, but because of the circumstances I am going to ask anyway. What happened to change you so?"

"War changes people."

"It certainly changed you."

"Before the war I saw things differently. Then, certain things happened and my eyes were opened. It's a different world than I thought it was. But what you said before is right. It's not your concern."

"You're right Ira. It is not really my business. That is between you and God and most certainly Sarah. I only wish you to know that if you think for a moment that I am anti-semitic or anything even close, then that offends me. It offends me a great deal."

"I didn't say you were anti-semitic Katalin,! But within your faith there are many who are!"

"I don't agree.."

"You don't agree, Katalin? You want examples!? Should I give you a detailed explanation of how I, Ira Katz, now perceive Christianity and all it has done to our people!?"

"Ira, I don't wish for this to continue. I think I should leave."

"I just want you to understand. Maybe you will learn something."

"Ira, really, is all this necessary?"

"I just want you to understand where I am coming from."

"I don't see what purpose it will serve, Ira, but I will give you the courtesy of listening."

"I'll try and keep this as short as possible. We can start with Saint Gregory of Nyssa who said that the Jews were slayers of the Lord and were advocates of the devil. Another beloved church hero, Saint John Chrysostom, stated that the synagogue was worse than a brothel and was a temple of demons. Chrysostom said he hated the synagogue and he hated the Jews.

Then you have one of the most heralded church leaders, Martin Luther. He was vicious. When describing the Jews he often spoke of us in vulgar terms. He maintained that we were a wicked and venomous people. In fact, Hitler often referred to Luther's tractate, "The Jews and their Lies' in his program of extermination.

There was a litany of others that I've forgotten. You might also remember a survey taken in this country seven years ago. It is why so many Jews feel another Holocaust could happen in America as well and why so many of us are still uneasy. In fact, I know Jews who barely escaped Europe or survived the camps that no longer will admit they are Jews, simply out of fear."

Katalin had a blank expression. She was already familiar with much of what Ira was telling her but knew nothing about the survey?

"The Survey, Katalin, was trying to get a fix on people's attitudes towards different nationalities and ethnicities. The survey question was, *Who are the people you consider the most dangerous in America?* For me, it drove the nail in the coffin regarding anti-semitism. Despite the fact that Hitler was ravaging Europe. Despite the fact that only several months earlier the Japanese had bombed Pearl Harbor, the survey revealed that only six-per-cent of the people thought that the Germans were the most dangerous. Only nine-per-cent the Japanese. Yet, fully forty-four per-cent thought that the Jews were the most dangerous people in America!

That was astounding to me Katalin! Here we are this "allegedly" Christian nation, where several Jews were instrumental in the founding of our nation if you researched the history of the Revolutionary War. Add to that that many Jews today are first and second generation Americans just struggling to survive like most other immigrants have in the past and yet we are supposed to be these noble people, these *Christian* people who willingly accept the poor, the hungry and oppressed!? That is why Katalin, the mere mention of Jesus, or better, Christianity, is an anathema to many Jews, and certainly is to me. We are often still referred to as the Christ killers and every century we are reminded of it."

As Ira paused for effect, Katalin felt compelled to respond. 'I'm not ignorant of the suffering of the Jewish people, Ira. I witnessed it first hand."

"I know you did and your parents died nobly and heroically in defense of the Jews. If all Christians were like you and your brave parents there would be no problem. But unfortunately that is not the case."

Katalin continued. "I also have no answer for all the wickedness in the world. Regarding Hitler, he was anything but a Christian and all too often Jewish people confuse being Gentile with that of being Christian, which is not the case. I will agree that Hitler started out a Catholic and an altar boy but he certainly did not stay one. In fact, Hitler harbored a real animosity towards Christians and once stated, "I consider Christianity the most evil, seductive lie that ever existed. The simple truth is that Hitler was heavily into black magic and the occult as early as 1918 and once told a friend that he heard voices telling him he would one day be Germany's messiah.

"I understand how Jews have been unmercifully and wrongly accused for Jesus' crucifixion when one considers that it was the *Gentile* Romans who actually did the crucifying. I'm fully aware of all the persecutions of Jews through the centuries and all I can say is that my precious Lord's name has too often been misappropriated by either ignorant or malicious people. It is blight and sad commentary on mankind. But my Jesus does not need a defense attorney, least of all me. But is some ways you are visiting the sins of the fathers on the sons and daughters of a new generation."

"Well, maybe I am being too harsh, Katalin, and not to change the subject, but you are still speaking of a dead messiah who committed suicide."

"The Resurrection, Ira! He's not dead! and until someone can come up with a body I will stand on that fact. Saying he committed suicide is no different than condemning the soldier who throws himself on a grenade in order to save his brothers in arm. It isn't suicide, Ira, it is courageous sacrifice. While in human flesh at Gethsemane, Jesus trembled and bled from fear of His impending death. Like all of us in human flesh, he had the human desire not to perish. Yet His faith was so pure and complete knowing all the while His Father would raise Him. Add to that His unquenchable love for mankind and the courage it took to face the cross, no matter how you feel about me, I will not permit you to denigrate my Lord."

"Sorry, Katalin...even though I obviously do not believe in the resurrection, or your stated reasons for the crucifixion, I apologize and will take back my suicide comment. But there is absolutely nothing in the *Tenach,* about a messiah dying or being raised from the dead."

"In the Babylonian Talmuds, Ira, Jewish scholars sometimes debated the issue of there possibly being two messiahs. It was obvious to some of your very learned people that one messiah was to be cut off or killed."

"A man cannot become a god, Katalin.."

"True, Ira, but God can certainly become a man or do we limit God?"

"And what If there is no God?"

Katalin was stunned by Ira's last remark. She had once known Ira to be very God fearing and deeply spiritual. She wondered, *Had the war affected his mind this much?*

"Ira, I so love and admire the Jewish people. Again, I don't know what has happened that has made you feel the way you do and even now to question God's existence? Regardless of your wanting to distance our relationship I care for you and it worries me that you are speaking in this manner. Of course there is a God! But that is something you need to talk with a Rabbi about, or with Sarah, but certainly not me. Ira, tell me plainly though! Do you now resent me so much that your desire is that I never see or be with your family again!?"

"No, not at all. I'm not sure what I'm trying to say or what I want, this is all so awkward. You and Sarah are so close that I sometimes feel as if I am married to two people. What I resent though is your religion and its undue influence on Sarah and I know, DeeJay. As a person I still really care about you which is what makes all this so difficult. Can't you see? Sarah and DeeJay are so admiring and loving towards you that you can't help but be an influence on them and I really do think that Sarah's opposition to moving to Arizona, even though she won't admit it, is because she feels so obligated to you as a friend, especially because of all you've been through together."

Katalin resigned herself to the inevitable as tears again welled up in her eyes. "Okay Ira...tell me what you want of me?"

"I am only asking that for the foreseeable future that you spend less time with us. At least until I can convince Sarah of our need to move to Arizona. With you busily involved in other things, the finish of your schooling, your helping out at church, your work as a proof-reader and writer at the newspaper, Sarah might not think she is abandoning you if your life is already full."

"Okay Ira...I will heed your wishes. I can't talk any more. Right now I just want to go home and cry my eyes out...goodbye." Emotionally distraught, Katalin scooted her chair back, rose and hurriedly left the delicatessen.

Ira was now left alone with his thoughts. He looked over where Katalin was seated and noticed that she had not taken one bite of her sandwich and felt remorse that he had so thoroughly reproached her. Tired and emotionally drained, he began to reflect on Katalin's tragic loss of her parents and how powerfully and courageously she had managed to cope with it over the years, rarely ever speaking of it. He no longer had to worry about Sarah feeling she would be abandoning Katalin because he just did. Ira's thoughts then turned back to a time in Katalin's life that made him feel even more miserable. He reflected back to two Christmases ago when Katalin, in an uncharacteristic and melancholy mood shared with he and Sarah, the depth of her loss and when her life changed forever. A time when Katalin was thirteen years old.

It happened, Katalin said, in the middle of a sermon by her father, on a hot August day in 1936. Four German SS troops had quietly entered her father's church. Imposing and intimidating, they stood with fearsome scowls, as one by one the frightened parishioners filed out of the pews and exited the small country church.

Ira remembered Katalin telling of a brash young SS lieutenant who had first seated himself and draped his arms over one of the pews. Reverend Zichy remained at the lectern where his wife, Katalin's mother, fearfully joined him. Katalin had started walking towards them when her mother caught her eye and with a quick head motion, warned her off. Katalin then stood by the side exit trembling as she listened to the verbal exchange between her father and the smug lieutenant.

The officer soon grew impatient with Katalin's father and got up and swaggered towards him. Standing eyeball to eyeball, the overbearing Nazi told Reverend Zichy that he was no longer interested in his theological discourses, that he was to give the Nazi salute and condemn the Jews if he wished to live.

Undaunted, her father refused, and the irate lieutenant then straight armed a salute above the pastor's head and clicked his heels. In his pompous arrogance he shouted in Reverend Zichy's face. "Heil Hitler! Reverend Zichy! Heil Hitler! Heil Hitler!"

In her thirteen years, Katalin had never heard her father utter a contemptuous word towards a soul. She didn't then. "I could never do that," her father had said solemnly, although his face had become a pasty white.

The enraged lieutenant then pistol-whipped Katalin's father to the ground. Her terror-stricken mother screamed in her direction. "Katalin, run!"

For a brief moment, Katalin stood frozen, fearful of leaving her parents in their moment of desperation. Then she detected a pungent odor and realized she had no choice. While two of the SS men were emptying large cans of petrol inside the perimeter of the church, the fourth one eyed Katalin and began moving towards her. She bolted out the side door as fast as her legs would carry her and fled away until at times she thought her lungs would burst.

No sooner had she safely reached a forested area a couple hundred yards away when she heard a volley of shots ring out. She stopped and slowly turned, horrified at the thought that her parents had just been murdered. Then smoke began rising from the church and within minutes it was engulfed in flames.

Katalin said she stood paralyzed. Her grieving heart having been ripped apart, hoping on one hand that her parents were still alive while, simultaneously hoping they were dead so that they would not die by fire.

Ira tried to imagine, now as then, how Katalin survived such a horrendous experience. Her tragedy compounded when spending the next, almost two years surviving on her own in the streets and in the sewers, with the barest of subsistence. Then came the time when she was spotted by Mrs. Forguet, eating scraps in the rear of the Schooner Bar and was taken in.

Ira rose from his chair to go back to work. He also had left his sandwich uneaten. His feelings for Katalin were mixed. At once, he had great empathy and compassion and even a great fondness for her. Still, he had the best interests of his family to consider and knew it was time to move in another direction. As difficult as it was, he was convinced that putting space between his family and Katalin had become an absolute necessity.

Chapter 7

September brought the first respite from the suffocating heat wave that had gripped New York for much of the summer. What started as a crisp gentle breeze was forecasted to be a full-fledged storm by midnight. As the hour approached six o'clock, the evening sun winked its eye over the rooftops of the brownstone apartment buildings in the Williamsburg section of Brooklyn.

This was Bedford-Stuyvesant, the area where Ira and his family had lived for four years, generally referred to, however, as *Bedford-Stuy-returned* by those who came back to the same impoverished neighborhoods they had left when they went away to war. Now, at sunset, on the night of Rosh-Hashanah, known as the Head-of-the-year [Jewish New Year], Bedford-Stuy was the place Ira Katz wanted to leave.

Both Katz families, along with Elsa and Sam Rosen—Ira and Sarah's older neighbors from across the hall—milled around the living room engaged in conversation. A dinner table with tablecloth and place settings occupied much of the space in the middle of the room. The centerpiece was two unusual brass candlesticks, their candles waiting to be lit. These candlesticks had turned out to be an object lesson and a humbling experience for Ira. Sarah had purchased the once badly tarnished items at an antique shop three years ago, paying twenty dollars for the pair because they reminded her of candlesticks her parents once owned.

Upon seeing them, Ira slapped himself on the forehead. "You paid twenty dollars for those!?"

Sarah felt embarrassed and offered to take them back, but Ira, seeing the tears in her eyes, suddenly realized the sentimental attachment that prompted her to purchase them. After being scrubbed and polished, the candlesticks—found to be of Austrian origin—revealed a handsomely decorated mélange of medieval, baroque and art nouveau forms with Hebrew inscriptions dating back fifty years. When offered five hundred dollars by the state Jewish museum, Ira bribed Sarah with a dinner out if she promised to quit waving them in front of him with a triumphant grin.

Sarah and Ruth began bringing in the food from the kitchen. The sweet-scented aroma of honey-almond chicken and freshly baked challah loaves filled the air. Last to be brought in were the sectioned apple slices and bowls of honey in which the apple slices were to be dipped. At a certain point, everyone would dip the slices and wish each other a "sweet" new year.

When he thought no one was looking, David-Jacob, his eyes darting back and forth, stretched his arm across the table and grabbed one of the slices. Ira saw him out of the corner of his eye and reminded himself to speak to his son before putting him to bed. He then went to the kitchen to refill his drink, returning with a full glass of ginger ale. Tired from a hard week's work and observing that everyone else was still standing and talking, Ira casually leaned against the wall and let his mind drift, thus allowing himself to become detached from the proceedings. In his distant thoughts he tried to determine in quick synoptic flashes how each personality had been scripted into his life and times.

Watching Ruth Katz, his sister-in-law, as she assisted her daughter Rachel in placing the candles in their holders, Ira concluded that Ruth was the type of woman who would go unnoticed in a crowd of one. Like the small nondescript blue sofa at the other end of the room or the walnut-grained glass-enclosed bookcase in the center, Ruth Katz was just like another fixture—always there but hardly ever noticed. Yet everyone who knew her held her in very high esteem.

Tonight she was wearing a simple black skirt with white blouse and red scarf. On her blouse was pinned a gold letter pendant *L'chayim*, meaning "To your health" or "Cheers." Ira was aware that his brother Marvin had brought with him the customary bottle of Dom Perignon, the champagne now being hidden in a brown paper bag beneath his chair. At some time during the evening, Ira knew, Marvin would offer another of his lengthy discourses, longer than a filibuster, but otherwise known as a toast.

Ruth, with her thin eyebrows, thin lips and straight brown hair that curled into a flip, was by most standards considered homely. At thirty-four, her droopy eyelids lent to an always tired looking appearance. However, her unassuming and unobtrusive nature belied a surprisingly highly charged, accomplished and energetic person with a distinctively sharp wit. A graduate of CUNY (City University of New York) with a degree in Liberal Arts, she was very active in Hadassah and a woman often sought after to be a sounding board for Jewish women with troubled marriages. Her confidential, sisterly advice was often helpful for those whose ex-soldier husbands had difficulty readjusting to civilian life. Ira liked Ruth but realized, like everyone else, that it was easy to take her for granted.

Turning his thoughts towards his brother Marvin, Ira's initial impression was of a man determined to occupy center stage. Extroverted, overbearing and argumentative, Marvin was nonetheless a loyal friend to those who needed a friend. A member of the B'nai B'rith men's group, he could always be found on committees dealing with the group's charitable functions.

Although the owner of a hugely successful floor covering store and an Orthodox Jew, Marvin was both unconventional and opinionated. Tonight, his choice of wardrobe would have been considered unconventional, if only because of his normal slovenly appearance. He was wearing a blue twilled, striped seersucker suit and a neatly pressed white shirt, open at the collar, with a gold stenciled "MK" on the left pocket. His receding hairline literally gleamed, glue-slicked back with, Ira thought, at least a gallon of alcohol-laden Vitalis. The overpowering aroma of greasy hairdressing competed strongly with the smell of the honey-almond chicken and challah bread.

The blustery Marvin was an ardent admirer and frequent reader of biographies of ex-President Theodore Roosevelt. Ira regarded Marvin as an anachronism. He was certain that his older brother would have been much happier living a hundred years ago as a mountain man, blazing trails and hunting bears.

Ira both loved and respected his brother but was bothered by that part of his character that came across as condescending. His brother was never shy about reminding people of his generosity and what he had done for them, generally implying a kind of servitude. He was not the type Ira felt would understand why his brother wanted to move 2500 miles away to get out of his shadow. Marvin was totally unaware that after months of discussion and outright arguing, a decision to move to Arizona was close at hand for Ira. If indeed Sarah could be convinced, telling Marvin would be a loathsome task. Ira dreaded the mere thought of it, thinking now—if given the choice—he'd rather steal pennies from a beggar.

While straightening the tablecloth, Sarah looked up and caught Ira's stare as he leaned against the wall sipping his drink. She smiled coquettishly, her lips forming the unspoken words, "I love you."

Sarah was wearing the new outfit Ira had surprised her with last week. Ruth had mentioned to him how much Sarah admired the new 1949 Paris-look dress with fitted waist and lower hemline. With his sister-in-law's help in color coordinating, he also purchased for Sarah the high heeled shoes to go with the dress. Fourteen months had passed since she had had any new clothes and with Rosh-Hashanah coming up and then Yom Kippur ten days later, Ira felt the time was appropriate. Despite their tight budget, he knew she was certainly deserving of a new outfit and it was unlikely she would ever have purchased one for herself. When she opened the packages from Macy's eight days before, she squealed with delight. That night they went to an Italian restaurant and it was the happiest he remembered Sarah in years.

Now as Ira stood eyeing his wife of seven-and-a-half years, he realized how blessed he was. There was no doubt in his mind that she was far prettier than he was handsome. He mused that at twenty-eight and after two children, she was even more attractive than when they first met. Ira's mind went back to that cold January day in 1942. . . .

Ira and two Army buddies, all in uniform and with weekend passes from Fort Dix, New Jersey, had decided to take the bus and check out the girls at the ice skating rink at New York's Central Park. It was no contest. The two prettiest girls, hands down, were Sarah and Katalin who were there with their dates. Sarah was the last link in a four part human chain being whipped around the oval surface.

Ira remembered barely stepping onto the ice and kneeling down to retie the laces on his skates when he heard a loud scream, "Look out!" Sarah's sailor companion had lost hold of her hand and she went skating wildly out of control.

Trying desperately to keep her balance, lifting up one leg and then the other, she was headed straight for Ira. No sooner had he shot to his feet than he felt as if he'd been hit by a Mack truck and slammed hard to the ice. While on his back, Sarah rode him like a sled into the wall and he hit it so hard he momentarily blacked out.

Once he shook out the cobwebs, he felt her warm soft body on top of his. She was dazed herself, breathing hard, her mouth pressed against his cheek. Apologizing and blushing over their compromising situation, she looked relieved when she was finally helped up. Amid the concern, laughter and innuendos the two groups made friends but neither he nor Sarah skated the rest of the evening. No amount of coaxing would get either of them back on the rink. The easily embarrassed couple were too busy getting to know each other over cups of hot chocolate and staring into each other's eyes.

Sarah had soft rounded cheeks, still with the blush of youth. Together with her smooth olive skin and well defined, what Ira called, sensuous lips, people often confused her for being Italian. But it was Sarah's eyes that intrigued Ira—those deep set, haunting and penetrating, green eyes that contrasted boldly with her silken, auburn-brown hair. Yet he knew that Sarah would never see herself for how pretty she really was. The scar on her chin left wounds that would never heal. Sarah's eyes revealed a woman of tremendous complexity—pain, passion, vulnerability and doubt. She was a woman wanting desperately to trust but always questioning motives.

His wife had witnessed the most vile of cruelties. She had also witnessed incredible acts of selfless love. She now lived in a kind of purgatory, wondering endlessly, *For what divine purpose did people choose to become evil or good?* When Ira noticed her occasional expressionless stares, he concluded that what her eyes revealed most were confusion, the bewildered look of a deer caught between the headlights of a car, anxious to move in one direction or another but unable to do either.

Sarah had seemed happy though the last two months. Most of that time had been spent doting over Joshua-Caleb and wheeling him all around the city in his buggy. In the process, many strangers who stopped to admire her new infant and had become her friends. As a side benefit to what she jokingly referred to as BBP (baby buggy pushing), she managed to lose all the pounds she had gained during pregnancy.

Other than the conflict surrounding their potential move to Arizona, Sarah's only concern seemed to be the absence of Katalin. Ira still wasn't sure how to downplay that issue. Normally his wife and Katalin were together two or three times a week. In the last two months, they had seen each other twice . . . period.

Katalin maintained to Sarah that her schedule entering her senior year of journalism at Brooklyn College had become more hectic. In addition, her work as a part time writer and proof reader at the Brooklyn Daily Eagle often had her stressed out and tired. "Something about Katalin is different," she mused aloud to Ira. "She's not so bubbly or confiding anymore. I wonder if something is wrong. But if there is she won't admit it."

Only Ira knew what was really bothering Katalin. Maybe, Ira thought, he miscalculated how much trying to push Katalin out of their lives would affect his wife but he really was tired of competing with Katalin in occupying Sarah's time and thoughts.

Ira could only admit to himself, that his concern over Katalin's undue Christian influence was only part of the problem. He had other reasons for wanting to move across country. In Arizona there would be the opportunity to adapt to a more liberal practice of Judaism. When there, he would still observe the traditions of the faith. This was necessary for several reasons, not the least of which was to avert any discussion over his own lack of faith. He knew that tradition was also necessary as a reminder to his children that there was no shame in being a Jew—only that his present version of being a Jew meant walking on the ashes of suffering Jews of previous generations, unremitting anti-Semitism, forced conversions, the popular form of entertainment in 17th century Spain known as auto-da-fe's, when those Jews who were forced to convert, were found reverting back to Judaism, then branded as heretics and burned at the stake, and of course, the so very recent genocide. Certainly there were other races of people who suffered, but few who suffered so tragically or for so long.

Yet paradoxically, Ira was forced to live a lie. As an atheist, he knew that any proclamation of his non-belief in God would cause friction, both within his family and the community of people he lived and worked with. Why buy trouble when it was easier to play the game. His brother Marvin didn't know. Even his precious wife, who knew him intimately, didn't know. They didn't know that his God was dead. The one person he suspected did know, who saw through the facade of his still being a resolute Son of the Covenant people, was Katalin. Ira felt relieved when she had phoned Sarah earlier in the week to apologize for not being able to come over that night for Rosh-Hashanah. Her excuse was in keeping with her previous excuses the past two months: too much work to catch up on and too little time to do it.

Ira noticed Sarah's disappointment at the time of the call; however, the two women did agree to meet later in the month over lunch. The Rosens also committed to watching the children, giving Sarah a well-deserved break. Still, it would be the first Rosh-Hashanah that Katalin would miss in what was now going on five years, since 1945, when Ira got out of the Army.

It was an off-the-cuff irreverent remark made during casual conversation with Katalin last February that kick-started it. Katalin was at the apartment and she and Ira were at the table drinking coffee, waiting for Sarah to finish tucking David-Jacob in. They were talking about Israel and how by only a scant one vote of the United Nations, Israel had become a country again.

Katalin attributed its nationhood to God's miraculous intervention on behalf of the Jewish people, starting in on the famous dry-bones prophecy written of in the book of Ezekiel some 2500 years earlier. She exulted in her declaration that Israel's return to her land was not only a grand fulfillment of prophecy but perhaps one of the Bible's three greatest miracles. (Without asking, Ira instinctively knew that she regarded the resurrection of her Savior as the single greatest.)

Ira's cynical response seemed to take her by surprise. "Isn't it amazing, Katalin, that it took God almost 2500 years to fulfill that alleged prophecy? In the meantime, by 1882, as many as 25,000 Jews had already emigrated back to Palestine. Seems to me that we Jews, without God's help, accomplished more in the last seventy years than God did in 2,500."

"You're confusing the issue, Ira. God is the One who put it in the hearts of His people to want to return to their land." At that point Ira changed the subject.

He didn't regard Katalin as any less a person worthy of his highest respect. He just wanted to respect her from a distance. Now it appeared he was getting his way since his non-lunch with Katalin some two months ago. He wearied of conversations with her that always evolved into matters of deep introspection and personal belief. Sometimes Sarah would take him to task for being so uncommunicative but he argued that it was just his nature. He convinced himself that some things in life were too fraught with emotion and pain to talk about.

Now Ira just wanted to attempt the geographical cure by changing his surroundings. Brooklyn had a population of three million people, half of which were Jewish. Although he loved its people and had established strong relationships, too much of the city's social life centered around the synagogue and a God he no longer believed in. It made it that much more difficult to cast aside the dispiriting and resurgent memories of what occurred four years ago in Ohrdruf, Germany.

Try as he might Ira couldn't forget nor bring himself to talk about what he witnessed on that day. On more than one occasion he came close to telling Sarah, and he wanted to, but then thought better of it. After what she had endured in her life, how could he add his burden to hers? How could he share his own horrifying experience as a corporal in the 89th Infantry Division, 353rd Regiment, when he was required to help liberate a Nazi death camp, an act which had a profound and devastating effect on him. Amid the torture chambers, the cordwood stacks of emaciated bodies and the dazed and terminally ill walking dead, Ira sought to take out his revenge on one of the captured SS guards. It was a dehumanizing experience and one that made him realize he was capable of murder.

April 4, 1945, was now forever etched in his memory. It was the day, month and year that Ira Katz buried his God. The alternative was too difficult to accept: that the God who did exist had either abandoned or now hated the once chosen people.

Chapter 8

Sarah noticed that the Scrabble game had started without her: Ira, Sam and Elsa on one team; Marvin, Ruth and daughter Rachel on the other. Joshua-Caleb was beginning to stir in his buggy and Sarah was surprised to see that he had already been changed and given another warm bottle of milk.

Ruth looked up and smiled at her. "He's just darling, Sarah, not even a whimper. If my brilliant husband wasn't complaining and getting trounced over here, I'd still be holding him."

Sarah thanked Ruth and lifted her infant son from the buggy. Still clutching on to his bottle with his right hand, her baby wrapped his chubby left arm around Sarah's neck and pressed against her.

Sarah took baby Joshua to her room and put him in his crib. Returning five minutes later, she observed her older son being admonished by Ira for eating an apple slice before prayers—warning him not to do it again, but for now, Ira would let it pass.

Ira turned back to the game and picked up seven tiles to place on the board for bonus points. Marvin shook his head, "Ira, either you're the luckiest man alive or you cheat. Which is it?"

Ira retaliated. "Neither, I was just born smarter than you."

"Yeah, sure, and mice give birth to baby elephants."

David-Jacob rose from the floor and walked about the scrabble table to get the best view. He soon found himself observing the scrabble game while standing next to his Uncle Marvin. Taking notice of his nephew, Marvin turned his chair slightly sideways to face David-Jacob and affectionately pinched his cheeks. Marvin then waved his index finger in David-Jacob's face to instruct him. "*Boychik*! You've got a lot of enthusiasm and you need to put that energy to work and learn, especially about being a Jew. I know your father works very hard, but when he is too tired, make sure that you find someone else to take you to Temple. Someday, before you know it, you'll be thirteen years old and be having your Bar Mitzvah." Marvin reached behind him for his glass of champagne.

While his uncle sipped his drink, David-Jacob responded, "I'm not going to Temple anymore because I'm not going to be Jewish anymore."

Marvin gagged on the champagne, spitting some of it on David-Jacob. Everyone looked on with stunned expressions. Marvin finally regained his composure. "Oh, so! the little pisher boy, son of my brother who is not yet seven years old, decides in his great wisdom that he no longer wishes to be Jewish. Perhaps you are planning on becoming a Presbyterian?"

"Nope, I'm gonna be a monkey people."

Cousin Rachel broke out laughing. Marvin, meanwhile, stuck his pinkie finger in his ear and screwed it in hard, pretending to clean out the wax in order to hear better.

Ira was perplexed and turned in his chair to look up at his wife standing behind him. Sarah, puzzled, shrugged her shoulders, suspecting that her son's remarks had something to do with his telling her yesterday about some older boys taunting him.

The Rosens looked on with intense curiosity as Marvin squinted and grilled his nephew further. "So, David, tell me. What's a 'monkey people' and where do these people live? Not in trees I hope, although experience leads me to believe that you'd enjoy swinging from branches." Ruth jabbed her index finger into Marvin's back.

"Aunt Katalin told me about 'em, Uncle Marvin. They are these people that pray all day and aren't allowed to talk to girls. They wear funny clothes with ropes in the middle and live in places called monster-aries."

Marvin raised his eyebrows and stared at his wife. "You hear, Ruth! He's going to live in a monster-airy. If I'm correct, I think that is where little monsters grow into great big monsters."

"Dear, I think that your nephew is referring to monks and monasteries."

"Naw-w-w, not my precious little nephew. Monks pray to the gentile God named Jesus." Marvin gazed into David-Jacob's eyes anticipating a response.

"I know that, Uncle Marvin. But Aunt Katalin said that Jesus was Jewish. So if I'm nice to him and pray a lot and tell him that the Jewish people are sorry, then maybe he'll tell all the other people to quit calling all the Jewish people names."

Marvin's expression was now one of incredulity as he looked across the table at Ira and Sarah. "May I compliment the two of you, and may I ask if you are planning on raising your second son to become a Catholic priest?"

"Enough with the sarcasm," Ruth implored. "Since when are you Mr. Perfect? I'm sure that Ira and Sarah will talk to David-Jacob and explain things properly to him."

"What's to explain! They're raising their children to be *Goyim* [gentiles]."

Ira interjected, "Marvin, trust me, this is news to Sarah and me as well. Apparently Katalin has given him some fanciful ideas."

Sarah took offense to Ira's remark. "Ira, please! Quit blaming Katalin for every little thing. I've never heard her try to proselytize DeeJay!"

"Sarah, he just said that his Aunt Katalin told him about these things."

"It doesn't mean she gave him instructions." Ruth sided with Sarah. "Ira, I'm not trying to interfere and I'm only making an observation, but Katalin cares too deeply and respects all of you too much to attempt to influence your son towards Christianity."

Ira smirked and shrugged his shoulders. A still chomping-at-the-bit Marvin continued his interrogation of David-Jacob. "Okay, boychik, when is all this going to happen? That you're going to monster-airy school."

"When I'm ten years old."

"What's so special that you have to be ten years old?"

"Because, Uncle Marvin, I'd be too little before ten and they wouldn't take me. You have to be old enough to take care of yourself."

"Oh, well, pardon me. I should've known."

"That's okay, Uncle Marvin, but it's in all their rules."

"Of course!" Marvin responded, rolling his eyes. "Well, boychik, I hate to tell you but I don't think they have any monster-airy schools in Brooklyn and they're not likely to have any, even when you're ten."

"I know, Uncle Marvin, but they do in Arizona."

"Huh!?"

"In Arizona! Where we're going to live!"

Marvin looked back at Ira and Sarah, bewildered. "I'm sorry, I can't keep up with your kid. He makes up more fairy tales than Mother Goose." He leaned forward in his chair, his face only inches from his wildly imaginative nephew. "David-Jacob, let me inform you about Arizona, this place of make-believe that you're pretending to move to. Nothing lives there but rodents, centipedes and a few million rattlesnakes. And they're not exactly thrilled about it."

"Uh-uh, Uncle Marvin. People live there too."

Marvin again waved his index finger. "Boychik, you don't understand. In the summer it gets so hot there that your brain shrivels up and becomes a french fry. Nobody normal wants to live there."

"Mommy and Daddy do!"

"Case closed. What? Wait! What are you talking about!?"

David-Jacob looked over at his mother who was gritting her teeth. He nervously bit his lower lip, suddenly remembering being told several times not to mention Arizona to anyone until a final decision was made. No use in causing anyone concern, his parents said. Now he was in trouble again as he anxiously tried to extricate himself. "Well . . . I think Mommy does . . . want to . . . live in Arizona . . . sometimes . . . but not really."

Sarah muttered under her breath but the sternness of her voice was unmistakable. "DeeJay! To your room! Now!" Without any hesitation, David-Jacob beat a hasty retreat.

An awkward silence filled the room as Marvin eyed his brother and sister-in-law across the table. Ira turned and looked up at his wife who was still standing behind his chair. Both were apprehensive, not knowing quite what to say. Their son had spoken presumptuously and now that the cat was out of the bag, Marvin was sure to be furious.

The Rosens had become interested observers. Both sat stiff as boards, sensing the tension in the air. Earlier Rachel had moved to the sofa where she was almost asleep.

Ira's mind was awhirl as he contemplated what to say. Moving to Arizona had been his idea from the beginning. Sarah had recently and only reluctantly begun to give in. He felt strangely embarrassed for not confiding in his brother earlier, especially considering the time and resources Marvin had poured into letting him run the store without interference. The newly-established profit margins, the turnover time for floor stock before markdown and the setting in motion of a newly constructed advertising program taking them through the current fiscal year were entirely Ira's decisions.

Marvin had also given him the go-ahead to train two new employees for future management as part of a five-year plan of growth that would hopefully lead them to open a second and possibly third successful store. Now he had to tell his brother that he was bailing out and that the faith he had placed in him wasn't justified. He felt like a traitor. Measured against that was the fact he was miserable living in the big city and needed a change.

He took a deep breath. "Marvin, what DeeJay mentioned about our moving to Arizona is maybe yes, maybe no. The truth is, Sarah and I still haven't come to a meeting of the minds."

All eyes were on Marvin, anticipating a major outburst. Ira continued, "You remember Barry Greenberg? He and I used to lay tile for you before we joined the Army together."

"Of course. I also knew he lives in Arizona because his parents are still customers. But then Barry wasn't exactly a whiz kid. He and Arizona probably deserve each other."

Sarah became mildly irritated at Marvin's steady stream of caustic remarks. "Marvin, do you practice being obnoxious or do you just come by it naturally?"

Marvin broke into a wry grin. "Sarah, if the two of you are truly thinking of moving to Arizona, let me first do you a favor. Tomorrow I'll buy you a cactus. You can sit on it while sticking your head in the oven and just pretend you're in Arizona."

Sarah proceeded to answer her own question. "You come by it naturally."

Despite his sarcasm, Marvin was still surprisingly calm as he gestured towards Ira. "Nu! You still haven't explained to me about Arizona, except to say that muttonhead Barry lives out there frying his *tuchis* [posterior] off."

"Well, Marvin, during the war, Barry met an Arizona girl who was part of a USO troupe. They corresponded and after the war they got married in Arizona and settled there. He went back to installing, but then his knees started giving out. On a shoestring he opened a small floor covering store and he said he's done quite well."

"Who does he sell to? Mr. and Mrs. Gila Monster?"

"Marvin, you might find this hard to believe but almost a quarter-million people now live in Arizona. Anyway, he's decided to sell the store and go back to school on the GI Bill. He wants to learn electronics."

"So what does this have to do with you?" Marvin inquired.

"I was curious. I asked him what contracts he's got lined up, what kind of walk-in traffic, store displays and so forth, and he leveled with me. He made me a very generous offer because he'd love to have us move there. I don't know, it's just something that appeals to me. I say that, knowing and despite all that you've done for me. No matter what happens, I'll always be indebted to you. Anyway, I knew you'd be upset, so I couldn't bring myself to mention it to you."

"Why should I be upset that you want to waste your life living in the God-forsaken desert?"

Elsa Rosen became suddenly alarmed. "Ira! My goodness! There's indians living in Arizona!" Shouting her peculiar concern caused the four Katzs to exchange blank stares. Seizing the opportunity, Marvin facetiously and tongue-in-cheek echoed her fear. "Yes Ira, the indians. You'd no sooner get out there than you'd have a face-off with Geronimo. Don't you care at all about your family?"

Ira wasn't in the mood for jesting, anxious instead to resolve the previous issue with his brother. "I believe they caught Geronimo."

Elsa looked quizzically at Ira. "They caught Geronimo? Why didn't I hear?"

"The news is slow coming out of Arizona, Elsa," Marvin volunteered. "In fact, they're still delivering mail on the backs of tarantulas."

Ira smirked, "Elsa, Geronimo was caught decades ago. Indians haven't been on the warpath for seventy years. They're good citizens just like everyone else, wearing a white hat and driving their Desotos and Henry J's."

Elsa still persisted in an admonishing fashion. "I wouldn't be so sure. I hear stories still . . . and see in the movies. And how do you know for sure that this Geronimo, he is no longer around? He might be old but still telling his people what to do. I think it is very dangerous your wanting to live in Arizona. Leopards are not so quick, you know, to change their spots."

Ira closed his eyes, wondering how in the world this conversation ever got started. Opening them again and looking around the table, his wife was now sitting next to him while Marvin and Ruth were sitting across from him. The three were restraining themselves to keep from bursting out laughing. Sam Rosen, meanwhile, was tapping on his hearing aid, having a difficult time picking up on the conversation.

Ira surmised that any argument with Elsa would be ineffectual and his mind raced to concoct the most plausible story she might accept. "Elsa, the last time I wrote Barry, I asked, 'Barry, what about Geronimo, is he still on the warpath?' Barry wrote back, Elsa, and told me that the Apache chief had become a model citizen and has been allowed off the reservation."

"To do what?" Elsa exclaimed.

"To um-m-m-mm, ah . . . to ah . . . move to Tucson. I believe that Geronimo is now living in Tucson and managing a bowling alley."

Marvin cast a glance at his younger brother, rolling his tongue on the inside of his mouth, attempting to keep a straight face. Sarah quickly excused herself, saying she had to go to the kitchen to do dishes. Ruth, just as quickly, shot from her seat, offering to help. Once on the other side of the kitchen door, the two women fell into each other's arms laughing hysterically. Neither could believe that the stoic, never-tell-a-lie-Ira, would fabricate such an outrageous story.

Just as suddenly, Sarah's countenance soon changed and she became strangely quiet.

"You okay, Sarah? If you've developed a headache, I have some aspirins."

Sarah didn't reply but walked towards a small circular table in the corner and sat down. She appeared pensive as Ruth took the seat next to her and placed her hand on top of Sarah's.

"Sarah, are you disturbed over possibly moving? Is it upsetting you?"

Sarah looked at Ruth and shook her head no. "Ruth, it occurred to me that a short while ago we were laughing over Ira and Elsa's conversation."

"Are you concerned that we offended her?"

"No, I think we were careful not to, in that we left the room. But it just struck me that Elsa's attitude towards the Indian people is not really a laughing matter."

"I don't understand."

"Well, Elsa's such a kind, sweet and decent person. Yet she's stereotyped the Indians in much the same way that many people stereotype us as Jews."

"If people choose to be ignorant, Sarah, there's not much you can do."

"I know, but it troubles me that it has to be this way."

"Sarah, why is this bothering you now?"

"Because last night, when I was putting DeeJay to bed, he asked me if the Jews are the devil's people because they killed Jesus."

"Oh dear! Where did he pick up that idea?"

"Some boys that he's been playing with."

"Well, it's likely that their parents have taught them that."

"Oh I'm sure, and that's what's really bothering me. It started me to thinking. Ruth, let's say that I wasn't Jewish but instead was born into a family that hated the Jews or the coloreds. If I was taught to believe that way, then I would be no different than those who hate us now. The only reason I don't think like that is just an accident of birth. Am I making sense?"

"Sarah, why do you burden yourself with questions no one can possibly answer?"

"Don't you see, Ruth? I was fortunate enough to have been born into a loving family. I wasn't taught to hate. By the same token, how can I criticize or blame others who do hate because of their upbringing. If I had been born into a family of anti-Semites or Nazis, maybe I would think the same way. I was going to talk to this family that DeeJay mentioned, the family who thinks we're the devil's people. But who am I to stand in judgment of them, or anyone for that matter?"

"Sarah, I'm surprised at you."

"Why?"

"You of all people should know that regardless of what people hear or are taught, they have the freedom to choose what to believe. Your German soldier, Sarah. He was taught to be a Nazi and to persecute the Jews, yet he saw that it was wrong and risked his life for you. Bad people can be born into good families and vice-versa.

"God gave us all a conscience, Sarah. That is what makes us higher than the animals. Animals operate on instinct but man is capable of rational thought and knows the difference between right and wrong. To make sure we know the difference, God gave us the Ten Commandments.

"No Sarah, everyone is responsible for his or her own actions, which is why I am convinced there must be some type of afterlife. Also justice in the afterlife requires judgment, and for judgment to be fair, mandates that there be a supreme judge who knows both our thoughts and deeds and holds us accountable. It is the only thing that makes sense to me.

"Remember, Sarah, God created us in His image! His! We are to be like Him. Sadly and too often in this world we get it backwards. Man does as he pleases and then creates a god to his liking—one that will give him a stamp of approval regardless of his actions. Trust me, Sarah, the one true God, who I believe to be the God of the Bible, is observing how we treat others."

A smile returned to Sarah's face. "Thank you."

"For what?"

"For putting things back in proper perspective."

"I didn't know I said anything that profound."

"You did though."

Embarrassed and not desiring credit, Ruth deflected Sarah's compliment by resorting to her occasional offbeat sense of humor. In her throaty voice imitation of Sylvester the Cat, she said, "Well, sufferin' succotash! I kept tellin' everyone that Tweety Bird was really a cow-eating buzzard in disguise but no one would listen!"

Sarah laughed out loud. "How'd you do that?"

"You live with Marvin as long as I have, you find different ways to amuse yourself."

While finishing the dishes, Ruth provided the entertainment with more of her cartoon character imitations, keeping Sarah in stitches. It was a side of Ruth that Sarah had never witnessed. Suddenly she felt closer to Ruth than she ever had before. As thoughts of Arizona kept flashing in and out of her mind, her newly, stronger-formed bond with her sister-in-law made the possibility of moving that much more difficult to contemplate.

Chapter 9

As the evening grew late, David-Jacob and his cousin Rachel were sitting cross-legged on the linoleum floor spinning a *dreidle,* a four sided toy top with Hebrew lettering.

The *dreidle,* a favorite toy among Jewish children and adults, was normally associated with the December holiday of Chanukah. The spinning game of chance had a history going back to the rule of Antiochus Epiphanes, before the Maccabean revolt in 150 B.C., a time in Jewish history when soldiers executed any Jew practicing or studying their faith. Whenever those Jews heard soldiers approaching, they quickly hid the scriptures and took out and pretended to be playing with the *dreidle.* Sam Rosen, who was now sitting on the edge of the sofa kibitzing with the children, had brought the object for the children to play with. It had been in his family for three generations and he took delight in showing it off and telling of its history.

With the dishes finally done, the two women returned to the living room and drew up chairs next to their husbands. Sarah smiled at Ira who was near enough that he draped his arm around her shoulder. When Sarah looked across the table at Marvin, he was casually toying with his fork at cake crumbs left on his plate

Marvin appeared as relaxed and laid back as Sarah had ever known him to be. How odd, *at a time she most expected him to blow a gasket, that he would be so at ease.* She found herself feeling offended over his seeming indifference. It was as if he could care less that Ira might leave his employment. *He'd be lost without Ira,* she mused. *Why is he pretending to be so unaffected?*

Her curiosity finally got the best of her. "Marvin, I don't know what you and Ira were discussing while the two of us were in the kitchen, but would you answer me something?"

Still preoccupied with toying at the cake crumbs on his plate, Marvin answered but didn't bother to look up. "Sure, Sarah honey, what's on your mind?"

Honey!? The very word rattled in her brain. Sarah couldn't remember Marvin ever calling her "Honey." "Marvin, what's on my mind is, if we move to Arizona, won't it have a major effect on the operation of your store?"

Marvin looked up. "Why's that, Sarah?"

"What do you mean, 'Why's that?' You know 'why's that'! 'Why's that' is because Ira wouldn't be working for you anymore."

Marvin looked across at Ira. "Is that true, Ira. You wouldn't be working for me anymore?"

"Yep! it's as true as true can be. Can't be in two places at once and don't ever plan to be."

Sarah lifted Ira's arm from her shoulder in a mild fit of pique. "I don't know why the two of you are taking this so lightly. This is serious! I have struggled for months in an attempt to reconcile myself to possibly moving to Arizona and the two of you act like it's a big joke. Marvin! Why aren't you angry?"

"What, did somebody just pass a law that I'm supposed to be angry?"

"You know what I mean. How come you're not angry that we may leave? I thought you'd be furious if you found out. And how are you going to run the store without Ira?"

"What, you think I can't run my store without your so-called genius of a husband. I'll have you know, I managed quite well without him when he was in the Army."

"Well, Ira works very hard for you and, if we do move, you'll never find anyone as loyal or honest!"

"So . . ."

"So! Oh, you irritate me, Marvin Katz." Sarah turned sharply towards Ira. "Ira, why aren't you defending yourself? Marvin's as much as said he doesn't need you."

"Because Sarah, I don't want him to take this back, number one." Ira handed Sarah an envelope. "Number two, unbeknownst to us, the sly fox has known about our possible move to Arizona for months. That's why he allowed me to hire two new people as potential managers—one for the eventual second store and the other to take my place. He only pretended to learn about it tonight when DeeJay spilled the beans."

Sarah was in a mild state of shock as she peered at Marvin. "That's not possible. We didn't tell anyone."

"My dear sister-in-law. I was born at night but not last night. As early as last May, Barry, who you secretly planned to buy the store from, called me from Arizona asking me for financial advice in the selling of his store. In confidence he shared with me that although Ira was happy with the money he was making, he wasn't happy living in New York. He also mentioned Ira's interest in his Arizona store.

"At first I was shocked that Ira was thinking of moving. I was also hurt that your husband, Sarah, wouldn't tell me how he felt. But now I understand a little better.

"Anyway, since I was told in confidence, I wasn't in a position I could discuss it with either of you. Besides, if Ira's not happy living here, I can't change that. I love Ira. I love you, too, Sarah, and the kids. Ruth and I would miss all of you. But Ira's a grown man, Sarah. He's seen more of the world than I have and he knows himself better than I do. Who am I to tell him what's good for him.

"What Barry had told me over the phone became more obvious when I'd be searching for invoices on Ira's desk and would see real estate brochures like, 'How to buy a home in the growing southwest,' or, 'Come to the beautiful open spaces.' I thought perhaps if the two of you attended synagogue more, you would meet people and do more socializing. Maybe you would change your mind. You don't get out enough. But I couldn't get my brother out of the store."

"Ruth, did you know all this?" Sarah inquired.

"Yes, but Marvin made me promise not to say anything."

"I see. Why do I feel so very foolish? How do you feel, Ira?"

"Same as you. I misjudged Marvin and should have trusted him more rather than keeping everything a secret. But if you really want to feel foolish, look inside the envelope."

Sarah had totally forgotten the envelope she still held in her hands. Once she opened it and saw the size of Ira's bonus check, she covered her mouth and broke down in tears. The amount was fifteen hundred dollars—the equivalent of a third of Ira's annual salary. It was the largest single check she had ever seen in her life. Overcome with emotion, Sarah could barely speak through her tears. "W-w-we can't accept this, Marvin . . ."

"Okay, give it back."

"No!" she shouted back emphatically, crying and laughing at the same time. She slowly rose from her chair, walked to the other side of the table, and was swallowed up in the embrace of her large brother-in-law.

Marvin couldn't help but comment. "Eh! women! All night this one wants to bite my head off, now she's hugging me."

Ruth, wiping away her own tears, retorted. "Hey, big-shot money giver, for fifteen hundred dollars, I'd even hug you."

Releasing Sarah from his embrace, Marvin sat again and turned to his wife. "You I can hug for nothing. You're easy."

Sarah excused herself to bring back coffee from the kitchen and regain her composure. When she returned and sat again next to Ira, Marvin addressed her. "Sarah, as much as I hate to say it, I truly believe that moving to Arizona would be an excellent opportunity for you both."

"But I'm scared. Except for Barry, who you two know but whom I've never met, we don't know anybody out there. I have so much security here, which is all I ever wanted. Also, I'm worried about the little money that we've managed to save over the years and the cost of re-settling. What if it doesn't work out? Four years of earnings down the drain. It's all so risky when all I've ever wanted was to have family and friends and secure a decent future for my children."

Ruth empathized but cautioned, "What you say, Sarah, is well and good but the two of you have to be happy together. Far more than your friends, Ira is your real security."

"I have such deep devotion to you, Sarah. As your sister-in-law, I love you immensely and I can't, in my wildest imagination, conceive of having endured what you have already lived through. Yet as much as I admire you for your courage, I admire you as much for your sweetness. Wherever you go, Sarah, the last thing you'll ever have to worry about is making new friends."

Sarah bit her lip to again keep from crying. She barely managed an audible "Thank you."

The emotion of the moment had drained them and fatigue was showing on all their faces when Ira began to yawn.

"Don't let us keep you awake, Ira," Marvin teased.

"Sorry, what time is it anyway?" Marvin and Ira simultaneously checked their watches. The time was approaching ten o'clock. Outside they could still hear the faint sound of raindrops pleading their case for tranquility. The rain had a somnolent effect, turning each person's fatigue into drowsiness.

Ruth and Sarah looked over at Rachel, asleep on the sofa. "We better get her home," Ruth remarked. "She'll need all her energy for her next go-round with David-Jacob."

"Those two!" Sarah replied. "They're like cats and dogs."

"Oh, that's just their silly way of not wanting to admit that they really like each other."

Marvin had been deep in thought and then, remembering, his face suddenly brightened. "Sarah! I was thinking about what you said earlier, about the risk involved should you move. It brought to mind something Theodore Roosevelt once said. May I quote him?"

Sarah, feeling more spirited, tilted her head as if scheming, "If we listen, can we have another fifteen hundred dollars?"

"Keep it up. That can be canceled, you know. Besides, you'd only start crying again and I couldn't handle that." Marvin then turned serious as he began to speak. "Roosevelt was a man who also had to overcome great odds and take risks. He was quite sickly as a child and had terrible asthma. Yet he eventually became an outstanding soldier, an out-doorsman and, of course, a great president. He was a strong and bold leader and worthy of admiration. This is what he said. I hope I get it right:

"It is not the critic who counts, not the man who points out where the doer of deeds could have done them better. The credit belongs to the man who is actually in the arena, whose face is marred by [the] dust and sweat and blood; Who strives valiantly—Who errs and comes short again and again—Who knows the greatest enthusiasms, the great devotions—Who spends himself in a worthy cause—Who, at the best, knows in the end the triumph of high achievement—and Who, at the worst, at least fails while daring greatly, so that his place shall never be with those timid souls who know neither victory nor defeat."

"Those are inspiring words, Marvin. I can see why you admired the man so much," Sarah said gravely.

"Then I hope you'll take them to heart. I think those words apply to both you and Ira."

"Perhaps to Ira. I have little reserve left."

Ruth attempted to encourage Sarah. "What is it that Katalin always says? 'God will not give you more than you can bear,' and, 'All things work together for good for those who love God'."

Ruth's quoting of scripture irritated Ira. "You're quoting New Testament, Ruth!"

Ruth deflected his remark. "What difference does it make? You don't have to believe in Jesus for something to be true."

Ira remained silent, ignoring her response, while Marvin quickly changed the subject. "Sarah, about what we were saying before. Ruth and I hate the thought of your family moving. But if Ira is miserable living here, his disposition is bound to affect you and the kids. On the other hand, there's the possibility that your moving to Arizona might work in all our favor."

"How's that?" Sarah asked.

"Reading some of the brochures that Ira left on his desk, I was intrigued by how cheap land is in Arizona. When you and Ruth were in the kitchen, Ira and I discussed the possibility of actually buying some land. You never know, someday it could make us rich."

Sarah became resigned to the inevitable. Exasperated, she took a deep breath. "Well, I guess everyone has me moved already. And I suppose I love Ira too much to keep arguing over it." She turned towards her husband. "By the way, Ira, what did Barry say in his letter?"

"Which one?"

"The one that came today. I put it on our dresser."

"I haven't opened it yet. I will later. Of late he's been pressuring me for an answer, especially since he's had another offer."

With everyone tired and anxious to call it a night, hugs and kisses were exchanged. Ruth asked to borrow an umbrella as Marvin lifted his sleeping daughter to his shoulder. Once they had gone, Ira offered to clean the living room and vacuum.

By eleven-thirty, Sarah had already showered and was in bed reading when Ira came in. He began unbuttoning his shirt, then, remembering Barry's letter on the dresser, he grabbed it and sat on the edge of the bed where he opened it. Sarah sat directly behind him and began massaging his back. His muscles about the neck and shoulders felt tight and rigid.

As Ira began reading the letter, Sarah could sense immediately that something was wrong. He finished the letter, gently placed it on the night-stand and removed his glasses, then rubbed his forehead with the back of his hand, remaining strangely silent.

Sarah was curious. "Ira, what did he say?"

Ira didn't bother turning around but there was no mistaking his subdued tone of voice. "Barry sold the store to someone else. He said he couldn't afford to wait any longer." Looking resigned and depressed, Ira headed to the kitchen, telling Sarah he was going to get a drink.

Sarah sat in bed stunned by the sudden turn of events. *How could he do that to Ira, his friend and Army buddy?* she thought. She reached over to the dresser to read the letter for herself. It was just as Ira said. Barry indicated that he was offered thirty-five hundred dollars more on a cash transaction. He wasn't going to have to carry paper for five years as was the case in his deal with Ira.

Before putting the letter down, Sarah couldn't help but notice a line towards the end of the letter: "Do you still think about Ohrdruf?" At first it sounded like an odd name of some person, perhaps of some girl. Then she remembered a small city by that name in the southern part of Germany. The mention of the city must have had something to do with the war, Sarah reasoned, since that was the only time Ira was in Germany. Whatever significance Ohrdruf held, now wasn't the time to bring it up, especially given Ira's reluctance to talk about the war.

Sarah's heart ached for Ira. She began to feel remorse for the part she played in his despondency, reflecting that Ira had worked himself to the point of exhaustion to make a better life for her and the kids. Now her stalling and arguing had cost him a golden opportunity to realize one of his dreams and to be his own boss.

Sarah brushed back tears and slammed her fist into the mattress several times. "No! no! no!" she cried to herself. "We're gonna do it anyway, Ira!"

She got out of bed and walked quietly into her children's room, taking David-Jacob's red cowboy hat from high atop the closet shelf. She then bundled her hair and worked the small hat until it finally fit, tilting it over her forehead and tightening the drawstring underneath the neck.

Wearing her white flannel nightgown and child's hat, she proceeded to the kitchen where Ira was seated at the circular corner table. In the middle of the table was a half empty bottle of Mogen-David wine. He was looking straight down, nursing his second full glass. Sarah put the bottle back in the refrigerator, pulled out a chair and sat across from him.

Although aware of Sarah's presence, Ira had still not acknowledged her. He stared trance-like into his glass of grape wine, tipping the tumbler one way and then the other.

Sarah cleared her throat and tipped her cowboy hat further over her brow. "S'cuse me stranger! This h'yar saloon open to wimmen!?"

Ira rolled his eyes upward and looked hard at Sarah. Seeing her in her nightgown and son's red cowboy hat caused him to close his eyes again, shaking his head. "Sarah, I'm not in the mood for your silly humor right now. Besides, wearing that outfit, I think you're ready for the men in the white coats."

"Varmint! I don't cotton to your funnin' of me. The last critters thet done that are now in residence in Boot Hill."

"Sarah, please go to bed, read a book. Do something but leave me alone."

"Kin't leave ya' lone, podnah. I got this here ol' hitchin' ring on my finger thet tells me we're stuck together much like a tumbleweed caught in barbed wire."

"Poor Sarah. I took you to too many western movies and now your brain's gone kaplooie."

"Another thing, podnah. My name ain't Sarah. I think yer confusin' me with some a yer other wimmenfolk."

"Okay, Sarah, I'll play your stupid silly game and then maybe you'll leave me alone."

"Told ya podnah, name ain't Sarah."

"What is it?"

"Name's Calamity Katz!"

Ira brought his hand over his face. "Oh God help me. Where's my bottle of wine."

Sarah had thus far deadpanned every response, surprising even herself. She had something important she wanted to tell Ira but not in his present mood. "Ya know, stranger, yer about as down in the mouth as a polecat with his paw caught in a bear trap."

"Boy, where's Elsa when you need her. Talking to her about Geronimo running a bowling alley in Tucson made more sense than my talking to you. Sarah, let's be serious. I wanted that store as much as I've ever wanted anything in my life. Barry had contracts for two tracts of houses numbering over a hundred homes. He said his store was in a prime location and he was already starting to get good referral business. We could have stepped right in.

"We blew it, Sarah. And frankly I'm tired. I'm real tired and I'm not having much fun. So go chew on a locoweed or something; that is, if you haven't already."

Sarah decided it was now her turn to play it straight. She removed her hat, laying it on the table. Then shaking her head to let her hair fall about her shoulders, she spoke with a determined voice. "Ira! listen! We can do it! You and I. We don't need Barry and his lousy store. You don't know how much money he's making off those tracts? Maybe he's only making zilch and you would have been stuck with the contracts. You need to fly to Arizona immediately and find us a place to live. Once you've done that, we can give Marvin proper notice. With the money we have in the bank plus what Marvin gave us tonight, we'll have enough to get by for the short term. Time enough to allow us to find a building and get set up with samples and the like.

"So we start out new, who cares? That will only make it more fun. I can help you in the store, Ira. I'm good with figures. You can hire an accountant to teach me how to do the books. We'll put a playpen in the store for Joshua. At other times, DeeJay and I can go into the neighborhoods and deliver flyers.

"Maybe Barry's selling the store was a blessing. Even had we bought his store and made money, we would always know that it was his store.

We would never have that sense of accomplishment. We can start our own store and be successful. We can do it, Ira. You and me."

Ira looked puzzled. "Sarah! I don't understand you. For months you've fought me over this. Why now? Why after all this time the sudden change?"

"Because Ira, before it was just your dream. You wanted to fulfill your ambition. My needs were just an afterthought. But now, if you'll let me be part of your dream, there's nothing in this world that would make me happier."

There was a pause as Ira let what Sarah said to him sink in. In the meantime, Sarah could see in Ira's eyes a spark of renewed hope and anticipation. "Sarah, you've got to realize it won't be easy. It's real tough getting a new store off the ground. It may take several months, maybe even a few years. But Sarah, if you're serious, I'll work my tail to the bone."

"We'll work our tail to the bone, Ira," Sarah corrected him. "And once the store is on its feet, then I can stay home again. But I'll always be there when you need me."

"Okay, Sarah, let's do it! And tomorrow night, let's celebrate and go out to dinner. We'll ask the Rosens or someone to baby sit."

"What about tonight?" Sarah countered.

"Huh! tonight . . . we can't go anywhere tonight?"

Sarah plopped the red cowboy hat back on her head. "Yer gettin' kinda slow on the draw, ain't ya, slim?"

"Whaddya mean?" Ira was confused but smiling.

"Yer not a cowpoke, yer a slowpoke. Let me put it to ya this way. Ya ever kissed a cowgirl before?"

Ira felt stupid and slightly embarrassed, realizing now the intent of her statement and invitation. He stared admiringly at Sarah. Despite all that she had been through she was still full of spunk. More than that she was a devoted mother, wife and friend. Again he was mesmerized and captivated by her misty green eyes that were both seductive and alluring. "Nope, never kissed a cowgirl before. Not in this century. Not on this planet. Certainly not a cowgirl as pretty as you."

Sarah drew her hat down again over her forehead where it practically covered her eyes. "Then podnah, you got a gap in yer life thet needs fillin' and it's gettin' late. We oughtta get to it. Ya mind followin' me to the bunkhouse?"

She reached across the table and allowed Ira's hand to grab hold of hers. As they rose, Ira brought Sarah next to his body and they kissed.

Sarah felt gloriously alive. She was consumed with love for the man she most admired. Her feelings tempered slightly in the knowledge that there was still part of her husband that remained hidden and mysterious, something deep inside that she knew was churning in his spirit.

Still, however, she was satisfied for the moment. And the moment was one minute after twelve-midnight, on the day after what was the first night of Rosh-Hashanah. It was that rarest of moments for Sarah, one of those moments when all was right with the world.

Chapter 10

It was the typical Friday evening rush with the stampede of people pushing and jamming against one another, attempting to get on the A Train before the doors shut. Katalin then saw a golden opportunity where she could use her five foot two inch, one hundred and five pound frame to its greatest advantage. Two excessively large men with wide girths were both trying to squeeze in sideways and, in so doing, were preventing one another from getting on. As the doors started closing on them, Katalin made a mad dash and ducked between the space beneath their protruding bellies and accomplished her mission. Once on the train and looking back, she observed both men still on the platform, slamming each other with newspapers.

With her first objective in hand and feeling too exhausted to stand for the twenty minute ride to the Pulaski Street station a block from her apartment, she quickly sought to accomplish objective number two. Scanning her crowded car with its many people holding onto the ceiling straps or vertical poles to maintain their balance, she spotted an older teenager sitting along the row of lengthwise seats and staring at her. Reminding herself that the Apostle Paul wasn't averse to using both wit and skill to his advantage, especially when it served his missionary purpose, she rationalized her situation. In a city where people made tents, Paul became a tentmaker, thus endearing himself first to the populace. So on a subway car, where some teenager was ogling her, she would edge closer to him and feed his ego by returning him her brightest smile. Half a minute later, she was sitting in the seat the teenager once occupied. And it worked again.

Passing rapidly through tunnels and stations created a Klieg light effect as the subway car flickered light and dark from the remaining sunlight cascading down platform stairwells. Turning slightly sideways, Katalin looked over her shoulder, out the window and wished she were already home. She wasn't sure why, but as was often the case lately when weekends approached, she felt like crying.

It wasn't the hectic weekday schedule that bothered her. In fact, she usually looked forward to it with enthusiasm. She liked being busy and being around people.

What kept her spirits at a low ebb was trying to fill the void in her non-existent social life. She had friends from church, but two hours every Sunday morning gave her little time to know anyone well. The lone exception to her weekend miseries was a prominent and successful male friend from work who, after two months of dating, boldly asked her to marry him. But turning Neil Simmons down had apparently ended their relationship. He hadn't asked her out since.

Neil was thirty-four years old and already the assistant managing editor of the *Daily Eagle*. Bright, handsome and ambitious, he and Katalin had first met in the coffee room and were immediately attracted to each other. But Neil was a man who didn't want children and indicated to her that his religious beliefs floated somewhere between the Dalai Lama, Buddha and Superman. Katalin liked his wry sense of humor, however. She found him also to be a gentleman and a stimulating conversationalist who made her feel good about herself.

But still there was no one with which she could share intimate thoughts and feelings. Katalin felt awash in a sea of people, in a world of strangers. Even her prayer life began to suffer as a result of her despondency. Last weekend was the absolute worst and, for the first time in her entire life, she experienced thoughts about suicide. Even though temporal and fleeting, the morbid thoughts nonetheless invaded her consciousness and frightened the wits out of her. She spent hours crying and pleading with God to change her circumstances. During this time, the Lord revealed to her that her heart was filled with bitterness and anger—all directed at one Ira Katz.

Up until three months ago, Katalin had always held Ira in high esteem, considering him a strong, honest, decent and hard working man, and she had never felt the slightest tinge of jealousy over his marrying her dearest friend. Instead, she felt comforted that someone had finally lifted the burden from herself in trying to keep Sarah's life on an even keel. Ira was her answer to prayer in bringing stability and meaning to Sarah's life. In turn, she felt that she acquired yet another best friend.

Then Ira had turned on her, fearing her influence on Sarah and possibly DeeJay. Something that had never been a problem before, but Ira was not the same person she once knew and trusted. When she heard Sarah's voice on the phone that afternoon, it was a blunt reminder that in three weeks she would likely never see Sarah again.

After all their shared struggles and all they meant to each other, it was a difficult burden to bear.

What made matters even worse is she could sense Sarah's displeasure with her, thinking perhaps that their declining relationship was all Katalin's fault. Two and a half weeks ago, just after Rosh-Hashanah, they were to have gotten together over lunch, but Katalin had become ill with the flu. Sarah accepted the fact that she was sick but Katalin knew that it sounded like just another excuse in a long line of excuses over the past three months. They didn't even try to get together after that.

Katalin searched her mind, wondering what else she could do. Ira had put her in a no-win situation. Even if she had revealed to Sarah the reason she was avoiding her, it would make Ira that much angrier and, at the same time, make herself look petty. She had become a problem in Ira and Sarah's life and she had no way of defending herself. Inwardly, she felt ripped apart.

After entering her apartment, Katalin was famished and was disappointed to find little food in her cupboard or refrigerator. She changed into more casual clothing and thought to grab a sandwich at the corner deli. While she was out she would spend time at the used bookstore and maybe treat herself to an ice cream soda.

It was then that her phone rang and she was surprised to hear Neil's voice on the other end. She confessed to him that she indeed hadn't eaten yet but was about to step out. He convinced her to wait, saying that he had something he wished to discuss with her and assured her it wasn't of a personal nature. He would also be bringing over her favorite Chinese food.

Katalin's spirits soared. She admitted to Neil to have been feeling in the dumps and that she looked forward to his company.

Looking back later, Katalin realized that what had the earmarks of a dull evening at home had instead turned into a memorable and happy occasion for her. Neil Simmons had shown up carrying a giant-sized paper sack with no less than eight containers of Chinese food.

Katalin laughingly teased her friend, co-worker and boss, that he must think of her as some type of glutton. He, in turn, reminded her that one of his heroes was the philosopher Epicurus who gave himself over to a passionate and hedonistic lifestyle. He assured Katalin that Epicurus would approve of gorging oneself with all manner of Chinese food whenever possible. Katalin countered that God, in His infinite wisdom, was aware of people like Epicurus and Neil Simmons and

consequently gave mankind the formula from which to invent Bromo-
Seltzer.

While they feasted, they talked mainly of the newspaper business.
It was mostly lighthearted banter when Neil broke his promise and
commented on how attractive he thought Katalin to be.

Katalin shyly replied, "Thanks, kind sir, and you're not exactly
short in the handsome department."

He followed by asking her if he were to change his mind about
having kids and going to church on Sundays, would she change her
mind about marrying him.

Katalin thought for a second on just how to respond. She had hoped
that Neil wouldn't ask her again, yet she felt flattered by his interest
in her and didn't want to offend him. "Just having kids wouldn't make
you happy as a father, Neil, no more than your going to church would
make you a Christian when you don't believe in Christianity." Then she
added, "Neil, I know there are a hundred women out there who would
jump at the chance to marry you."

"But Katalin, I'm only interested in number one-hundred-one."

"Tell you what, let me clean up and do the dishes and then we'll go
for a walk."

Neil nodded and smiled, but with a certain look of disappointment
and resignation. During the ensuing conversation, while Neil helped
Katalin clean the kitchen, he reminded her that they had forgotten
to read their fortune cookies sitting on the kitchen sink. Katalin
remarked as to how she didn't believe much in fortune cookies, that
reading fortunes sounded too much like astrology. He offered that she
took everything too literal and too serious in adherence to her religious
beliefs. Then he began quoting from various philosophers he had read
and studied about in college: Boehme, Schelling, Leibniz, Aristotle and
the hardened atheists, Spinoza and Nietzsche.

Katalin, impressed by his ability to remember, listened intently
and without response for several minutes as he concluded his lecture
to her with a rhetorical question. "All these brilliant men, Katalin. They
searched for God and came to conclusions other than Christianity,
including the belief of there being no God. In fact, most writers and
newspaper people I know today no longer regard the Bible with any
substance. They relegate the Bible to myth. Times are changing."

Katalin was unruffled by his arguments and used her fingers to
wipe off suds from Neil's chin. "For a minute there, Neil, you started
looking like Santa Claus," she remarked, then continued, "Neil, as to

what people believe today compared to what people may have believed in times past has little relevance. If Christianity was true a hundred or a thousand or two thousand years ago, then nothing changes. Since when have we acquired the ability to determine truth by looking at a watch?

"As for all the philosophers you mentioned who failed to discover God or figure out if life truly had meaning, they remind me of the story poem, 'The Blind Men and the Elephant.' Each blind man attempted to describe what an elephant was like by touching him. One touched the tail, one the leg, another the tusk and they all arrived at different conclusions—describing the elephant as anything from a snake to a tree.

"You know, Neil, my father was always fond of a quotation of Jonathan Edwards, 'How impossible is it, that the world should exist from Eternity, without a Mind.' As far as I'm concerned, Neil, these otherwise brilliant men, when it came to matters of a spiritual nature, couldn't see the forest through the trees. Now let me ask you something. All these philosophers, where are they?"

"What do you mean, where are they?"

"Well, if I wanted to hear them speak, where could I go to listen?"

Neil was befuddled. "Katalin, they're all dead! Most of them lived a long time ago, you know that!"

"When one of them is raised from the dead, let me know."

"You're right, Katalin. I could never marry you. I would never have the last word. Not to change the subject, but besides the challenge of your smarty-pants intellect, there's another reason I wanted to see you tonight."

"Oh I forgot! You did mention something over the phone. Why don't we go for a walk and you can tell me."

"It's in the fortune cookie, kiddo."

"Huh?"

"Katalin, I was trying to get you to read your stupid fortune cookie. I spent twenty minutes, using tweezers, inserting my own fortune in one of those lousy misshapen things."

Katalin laughingly apologized. She put down her dishrag and leaned over to peck him on the cheek. Neil was a foot taller and had an angular face with smooth untanned, skin and thick straight light-brown hair which he wore swept back.

Neil grabbed her fortune cookie as they walked back into the living room. Handing it to her, he watched intently as she unfolded the wadded, neatly inserted note. Katalin read the words aloud:

You are kind, compassionate, hard-working and intelligent. You are also the newest *full time* Feature writer for the Brooklyn Daily Eagle. Congratulations.

Love, Neil

"Neil! Do you mean it? You want me to write for the newspaper full time and permanently!? I can't believe . . . my whole life I've dreamed . . ."

"Believe it, Katalin. We're always looking for fresh new talent. When you showed me the columns you wrote for your college newspaper, I called the head of your journalism department. He told me how impressed he was by you, how, despite your hectic, daily schedule, you were the most diligent and resourceful student he had."

"You were checking up on me?"

"I wanted to be sure that my thinking wasn't being clouded by emotion. Basically, all your professor did was to confirm what I already knew. You also write with a great passion. Sometimes our writers get a little jaded from the stories they are forced to cover and they fall into a rut. You can read a lot of pessimism in their articles. They need to be transfused with renewed enthusiasm and reminded of the ideals they had when they first started writing. Bringing on fresh blood will sometimes accomplish that purpose.

"You'll get a lot of advice from other writers on our staff, Katalin," he added. "They're all good people or we wouldn't have them working for us. But sometimes they can become a strange and brooding lot. Listen to them. They'll be an invaluable resource to you. But stay close to your principles and what got you this far.

"In the meantime," he explained, "what's happened to bring this about is that we are losing two of our writers. One is going over to the *Times*, the other is going to be on overseas assignment for up to six months. There's trouble brewing in Korea and we want to stay on top of it."

While overwhelmed and feeling grateful, Katalin couldn't help feeling a little suspicious. "But why me, Neil? Why are you doing this for me?"

"I thought I just explained it to you." Katalin's question to Neil suddenly became more obvious. "Oh, I get it. It's not what you think. I wouldn't compromise the integrity or the quality of the product we publish by playing favorites. Don't forget, I'm already aware of your work habits and what benefit you might be to us. Our friendship may have brought you to my notice but if it turned out you did lousy work, I wouldn't hesitate to fire you in a New York minute. I mean that! At the same time, I think you have great ability and a bright future in this business and I wanted the *Daily Eagle* to get you before one of our competitors did. In baseball parlance, you call it good scouting."

"I apologize to you, Neil. I wasn't meaning to impugn your integrity."

Neil broke into a wide grin. "Hey, I already knew you'd be thinking that. And, to be honest, I fantasized that hiring you might change your mind about marrying me— seeing what a wonderful guy I am and all. Being pragmatic, however, I value our friendship, and politically and philosophically we are at opposite ends of the spectrum. I think eventually we would drive each other insane." He stopped, then continued, "Two things we need from you, Katalin . . ."

"What's that?"

"We need you five days a week after school until you're finished and also Saturdays beginning in November." Neil awaited her response.

"And the second thing?"

"Well, you're not going to be given choice assignments right off the bat. You're going to have to pay your dues. That means covering city council meetings, writing obituaries and the like."

"Neil, compared to proofreading half the time, it will all be an adventure, I assure you. I don't mind. I'll do whatever is necessary and required of me."

"I figured you'd say that. However, in mid-November, we will be running a series of human interest stories dealing with survivors of the recent holocaust in Germany. I've suggested to the managing editor that you be allowed to run the series with your byline since you have firsthand experience. He concurred, allowing as how your own unique and tragic circumstance would bring out the emotional appeal we want and that survivors would be willing to talk to you more freely. As a way of introducing you on a wider scale to our readers, we want your story to run first."

"You're kidding!?"

"No I'm not! However, I want you to give it deep consideration before committing yourself. As I said before, you have a unique story to tell. But if it's too painful for you to dig up the past, you don't have to do it."

"Neil, you can't expect me to drag out the heart-rendering experiences of others without having to recount my own. Why should I be spared any emotional torment when they aren't? Besides, you said before that you thought I wrote with passion. Writing with passion,

Neil, involves writing with pain. In a way, it will perhaps be a catharsis for me. I can handle it, honest I can."

Neil took a deep breath and sighed. "Okay, Katalin, let's run with it. I need an outline or even a rough draft of your account within two weeks. Afterwards, I'll ask you for names of people you think you may interview. We're expecting a lot from this series, Katalin. It's important to us. If at any time you feel overwhelmed, please come to me."

"Neil, I'm eternally grateful to you."

"Don't be. You may hate me before this is all over."

"I don't think so."

"Oh, one more thing. When writing your personal experience, it's important that your friend . . . what's her name . . . ?"

"You mean Sarah?"

"Yes, when writing your story, I think it will have greater impact by stressing the dichotomy of the Jewish/ Christian relationship, how, despite your differences, you managed to draw strength from one another."

"No dichotomy existed, Neil. We thought only of the blending of our faiths and how much we had in common. The strength we drew from each other was simply because we loved each other as individuals. To me, it didn't matter what religion she was. Nor my religion to her."

"Then that's what the people need to read about, Katalin. There's a lot of bigotry out there. Do you still want to go for that walk?"

Katalin nodded and extended her hand for Neil to take in his. He clasped her hand and, with a slight tug, gently drew her close to him. Their eyes locked and as they stared at one another, he released her hand and laid both his hands on her shoulders. He drew Katalin next to his body and they kissed. Initially, Katalin made little attempt to resist him. The second time they came up for air, she gently laid her hands on his chest and, with a small push, managed to back off his embrace. She smiled, while looking up at him. "I thought we were going walking?"

"Still no bombs bursting in air?"

"Neil, when it comes to kissing, you don't have to take a back seat to anyone. I just know that for us it would be wrong. You said so yourself."

"I was hoping I might be wrong about being wrong."

Katalin laughed. "Neil, I just want to be careful and not let things go too far."

"It's hard being around you, Katalin, just being friends. You're beautiful, you're warm, you're smart. I really envy whoever ends up with you."

"Neil, I have the deepest admiration and affection for you. But I love you in a way different than the way people who are 'in love' love each other."

"Boy, that's the kiss of death if I ever heard it. But, *c'est la vie!*"

"That's the same remark the young couple from the French Resistance uttered when helping us escape into France."

"You know, Katalin, you've told me everything else about your escape, except the time you actually were in France."

"I'll tell you during our walk."

Once outside, a brisk cool wind foreshadowed the onset of fall. Twenty-foot-tall silver linden trees—that five years ago were planted between widened cracks at the sidewalk's edge—now swayed in the wind. The crest of uppermost branches were leaning, as if in prayerful oblation to God, whispering a song through the spent and falling leaves.

Casually strolling down Pulaski Street, Neil and Katalin cordially acknowledged the many people sitting in folding chairs in front of their apartment buildings or reclining on stoops. Then, for the better part of an hour, Katalin shared with Neil her and Sarah's ten months in France.

She described in detail how, after they scaled the border fence that night in 1938, they dashed across an open grass field until they came to a small wooded area. Reaching the forested area, they were immediately halted by someone who called them by name. That someone was a Roman Catholic priest by the name of Jean Rouault.

Monsignor Rouault was a sturdy, compactly built individual, about five foot seven or eight. He was middle-aged, bald on top, but distinctive looking with a short goatee. The monsignor, it turned out, was part of a growing sanctuary movement which happened at times to coordinate its efforts with the French underground. Despite being a priest whose job it was to teach love and forgiveness, he had an overt hatred of Adolph Hitler and his entire party apparatus. He insisted that Hitler was possessed of the devil and an embodiment of consummate evil.

Later that night the monsignor told how his sister had been married to a Jewish physicist in Germany. Both the sister's husband and two children—a boy and a girl—had been missing for six months and were likely dead or in some concentration camp. With an obvious bitterness, he maintained that his sister was so distraught she was considering taking her own life. The monsignor went on to say that if given the opportunity he would choke Hitler to death with his bare hands, confessing that his anger had gotten so bad he could no longer preach but he would do whatever he could to save people from the Nazi monster.

Katalin shared how Rouault secured work for her and Sarah at a large farmhouse with nearby vineyards. It was in one of the more depopulated areas, just west of Clermont-Ferrand in the Auvergne region. Although they did housekeeping chores and fed animals, their primary work was in the cutting of grapes. Usually Andre, the farm owner's sixteen-year-old son, would patrol their rowed area of vines carrying a large wicker basket into which the grapes were placed. The grapes were poured into wooden vats and taken by cart back to the farmhouse.

She described that while they worked at the farm and vineyards, preparations were being made to smuggle them into Holland. When the escape routes to Holland became known and reported to the Germans by Nazi sympathizers, they were forced to scuttle their original plans. After a while, she and Sarah were given another option. They were advised that a local teacher was tutoring people in English for a small fee. Sponsoring agencies in America also offered their help to refugees.

Ten months later Katalin and Sarah arrived at Ellis Island in New York. They became naturalized citizens in 1944, although by then Sarah's citizenship had already been secured through her marriage to Ira.

Katalin went on to tell of the various landmarks they visited when in France, also commenting on the fun-loving French people. She mentioned that twice, from a distance, she managed to see the famous writer Ernest Hemingway. He was much taller than she had originally imagined and she described him as looking very stalwart with a large and bushy mustache. On each occasion, Hemingway had a beautiful but different French woman hanging on his arm. As the hour approached eleven o'clock, Neil walked her back to her door where he gave her a gentlemanly kiss on the cheek. Katalin thanked him for a wonderful evening, an evening she said she would never forget. Also, with his permission, she offered to start praying for him that he would find the brightest, most wonderful and beautiful girl in all of New York to marry. Neil commented that if that were truly her prayer, then she should concentrate instead on the second brightest, most wonderful and beautiful girl in New York, given that he was already looking at the first. Katalin gave him another quick goodnight kiss on the cheek, then ran inside.

Chapter 11

When dawn broke on Saturday morning, Katalin pulled a pillow over her head to block out the noise of rambunctious children yelling, screaming and running down the hallways. She had finally fallen asleep after three a.m., exhausted from crying all night.

Last night's excitement over becoming a full time writer, with her own bylines, for the *Daily Eagle* had quickly dissipated. Suddenly she felt apprehension and doubt, questioning her own abilities. *What if I'm not as good as Neil thinks I am?* she asked herself. *What if I fail? What would Neil think of me then? How embarrassing after recommending me.*

Turning over and propping herself up on her pillow, she looked heavenward and prayed,

"Oh, Lord, you are my creator. You know me better than I know myself. You know what I have need of even before I ask it. My spirit groans. I am filled with foreboding and loneliness.

"I also fear that I will let Neil and the newspaper down. Writing is a creative skill, borne of inspiration and, at present, I can't feel anymore. I am besieged with morbid thoughts that I've never before encountered. I don't understand what's happening to me.

"Hear my cries, O Lord. Lift me from this valley of depression and carry me on your wings of glory. I would rather be walking streets of gold, living with my beloved parents and my precious little brother, Stephen, than to continue living this life of emptiness and heartbreak. Minister to my heart, O Lord. Give me strength to carry on and do your will.

"In Jesus' holy name I ask these things."

Katalin managed finally to drag herself out of bed to freshen up. She dressed casually in white pedal-pushers and a navy-blue chambray shirt which she didn't bother to tuck in. Slipping on sandals, she realized she'd soon have to shop for new outfits to wear at her new job.

After eating corn flakes and toast, she went back to her bedroom to call her pastor, thinking perhaps a little counseling might be in order. She had just begun to dial when she remembered he was on vacation and would be gone for two weeks. She then tried calling Clara Johnson who had, years before, sponsored Katalin and Sarah in Brooklyn Heights after their arrival at Ellis Island. Clara always had a sympathetic ear.

After several rings and no answer, Katalin wondered if there weren't some kind of unnatural conspiracy at work. She just wanted to talk to someone, anyone who cared about her, realizing she had no one to even share the joy of her becoming a writer.

Then thoughts of her previous night's conversation with Neil, when he asked her about her and Sarah's escape into France in 1938, caused her to get an old photograph album from her dresser drawer. In it were several pictures from that year, taken when they both lived at the farmhouse in Clermont-Ferrand.

Stretched across the bed and turning the pages of the album, Katalin allowed her mind to drift back eleven years and it brought a smile to her face. Despite the German army readying to invade France, despite their concerns about the future, or even if there would be a future, 1938 and '39 in France was a breath of fresh air.

The first pictures she noticed were of Sarah, her face and dress caked with mud after having fallen in the slop-bucket trying to feed the pigs. She appeared astonished while looking down at her dress with her arms outstretched. There were pictures of Katalin and Sarah taking turns sitting on a small stool milking the cows while happily posing.

Several pictures, taken by other workers, were of the two of them working in the vineyards, cutting grapes and placing them in the wicker basket Andre had strapped to his back. Still more pictures showed Katalin and Sarah laughingly throwing grapes at each other as if they were miniature snowballs. Another picture had the two, then teenagers, on either side of Andre, simultaneously planting a kiss on his cheek. He was smiling, but even in black and white he looked to be turning a crimson red. The German fuehrer and his minions had dramatically changed their lives, but even the Nazis couldn't destroy their zest for living, their love for freedom, nor their desire to dream.

During those ten months at least, from November 1938 until September 1939 — only months before the German blitzkrieg rolled into France — God allowed Katalin and Sarah refuge and renewal in a country most blessed.

France had been apportioned great rivers to keep its fertile valleys always resplendent, capable of supporting every imaginable type agriculture. Its broad landscape and sweeping prairies were merely the cast molding before the Master Sculptor's vision arched the rich sodded clay into the templed snow-capped peaks known as the French Alps. At the Alps' apex was Mont Blanc, addressing the heavens at over 15,000 feet.

France had its fishing villages and it had its sheik Mediterranean resorts. It also had its share of world-famous landmarks—the Arc de Triomphe, Chaillot Palace, Notre Dame Cathedral, Eiffel Tower and Louvre Museum being just a few.

Looking through the album and its many pictures, Katalin was amazed at all the sites they had visited in so short a time. It was as if she and Sarah had discovered heaven on earth, a land yet unfettered and unspoiled by the ravages of war beginning to take place just outside their borders. It was a time to breathe free and learn to deal with their grief and think of their future. In the eye of the hurricane, God found them temporary safe haven and had given them rest.

Katalin closed the album but stayed with her memories. As past and present began fusing together, the real reason for her fond memories of France began to focus. She remembered that hardly a night went by while living in their small cottage on the farm, that she and Sarah didn't stay up well into the night. During that time a deep familial bond developed where they would share their most intimate emotions. Nothing was sacrosanct.

There were nights they discussed their parents and how they missed them, which inevitably led to one or the other of them breaking down in tears. Yet curiously, when one was down, the other became a strong shoulder to lean on.

It now occurred to Katalin that it wasn't so much the country of France that made France so special . . . it was the person of Sarah. She realized now the true depth of their friendship and how much she presently missed her and desired her company. They had been God's provision, filling a void in each other's life.

Sitting by the side of her bed Katalin thought even more about throwing caution to the wind and disregarding Ira's strong rebuke of her and contacting Sarah. Still, she knew she had to choose her words carefully and not put Ira in a bad light and make things worse. His relationship with Sarah was obviously far more important.

"Oh Lord," she prayed, "give me the wherewithal to speak to Sarah and re-establish our relationship in a way that won't cause conflict. I hope it's not too late. Should I even call her? Oh Lord, what am I to do? In three weeks I might never see her again and I don't want our friendship to end. And if it were to end, certainly not this way by so ungraciously avoiding her. Lord, please help me to understand Ira and work things out between us. Oh why did stupid me let this go on so long?"

Reaching for her phone, Katalin picked up the receiver and started dialing. The voice that answered on the other end was that of a young male. "Hello . . ."

"DeeJay, is that you? You sound all grown up, sweetheart."

"I am grown up. I'm almost seven. Hi, Aunt Katalin!"

"Hi, DeeJay. I'm surprised you still recognize my voice."

"Aren't you going to come by and see us anymore. Mommy says we're moving to the other side of the world. I miss you, Aunt Katalin."

"I miss you, too, Precious. How are you!?"

"I had to go to the hospital where Nurse Annie took care of me. She believes in Jesus, too, like you do, and then Mr. Sergeant Connor brought me home and Mommy got real scared on account of I had this big black eye but it's okay because I broke Jamie Shlee's nose and all." Katalin couldn't believe all that she was hearing and quickly realized how much of DeeJay's life she had already missed in just three short months.

"Sweetheart, I'm glad you're okay. But I wish you wouldn't get into any more fights. How's your little brother?"

"He's okay, except Mommy calls him a little stinkpot because he's always pooping in his diapers."

Katalin laughed. "Well, DeeJay, that's what little babies do. Now could I talk to your mommy."

"Okay, I'll go get Mommy. I love you, Aunt Katalin! Thanks for always taking me to the zoo and buying me stuff. I hope you can come to Arizona and see us."

Before Katalin could respond, she heard the crash of the receiver banging around and David-Jacob yelling for his mom. She felt choked up inside, realizing that she wouldn't be around to watch Sarah's children grow up. She may have been an aunt in name only, but her love and concern for the Katz children was the same as if they had been related by blood.

Sarah got on the phone. "Hello. . . hello." There was a measured pause. ". . . Hello, Katalin, is that you?"

Katalin's mind suddenly went blank as she struggled to answer. "Yes . . . Sarah, it's . . . it's so good to talk to you again."

"Well, that's a surprise."

Katalin immediately felt on the defensive as she bravely attempted to keep her composure. She knew that Sarah was never one for mincing words and this time she couldn't fault her. "Why do you say that, Sarah?"

"Well, Miss Amelia Earhart, you've been missing for quite a long time. I'm only a phone call and a short bus ride away and for almost three months now you've acted as if I had the plague. I thought . . . well . . . never mind, I've just felt hurt is all. But I'm glad anyway that you called. How are you doing?"

"Good . . . I mean . . . well, I've got my first real promotion at the paper. I'm now a full time Feature writer for the *Brooklyn Daily Eagle*."

"Great! How exciting!"

Katalin didn't feel excited though and was close to tears. "Sarah . . ."

"Uh-huh?"

"I need to see you desperately . . ."

"Why? . . . you pregnant?"

"Sarah, don't be silly . . . please I'm . . . I'm . . ." Too choked by emotion to complete her sentence, Katalin slammed down the receiver, turned face down on her bed, drew the pillow to her face and started flooding it with tears. Within seconds, the phone rang back. She turned slightly and reached over her side to the nightstand, lifting the receiver from the hook. "He . . . hello. . . Sarah?"

"No . . . Mahatma Gandhi! Of course this is Sarah. Katalin! What in heaven's name is going on!? What's happening to you?"

"Nothing . . ." Tears were still running down Katalin's cheeks. In a rush of breathless emotion her words ran together while, at the same time, she developed the hiccups.

"Except(hic) except that I'm an emotional wreck and I miss my (hic) best friend who I'll probably never see again the rest of my life (hic) . . . and I should be hap-happy for you . . . and I can't. . . can't marry my new boss because he thinks Superman is God and I'm going to die an old maid . . . and I know you hate me too and I don't blame you . . . so will you see me? . . . please."

"Katalin! Take it easy. We do need to talk. Look, let me see if the Rosens can baby sit the kids for a while. I'll call you back in five minutes. Sister Sarah's here to help! Meanwhile, go pour yourself a glass of wine."

"I don't have any wine, Sarah! And besides, I don't drink. You know that."

"Well, then go get some grapes and pour rubbing alcohol on them or something. But stay calm and cheer up. I'm coming to the rescue! I'll be right back."

Katalin hung up the phone and, just as Sarah promised, the phone rang again only minutes later. In the meantime, Katalin had splashed water on her face and was able to pull herself together emotionally.

Sarah sounded almost jubilant at the other end. "Katalin!"

"What?"

"Are you okay?"

"No!"

"Congratulations!!"

"On what?"

"On being miserable! Remember at the *bris* I was so frustrated with you because I was depressed and you weren't? I asked you, 'Why can't you be miserable like me?' But you seldom are or were."

"Sarah, you've always been a little strange but I never realized just how much until now."

"Well, don't you see, Katalin? Now that we are more like each other, we can celebrate. Let's see, we'll call ourselves the Sob Sisters."

Katalin chuckled, having forgotten how humorous Sarah could sometimes be. "What do you mean celebrate?"

"The Rosens are going to watch the kids awhile. We can have lunch together. Why don't we meet at noon at G&T's. Afterwards you can come back to our apartment and see the children. DeeJay always asks about you. Then have supper with us. It will be just like old times."

"But wouldn't Ira object? I mean tonight, wouldn't you two rather go out together?"

"Why should he object? Besides, he's been in Arizona all week finding us a place to live. He won't be home until tomorrow. At noon . . . okay?"

"Okay, Sarah! . . . and Sarah?"

"Yes?"

"Thanks . . ."

"For what?"

"For caring about me. For being my friend. I've missed you a lot."

"I've missed you, too, Katalin. Love you . . . we have a lot to talk about."

Gage & Tollner's advertised itself as "The Very Famous Restaurant in Brooklyn". It had been around since the late nineteenth century and was well known for its unique atmosphere as well as for its steak and chops. Its seating arrangement consisted of rows of mahogany tables and lighting was supplied by brass and cut glass gas lights. Much of its interior was walled by arched mirrors.

Being close to the Navy Yard, it had a long established tradition of its waiters wearing hash marks on their sleeves indicating years of service. A gold bar meant one year. A gold star five years, and a gold eagle twenty-five years.

Katalin arrived first exactly at noon and was escorted to her table. For ten minutes she anxiously awaited Sarah's arrival. Before leaving the apartment she had donned a blue skirt and heels and put her casual wear in a tote bag she now carried with her.

When spotting Sarah being led to the table, her friend looked to be ebullient while conversing with the waiter. Seeing Sarah in such a happy mood made Katalin feel more at ease. She wanted this to be a happy occasion, a valuable reminder of their long-standing friendship, and she had prayed hard on her way over that Sarah would still enjoy being with her.

Rising from her chair, she greeted Sarah. There was an awkward silence as they stared at each other. Sarah looked as though she was about to cry, then they simultaneously opened their arms and for the next several seconds they engaged in an emotional embrace. Meanwhile, their waiter patiently stood by and finally seated them.

Wiping her eyes and taking a deep breath, Sarah spoke first. "Well . . . I didn't realize how much I missed my little Hungarian friend."

"Not half as much as I missed my dear friend from the once shtetls of Poland, a friend who's closer to me than any sister could be."

"Well, thank you. And to avoid being any more maudlin than we already are, let's get the most difficult question out of the way first. Why in the world have you avoided seeing us all this time? DeeJay has been asking, 'Where's Aunt Katalin? Doesn't she like us anymore?'"

Katalin came up with the best explanation she could without having to lie and without casting aspersions on Ira. She roughed out the excuse that she felt she was being an imposition on their family, that they had their own lives to lead and she worried she might be wearing out her welcome. She stammered that with Ira working so hard, and them with a six year old and a baby to raise, they needed to spend what little free time they had together without her being an interference.

Sarah countered by reminding Katalin that she was like family. They never thought of her as being an interference, rather, she had always been of great assistance to them. She not only helped watch the kids, but took time on occasion to feed them, do laundry, take David-Jacob to the zoo and a myriad of other tasks which served to make Sarah's own life easier.

Once they had cleared the air, the next two hours were spent talking about everything that had occurred in their lives since they last met. Sarah was especially interested in hearing about Neil, asking why Katalin had taken to dating a non-Christian.

Katalin's reply was that Neil had asked her out on the spur of the moment and his being her boss made saying "no" very difficult. "I didn't have time to hand him a questionnaire asking him about his religious beliefs," she laughed, added that she never intended that they would be involved romantically but Neil, despite his offbeat religious beliefs, had turned out to be a delightful person, and a person she sensed was as lonely as she was. However, she admitted to Sarah, that if Neil persisted with his marriage interest in her, it might cause her to leave her new and promising position as a writer.

She then told Sarah of her pending human interest project in November and asked Sarah if she would mind her writing of their shared experience. Sarah assured her that it would be okay, but if it came to the point of mentioning the German soldier, they should use a fake name. "If he were still alive," she said, "regardless of how remote he might be from the article mentioning his name, we might make trouble for him, even now." She admitted that only Ira knew the soldier's name, besides themselves. In saving her life, the German soldier had exacted one promise from her—that he remain anonymous.

It was nearing 3:30 p.m. by the time she and Sarah arrived by subway back at Sarah's apartment.

The Rosens had met Katalin on several occasions and were delighted to see her again. After greeting the Rosens, Katalin heard David-Jacob screaming her name from his bedroom. As she dropped to one knee, Katalin's "nephew" ran into her arms and she could tell immediately that he had grown some.

"Well, big boy, how's the present and future heavyweight champion of the world?"

"I'm gonna be a baseball player, Aunt Katalin, not a boxer."

"Well, I'm glad to hear it. But just in case, I think that someday I'll just have girls. Raising boys seems awfully dangerous. DeeJay! that's an awful black eye. No wonder your mother is concerned."

Katalin looked questioningly up at Sarah who grimaced and nodded affirmatively.

Katalin stood up and then David-Jacob began tugging at her dress. "Aunt Katalin?"

"What, DeeJay?"

"What if you don't get married? Then you can't have girls or nobody."

Sarah felt embarrassed by her son's unwitting and questioning remarks, especially after hearing about Katalin's bittersweet relationship with Neil Simmons and knowing that marriage had become such a sensitive subject with her.

Katalin retorted, "I can have whatever I want, tough guy!" as she grabbed him and began tickling him in the ribs while he squealed and laughed.

Sarah immediately warned him not to run screaming into the bedroom for fear of waking the baby. Obeying, he turned facing Katalin and, at a safe distance, reciprocated with, "No, you can't, Aunt Katalin! You can't have silly dopey girls if you don't get married first. What if no one ever marries you!?"

Sarah rolled her eyes while the Rosens looked on quietly amused. "DeeJay, why don't you go outside now and play stickball while your aunt and I talk."

"But I want to stay here and talk, too."

"Then quit pestering your Aunt Katalin. No wonder she's waiting so long to get married when she sees what an annoyance children can be."

Katalin was taken aback by Sarah's statement and looked at her astonished. "So long!? Waiting so long-g-g!?"

Sarah suddenly recognized her faux pas. "I mean . . . not so long . . . really . . . just waiting for the right man is all."

Katalin wasn't nearly as offended as Sarah was embarrassed. Walking up to Sarah, she whispered in her ear. "Take your foot out of your mouth. I can handle it."

Sarah whispered back, "I didn't mean it the way it sounded." Katalin grinned at Sarah, relishing in her sudden discomfiture. She then walked to the sofa and, after sitting, asked David-Jacob to take the seat beside her.

Complying, David-Jacob looked curiously up at her. "What, Aunt Katalin?"

"DeeJay, it doesn't matter if no one ever marries me. You know why?"

"Why?"

Katalin smiled and touched the tip of her index finger to the tip of his nose. She then recited a poem which seemed perfect for the occasion:

If no one ever marries me
I shan't mind very much;
I shall buy a squirrel in a cage
And a little rabbit-hutch:

I shall have a cottage near a wood,
And a pony all my own
And a little lamb quite clean and tame
That I can take to town:

And when I'm getting really old,
At twenty-eight or nine,
I shall buy a little *orphan girl*
And bring her up as mine.

"That's neat, Aunt Katalin! Did you make that up by yourself?"

"Nope, someone by the name of Lawrence Tadema made it up."

"My mom was an orphan girl, Aunt Katalin. You were, too, huh?"

After Katalin and Sarah exchanged glances, Katalin answered him. "DeeJay, one thing you have to remember for always. In God's house, there is no such thing as an orphan."

A baby's cry interrupted their conversation and everyone went into the bedroom to admire Joshua-Caleb. While Sarah took Joshua-Caleb out of the crib and changed and fed him, Katalin used the time to put on her casual clothes and converse with the Rosens who asked Katalin and Sarah to come over to their apartment that night for boiled corned beef and cabbage. They also invited them to stay and watch the new seven-inch television that their grown children had purchased for them. They were the only ones in the apartment building with the new invention.

After the Rosens left, Sarah and Katalin took folding chairs outside to sit and talk while watching David-Jacob play stickball. Joshua-Caleb was placed in his carriage, wrapped in a cocoon of blankets.

Once the two women started talking, the time flew by. Although Katalin appeared to Sarah to be her old self, Sarah remained suspicious about her excuse of staying away so long. She was convinced she hadn't heard everything that was to be said. She had known Katalin too many years and could recognize when her friend was being evasive. When they were at Gage & Tollner's, Katalin had explained herself while nervously tapping her fingers against the table and gazing elsewhere.

Mrs. Rosen's corned beef was exceptionally tender and, although the cabbage had its usual rank smell, it also tasted good. Watching the newest novelty of entertainment, television, was also an enjoyable experience, although it was a strain on the eyes as the reception—via use of rabbit ears—wasn't great. A half hour show—"Man Against Crime" starring Ralph Bellamy came on at 8:30, then from 9 to 10 p.m. the Ford Television Theater presented one of its twice monthly dramas "Arsenic and Old Lace".

By 10:30, David-Jacob had to be awakened whereupon he walked zombie-like back down the hall to their apartment. Katalin warmed to the task of carrying Joshua-Caleb back.

Once the two children were put to bed, the two women sat at the kitchen table and talked over coffee. Meanwhile, a cab had been called to arrive at 11:30, the driver instructed to buzz their apartment. Minutes before the cab driver arrived, Sarah looked her friend squarely in the eye and confronted her. "Katalin, I've known you too long and too well to know that there's more to what you told me this afternoon."

Katalin was caught off-guard and felt uneasy. "About what, Sarah?"

"About why you stopped coming around."

"Sarah, what I told you was the truth. I don't lie to people."

"I didn't think you did—only that I feel there's more to tell. Why, after all these years of practically being a part of our family, would you suddenly decide that we didn't want you around. I'm sorry, it doesn't make sense. Something or someone caused you to think that?"

"Sarah, I just overreacted. Let it go."

"You're not leaving this apartment until you tell me."

"Sarah, quit being ridiculous!"

"I mean it! I'm not letting you out the door."

"Well, I'll have you know that I've been taking boxing lessons from a male classmate at Brooklyn College. He fights Golden Gloves and he's taught me how to do a jab, a right hook and an uppercut. So if you don't let me out the door, I'll just punch you in the nose." She doubled up her fist and the two of them broke out laughing.

Katalin's cab arrived and the driver announced over the intercom that he'd be waiting outside. The two women hugged and Katalin left the apartment, promising she'd call during the week to make plans for next Sunday afternoon.

Alone, Sarah returned to the kitchen table and sat to finish her coffee. A minute later, there was a gentle rap on her door. Opening it, she was surprised to see Katalin again, having forgotten her tote bag.

She noticed Katalin's eyes were wet with tears. Concerned, she stopped her at the door.

"Katalin, what's wrong? A moment ago you walked out of here happy as a lark, now you come back and it's obvious you've been crying."

"Sarah, I'm not sure about calling you this week, or getting together again."

"Uh-uh, Katalin! You called me this morning . . . remember! I'm not playing this fickle game with you anymore!"

"I'm sorry, Sarah. . ."

As Katalin reached for the doorknob, Sarah shoved her hand away and squeezed between Katalin and the door, her arms folded. "This time I mean it, Katalin! I demand to know what's going on!"

"I can't tell you . . ."

"Can't or won't!?"

"Either way. In three weeks you'll be gone and I'll never see you again."

"Baloney! Katalin, you've changed in the last few months. I always thought of you as being the most stable and unshakable person I ever met. With your limitless faith I thought you capable of handling anything. Now you look like some confused, helpless, teary-eyed little waif!"

"Thanks for the compliment. I told you before that I spend more than my share of nights crying myself to sleep. You're not the only lonely person in this world, Sarah! At least you've got a family!"

"I don't believe I'm hearing this from you. You sound like you're jealous."

"Not jealous . . . but envious. You have a family to surround you with love and all I have is me—Sarah. For thirteen years now, all I've had is me. I don't begrudge you, Sarah. I'm thrilled for your happiness but I'm dying inside. I just feel a great big emptiness and now with you going, I'm not sure I can bear it much longer."

Sarah wrapped her arms around Katalin in a desperate attempt to comfort her. She felt like a mother abandoning her only child and she fought back her own tearful emotions. She had never seen Katalin so despondent and it bothered her. "Katalin, do you have any idea how loved you are? Not just by me but by everybody I know that's ever met you."

"Thanks Sarah, but I'm beyond cheering up right now. I really need to be going."

Sarah shakily grabbed Katalin's wrist and gently but firmly held on to her with both hands, worried about her leaving in her present mood. "I mean really loved, Katalin!"

"Please Sarah, it won't do any good and my cab is waiting."

"Katalin, think! Just tonight the Rosens told me that you're the only Gentile girl they've ever met that they'd want for a daughter."

"The Rosens are sweet people, Sarah. I appreciate their saying that."

"Sure, and Marvin and Ruth love you tremendously. You really should get together with Ruth. She's a fun person to be with. They really missed you at Rosh-Hashanah." Sarah felt she was making progress. "And David-Jacob idolizes you. He's always talking about you. He loves you a lot."

"I love him, too, Sarah, but I really, really have to go."

"And Ira! Ira loves you, too, Katalin!"

Katalin immediately jerked her head away. Sarah released her wrist and, with her left hand, she tenderly turned Katalin's face back towards her. Looking her in the eye, she repeated, only with more emphasis. "Ira loves you, too, Katalin!"

Katalin looked at Sarah with a pained expression. Neither of them spoke a word. They didn't have to. They read it in each other's eyes. Sarah had the answer she was looking for, but not the one she hoped for. Something had happened between Ira and Katalin that threatened Sarah's relationship with her.

Katalin didn't respond. She couldn't, except to whisper goodnight, which is all a shocked and surprised Sarah could do in return.

Chapter 12

Sunday evening Marvin picked Ira up at the airport and drove him to his apartment. When they arrived, Sarah and David-Jacob greeted them warmly, but Ira and Marvin both stared in shock at DeeJay's black eye. Over coffee and sponge cake, Sarah told them of David-Jacob's misadventure.

Before leaving, Marvin advised Ira and Sarah that they should call the Chamber of Commerce in Phoenix warning them to tell their citizens that David-Jacob was coming in three weeks, and life in that city would never be the same.

After David-Jacob was in bed, Ira told Sarah he had located a 2500-square-foot building for a floor covering store.

After sharing with her some of Arizona's unique points of interest, including its ghost towns, he presented her with a genuine cowhide cowboy hat and placed it on her head—a sentimental reminder of their night of mutual agreement to move.

When he asked Sarah how her week went, she replied that with the exception of David-Jacob's street fight with two other children and worrying about Joshua-Caleb coming down with croup, it was just a normal week. However, after they were in bed with the lights out, she made one last comment. "By the way, Katalin was over on Saturday. She spent the day. We had an interesting talk."

When Ira nervously inquired what they talked about, Sarah yawned, "Oh, we can discuss it tomorrow night. I'm really tired . . . good-night. Glad you're home."

Although only married seven and a half years, Ira learned that when Sarah said, "By the way..." the interpretation was, "Ira, you're in big time trouble. Think fast, because the hammer's about to fall!" For the next two hours he tossed and turned, imagining every possible conversation that could have taken place. Once he was convinced that he had a defense strategy for each, he finally fell asleep.

When dawn broke Monday morning, Sarah rushed to change and feed Joshua-Caleb while, urging David-Jacob to get dressed. By 6:30, he had also been fed and the three of them were ready to leave the apartment, both children having early morning doctor appointments.

Mostly, Sarah wanted as little conversation with Ira as possible, until that night when the children were asleep. Timing was everything. Whatever animosity Ira was harboring towards Katalin that had caused a break in her own relationship with her was too serious a matter to be resolved over breakfast. Perhaps it was only a minor misunderstanding and she was allowing it to fester unnecessarily. At least that's what Sarah hoped. Woman's intuition, however, based in large part on contending remarks Ira made towards Katalin the past few months left Sarah with the impression that things were far more serious.

Hearing the alarm go off in their bedroom, she walked in to see Ira sitting at the side of the bed rubbing his eyes. She told him she had to catch the seven a.m. bus in order to be at her eight a.m. appointment. The truth was that her first appointment wasn't until nine-thirty, but she didn't trust her present emotional state to not confront Ira immediately if she remained much longer.

Once Sarah left with the kids, Ira showered and made himself breakfast. He thought how rare it was when Sarah didn't have breakfast already prepared for him once he had dressed and was ready for work. He missed that ritual as well as their general discussion on what was written in the morning newspaper.

At the same time he cringed, thinking what their conversation might be like when he got home. Then a smile crossed his lips and he thought it a stroke of genius to stop at the flower shop after work. There was no way Sarah could be angry with him if he arrived tonight carrying a bouquet of red roses. And if he happened to pick up a box of Whitman's Samplers to go with the flowers, all the better. Ira whistled as he left the apartment.

Once at work, Ira found himself playing catch-up resulting from his week in Arizona. He had to order several skids of tile as well as linoleum rugs and items of carpet to put on sale. There were floor measures and complaints to handle as well as preparing final inventory sheets before moving.

At five o'clock that afternoon, Ira called Sarah and told her he was going to stay at the store an additional two hours to finish up some work. She told him that the children's doctor's appointments came out fine, although Joshua-Caleb did have a mild case of croup and she was given medicine for him. David-Jacob's eye should heal fine. Sarah then reminded Ira that there were some serious matters weighing heavily on her mind that she wished to discuss after the children were asleep.

After hanging up the phone Ira looked at the seven long-stemmed red roses he had had delivered to the store in an attractive Wedgwood vase. He had also picked up a box of Whitman's chocolates at noon.

Ira thought Katalin to have a sixth sense about him, a type of discernment that allowed her to read him like a book, or worse, that she could somehow peer into his soul. Pride had thus far prevented him from sharing with Sarah his deepest, most innermost struggles. Foremost amongst those struggles was why God was conveniently absent while the Jewish people were being unmercifully slaughtered.

Ironically, while helping to liberate the concentration camp at Ohrdruf, Ira had wrapped himself in spiritual chains. While admitting to no one that he had since become an atheist, he knew that Katalin knew. She had become a catalyst for releasing his hostility towards his now non-existent God. In effect, she had become too close to him and Sarah, so close that he started to tense up around her. Sometimes he actually envisioned her reading his mind. However, despite all his apprehensions about Katalin, Ira knew he still greatly admired her and reluctantly admitted to himself that she had often been a great stabilizing force in his and Sarah's life, especially when Sarah was troubled and needed encouragement by someone other than himself. Add to that, her intellect and quick wit often presented a challenge to him. Katalin loved history as much as he did and with history came the usual politics of history.

Ira decided to walk the several blocks home rather than wait for the bus or take a cab. He wanted more time to gather his thoughts. When he eventually arrived at his apartment door, he took a deep breath and entered. Sarah was in the kitchen washing dishes and he could smell the chicken soup keeping warm on the stove.

He took the gifts out of the large paper sack, placed the vase on an end table in the living room and walked into the kitchen with the flowers and box of candy hid behind his back. Bussing Sarah on the cheek, he sprung the gifts on her.

"Ira! Why thank you! What's the occasion?" Sarah wiped her hands on her apron and took the gifts.

"Why does there always have to be an occasion? I just missed you when I was gone, that's all."

Sarah reached around Ira's neck and gave him a warm hug and kiss. He then went in the living room to retrieve the blue and white sculpted vase. Upon seeing it, Sarah's eyes widened in still more surprise. "Ira, it's gorgeous! Come now . . . you didn't miss me that much. Are you trying to bribe me?"

"Just like a woman. You don't buy them something and they whine. You buy them something and they become suspicious."

"Well, Ira, would you like a substitute? Like, say, a monkey or a kangaroo?"

So far Ira felt everything was going as planned. He left the kitchen to change clothes and wash up while Sarah prepared the table. She would usually stuff his bowl one third full of rice into which she ladled the soup. Ira preferred the soup with generous portions of cut carrots and boiled chicken. While Sarah continued with the dishes, a famished Ira proceeded to eat a second, then a third and last bowl.

While eating, they talked of Ira's day at work and the children's doctor's appointments. Sarah then took off her apron and carried the vase with roses to the living room. Returning, she pulled out the chair next to Ira. "How is it . . . the soup?"

"Great as usual. Something about chicken soup, Sarah, makes you feel healthy all over. I'm convinced that there would be no sickness in the world if everyone could be vaccinated with real homemade Jewish chicken soup, alias, Jewish penicillin."

Sarah smiled, then bit her lip and looked pensively at Ira. Seeing her expression, Ira sensed that the inquisition was about to begin. Hopefully, the flowers and box of candy had softened her mood.

"Ira, did you look in on the kids?"

"Yep! DeeJay was just drifting off when I walked into his room. The baby's doing fine."

"The 'baby's' got a name, you know."

"Are you accusing me of playing favorites?"

"Only that last night, after a week of being gone, you never asked once about little Joshua. Nor did you even peek in his crib."

"Sarah, I was tired. It was a long flight and then the first thing I see is DeeJay all messed up. I'm sorry, I was just distracted."

"You do love him, don't you, Ira?"

"Sarah! What a ridiculous question! Of course I love him! Why would you even insinuate that I don't?"

"I just want to be sure. Lately I'm not sure about anything anymore."

"What are you talking about?" Ira shoved his empty bowl aside and folded his hands on the table while looking straight at Sarah.

"I'm talking about us—about what we're doing, moving to Arizona. Why we're doing it?"

"We went through that, Sarah. In fact you're the one who finally convinced me. Remember?"

"That was before last week."

"What's changed, Sarah?"

"You! I just want to be sure I know and understand you. I want to be certain of the reasons why we're doing this."

Ira got up from the chair and threw his hands up in the air, while staring at the ceiling. "Sarah . . . we've been married going on eight years. I sleep with you every night. What more do you need to know and understand?"

"You tell me. You're the one with all the secrets."

"I don't believe this! I swear, Sarah, all year we've been having these same stupid arguments. Every question a woman asks comes attached with a free puzzle piece. First you have to solve the puzzle before you can answer the question and may God help you if you come up with the wrong answer!"

"We aren't playing games now Ira. This is about you and me and about our future together."

Ira stiffened as he detected an implied threat. He had no idea what Sarah was leading up to. What confused him more was that he knew that Katalin's visit on Saturday had something to do with Sarah's searching questions but, as yet, she hadn't even brought up her friend's name. He hated when Sarah enmeshed him in mind games because it always allowed her to steer and control conversations.

"What about you and me, Sarah? We've got a good marriage. I work hard to support you and the children. The three of you are the focal point of my life. And now we have the prospect of starting our own business in a growing and beautiful state. We've got everything to look forward to. I don't know what your problem is."

"You do work hard, Ira. You're also a good husband and father. I love and admire you for all that. But I've come to realize during our week apart that I really don't know you. You're like a stranger to me."

"Stranger? What are you talking about? And that stupid remark you made earlier about secrets. What secrets?"

"Ira, whenever I think that I know you, something happens to make me feel that I only know the part of you that you want me to know. You keep all your deepest feelings and emotions so hidden that essentially I don't know you at all. In three weeks, we'll be leaving Brooklyn, the city I love more than any city in this world. Part of the reason I love it are the people here who are so much a part of my life. And although I love you dearly, I keep asking myself, 'Why am I moving to Arizona with someone who keeps shutting me out of his life?'"

Ira was incensed and thumped his chest with his fist to punctuate his response. "I'm Ira Katz, Sarah! Remember!? We met at a skating rink where you crashed into me, almost knocking me unconscious. Correct me if I'm wrong, but I believe for the both of us it was love at first sight! We got married! Granted, we didn't date very long, but we more than made up for it by sending hundreds of letters to each other, especially when I was in Germany fighting the war. Fortunately I survived. I came home to a new son. Now we have two sons. And here we are several years later, arguing about God only knows what!? Because I sure don't!"

"Did you really survive the war, Ira?"

"I'm here, aren't I?"

"But you were a lot different before you went to war. You were happier and because you always seemed happy, I felt confident in our marriage. When you came back, even your brother noticed how little you smile anymore."

"Well, pardon me, Sarah, but war has a way of changing people, okay? There are things you try and forget."

"I understand what you're saying, Ira. I anticipated that you might change, but I hoped not so drastically. You see, I've told you everything about myself—not only because you insisted on knowing, but I wanted you to be there for me when the memories overwhelmed me. I'm only asking the same thing of you, Ira, that you tell me what it is you're trying to forget."

Ira contemplated Sarah's remarks and became more subdued. "Is it so necessary, Sarah?"

"Yes."

"Why?"

"Well, for one reason, it might help explain why you never go to synagogue anymore. When I first met you, you were always quoting from the Torah. You even expressed a desire of someday devoting yourself to Talmudic studies. Becoming a rabbi wasn't totally out of the question for you."

"I was just indulging in fantasy, Sarah. I didn't know what I wanted to do with the rest of my life. My reasons for wanting to be closer to God were selfish reasons. There was a chance I could be killed and I wanted to get on God's good side."

"How do you feel about being on God's good side now?"

"I don't think about it at all."

"You don't believe in God anymore, do you, Ira?"

Ira looked at Sarah who was still seated. He was surprised that he hadn't fooled her at all and how coolly detached she seemed to be.

Then he thought, *Why shouldn't she be? She's not the one on trial here.* He couldn't escape the truth of her question without lying. He also knew that sooner or later his antipathy towards God would become evident. "No Sarah. I won't lie to you . . . and I won't pretend anymore."

"Well, when we get to Arizona, I will personally take our children to Hebrew school and synagogue."

"That's fine. I want them to go. I don't believe in God, but I believe in being Jewish. Our children must be raised Jewish."

"You're a real contradiction, Ira."

"I'm sorry. I should have told you a long time ago."

"You didn't have to. I guessed it not long after you got back from Germany. I just wasn't a hundred percent sure. I also hoped that I was wrong or that it was something you could work out by yourself. What happened, Ira?"

"What do you mean?"

"What happened to make you hate God?"

"The God that I thought existed wasn't there when the Jewish people needed Him most. The only alternative was the Christian God, the One whose people helped persecute ours."

"You can't condemn Christians, Ira. The true Christians weren't at fault. Many of them, like Katalin's parents, stood by the Jewish people, even at a cost of their own lives."

"Someone's to blame, Sarah."

"From personal experience, Ira, you can't live choosing who you want to hate."

"Let's drop it, Sarah. Okay?"

"No, it's not okay. Because this is what our whole discussion is about, Ira. I love you so much and you keep pushing me away. You've always been there for me, but you won't let me be there for you, Ira, and it hurts." Sarah started wiping away falling tears.

Ira shook his head. "I can't talk about it, Sarah."

"Why?"

"You've gone through enough. Why should my pain have to carry into your life?"

"Because you are my life. Please tell me, Ira. I beg of you!"

Irritated, Ira responded icily. "It's none of your blasted business."

Sarah was angered by his statement and clenched her teeth. "Then I'll make it my business. Because as much as I love you, I'm not going anywhere with you unless you open up. Things won't get better, Ira. They'll get worse. In the long run, these things that you're keeping from me can destroy our marriage. I won't live with that fear anymore. I demand to know, Ira!"

"Forget it, Sarah. You're really upsetting me. If you really love me, you won't keep prying."

"I'm afraid, Ira, that you have a distorted view of what love really is."

"But you do know, right?"

"I know that someone who once loved God, and now hates or doesn't believe in God, has a considerable problem."

"Women . . . bunch of nosey bodies. Think they know everything."

"Well, since I've already been included in your indictment, let's try this on for size. When Barry sent you his letter telling you he sold the store to someone else, you left his letter on the night-stand. After you left the room, I picked it up and read it, wanting to know what reasons he gave. Apart from his reasons, he asked a question that aroused my curiosity."

"What are you getting at?"

"The question was, 'Do you still think about Ohrdruf?' What happened, Ira, in Ohrdruf, Germany?"

Sarah's mention of the small German city caused a surge of adrenaline to course through Ira's veins. No matter how hard he tried to bury the memories, they continued to resurrect themselves, sometimes revisiting him in his sleep.

Ohrdruf was a testament to the utter depravity of man when devoid of conscience. To Ira's way of thinking, it was also an indictment against man's alleged Creator.

Trembling with rage, feeling he was about to lose control, he sought the closest object in which to displace his anger. Rearing his foot back, he then drop-kicked the wooden chair in front of him and drove it airborne, until it crashed inches below the kitchen sink.

Sarah gasped in stunned disbelief and bolted from her chair. First she stared at Ira and then towards the now badly demolished piece of furniture.

Still seething with anger, Ira jabbed his finger in the air in Sarah's direction. His chest heaving, and railed at her, "You just can't leave things alone, can you, Sarah!? When will you ever learn not to push me!" He stormed from the kitchen.

Numbed by Ira's sudden burst of emotion, Sarah walked over to the broken chair and knelt to pick up the pieces. She fumbled with parts of it, seeing if she could force-fit it together. It was part of the set of table and chairs given them as a wedding gift eight years ago. Now she feared it represented the state of their marriage.

Dropping the chair's shattered remains, she rose to her feet, walked out the kitchen and through the living room where Ira stood with his back to her, staring out the window. Ignoring him, she went into their bedroom to retrieve her purse. Seconds later, she was rushing out of the apartment.

Hearing her opening the door, Ira turned and called out to her. "Sarah! Where are you going?"

"As far away from you as possible!"

"Sarah wait! I'm sorry . . ." Ira hurried over to her and momentarily rested his hands on her shoulders. "Really, Sarah, I'm sorry. I'll buy a new chair first thing in the morning."

"Why? So you can break it too?"

"That's not fair."

"Fair? What do you mean, fair? Am I just supposed to stand around and watch our marriage deteriorate and you accuse me of not being fair? Fair to me, Ira, means communicating, talking to me rather than busting up chairs. It means loving me enough to risk being vulnerable, when all I want to do is get to know you better. It's not just the chair, Ira. I need to go for a walk and sort things out."

"Don't go!"

"Can you think of a reason why I should stay?"

Ira cast his eyes downward and slowly turned to avoid her gaze. Taking a deep breath in an effort to calm his nerves, he wrung his hands while searching for the right words. "I don't want to burden you with my problems, Sarah. You've had enough troubles in your life."

Sarah was now speaking to his back. "What do you mean, Ira?"

"I'm talking about Ohrdruf . . ."

"Did you meet another woman there, Ira? Did you have an affair? Because if you did, I'll try and understand."

Ira turned sharply with a look of astonishment. "Is that what you think? That I had an affair? Sarah, I would die before I would be unfaithful to you! I can't believe that you would think that of me!"

"That's the problem, Ira. I don't know what to think of you anymore because you won't share things with me."

"I love you, Sarah! I would never cheat on you!"

"Then what could be so bad that occurred in Ohrdruf that you won't tell me?"

Ira paused a moment while debating in his own mind whether to tell her. He then stared at the ceiling and closed his eyes trying to compose himself. "Okay, Sarah, you win. You've heard of Buchenwald?"

"Of course I've heard of Buchenwald. It was a Nazi death camp."

"So was Ohrdruf. It was a subcamp of Buchenwald. Our unit helped liberate it. I was there five days. I never wrote you about it because it was too painful and depressing. I was aware of what you had already been through and I didn't want to cause you further misery. After I returned from the war I still saw no need to bring it up. I thought I would just try and put it out of my mind, but even without your bringing it up, I continue to have nightmares about it."

"My God, Ira, you should have told me. I'm a big girl! I'm aware of what happened in the camps. When did . . ."

"1945 . . . April . . ."

"And you've kept this a secret for over four years. I'm your wife, Ira! Why are we even married if you can't tell me things!? My legs feel weak. I need to sit down." Sarah seated herself on the sofa while Ira remained standing.

"Sarah, sometimes there are things that you just want to forget. I didn't want my memories of the place to be part of our lives. I'm sorry if I've been wrong, but still I don't wish to talk about it. Things happened there. Things I saw . . ." Ira's voice drifted off.

"Ira, from what you're telling me, it isn't me you're trying to protect, it's you! You won't face living with what you saw and experienced and, what's worse, you won't let me help. You're still shutting me out. Don't you see!?"

Ira started breathing rapidly, his lips quivering. "I'm sorry, Sarah, it's something I alone have to deal with."

Sarah felt frightened. She had read accounts by those who had liberated the camps, and the profound effect it had on them, reducing many of them to tears. Ira's having so personalized it indicated to her that something beyond liberating the camp had disturbed him emotionally.

She rose from the sofa and faced her husband directly. "Tell me something, Ira, how many more years do we have to be married before you hit me with another bombshell?"

"What do you mean?"

"Ira, I feel like I'm in a dark whirlwind of secrecy and deception. I feel sick inside, Ira. Ever since I read Barry's letter about Ohrdruf, I worried about it. It weighed on my mind like a heavy shadow." Tears began falling from Sarah's eyes in rapid succession. "Maybe it would have been better had it been another woman," she continued haltingly. "I'd know then how to deal with it."

Sarah hesitated, then continued, "Ira, there's something else! The other day when I was with Katalin, I got this awful feeling that you had something to do with her vanishing from my life. It just swept over me when I was trying to grill her on why she had been so distant, so unavailable to me. Ira, help me, this inkling of distrust has snowballed into something that is out of control. I'm almost afraid of you."

Ira again rested his hands on her shoulder in an attempt to reassure her and took another deep breath before attempting to explain. "Sarah, there is a lot to unravel. I admit, I have some confessions to make to you. I'm afraid I did come between you and Katalin."

Sarah jolted backwards, as if she'd been hit. Her body trembled.

"Sarah, I was jealous for your time and concerned that Katalin was proselytizing both you and DeeJay. Almost three months ago I met with Katalin and over lunch I told her to not be so involved with us. Not to quit seeing us completely, just to back off a little. Apparently she took my suggestion much more seriously than I had intended. I never imagined she would be so hurt as to stop coming by altogether."

Sarah shook her head in disbelief. "Ira! How dare you go behind my back and hurt my friend and knock her support from under me! For heaven's sake! I'm your wife, not your child! I have feelings! I have rights! What has our marriage come to!? How could you, Ira!?"

She turned and grabbed her purse off the sofa. Clutching it, she brushed by Ira and headed for the door. With her hand on the doorknob, she paused. "Ira, I've got to go. I feel sick . . . and I feel very very scared. I need time to think. Please don't try and stop me!" A moment later she was gone.

Chapter 13

Dazed by the whole series of events, Ira turned and slumped horizontally on the sofa. Bringing his hand to his face and covering his eyes, he waited for his heart to stop beating inside his head. *What do I do now?* he asked himself.

David-Jacob entered quietly, rubbing his eyes. He huddled next to his father, then rested his head on his lap. Normally, Ira would ask him what was wrong and then carry him back to bed, but this time he was in no rush. He needed the comforting touch of his son. Gently stroking David-Jacob's face as one would a newborn puppy, he said quietly, "Couldn't sleep, huh, Tiger?"

"Uh-uh. I was all asleep, then I heard you and Mommy talking real loud. Did Mommy go away?"

"She just went for a little walk, DeeJay. Daddy said some stupid things and she's a little mad at me right now. She'll be back soon. Why don't we have some cookies and milk before going back to bed."

David-Jacob had already dashed off to the kitchen when Ira remembered the busted chair. Concerned at what his son would see, he entered the kitchen and witnessed David-Jacob on his knees next to the broken chair, trying to reassemble it.

He looked up. "Daddy, I've got some sticky glue. We can fix this real good so when Mommy comes back she won't be mad at you anymore."

It occurred to Ira that his son had not only heard but witnessed much of their argument. With a heavy heart, he knelt on one knee to look his son in the eye. "DeeJay, sometimes grownups do and say things they shouldn't. They act like little children. That's what I did tonight. I love your mommy very much and when she comes back I'm going to tell her how sorry I am and buy her a brand new chair."

"Daddy, I don't want Mommy to be gone."

"She'll be back soon. Even though she's mad at me, she still loves you children. She also knows I'm a lousy diaper changer. Why don't we have those cookies and milk and then I want you to go right back to bed. I'll take care of the chair later."

"Okay."

"One more thing . . ."

"What?"

"Do you still love your daddy?"

"Uh-huh."

"Then where's my hug?"

David-Jacob wrapped his arms around his father's neck and gave him a powerful squeeze. Ira was hoping his son wouldn't let go too soon or he would see the tears in his father's eyes. When David-Jacob did let go, his words pierced Ira's heart. "Daddy, when I grow up I want to be just like you."

Ira could only whisper back, "You be better than me."

After sharing cookies and milk, Ira tucked David-Jacob into bed. Smelling a rank odor, he went over to the crib where Joshua-Caleb was gurgling, changed and fed him and eventually rocked him back to sleep. Looking at the clock, he saw that it was ten-thirty. He grabbed a stack of magazines and threw himself back on the sofa to leaf through them, barely able to concentrate.

Still exhausted from his trip to Arizona and his long work day, he dozed off to sleep. When he woke again, it was nearing one a.m. and Sarah still wasn't home yet. He paced the floor for several more minutes and then, too anxious to wait any longer, he phoned Marvin and Ruth. Marvin demanded an explanation before dragging himself out of bed, but finally reassured Ira he would be right over. Half an hour later, he arrived at the apartment wearing a huge tent-like bathrobe over his pajamas.

Despite the seriousness of the moment, Ira couldn't help but comment, "That's a great outfit, Marvin, especially if you plan to go camel riding in the Sahara."

A very tired Marvin wasn't in the mood for any of his younger brother's sarcasm. "Real funny. At least I'm not the person with the brains of a nincompoop calling people at one o'clock in the morning." He then lectured Ira on the gross stupidity he exhibited in attempting to come between Sarah and Katalin. He was less critical of Ira's reluctance to speak about liberating the camp at Ohrdruf, although it aroused his own curiosity, concerned that his brother hadn't mentioned it to him either. Then, feeling Ira didn't need to hear any more, Marvin tossed him the keys to the car and wished him *mazel tov* (good luck) as he left to search the neighborhood.

For over an hour, Ira searched an area of several blocks, including walking in and out of three eateries. The last place he stopped was the emergency room at Bushwick Hospital, happy not to find Sarah there.

It was two-forty-five a.m. when he returned to the apartment looking haggard and concerned. Ruth meanwhile had called Marvin to tell him she had phoned two police stations in the area. Fortunately, there were no reports of anyone matching Sarah's description.

Ruth then suggested that Ira call Katalin's apartment. "Better yet," he grabbed his jacket, "I'll go over there." Ira headed for the door.

Katalin stumbled out of bed and groggily searched for her alarm clock to see what time it was. The person knocking on her door said he was Ira, but what would he be doing at her apartment at three o'clock in the morning?

She cracked the door open to the length of the chain. "Ira! What are you doing here?"

"Is Sarah here? I need to talk to her."

"Heavens no! Why would she be here at this hour? Wait, let me get my robe on." Putting a blue terry-cloth robe over her nightgown, Katalin let Ira in and offered him a seat on the couch. He first scanned the room.

"Ira, don't you believe me? What's going on?"

Ira then realized he offended her. "I'm sorry, I just assumed she was here."

"Well, you assumed wrong!" Katalin took a seat on the couch opposite Ira. "Did you two have an argument?"

Ira stared dejectedly at the floor. "I'm sorry, Katalin, I wasn't trying to accuse you of hiding her. I'm just worried sick about her. And yes, we did have an argument. A pretty bad one."

"Oh no, not about me I hope."

"A good part of it was about you. But it's not your fault, it's mine. I said and did some stupid things that I'm sure you're aware of. But can we talk about it later. I need to find her."

"How long ago did she leave?"

"About six hours ago. Marvin's over at my apartment now and I've borrowed his car. I've searched our neighborhood high and low, all the late night cafes. I've even gone by the emergency room at Bushwick Hospital. Ruth called both police stations in our vicinity. I don't know where else to look. She's never done this before."

"I have an idea where she might be. Let me get dressed and I'll go with you."

"You do! . . . you will! . . . where?"

"I'll tell you when we get to the car. I'm not having you dash off without me!" In a couple minutes Katalin was dressed and they were on their way. "Get on the Parkway and head towards Coney Island."

"Why Coney Island?"

"Ira, do you two talk at all?"

Ira didn't answer. Neither of them spoke until they reached the Parkway. Ira took a deep breath, trying to relax himself as he peered over at Katalin who was staring out her side window.

Ira, too, like all others who met her, couldn't help but admire her beauty. It amazed him how young she looked, thinking to himself that she could still pass as an older teenager.

It then struck him how ridiculous and paranoid he had been to think that she was any kind of threat to his relationship with Sarah. He reflected on the many times early on that the three of them had been together, enjoying each other's company. Prior to the last several months, he had always felt a big brother kinship with her, even offering her advice as to the type of people he thought she should be dating. Sometimes she listened, sometimes she didn't.

A feeling of guilt and shame swept over him as he realized how much she meant to Sarah and David-Jacob, and how devoted she might be to Joshua-Caleb, if given the chance. Worst of all, he instinctively realized that Katalin, of all people deserved better. She had suffered tragedy not unlike Sarah, yet bravely trudged on, with the Katz family being her strong base of loving support.

The more Ira considered how wrongfully he had spoken of her and treated her, the more depressed it made him. Finally he broke the silence. "Katalin, can I say something?"

Katalin turned and looked intently at him. "Sure."

"I ah . . . well . . . I'm not sure how to say this. As you can tell from tonight, with Sarah walking out on me and all, I'm not real good at apologizing. What I'm really trying to say is I appreciate your helping me find Sarah. It shows how much you really care about us. I've really stunk in my attitude toward you and what I may have done to hurt you."

Katalin could see that Ira was struggling for words and felt moved. "Ira, hush, we'll talk about it later. I appreciate what you're trying to say."

"No . . . no you don't. Because what I'm trying to say is how deeply sorry I am . . . I ah . . . gosh I feel like David-Jacob does when he says he 'feels bad all over the place'."

Ira's last comment caused Katalin to both smile and well up with tears. Also, for the first time, she saw what she thought were tears in Ira's eyes. She reached over and patted his hand denoting "apology accepted", then spoke gently, "You wondered why I feel Sarah may be at

Coney Island. Do you remember when you and Sarah were first dating, before you married and shipped out?"

Thinking back brought wistful recollections to Ira. "Yes, there were too few of those times. It was often difficult to get a pass."

"Do you remember the place you always went to? In fact, I occasionally went with the two of you on double dates."

"Yeah... sure... Coney Island. I remember we'd usually go there at night when the beaches and midway weren't as crowded."

"Well, before Sarah and I first met you at the ice skating rink, we often went to Coney Island by ourselves. It was very difficult for Sarah, our first two years in America, even more so than when in France. We were on an entirely new continent and so far from what was once home.

"For that matter, I, too, had difficulty adjusting. But it seemed that whenever we were at Coney Island, sitting on a bench on the boardwalk, or walking the beach, Sarah's whole countenance would change. She would become, oh I don't know, philosophical and introspective, on occasion even bringing a book of poems to read. With the ocean waves pounding the shore in the background, she found contentment and peace. She mentioned once that the rush of the ocean had a cleansing effect on her."

Ira grinned, "Katalin, the reason I liked coming to Coney Island with her is because it put her in a romantic mood."

"Men!" Katrina scoffed.

But the creases of Katalin's lips turned to a smile before she continued. "I believe what Sarah was experiencing was a sense of God's majesty. The ocean often has that type of mesmerizing effect on people. She didn't seem to be aware of its imperial nature, the fact that it can sometimes be foreboding and unforgiving, capable and powerful enough to swallow huge sea-going vessels with a mere lick of its tongue.

"Instead, she saw the ocean as peaceful and reassuring; it had been around for tens of thousands, perhaps millions of years and nothing man ever did was going to change that. It reminded her that a force higher than man was in control, regardless of how brutal and chaotic the world was becoming.

"By looking over the ocean she could see things on a larger scale, keeping her from dwelling on her own misfortunes. It gave her a sense of the eternal. Sarah may not talk about it often, but she has a deep reverence for God."

"Despite everything she's been through?"

"I think, Ira, that long before coming to America, Sarah gave up blaming God for what happened to her. She doesn't always understand God, none of us do, but she still very much depends on Him. In fact, keeping everything in perspective, as incomprehensible and beautiful as the ocean is, she marveled that it was but a mere thimbleful of water in the hands of God."

Ira contemplated all that Katalin was telling him. Dozens of seconds later, he responded. "Katalin, I once thought I knew God, but I've lost Him. He's gone."

Katalin wished desperately to respond but felt she would come across as self-righteous and preachy. No more was said until ten minutes later when they arrived at Coney Island.

The gentle sea breeze nipped at their cheeks. Surprisingly, even at the early morning hour, several people were either sitting along the boardwalk or jogging along the beach, just out of the reach of the lapping waves.

Katalin was the first to spot Sarah, sitting and talking with an elderly woman about a hundred yards in front of them. No sooner did they see her than her elderly companion rose to her feet, embracing Sarah before departing.

Though anxious, Ira was tremendously relieved to find his wife safe and, at least for a while, knowing she had company. However, he felt as nervous as a school kid on his first date. "Come with me, Katalin, it'll make everything easier and I know she'll want to see you."

"No, Ira, you're the person in her life that makes it work. You're the one she's thinking about right now."

"Why am I scared?"

"Well, if I can hazard a guess, I'd say it's because you realize how much you love her—and you're probably wondering if she still loves you. If I can take that a step further, let me reassure you that she does. She adores you, Ira, she always has, although," Katalin threw up her hands, "what she sees in you I have no idea."

"Katalin, would you like an early exit from this life?"

They grinned at each other. "Go to her, Ira!" Though Katalin was smiling, her eyes were tearing. Ira gave her a quick hug in a long overdue effort to thank her. "Hurry up, Ira, before you make me cry."

"Are you okay?"

"I am now! In fact, I'm more okay than I've been in a long time. I'll wait here for you two."

Ira walked the short distance to the back of the bench where Sarah sat, staring out at the ocean. He quietly seated himself next to her, not uttering a word. Still staring straight ahead, she spoke. "I love it here, Ira, did you know that?"

"I forgot, Sarah. I forgot how much you loved the ocean. In fact, I've forgotten a lot of things and I can't express to you in words how sorry I am."

Sarah smiled and reached her hand over for Ira to clasp. "I'm chilly, Ira, would you sit closer and put your arms around my shoulder?"

Ira gladly complied. "How long have you been here, Sarah?"

"I don't know, I guess for a long time." She finally turned and looked at him. "Who's watching the kids?"

"Marvin, he's at our apartment in his pajamas and a bathrobe. He looks like he's ready to lead a caravan across the desert."

Visualizing Marvin in her mind caused Sarah to shake in brief laughter. Then there was a pause as she became pensive. "What are we doing, Ira?"

"I don't know, Sarah. All I know is how much I love you, how much I need you. Other than that, I guess I just need to change. If you don't want to move to Arizona, I'll understand. We don't have to go."

"You know, Ira, up until you just said that, I've been hoping and praying that's what you would say. But oddly enough, now that you've said it, I don't think that's the answer. No Ira, we'll go. I think now the change would do us both good."

"Then what is it you're asking?"

"Don't you know yet, Ira?" Sarah's eyes gazed into his. Ira momentarily closed his and then opened them while nodding his head. "Yes, I think I now know the answer."

"And . . . ?"

"And the answer is 'Yes!' Yes, I love you enough to share with you my deepest fears and apprehensions, and also my deepest hurts."

Sarah's eyes flowed with tears and she buried her head in the crevice between Ira's head and shoulders. "I love you so much, Ira."

Ira then remembered Katalin. "By the way, I had help finding you."

"Huh?"

Ira stood and pointed in Katalin's direction. "That funny little lady looking back at us."

Sarah squealed, then stood and called for Katalin to join them. Katalin quick stepped, then jogged and soon tearfully fell into Sarah's embrace. While they talked, Ira quietly sauntered away across the sand in the direction of the ocean. Minutes later, Sarah and Katalin took off their shoes and rushed to catch up with him.

They locked their arms in his — Sarah on the right, Katalin on the left. Soon Ira's face began to quiver and he started breathing heavily. Sarah sensed something was wrong. She released her arm, as did Katalin, and then she stepped in front of Ira. There was moisture in his eyes.

Sarah grew concerned. "What's wrong, Ira?"

As Katalin backed away and to the side, Ira bent down and picked up a small broken shell, then walked purposely past Sarah and hurled it back into the ocean. With a glance at Katalin and a grave look at Sarah, he whispered, "No more secrets, right, Sarah?"

Sarah nodded. "Right Ira, no more secrets." She instinctively knew what was happening. "It's okay, Ira." She took his hand. "Katalin and I both know how painful memories can be. We can help you. Tell us about the death camp."

Ira paused, took a deep breath and began to speak.

Chapter 14

"On the 4th of April, 1945, our unit—the 89th Infantry Division—was advancing towards the southern German town of Ohrdruf. The area was very scenic with plenty of trees, flowers and rolling green hills. We were on the outskirts of town some five miles away when we started picking up a faint but distinct odor. At that time we were still unsure what the odor was.

"As we continued forward, several things struck us as odd. We began noticing large rock piles, along with stacks of wood and many large trenches—only recently dug. The citizens we passed were all reticent to talk to us. They seemed skittish and wouldn't look us in the eye.

"Getting closer to the actual town, we spotted an unusual site, a castle, with several additions being added to it. We also saw tall wooden platforms at the castle which at first led us to believe they were housing prisoners there. After searching the castle, we found no prisoners at all, but what struck us were the rudimentary tools that were being used for the additional construction. This was a modern castle, which even had elevators, yet all that was being used for construction were picks and shovels, and the area was also littered with hundreds of dirty and rusty cans.

"The castle's caretaker was a lone elderly man, as mysterious and tight-lipped as the rest of the townspeople. What he did volunteer, however, was that there was a camp located two miles down the road whose workers were being used to build the castle's additions. Other than that, he said he knew nothing of the workers or who consigned them. He claimed total ignorance of the people in the camps. Looking back, we soon realized that—like everyone else—he was a bold-faced liar. One couldn't ignore the obvious smell without being curious.

"Again we moved forward, only this time towards the direction of the camp. About a mile from the camp we all knew from the growing and noxious stench that what we were smelling was burning flesh. We finally reached the camp in a desolate and heavily weeded area, surrounded by a high barbed wire fence. Inside the fence we saw several wooden shacks.

"Then we opened the gates—the gates I can only now describe as the gates of hell! Immediately we saw hundreds of still smoldering pyres, littered with corpses. In fact, once inside the gates, what we saw was indescribable horror that defies human imagination. All around us were cordwood stacks of bodies, piled several feet high.

"Those who were walking around the camp, who by this time had taken some of the German guards prisoner, were so emaciated that you could only describe them as walking skeletons. Hardly a grown man left could have weighed more than sixty, maybe seventy pounds. Two days earlier most of the German guards had evacuated Ohrdruf. They had taken the healthier prisoners and marched them towards Buchenwald. Of those left, their skin was so taut as to expose every bone in their body. Their fingers and hands, claw-like. They were festered with vermin, many of them carrying typhus and we were immediately warned not to come in contact with them. Their teeth were mostly all blackened, their skin a splotchy red, their eyes bulging from deep and shrunken sockets. To look at them, one knew immediately that a goodly percentage were beyond saving. They were essentially the living dead.

"Rather than bury the bodies first, we fed those still alive all the K-rations and C-rations we had. They tried to rip open the cans of food with their bare hands. Meanwhile, all we could think to do to clean the inmates up was to bring in all the Lysol we could find to dump in water for them to bathe in.

"I was immediately drawn to one young boy who wouldn't take his eyes off me. He was barely able to stand. At seven or eight years of age, he was too weak to work his way into the desperate crowd, all anxious for food. He didn't look disease-infested, so I took the chance and walked over to him. He was bent on one knee, struggling to stand but unable to. I had him sit back down, cradled him in my arms like a newborn and fed him. He kept looking at me with those questioning and haunting eyes. Apparently I reminded him of someone familiar because, in his irrational state, he kept calling me 'Uncle.' He kept saying that 'they put Mommy and Daddy in a railroad car' and they were crying for him and could he see them again."

Ira took off his glasses and wiped the tears from his eyes while struggling to continue.

"What could I tell him? To give him hope, I lied. I said, 'Mommy and Daddy are fine and now they can't wait for you to come home again and make you well. They told me to tell you that they love you very very much.

"I continued to cradle him in my arms, saying whatever I could to give him hope. As emaciated as he was, I could tell that he was once a very beautiful boy. Someone gave me a washcloth soaked in Lysol and I wiped him off.

"Barry came by and I asked him to fetch me a basin of soap and water. Everywhere around me — brave soldiers, who were used to killing and accepted war for what it was — were now crying and cursing at what was done to these pitiful creatures. Many got sick themselves from retching so bad."

Ira again took off his glasses and nervously brought his hand down over his face. Composing himself, he shakily put his glasses back on and continued, "I asked the young boy his name and I thought I saw him trying to smile, thinking perhaps I was teasing him. He said, 'You know, Uncle Shimmon, I'm Dov. . . .'"

Ira's voice caught as he looked pleadingly at Sarah. "Isn't that a beautiful name, Sarah? . . . Dov?"

"Yes, Ira . . . It's a very beautiful name."

"Dov died, Sarah! He suddenly went into convulsions and died in my arms. You know why, Sarah!? I'll tell you why. Because those b_ _ _ _ _ ds had starved him so bad that his stomach shrunk to where he could no longer tolerate food. If someone would have told me — and the rest of us — we would have not fed them so fast, but we didn't know. I wanted to save him so bad but I didn't know and I killed him and hardly a day has gone by since that I don't see his face."

Sarah put her arms about Ira and openly wept with him. Katalin turned away from both of them, crying her own tears.

"Let's go home, Ira . . . we'll talk more at home." Sarah stroked the back of his head.

But Ira wasn't through. He had come this far, he wanted to get all the pain out while he still was able. He gently kissed his wife on the forehead and stepped away to continue.

"For two days, I helped bathe and feed those left. Then we were ordered into town to bring in all the residents of Ohrdruf to bury the dead and let them see what they allowed to happen. We brought many of them to the camp at gunpoint; they were furious with us. Unable to stand the sight any more than we could, they cursed us and we cursed them back. We hated them for their inhumane cowardice, far more than they could ever hate us.

"One of the leaders of the inmates—formerly a town mayor at Erfurt, fifteen miles away—told me of the immense brutality of one particular guard. That guard was now being forced to help with the cleanup. I gave the inmate my pistol . . . and I told him that he could kill the guard and the rest of us would look the other way.

"The time came when we all knew this was going to happen. Several of my army buddies concurred with what we were going to let take place. The inmate walked up to the sadistic guard and pointed the gun at his temple. The German guard stiffened, but half a minute or so later, the inmate handed me back my gun, saying, 'I cannot do it!'

"I could see the guard grinning, staring at me, as if mocking me. I read his look to mean, 'These people are so weak minded, they lack even the will to carry out retribution.'

"I became so enraged by his hardened stare that I immediately shoved the barrel of the gun down his mouth until he gagged on it. I told him, '*Ich bin ein Jude!*' so he knew that it was still a Jew who was going to blow the back of his head off."

Sarah gasped, as did Katalin. Ignoring them, Ira went on, "The inmate immediately grabbed my arm, forcing me to pull the gun away. He pleaded with me, saying, 'No, if you kill him, you will become like him. He has already forfeited his soul, don't do the same.' So that was that.

"The next day, that same guard, while locked in the stockade, tied some belts together and hung himself from one of the ceiling pipes. I felt he had cheated us. He didn't allow us to judge him for his crimes. I was even planning to talk to him myself to find out what made him so cruel and full of hate."

Ira's voice was ragged. "So . . . now I live each day with the face of a little boy which haunts me. And I live with the knowledge that I gave up the privilege of exacting revenge for him. I should have told the guard, 'This is for Dov,' and then pulled the trigger. Nobody would have said a word. Now instead, I carry the anger and remorse of not having done so."

Sarah placed her hands firmly about Ira's face, forcing him to look directly at her. "That guard, no matter how cruel he was, was not yours to kill. The inmate who prevented you from carrying out judgment was a thousand percent correct. Thank God for him! The camp guard was a victim of his own hatred. Don't you see, Ira! By not pulling the trigger, you proved yourself a far better man than that guard and people like him. In the contest of being human, you won, Ira! You won! Don't you dare blame yourself!"

Ira covered his face in his hands and wiped away the last remaining tears. Seconds later he turned and stared directly at Katalin. "Katalin, I respect and envy you so much your closeness to God. Why Katalin? Why did God let all this happen!? He could have stopped it, couldn't He, Katalin?"

Katalin had a perplexed look as Sarah quickly came to her defense. "Ira! Katalin doesn't know! I don't and you don't. It's not a fair question to ask her!"

Katalin seized the moment. "Yes it is, Sarah! It's a very fair question! And Ira . . . and you and I have the right to ask it."

A surprised Sarah looked obliquely at Katalin. The waves roared in the background, pounding furiously against the sloping shore, as if God himself were underscoring this brief space in time; His present brave spokesman being a young, beautiful Hungarian woman with unyielding faith.

"Always it is God's fault, never man's! God loves us is precisely why He didn't interfere. Where there is no freedom, there is no love. God allows us the freedom to choose, and so ties His own hands at what grieves and offends Him. He loves us enough that He gives us the liberty to choose to hate Him if that is our desire. He has not made us to be puppets and robots. Johannes Denck once wrote: 'God forces no one, for love cannot compel, and God's service therefore is a thing of perfect freedom.'

"But lest we forget," Katalin went on, "God reserves the right to hold us accountable for the choices we make. The book of Ecclesiastes says, 'God shall judge the righteous and the wicked.' From that statement alone, it is obvious that God neither causes evil nor turns a blind eye towards it. I only know that it shall be a fearful thing for the unrepentant sinner to one day stand before an angry God with the prospect of eternal Hell as his destiny."

Katalin's voice shook. "Now, if you two don't mind, I am cold, I am hungry and I am emotionally exhausted. I would like to go home." Almost miraculously, as if on cue, the tides began receding. The roar of the ocean waves became as a quiet symphony and, if one listened closely, there was a message left.

Chapter 15

The back yard of the house on Albemarle Road was over an acre of lush
green lawn spotted by two large cherry trees and bordered by hedgerows.
The house itself was a six bedroom, white Craftsman Style villa, built in
1910 of stucco and shingle. It belonged to a gracious and elderly couple
who were longtime members of Katalin's church. Today, as in past years,
they had offered their house and grounds for the annual church picnic.

Katalin hadn't been on a church picnic but once since she had come
to America and that was four years ago. She had forgotten how much fun
they were. Besides the enticing food--consisting mainly of fried chicken
and a variety of casserole dishes — the several dozen congregants who
showed up had participated in a number of competitive contests.

The temperature was in the mid-fifties and Katalin had dressed
in Levis, sneakers and an oversized sweatshirt rolled up at the cuffs. It
was a direct contrast to the chic and stylish apparel she normally wore
when attending church. As a consequence, she sensed that others in the
church saw her as someone delicate and maybe too refined. But most
only knew her casually and were unaware of the competitive juices that
flowed within her. This morning, looking in the mirror and putting on
makeup and earrings, she spoke to her reflection. "Well my precious
brethren, if you think your sister Katalin is just some unassertive, overly
prim young lady, come picnic time you are in for a surprise!"

Katalin knew she came from good genes and was proud of it. Her
father, before going into the ministry, had been a rising young soccer
star in Hungary. Even at the time of his death in his mid-forties he could
often beat men half his age in a foot race. Now at past three p.m., on
a balmy and beautiful Sunday afternoon, she sat on a spread blanket
with two other single ladies observing the festivities. Katalin's back
rested against one of the cherry trees as she finished off a piece of fried
chicken. Earlier she had raced against several men and one woman in
a hundred yard dash and finished third. She and her friend Barbara,
sitting next to her, also finished third in the wheelbarrow race and with

Patricia, her other friend sharing the spot under the tree, she finished second in the three-legged race.

Katalin had proved herself more than adequate at horseshoes, as well, and was on the winning badminton team. She then won the ladies softball throw with ease, receiving an apple pie for her efforts. In the process, she was acutely aware that several other unattached ladies were looking disdainfully at her. Her friend Barbara spoke, "You know what they're thinking, don't you, Katalin?"

"Oh, I'm not really paying them any mind."

"Well, I think their snobbishness is a little too apparent—turning their noses up at you at every turn."

Katalin was mildly amused by the attention she was apparently getting, but she was having too much fun to be bothered with pettishness.

"I'll tell you exactly what they're thinking," Patricia offered her opinion. "They're thinking, 'That overgrown tomboy. She's just trying to show off for the new assistant pastor, the Reverend Mr. Miller!'"

Katalin looked at her two friends and the three of them exchanged smiles. Barbara prodded her. "Well?"

"Well what? Why the silly grin?"

"C'mon, Katalin, we're *all* hoping he notices us! Admit it."

"I'll admit no such thing except that this food is quite good. I think Mrs. Draper makes the best fried chicken, don't you agree?"

"You're not getting off that easy, Miss Katalin Zichy." Patricia fueled Barbara's suspicions. "I've seen you cast a few glances his way, hoping he was watching you. Of course I would do the same if I was as athletically inclined as you are. So how about it, Barbara's right, isn't she, Katalin?"

"M-m-m-m, good fried chicken. I think I'll go get me another piece." Barbara and Patricia each grabbed one of Katalin's sleeves, not allowing her to rise until she answered their questions.

"Well shame on both of you! To think that I...that you two...would even insinuate that a proper Christian lady like myself would pay any attention at all to a perfect stranger, albeit a man of the cloth...dedicated to the Lord's service. About five feet eleven inches tall...slender build, 155-160 pounds. Rusty brown hair...perfect even white teeth which reveal a dimple when he smiles. Who grew up on a farm in South Dakota, is twenty-nine years old and born in the month of July. Has two younger sisters. Why I'll have you know I'm not even aware of his presence, or even that he has baby blue eyes. Again, shame on both of you!" Katalin grinned back at her two excited and saucer-eyed friends.

Barbara squealed at her. "When did you meet him, Katalin!?"

"Tell us Katalin!" Patricia demanded to know.

Katalin nonchalantly licked the fried chicken crust from her fingers. "Oh...a couple of days ago. Pastor Frey asked me to come by after classes and before work to introduce me to our Reverend Paul Miller."

In unison, Barbara and Patricia chorused a loud "Why!"

"We all met in the pastor's office where I was asked to do a short bio of Reverend Mr. Miller for the religion section of the *Daily Eagle*. But I was only there ten minutes. I didn't have time to notice that he was cuter than the dickens."

Katalin's two peers, both a year younger, then pressed her for every last detail as the three of them began giggling, gushing and laughing like teenagers.

By four p.m., some of the church crowd had left for home. Several of those remaining, including Katalin and her two friends, were watching a flag football game. The Reverend Miller was quarterback and captain of one team of six players ranging in age from fourteen to forty. They were opposed by an equal number of players of approximately the same age. In short time, one of the assistant pastor's players went down with a twisted ankle and he called out for a replacement. But of the men still at the picnic, their excuses ranged from, "I'm too stuffed," "I'm too old," or "Naw! I'm outta shape and somebody's got to finish off these pies. It would be a shame if they went to waste."

Meanwhile, unbeknownst to Katalin, her friend Barbara was whispering conspiracies into Patricia's ears. A moment later they both stood up shouting and wildly waving their arms! "Katalin will play! Katalin will play, Reverend Miller! She says she's as good as any man!"

Katalin was taken aback and embarrassed at suddenly becoming the center of attention! Almost all eyes turned her way. Several clapped and urged her on.

Katalin was furious at her friends for humiliating her but her protests and attempts to get the practical jokers to quiet down and quit waving their arms were futile.

Feeling as if she were now in the center ring of a three ring circus, she turned around red-faced and gritted her teeth. Many were laughing at her predicament as the Reverend Miller approached her. With the skill of a ventriloquist, Katalin then mouthed a veiled threat while looking straight ahead. "Barbara and Patricia, don't think for a moment that I won't get even with you two loudmouths."

The Reverend Miller stood a few feet away encouraging her. "Katalin, come on! you can do it. Flag football isn't like regular football. You just stick cloth strips in the waistbands. When someone pulls one out, it's the same as a tackle."

"B . . . but . . . I . . . I've never played football. I don't even know the rules, Reverend."

"So you'll learn. It's not that hard. Besides, I've seen how athletic you are."

"You have! . . . I mean I am . . . athletic . . . I mean . . . you think so . . . whatever."

Katalin became totally tongue tied in his presence and even began feeling goosebumps as the reverend smiled her way. At this point she knew she had little choice. "Okay . . . I guess . . . I'll play." With some trepidation Katalin started walking towards the playing field with Reverend Miller. Still seething, she glanced back over her shoulder and scowled at Barbara and Patricia, who were in raptures at the trick they had played on her.

Katalin was given a brief explanation of the rules of the game but it was still all like a foreign language to her. The Reverend Miller and four other men and Katalin were soon huddled together as the reverend called out the first play. "Okay, Mr. Graves! I'm going to fake the ball to you on a Statue of Liberty. Pete, check Mr. Conklin on the line then come back for the ball which I'll have behind my back. Okay . . . on three!"

When breaking from the huddle, Katalin was confused. "What do I do, Reverend?"

"I'm sorry, Katalin. You be our safety valve in case something goes wrong. Run straight out five yards, no more, then turn to the right and face me in case I have to throw the ball to you."

As fate would have it, Pete couldn't check the five foot, seven inch 220-pound Mr. Conklin at the line. Instead Pete got knocked to the ground and the reverend panicked when he saw Mr. Conklin coming at him like a human bowling ball. He then zipped the ball in Katalin's direction and it whizzed past her ear before she could even blink. It also unnerved her when she realized she could have been hit smack in the center of her face. Walking back to the next huddle, Katalin had a petrified look about her. "Reverend, I didn't know you were going to throw the football to me."

"Katalin, I told you that you would be our safety valve, just in case."

"Well, excuse me. I know what a safety valve means when one talks of plumbing. I do not understand its analogy to football."

"It means in case the play is in trouble, you take the pressure off by my throwing the ball to you. Understand?"

"And you expect me to catch it when throwing it a hundred miles an hour?"

The reverend apologized and so began Katalin's venture into the American game of football.

The game continued for another hour with several onlookers cheering Katalin on. Until the last play of the game she only managed to catch one of the five passes thrown to her but her speed on defense allowed her to "flag" tackle the opposing player several times. More importantly, she was actually enjoying herself.

Two situations became of significance during the game. The first occurred halfway through when the rather stout, belly-sagging Mr. Conklin was busily rushing the Reverend Miller. Two consecutive times he picked Katalin up off the ground and moved her aside with the apparent ease of lifting a feather.

While funny to everyone else, it infuriated and humiliated Katalin. Finally she confronted Mr. Conklin, telling him his actions were totally inappropriate for a Christian man. Mr. Conklin, in turn, advised Katalin that football was a man's game. As such, it meant that being a Christian, when playing football, was followed by "show no mercy" and "take no prisoners."

When Mr. Conklin did his procedure on Katalin a third time, it was more than she could bear. She felt he was intentionally mocking her and womanhood in general. Although aware that dispensing retribution was the province of the Lord, she apologized to the Lord and took matters into her own hands. Mr. Conklin was not about to belittle her anymore.

Minutes later, when he next rushed across the line and attempted to grab her and set her aside, Katalin stepped quickly backwards and smartly to the side, while sticking her foot out. The rhinoceros-charging Mr. Conklin stumbled over her foot and did a huge belly flop. When he fell to the ground on his rather large paunch, one could hear a loud whoom-m-ph! and some said later, they thought they felt the earth move.

While he was rolling on his back and trying to get his wind, Katalin fanned the palms of her hands and strutted around to the delight of everybody. She even bowed at the waist a couple of times to generous applause before bending over the flat-on-his-back Mr. Conklin and apologizing. "Sorry, Mr. Conklin. I sure hope you're okay and I really do mean that. I'm afraid I took your "show no mercy, take no prisoners" too seriously."

Still prone on the ground and looking up at the sky, Mr. Conklin addressed her. "It's okay, Katalin, I have good insurance and my wind is coming back. The question is, 'Would you do it again if you had the chance?'" When Katalin answered in the affirmative, Mr. Conklin congratulated her on passing muster and welcomed her to the fraternity of true football players. He also made a deal with her—not to pick her up anymore if she promised not to trip him again.

The most notable play, however, came at game's end. With the score tied, Katalin had not been thrown a pass for over twenty minutes. She had been running deep patterns, some twenty yards or more and getting in the clear but the reverend seemed determined not to throw her the ball. Exhausted and frustrated, wondering why she even bothered to run down the field, she moped into the huddle on an agreed-upon last play of the game. The five men in the huddle were already on the ground, on one knee, as the Reverend Miller was drawing a diagram in the plush flat lawn with his index finger. Katalin stood and listened while peering over the tops of their heads. She learned that the final play of the game was again slated to be a pass thrown to another player and it upset her.

Feeling inconsequential, before the huddle broke up, she decided to speak her mind. "Reverend Mr. Miller, may I say something, please!?"

From the tone of her voice, it was obvious to the reverend and fellow players that she was irked. He shrugged his shoulders. "Sure Katalin, what's on your mind?"

"With all due respect, I have run down that stupid field like some silly rabbit now some umpteen thousand times. Nobody's ever around me and yet you refuse to throw me the football and I don't think that's fair! Why am I doing it!?"

"Because it forces a player on the other team to watch you and frees our own player."

"You mean I'm being used as a decoy?"

"Yes, that's it! But you've played really well so far and we're all proud of you."

"Well thank you very much, but why don't you throw me the ball and then you can be proud of someone else?"

"Well . . . um-m-m . . . I would, Katalin, but you're never in the clear."

Katalin folded her arms and cocked her head. "Reverend Mr. Miller! I will have you know that if I was any more in the clear, you would have to send a rescue party to find me!" At this time, the other players on the team began chortling, enjoying themselves at watching the reverend's embarrassing attempt to extricate himself.

"Well Katalin, I apologize to you once again. I'm afraid I . . . ah . . . I just haven't seen you."

"Reverend, have you ever taken a class in anatomy?"

"No Katalin, I don't believe I have."

"Well too bad! Because had you...you would have learned that the two almond-shaped objects above the bridge of your nose are called eyeballs! Well, I've said what I wanted to say. I'll go running down the field again like you want me to, like some dumb dodo brain!" An irritated Katalin then walked brusquely away and took her position on the line across from Mr. Conklin. She took her normal stance, slightly bent over with a hand on each knee.

Meanwhile, the five men still in the huddle gazed at one another shaking their heads while barely containing their laughter. One of the players offered his advice. "Reverend, if I were you and I wanted to live long enough to preach my next sermon, I think I would change the play. It doesn't matter, Reverend. We still need over twenty yards for a touchdown and we're only out here to have fun. It would be the Christian thing to do."

Reverend Miller nodded his head. "Agreed! I'm throwing the ball to Katalin. Do some good blocking, guys. Give me a chance to get the pass off. Mr. Graves, when we get up to the line of scrimmage, whisper to Katalin that the ball's coming to her. And tell me—you guys know her—is Katalin always this way?"

One of the teammates was quick to respond. "Reverend, Katalin's one of the sweetest, most warm-hearted people you'd ever want to meet. Generally, she's kind of quiet. I don't know what's gotten her adrenaline pumping so."

"I do!" one of the other teammates blurted out. "It's been going on since the beginning of time. It's called, 'I'm a female and I refuse to be ignored.'"

Laughing, they broke the huddle and lined up for the final play. Reverend Miller was behind the center waiting for the snap when he briefly looked over at Katalin. He understood by the nod of her head that she was aware that the pass was about to come her way.

But something else happened in that split second. Their eyes locked. It was that communication of mind, spirit and soul that poets and writers have for centuries tried to describe—when the universe blinked . . . and only two people existed.

The ball was centered and Mr. Conklin, instead of rushing, immediately started chasing Katalin down the open field. He trailed her by a few yards as she anxiously looked over her shoulder and into the puffy, blue-white clouds. There, high above her, was a tiny odd-shaped speck that she knew in her wildest dreams she could never catch. As the football started its descent, Katalin ran to the spot where she thought the ball was coming down when suddenly, Mr. Conklin came crashing into her!

She screamed as they collided, with the force of their impact sending her flying into the row of hedges in front. Their striking together also caused the seriously overweight Mr. Conklin to lose his balance as he pirouetted and began doing a lopsided dance routine. While off balance, the football hit him on top of his head and ricocheted towards the hedges. It was just a simple reflex reaction that caused the mired-in-the-bushes Katalin to reach for the errant pigskin. Grabbing the football by her fingertips, she cradled it in her arms like a newborn baby.

Soon there was pandemonium everywhere! It sounded to Katalin as if the heavens had just opened and millions of angels and suddenly burst into song. Her wildly exuberant teammates and several in the crowd began rushing towards her.

Stupefied and speechless, Katalin tried in vain to extricate herself from the bushes but then decided to wait, reveling in the moment and clutching the football to her breast. By some miracle, she not only caught the ball, but had just scored the winning touchdown!

After her teammates rescued her from the bushes and heartily embraced her, Katalin began jumping up and down like a child receiving a new bicycle. Lost in the crowd was a dismayed, embarrassed Mr. Conklin, rubbing the top of his sore pate and nursing a bruised ego. A girl had just beat him for the winning score. Katalin then spotted him and threw her arms around his neck, thanking him for the use of his "beautiful" head.

Mr. Conklin turned crimson red but confessed that her hugging made him feel a lot better. He also made her promise that at next year's picnic, she would play on his team. In her fleeting moment of glory she couldn't help but notice the Reverend Miller's admiring glance.

Everyone worked to clean up the private picnic area before dusk settled in. Katalin's friends were two of the happiest for her when she made her miracle catch, but they left immediately for choir practice. She promised to call each of them later in the evening.

During cleanup, which took an hour, she secretly hoped that Reverend Miller would have approached her for conversation but he never did. He never had a chance to. Every time she turned around, some pretty girl, much younger than herself, was talking to him. Once again, she began feeling old at twenty-six. Disappointed, she also began chiding herself for acting so churlish and immature during the football game, yelling at the pastor like some shrew, jumping up and down like some silly adolescent. How embarrassing! How could she ever face him again?

Katalin couldn't get to the bus stop fast enough. The glow of what happened an hour earlier had worn off and was something she no longer wanted to think about. Except for that special moment when their eyes fixed on each other, the whole event was really a disaster.

Halfway to the bus stop, Katalin heard a voice yell out her name. Turning, she saw the Reverend Miller running towards her and she thought to herself, *Oh goodness, not now! I'm not ready for you!* A few feet away, the reverend stopped to catch his breath and soon they stood facing each other. Katalin felt extremely nervous and her insides were churning as she spoke. "Hi. I . . . ah . . . enjoyed the game. It was a lot of fun. I need to catch the bus home. I'm sorry if I acted silly and immature during the game. That's really not . . ."

"Katalin!"

" . . . not like me. I usually try . . ."

"Katalin!"

" . . . try to act more mature and ladylike. But I did enjoy meeting you and . . ."

"Katalin! I loved having you on the team. It added a lot of spark to the game. There's not a guy around that doesn't want to play his best when trying to impress a beautiful young lady. Besides, if anything, I owe you an apology."

"You do!? How come?"

"Well, I have to confess. I purposely wasn't throwing the ball to you because I was afraid you couldn't catch it. I got caught up in the game and wanted to win. I need to ask your forgiveness."

"Hm-m-m . . . let me think about it." Katalin stroked her chin.

"Well Katalin, while you're thinking about it, would you permit me to drive you home. My old jalopy is right around the corner."

"If I don't forgive you, will you still drive me home?"

"Sure, but if you don't forgive me, next time I definitely won't throw you the football."

"Oh dear! I forgive you then!"

It took half an hour for Reverend Miller to drive the distance to Katalin's apartment. During their ride the two of them filled in some blanks to their individual lives. At the same time, the reverend insisted that when not in church, that she just call him Paul.

Adding to the information Katalin had gathered two days before, she learned that Paul grew up in the Black Hills of South Dakota about sixty miles from the Homestead Gold Mine. His father would occasionally moonlight at the mine but otherwise was a farmer. He had two younger sisters, one twenty-two, one nineteen. On their farm they grew mostly corn and wheat and raised pigs. He had a very normal and happy childhood although his parents always scraped to get by.

Paul described South Dakota as God's country. All around where they lived were streams, rivers and lots of pine and birch trees. When it snowed, which it did often, the ponds would freeze over which allowed for a lot of ice skating. His description of South Dakota was of a winter wonderland. "At times," he said, "the snow seems so pure and crystallized that it glistens."

When asked why he left such a beautiful place, Katalin learned of two events in the young pastor's life that had a profound impact. He had been engaged for almost three years to a girl he grew up with. Paul spent two of his years in the Navy aboard an aircraft carrier as an ensign, then a LTJG, serving as a personnel officer. During that time, his fiance had gotten lonely and started seeing someone else. Soon after his discharge from the Navy, she broke their engagement.

After their breakup, and despite a degree in psychology, Paul felt the Lord's call into the ministry. He then attended Wheaton College in Illinois, graduating in June of 1948. Going back to South Dakota and living in the same town as his ex-fiance would have been awkward, he said, although he maintained there was no bitterness. It was a major setback in his life, however. He had hoped to be married by now and be raising a family.

Prior to that, the Miller family was struck by tragedy. On August 24, 1942, his family received a telegram from the war department stating that Paul's older brother, Thomas--a Marine lieutenant--was killed three days earlier at a place called the Tenaru River on Guadalcanal. Thomas was three years older than Paul and Paul had idolized him since he was a small child.

As he shared this part of his life, Katalin sensed he still missed his brother a lot and felt great empathy for him. She knew that pain only too well. At that point in their conversation, sitting in the parked car outside Katalin's apartment, she felt obliged to briefly share her own loss. She spoke of Sarah and how together they escaped Nazi Germany.

Since it was still early he invited her go to an ice cream shoppe for a chocolate malt. The next two hours were spent talking of their future dreams and sharing their mutual love of the Lord.

Katalin made three phone calls before going to bed. One to Barbara, one to Patricia, and the last and longest call to Sarah. For an hour, Katalin described to Sarah in great detail everything that happened. Three different times, Sarah had to tell Katalin to slow down so she could understand her. They made plans to have lunch the next day. Then Katalin remembered she already accepted an invitation from Paul to have lunch, and they decided they would make it a threesome. It was important to Katalin that Sarah approve her new knight in shining armor. Katalin couldn't sleep until the early hours of the morning. She couldn't ever remember feeling this way before.

Chapter 16

It was all coming together like clockwork as Ira reclined in his office chair, resting his hands behind his head, his legs on the desk. He was working alone and well after closing, preparing the store for final inventory before their family's move to Arizona in eight days. Only yesterday he was at Grand Central Station purchasing their train tickets.

Looking now through his mostly glass-enclosed cubicle and surveying the store, everything seemed in order. The pallets of tile were all stacked neatly in rows and by stock numbers. The one, three and one-half and five gallon pails of cutback and all purpose adhesives were all sectioned off. The rolls of linoleum rugs were measured and tagged, as were the dozens of area rugs. Only three rolls of Wilton carpet remained to be measured.

Ira checked his watch. It was after eight p.m. He had been at the store now going on fourteen hours. He told Sarah to expect him home between nine and ten o'clock, but tomorrow would be his last day before taking the final week off to help pack their belongings. Tomorrow they might meet with Katalin and her new admirer, Paul, and treat them to dinner. Ira had occasion to meet him once and both he and Sarah liked him a great deal.

Ira closed his eyes, suddenly realizing how tired he was. The last several weeks had not only been eventful but chaotic. Often he felt he was in a race downhill with no finish line. Yet, despite it all, there was at last a sense of victory and renewal in his life. Fighting a war in the Solomon Islands, then Germany a few short years ago, was one thing. But fighting the ghosts that had shadowed him since liberating the death camp at Ohrdruf was something else entirely. The memories had almost destroyed his marriage and, in the four years since V-E Day, had drained him both spiritually and emotionally.

He knew that without Sarah and Katalin's help, his sequestered rage and self pity would have certainly consumed him. But now that the demons had been exposed, he had his last and greatest enemy in the crosshairs, soon the victim of the power of unyielding love and a desire to continue hoping. After years of running from God and denying Him, Katalin's emboldened defense of God eleven days ago caused him to wonder anew. Perhaps God hadn't abandoned the Jews after all. If so, there was reason enough to consider believing again.

Ira walked over to the floor safe and made sure of the two hundred dollars they kept on hand to begin each new day's business. Below the cash-box lay a .45 caliber handgun. Twice in the past four years the store had been robbed and Ira swore, never again. Satisfied with the money count, he closed the safe and spun the dial. Feeling hungry and needing something to tide him over until he got home, he decided to go next door for something sweet. He turned the light out in the office which left only a fluorescent light in the front as the only illumination in the large, old building.

The El Train, rumbling high overhead, continued as always to make the walls shake. Ira once again shook his head in resignation. A dozen times a day, every day for countless years, the El caused flakes of paint chips and plaster to float down to the floor and accumulate like so much sawdust. Several times in the past year Ira had tried to convince his brother to give up the lease on the building. The area was growing too seedy and rundown. But his efforts had been futile. Low rent and a lot of repeat customers were Marvin's main reason for wanting to stay put.

Ira laughed to himself when thinking of Marvin's other reason. "Nu, Ira, I know the exact times when over the building the subway train comes. So, when Mrs. Himmelstein or Offermeyer comes by to *kvetch* [complain] that they don't like the color of the floor tile, I only listen to them when the train comes over. It makes living a lot easier."

Reaching the front door, Ira realized he had left his keys on the desk in his office. Too tired to walk back and knowing he'd only be gone a minute, he left the front door unlocked. While at the pharmacy next door, Dominick, the store's owner, stopped to wish him and his family good luck. After purchasing a small Hershey bar for himself, Ira also bought a twenty-five cent giant bar to take home to Sarah and David-Jacob.

Returning to the floor covering store to prepare the final inventory sheets, Ira didn't notice that the small light in his office that he had turned off only minutes before, was now on. He casually entered and sat once again in his chair behind the desk. As he took out a blank piece of paper and a ruler to draw up a mock inventory sheet, he was startled by a noise and a shadow.

Peering over the rim of his glasses, Ira saw standing before him a disheveled, unshaven Caucasian male, about thirty years old, wearing Levis, a dirty tee-shirt and an open green jacket. The stranger was of average height and seemed very nervous. That he appeared nervous was of great concern because the stranger had a Colt .38 special aimed directly at Ira's head.

With glazed and darting eyes, the intruder sneered at Ira. "Remember me, Mr. Katz?"

Ira searched his mind. The man looked familiar. Then it came to him. "You once worked for us."

"Yeah, brilliant Mr. Katz." The man's brow was beaded with sweat and he had a crazed look as he used the sleeve of his jacket as a handkerchief. It was the same wild-eyed gaze that Ira had noticed in soldiers during the war when suffering from battle fatigue or drug addiction. The man also reeked of liquor.

"So what do you want?"

"What do you think I want!? Open the safe!"

"Why are you doing this? There's not even that much money in there."

"Two hundred dollars, Mr. Katz! That may not be a lot to you but it is to me, especially since you cost me my job."

"How did you know there's two hundred dollars?"

"I installed for your crummy store once, remember! But thanks to you calling practically every other floor covering store in town, I can't find work anymore. Now open the lousy safe!"

It all came vividly back to Ira. Two years ago, the gunman standing in front of him was working a tile job at the house of a middle-aged couple. The husband and wife later complained of an expensive broach and bracelet missing from their jewelry box. Ira's store made good on the missing items. It was the second time in three months that the young man had been similarly accused. The first time, Ira had given him the benefit of the doubt. The second time he let him go and also called several other store owners, warning them about hiring him.

Using his gun as a pointer, the night intruder motioned Ira towards the safe. Ira hesitated a moment and then reluctantly complied. It then crossed his mind that since he could identify him, the gunman might decide after robbing him to kill him anyway.

Ira dropped to one knee and, with trembling hands, began to work the combination to the safe. With fingers awkward with dread and palms slick with sweat the first time he worked the dial he inadvertently went past the final number.

This agitated the gunman. "Hurry up you stupid Jew! I don't have all day!"

Ira had a difficult time thinking clearly and for some odd reason when turning the dial again, he forgot the second number of the combination that he had worked hundreds of times before.

"What are you doing, you lousy idiot!? Quit stalling or I'll blow your stinkin' head off! I don't have time for games."

"I . . . I'm sorry . . . I . . . ah . . . just can't remember. I guess I'm too nervous. The combination is on the underside of my first desk drawer, left side, if you'll pull it out."

Ira felt a sharp jolt and saw spots when his head was shoved hard into the top of the safe. His glasses fell to the floor and one of the lens shattered.

Mumbling incoherently, the maddened gunman jerked open the top drawer of the desk and screamed out the taped combination. "Okay Mr. Katz! You don't open it this time, you'll be floating on a cloud and playing a harp! Thirty . . . wait . . . no . . . thirteen . . . twenty-six . . . and then three. You got it! Because if *I* have to open it, I might as well kill you. You see Mr. Katz, I'm needing some horse [heroin] real bad!"

Ira took a couple of deep breaths and then worked the combination a third time, only much slower. His head throbbed as his jumbled thoughts ran together, knowing in moments he might be dead. The tumblers locked into place and he slowly turned the handle.

While tenuously pulling the door open, he sought help from a previously unlikely source. *God, forgive me! I don't want to die. Sarah and the children need me. Whoever you are, God, please don't let this happen.* He removed the cash-box and, without turning around, handed it over his shoulder. He then heard what he was sure was the click of the gunman's revolver! Instinctively, he reached for the .45 hidden from view at the bottom of the safe. His immediate concern was to distract the gunman, if only for a few seconds.

"Is . . . is the money all there? The two hundred dollars I mean?"

"What do you care? You're a dead man . . ."

"Wait! There's more money in my desk in a locked drawer. I . . . I . . . Let me get it." Ira rose cautiously to his feet with the .45 in his hand. Then, faking a move towards the desk, he quickly whirled. Two loud pops! Two quick flashes! and the gun went flying from Ira's hand as he fell prostrate across the chair, then crumpled to the floor, clutching his stomach. He brought his knees up into a curled position and grimaced in excruciating pain. Struggling to breathe as blood streamed through his shirt, he could hear the gunman cursing while rifling the cash-box.

Pressing his left hand against his midsection, Ira tried to spot his broken glasses but couldn't. He then scooted his body in the direction of the gun on the floor, finally reaching it. As quietly as he could, with all his remaining strength, he labored to his knees.

Still gasping for air and starting to hyperventilate, he peered over the desktop, using it to support his right elbow and gun hand. Struggling to focus anew, he saw everything in double, including two gunmen. One was an apparition but he couldn't tell which. He could only point his .45 in the general direction of his assailant who was attempting to exit.

Ira yelled a warning. "Stop! St . . . stay where you are! I'm calling the p . . . po . . . police."

"No, you're not!" As the gunman again raised his weapon at Ira, Ira squeezed off four rounds in rapid succession. In a spray of blood his adversary was hurtled backwards, crashing through the glass window. His lifeless body lie draped across the sharded sill like a limp rag doll.

Still bleeding profusely, Ira dropped weakly back to the floor where he frantically pulled on the phone cord. Eventually, the phone toppled from the desk and the receiver fell off the hook. Inching over to the phone, Ira dialed "O", put his mouth next to the receiver and whispered, "Yes . . . op . . . operator . . . I've been shot. Help . . . help me please! Katz's Floor . . . Cov . . . El . . . Elevated Station . . . Myr . . . Myrtle Avenue. Oh God! Please hurry!"

Ira could hear his heart pounding in his head as he lay crumpled on his side, knowing that with every heartbeat, he might lapse into unconsciousness and die. Desperately he tried to stay awake until someone came, but he wasn't sure he could. His life was ebbing and the burning, searing pain in his midsection was so bad that his body started shaking spasmodically.

Got to live for Sarah! Got to! Got to! he chanted to himself. After what seemed an eternity, he finally heard what he thought were sirens. Then he heard voices and footsteps approaching as everything around him started spinning. Suddenly he saw something strange. While writhing on the floor, the blood exiting his wounds had formed perfect and symmetrical lines in the shape of a cross.

Was he hallucinating? He knew of stigmatas where people claimed that a mark of the crucified Christ appeared miraculously on their bodies, raising or restoring their faith. But he didn't believe in such things, especially being a Jew. Yet he couldn't shake from his mind's eye the vision of the smeared blood on the floor. What did it mean?

Someone was now in the room and shouting, "Over here, Tim. Hurry!" Then a second person entered the space. "You can call the coroner for this one! Amazing! Looks like all entrance wounds to the heart."

Ira saw faces encircling him, touching him, but could no longer see well enough to distinguish their features or tell who they were. Then the first voice spoke again, only in a more hushed tone. "This second guy's barely alive and bleeding like a sieve. I just gave him some morphine to ease his pain. At least he's stopped shaking. Help me plug him up and get him in the ambulance."

"It'll be a miracle if he makes it to the hospital," the second voice responded. "Have one of the policemen coming in to phone Bushwick and have a surgery team ready in case he does. Boy, talk about your shootout at the OK Corral!"

Ira was aware enough to know they were talking about him. He was obviously dying, but he didn't want to. Despite all the pain and tiredness, he just didn't want to. He wanted to be with Sarah again — and to love and hold his children.

Something cold was touching his forehead and he rolled his eyes upward. Now he was seeing, yet again, something as strange as before — a gold cross hanging in midair! Desperate for any kind of hope, he tried to grab it but couldn't raise his arm.

Then he heard the first familiar voice. "Tim, I think he wants the cross and chain you're wearing around your neck." A moment later, Ira felt an object being pressed into his right hand. His mind started floating in and out of sleep. He could sense that he was now somewhere else because the sirens became deafening and he heard the squealing of tires. Someone with a blank face was hovering over him.

Ira was even more weary than before but he had to stay awake — for Sarah and the kids! The person over him then cried out in distress, "He's eighty over fifty! Speed it up! I think we're losing him!" Then in a softer voice, that same someone whispered in his ear, "Hold on, mister. Just two more minutes and we'll be at Bushwick. Keep thinking about the cross of Jesus in your hand. He can help you! Don't give up!"

Ira wanted so badly to sleep. He was so tired, but he knew it still wasn't time yet. He felt people touching him again as they put him on some type of bed. Now there were more faceless people standing around him and murmuring. Moments later, the bed was moved quickly down an endless corridor of brilliant lights. Someone then took the object from his hand. The voices, though clear, now sounded more like a distant echo. "A cross! I thought Katz was a Jewish name! What's a Jew doing holding on to a cross?"

Another strange voice responded, "Hey, any port in a storm, right?" The word "storm" kept reverberating in Ira's mind until he slipped into precious, painless sleep.

Chapter 17

After work Katalin showed up unexpectedly at Sarah's apartment. Although she was tired, there were only eight more days for her to spend with her closest friend and soul-mate. At the apartment she helped Sarah with the beginning phases of packing, starting with the china and then the silver service items. In between, she played a game of checkers with David-Jacob before he was put to bed, and also changed and fed Joshua-Caleb. Holding Sarah's tiny infant, Katalin still marvelled at God's miracle of recreating part of Himself.

After sealing the corrugated boxes, the two women relaxed on the sofa over coffee and angel cake. Sarah looked at her watch and realized that Ira was almost an hour late but she wasn't concerned. She was enjoying her talk with Katalin as they reflected on old times. If Ira wasn't home in another fifteen minutes she would call the store.

Immersed in their conversation, the past and present soon led to talk of their futures and the excitement of new beginnings. Certainly they would miss each other but at least for Katalin, her budding relationship with Paul would help ease the pain of Sarah's family moving to Arizona.

At odd moments there were brief pauses as each strained to tell the other of the void they were starting to feel inside. They knew they were going to miss each other terribly and the best thing they could do was not even discuss it. There would be plenty of time for tears when saying their good-byes a week from Saturday at Grand Central Station. Both putting on their best face, they continued to talk of what lay ahead and whenever the Reverend Paul Miller's name came up, Katalin was one big happy smile.

Sarah and Katalin had arrived at a point in their lives where they had both found contentment. Two orphaned teenagers — once desperate and alone, penniless and with little hope for the future — had defied the odds. Arriving at Ellis Island in 1939, able to speak little English, they parlayed their combined strengths, desires, ambitions and individual faiths into acquiring their part of the American dream.

Katalin was only slightly more altruistic in that she gave all credit to God for any of her achievements, willing therefore to give freely of herself. Sarah, on the other hand, allowed that God was a guiding force but maintained that He hadn't made life all that easy. She merely gave of herself out of a learned process.

When Sarah insisted that her own self-reliance and inner strength was the primary source of her present peace of mind, Katalin cautioned her. "Dear Sarah, be careful. For apart from total dependence on God we accomplish nothing except to become boastful and proud." As usual, their differing philosophy and faith remained the one sticking point in their long relationship. It was the one constant that was never resolved and too sensitive to be engaged by prolonged debate.

Only once before in their eleven years of knowing each other had they effectively crossed swords over their conflicting beliefs. It happened in France while still in their teens. Katalin had boldly confronted Sarah over the issue of eternal salvation through Jesus Christ.

After a period of time, Sarah railed at Katalin, "Miss Zichy! to deny my Jewish heritage, to offend the memory of my dead parents and the God they believed in, is so reprehensible to me in both thought and action, that should you persist in this manner of trying to convert me, I shall no longer remain friends with you!"

Although Katalin enjoyed witnessing to others, she never again broached the subject of salvation with Sarah. She knew that her most effective witness to her was to remain transparent in her own life, to love Sarah because she was Sarah and not worry about taking scalps. Henceforth, she only talked of her beliefs when Sarah inquired, or when she felt it necessary to defend her own faith. Yet hardly a night went by when Katalin didn't silently cry out to God to make Sarah a daughter of the Right Hand.

A side effect of Sarah's core belief was her assurance that she had already withstood and survived the worst that life could dish out. Accordingly, she grew confident that she could adequately deal with any future crisis that might come her way. Her thinking partially stemmed from having lived in America now for almost a decade. Her adopted homeland was born out of opposition to religious and political tyranny. She wasn't so naive to think there wasn't prejudice in America but the example of Germany had for most people left a sour taste and a growing antipathy towards intolerance. Accordingly, one third of the world's estimated, and still remaining fifteen million Jews, now lived in America.

Katalin thought along the same lines as Sarah, except to be more guarded. To her, there was cause to rejoice for what God had done in their lives but it was still a sin-sick world and a world that offered no guarantees. Life remained a series of peaks and valleys. To run and finish the race, as the Apostle Paul described, it was always necessary to stay focused on God. One's strengths and abilities were part of God's largesse and only meant to be temporal. Living on the mountaintop was great but it also clouded one's view of reality. A fall from the mountaintop to the chasm below was often inevitable and could be devastating, especially without God as a safety net.

A sudden knock on Sarah's door caused her to raise her eyebrows. Had Ira lost his keys? Who else would be knocking on her door so late? Katalin remained on the sofa while Sarah got up to open the door. She found two policemen standing in the hallway.

Sarah was startled. "Yes officers, is there something wrong?"

The two officers glanced at each other and one finally spoke. "I'm afraid there is, ma'am. You are Mrs. Katz, correct?"

"Yes, what is it?"

"Mrs. Katz, we just took a call over the police radio. . ."

"A call? What are you talking about?"

"There's been an attempted holdup at your husband's store. Your husband's been shot and rushed by ambulance to the hospital."

"Oh no!" Sarah gasped. "No, not Ira! Please, not my Ira!" Her body began quivering as she broke into loud intermittent sobs and wails.

Hearing the commotion, Katalin immediately rushed out. "Ira's been shot!" Sarah buried her head on Katalin's shoulder.

"Is he okay?" Katalin questioned in a broken voice.

The policeman explained again of the attempted robbery but said that they weren't sure of Ira's condition, only that the apparent perpetrator was killed in the exchange of gunfire.

Several residents of the apartment building had started spilling into the hallway, curious as to the commotion. Sarah, her face flushed with tears, began mumbling, "It's happening all over again! It's happening again!"

Among those who had gathered in the hall were Sam and Elsa Rosen, both realizing immediately that something had happened to Ira. Elsa edged closer and Katalin told her the awful news. Elsa shivered and, in turn, told Sam and the other neighbors in the hall. An almost simultaneous gasp went up and some closed their eyes and looked heavenward.

Elsa walked back to Sarah, her own heart heavy with grief for her young friend. With gentle strokes she brushed away the tears from Sarah's face. In a soothing voice, she comforted Sarah as a mother would a small child.

"This isn't supposed to happen here!" Sarah cried out. "This is America! Maybe in Germany but not in America!"

The two policemen were anxious. "Mrs. Katz, we're prepared to take you to the hospital."

While choking back her tears and breathing hard, Sarah nodded. "Yes, would you please! And can we hurry!?"

Elsa urged Katalin to go with Sarah. She and the other neighbors would take turns watching the children as long as was necessary. Katalin rushed back into the apartment to retrieve her and Sarah's purse. She then quickly followed down the flight of stairs behind Sarah and the police.

Once in the squad car, the sirens and lights were turned on and they peeled away from the curb. Other than the sound of the siren and the scratchy voices coming in over the police radio, there was stunned silence. Nobody said a word. Nobody knew what to say.

If ever time stood still, it was every painstaking minute that Sarah and the others sat anxiously waiting, praying, fearing, hoping, dreading—all trying to keep each other's spirits up while themselves anguishing. Their being in the lobby waiting area at Bushwick, when only hours before they were going on happily about their lives, only added to the surreal atmosphere. Now, three and a half hours later, at 1:30 in the morning, every stress-filled, hand-wringing moment was spent anxiously anticipating the precise instant when one of the surgeons would step into the waiting room.

It was almost too much for Sarah to bear. After two hours of emptying herself of tears, she sat numbed and motionless, staring into a void. Her last comment to Katalin, sitting next to her and clasping her hand, was, "It's like waiting for a pronouncement from God."

That was almost an hour ago. Katalin meanwhile continued to try and bolster her friend's spirits. Katalin repeated to Sarah several times that Ira was in the hands of other very skilled doctors. She wanted desperately to tell her of God's overwhelming concern but was worried about Sarah's present concept of God. Katalin chose discretion instead.

Sitting on the other side of Sarah were Marvin and Ruth. As the owner of the store, Marvin had been called immediately, once the police came on the scene. Stunned and distraught, he refused to meet the detectives at the store, offering instead to meet them at the hospital where he spent an hour and a half talking to them. He said he would go back to the store with them once he found out how his brother was. He was now having misgivings about not listening to his brother the several times Ira suggested relocating the store.

Ruth was holding up only slightly better than Sarah, but was still a nervous wreck. She wept not only for Ira, but her heart literally ached for Sarah and the children. She couldn't understand why God would put Sarah through something so tragic a second time.

For a short time, Ruth herself became a source of concern. At about 11:30 p.m., she mysteriously disappeared. Forty-five minutes later she returned, saying she just needed to be alone to pray.

Marvin questioned her, "So we're not worried enough? You go off alone in the middle of the night to God knows where to pray?"

Her own emotions strained, Ruth just told Marvin to "drop it." Marvin then watched his wife take an envelope out of her coat pocket and stick it in her purse. He was curious what was in the envelope but decided to leave well enough alone. The rest of the waiting time Ruth seemed more relaxed and at peace.

Katalin had called Paul soon after reaching the hospital and he rushed down immediately. Not wanting to be an intrusion, he chose to sit a short distance away, praying alone. Earlier, he had spoken a general prayer with the family. He also made himself available for food runs and other errands and whatever support he could offer.

Soon after praying with the family, he asked Katalin to take a quick walk around the hospital grounds outside. Halfway through their walk, Katalin broke down in a torrent of tears. Paul held her close for the first time. Minutes later they passed an old sycamore tree where they both felt compelled to kneel and pray together, their hands clasped.

Walking back to the lobby, Paul surprised Katalin with a bold statement. "Katalin, I'm absolutely convinced in my spirit that Ira's going to pull through this. At lunch the other day, when you and Sarah were away from the table, the two of us had quite a discussion about God. I can't tell you the text of what we talked about, except to say that I feel God is very much at work in Ira's life. When I just prayed with you, I again felt God's presence in a powerful way." Though still concerned, Paul's words of hope buoyed Katalin's spirits.

Chapter 18

Almost four hours after Ira was rushed to surgery, the moment finally arrived when—at least for Sarah—the world stopped on its axis.

"Which of you is Mrs. Katz?" The surgeon's voice jolted Sarah as the reality of the moment set in. Katalin, Marvin and Ruth rose to their feet to face the doctor with her. Paul also got up from his chair and stood within earshot. Sarah's lone thought was *Just be alive, Ira! Just be alive!*

The surgeon looked somber and bleary-eyed as he asked them to follow him into a more secluded area of the lobby. He then turned and faced a trembling Sarah with Katalin gripping her upper arm for support. Ruth was near tears and held tightly to Marvin.

"Mrs. Katz?"

"Y . . . yes? . . . how . . . how is he!? Is he . . ." Choked with emotion, Sarah covered her mouth, feeling as if her insides were tied in knots. She wanted to scream from the sheer torture of not knowing.

"I'm Dr. Merodious, the trauma surgeon. At this point, Mrs. Katz, I can tell you that your husband made it through the operation and is in recovery." Tears of relief ran down their faces, even Marvin's and Paul's as they continued to listen. "...but he's still in critical condition. The next twenty-four hours will likely determine if he pulls through or not. I hate to sound so ominous, but I won't lie to you. It's a miracle he's made it this far. His excellent physical condition as well as an apparent tremendous will to live are probably the two main reasons he is still alive."

Marvin was trying to read between the lines. "So what are you saying?"

"I'm just saying that there's reason for hope. That's all I'm saying."

"Well, hope isn't good enough, doctor!" Marvin interrupted loudly. "That's my brother you're talking about!"

Upset at her husband, Ruth quickly intervened. "Marvin, settle down! If it weren't for the doctor, Ira might not even be alive!"

Marvin took a deep breath and nodded. "You're right, I'm . . . I'm sorry. What are his odds?"

"I'm not in the odds business. As I said before, there's reason for hope. It's no longer in our hands. Can we all sit down a minute." The doctor pointed towards a cushioned bench. Katalin reached in back of her and Paul took her hand.

Once everyone was seated, Dr. Merodious elaborated. "Let me tell you what we're dealing with, what we've done, and what we as doctors can and can't do. You see, the human body is the most remarkable invention in the world. The only problem is, man didn't invent it. In the process of discovery, we find ways of keeping the body running. It's just like a car. The manufacturer is always going to know more about it than even the best mechanic."

Katalin's face lit up. Paul was right! The doctor's humility and oblique reference to the majesty of God was more than she could have hoped for. *Could it be that God had picked this particular surgeon to save Ira's life!?* If so, there was no way now that God was going to let him slip into eternity. She suddenly became convinced of what Paul instinctively knew. Somehow, God was going to use what appeared to be a senseless tragedy to bring glory to Him!

Paul was seated next to Katalin, still gripping her hand. Neither of them looked at each other but were listening intently as Dr. Merodious continued. ". . . anyway, let me explain to all of you what's going on. Your husband, Mrs. Katz, suffered two bullet wounds in the abdominal area, in the right upper quadrant. When we first opened him up, he had severe bleeding from the liver. That's where one of the bullets penetrated. Fortunately, after we removed the bullet and repaired that area, the bleeding stopped. However, the second bullet we removed had put a hole in the colon. It did a lot more damage and we had to do what is called a diverting colostomy. There was also large spillage during surgery which required ten units of blood. Although we've packed the skin, we left the wounds open in case we have to go back in unexpectedly.

"Now here's what makes his condition so critical," the doctor continued. "We had to put in a tube on the right chest to evacuate the blood and air from the right thorax. In order for your husband to breathe, Mrs. Katz, the lung needs to expand. An over accumulation of blood or air can compress the lung to the point where it can prevent him from breathing. Too much air we call a pneumo-thorax. Too much blood accumulation is called a hemo-thorax. If, somehow, the chest tube is not able to draw out all the excess bleeding or excess air, then we have a major problem. In blunt terms, if that happens—and in his present condition—we could lose him. We've also given him massive doses of antibiotics to prevent infection."

Although greatly relieved, Sarah was hedging on being too optimistic. Looking at the doctor with swollen eyes, she asked, "When can we see him?"

"Once he's put in intensive care, perhaps in the next hour or so. I would recommend that only you see him, Mrs. Katz, and only for a minute or two. If he gets excited and exerts too much energy trying to talk too soon, it might weaken him and worsen his situation. He'll also be heavily sedated. To put you somewhat at ease, I've ordered around-the-clock nursing care for the next twenty-four hours.

"I know this has been a terrible blow to all of you, as well as your friends," he added. "The best thing you can all do for Mr. Katz now is to take care of yourselves. Get some sleep . . . and if you're people that pray, praying wouldn't hurt."

After shaking the doctor's hand and thanking him, the family and Paul headed outside for some fresh air. Katalin had only taken a few steps when she turned around and paced quickly to catch up with the doctor. "Dr. Merodious! Could you wait a second!"

The doctor turned. "Yes?"

"Doctor, I'm Katalin Zichy. Mrs. Katz and I are close friends. I . . . . I just wanted to thank you for . . . well, for including God in what you do."

"I wouldn't do an operation without Him. Do you mind if I ask you something?"

"Sure."

"The family is Jewish, right?"

"Very Jewish. However, I'm a Christian."

"Well then, I can ask you without worrying about offending anyone."

"Ask me what?"

"Apparently when they wheeled Mr. Katz in on the gurney, I was told they practically needed a crowbar to take an object from his hand."

"What kind of object?"

"A gold cross and chain."

Katalin's mouth fell open. "You've got to be kidding! Maybe one of the people wheeling him in, a nurse or somebody, put it there."

"No, I asked. It's no big deal. I was just curious is all. Anyway, we gave it to the hospital chaplain to hold. We suspected the family might be Jewish and thought it best that the chaplain handle the matter, giving the item back to the patient when he recovers. I was concerned it might cause problems within the family. I don't know, it seemed unusual for someone Jewish to be clutching on to a cross."

Katalin didn't hesitate. "Jesus did!"

The doctor smiled at Katalin's sharp retort.

"At the same time, Doctor, what you've told me takes my breath away."

"Well then, all the more reason to get some sleep. I know that's what I'm going to do. Good-night, Miss Zichy."

Katalin walked away scratching her head and talking to herself. *Lord, you do indeed work in mysterious ways, but none more mysterious than now. What is going on?*

The next two days were nerve wracking for all concerned. When Sarah entered Ira's room the first time and saw him hooked up to the chest tube, the IV, catheter and heart monitor, she had to fight away the tears. She couldn't bring herself to leave.

Finally, after ten minutes of holding her sleeping husband's hand, the nurse on duty put her arms around Sarah's shoulder, urging her to leave. She assured a disconsolate Sarah that she could return as soon as Ira awoke. That didn't happen until hours later, at daybreak, when he awoke moaning in severe pain. He was immediately given more morphine after which Sarah was called back in.

While in the room the second time, Sarah struggled but stayed strong and didn't cry. Ira appeared to her to be in a fog as he anxiously surveyed the room, attempting to take everything in. His eyes seemed to float inside their sockets, the way a baby's eyes sometimes did when awakening. Sarah drew a heavy lounge chair next to the side of the bed, leaned over and whispered gently into Ira's ear how much she loved him and that everything was going to be fine. She cautioned him to save his strength and not try to speak.

Sarah wasn't sure how much Ira understood, yet she was encouraged when he turned his head and smiled at her. Her heart then melted as Ira slowly slid his hand towards the edge of the bed. She took his hand in hers and raised it to her lips and kissed it, then rubbed his hand against her tear-stained cheeks.

When Marvin returned to the floor covering store to meet with one of the detectives, it was still dark outside. Entering the blood-splashed office where the gun battle took place, his mouth dropped open in astonishment. It was enough to see the shattered glass and spilled blood where the gunman was shot, but peering behind the desk and seeing for the first time the amount of blood that had poured from his brother's wounds horrified him. He shook his head in disbelief wondering how in the world Ira ever survived. There wasn't a bare spot on the tiled floor that wasn't soaked in blood.

At first sickened, Marvin then became angry and pounded the side of the wall with his fist. When he was initially informed at the hospital that the gunman had been killed in the shoot-out, Marvin had expressed regret that a life was lost. Seeing now how his brother must have suffered, his feelings changed dramatically. Muttering under his breath loud enough for the detective with him to hear, ". . . the stinkin' bum got what he deserved!" Marvin decided to shut the store down for at least a week. He would only complete the jobs already scheduled. His thoughts now centered totally on Ira and the family.

Katalin and Ruth were constantly at Sarah's side. When one or the other of them needed a ride home to shower, change clothes or check on the children, Marvin provided transportation. Paul showed up in the evenings and late each night drove Katalin back to her apartment. She returned by bus in the mornings.

Katalin had notified her instructors at Brooklyn College that she would be absent during the week, advising them of the situation. Like everyone else she talked to, they sent along their heartfelt prayers. Neil, at the *Daily Eagle*, was also more than gracious to her and told her to take as much time off as she felt necessary.

Twelve hours after Ira's surgery, Sarah had gone home briefly to check on Joshua-Caleb and to talk to David-Jacob. As expected, he was very upset but managed to hold back his tears. He wanted desperately to see his father and Sarah had to explain to him, "Daddy will be able to see you real soon. He loves you very, very much. But right now, DeeJay, he needs a lot of sleep so he can get better. Later in the week you can go see him."

David-Jacob became tense and angry, shouting, "I'm glad the bad man is dead!" Sarah was disturbed over his remark but understood it enough not to reprimand him.

Friends and neighbors constantly called the hospital and sent cards and flowers. The many floral arrangements filled the room to overflowing. Sarah had to finally ask one of the nurses to distribute some to patients in other rooms.

Ira's condition steadily improved with only one minor setback. Late Saturday night, the first full night after surgery, a fever set in, causing his temperature to rise to 103 degrees. For three hours the nurses continually applied cold compresses. Despite the antibiotics, there was fear that Ira had an infection. Sarah became concerned enough that she asked Katalin and Paul to pray for him again. In her consternation, she would even accept help from their Christian God. The fever broke.

Ira drifted in and out of sleep. When he did speak, his sentences were often fragmented and slurred, a result of the heavy medication. As the hours passed, the pain decreased enough to allow the nurses to cut back on his dosage of morphine. Slowly, he became more aware of his surroundings.

From what Sarah observed, Ira understood *what* happened but had difficulty believing that it *did* happen. For Ira, everything was a haze, and certain details about why he was in the hospital still escaped him. However, as his mind became clearer, he started to remember the intense fear and dread of three days earlier when forced at gunpoint to open the store safe. He couldn't recall the actual shots but remembered writhing on the floor in agony with his guts spilling out, and remembered pointing a gun at a blurred vision of someone he once knew, then firing several rounds in his direction.

Ira also recollected seeing the perfect symmetrical shape of a cross, depicted in his own blood on the floor, and the shining gold cross suspended in mid-air radiating brightly from above and in back of his head. *How could it be that he saw these things so recently after his pleading to an invisible God? And if he really did see these things and wasn't imagining them, what kind of God even took the time to respond? And why, not once, but twice, did this unknown God respond in the way of a Cross?*

Though weak and bewildered, his life still hanging in the balance, Ira felt the overwhelming presence of something supernatural, a warm inner glow, a stirring in his spirit that screamed to tell the world that God was not a figment of people's imagination, that He *literally* existed.

Ira wanted to talk to Sarah alone and without the nurse in the room. He had to tell her, regardless of her reaction. He knew he had had a profound religious experience, only he wasn't sure how to deal with it. Previously, his plaintive cry to God was the same to him as wishing upon a star. Yet, in his moment of greatest desperation, God came through. What was most troubling was that it wasn't the God he expected? He still couldn't think clearly. His mind was one big question mark--*What now?*

Peering beyond the foot of his bed, Ira observed the room nurse seated against the wall reading a magazine. He had kept her pretty busy, both with his fever and her constantly having to change his dressings, empty his catheter, draw blood and administering morphine. While in elementary school, one of Ira's heroines was the young nurse of the

Civil War, Clara Barton. Since that time, he regarded nurses as angels of mercy and the nursing profession as one that ennobled women.

Turning his head, however, he saw the woman he adored-- equally for her courage, gentleness and sensitivity as well as for her sustaining and suffering love. Sarah was seated next to the bed, busily engaged in working the *New York Times* Sunday crossword puzzle. Sensing her husband staring at her, she laid her pencil aside and smiled at Ira over the top of the folded newspaper. He whispered her closer to the bed.

Sarah scooted her chair, leaned over and squeezed Ira's hand. His voice was barely audible but more distinct than before. "Sarah . . ."

"Yes, Ira?"

"I thought I was going to die, Sarah, I really did. I can't remember ever being so scared, even during the war. I kept thinking, 'I'm not going to see my wife or kids ever again.'"

Ira's eyes were watery as he continued speaking. "I tried to stop him, Sarah, I did. I yelled at him...and he just aimed his gun at me. He wanted to kill me. I had to shoot! I had to! He's dead, isn't he, Sarah? The man I shot...he's dead?" Ira's voice cracked with emotion.

Sarah wished, even by osmosis, she could take away some of her husband's anguish, but knew she couldn't. She swallowed hard and nodded yes, then tried to assuage his feelings of guilt. "Nobody blames you, Ira, not even the police. They said he already had a long arrest record. If you hadn't stopped him, he would have gone on robbing and hurting people. Ira, you didn't have any choice. It just happened. I'm just so glad you're alive. I need you, Ira. The children need you!"

Sarah allowed herself to cry as she cautiously embraced him, pressing the side of her face against his. Her solace became a comfort to him while he stared blankly at the ceiling. He had killed people in war but this was the first time that killing had a face.

After their brief exchange, he grew tired and closed his eyes. Sarah sat staring at him for several minutes, gently stroking his face. He looked so different without his glasses, which the police found smashed. Her heart heavy and burdened for her now sleeping husband, Sarah whispered gently into his ear. "On the outside, you're one tough cookie, Ira. But inside . . . inside beats the heart of a lamb."

Chapter 19

The good news came on Wednesday afternoon. The bucket beside Ira's bed measuring the outflow of blood now registered 50 cc's, down from the original 1500 cc's. The bleeding had virtually stopped and the chest tube was removed. Dr. Merodious gave Sarah a thumbs-up. Her husband was out of danger and well on his way to recovery. Sarah's voice caught in her throat but her lips were saying, "Thank you." Before leaving, the doctor indicated he wanted Ira out of bed to begin walking again. He warned her it would be a slow, painful process at first and Ira would need a lot of assistance.

When Marvin, Ruth and Katalin returned from the lunch room, they discovered that Ira had been moved from intensive care into a private room. They were as elated as Sarah to hear the doctor's report, and the women shared hugs and tears. Although excited himself, Marvin pretended to be blasé. "Eh! I knew he'd be fine. He's a Katz. Another week, Sarah, he'll be chasing you around the apartment."

"Well, Marvin, I can promise you one thing, he won't have any trouble catching me!"

Marvin then heeded his sister-in-law's request to go back to the apartment and bring back the children and the Rosens. An anxious David-Jacob, already knowing his father's room number, jumped from the car before it came to a complete stop. He made a beeline into the hospital, down the corridor, up the one flight of stairs, into the room and carefully into his father's arms. There until nightfall the room would remain happily crowded and would also smell of baby powder and diapers.

Marvin's daughter Rachel was being watched by next door neighbors while he and Ruth were at the hospital. The eight year old girl had made a tremendous sacrifice. She had her parents deliver to her Uncle Ira the favorite of her collection of five teddy bears. In gratitude and to lighten things up, Ira placed the teddy bear next to his bed, propped up on a pillow.

Paul had been amusing everyone with humorous anecdotes and stories about his being a pastor when everyone realized that Ira needed more rest. Previously, Sarah had stayed overnight by Ira, on a cot. Tonight would be her first night home in five days.

Before everyone left en masse, Paul insisted on telling one more amusing story. Marvin raised his arms in the air. "All of a sudden we have a gentile Jack Benny."

Paul scratched his head. "Well, you're all such a terrific audience and I've got to practice ways of keeping my congregation awake. He grinned and began:

"This is a true story told to us by one of our professors in seminary. It seems there was this pastor, years back, who kept getting angry letters from one of his parishioners. He'd been a pastor for some twenty years at this church, and knowing his sermons weren't always going to please everybody, these letters eventually became no more to him than water off a duck's back.

"But then he gets the strangest letter of them all. The only thing it has written on it is the word "FOOL", followed by several exclamation marks. This time the pastor decides to share the contents of the letter with his congregation, so Sunday morning comes and he steps to the pulpit and says, 'I've received several letters in the past from a certain person, always going into detail how he or she doesn't like me or my preaching. Never has this person been willing to sign their name. However, this letter is most remarkable. This time the letter writer signed their name but forgot to write anything.'"

Most of the room was laughing, then noticed Ira with his eyes half closed.

Ira admitted to being tired and in a broken voice, thanked everyone for being there and how everyone there meant so very much to him. Each person walked to his bedside and lightly embraced or hugged him. Marvin affirmed that he needed to spend some time at the store doing bookwork and fixing the office. Katalin felt the burden of missing work at the *Daily Eagle*. She didn't want to take advantage of Neil's good graces. Sarah and Ruth were concerned about the older children, especially, and how they were handling everything emotionally. Now that Ira appeared to be out of danger, perhaps they should be spending more time with Rachel and David-Jacob.

With the exception of Sarah, they all agreed not to visit again until the weekend. Sarah could stay in touch with them by phone. The nurses' station would be instructed to refuse any more visitors.

Knowing he would miss both family and friend, Ira still welcomed the prospect of spending the next two days alone with only Sarah at his bedside. Part of that desire was his wanting to discuss with her his confusing and possibly life-changing spiritual experience.

The next to last to leave, Katalin gave Ira a quick hug, then stood at the doorway waiting for Sarah. Everyone else waited in the hallway as Katalin watched Sarah lean over the bed and tenderly kiss her husband.

Once Sarah turned to walk out, Katalin observed Ira looking past his wife and directly at her. Something about his countenance puzzled her. He looked different. It wasn't just his missing glasses or that he'd suffered tremendous trauma from being shot. There was an aura about him, a transcendent look of peace and contentment. Before walking out of the room with Sarah, she noticed Ira nodding at her, a strange smile creasing his lips. It was as if he was trying to impart something to her, but . . . what?

This was a different Ira than she had known for almost seven years—the one with the nervous energy, seldom able to relax, stubborn, often temperamental and detached, especially the last four years. Perhaps, she thought, it was the effect of the morphine that caused the seeming change in his personality. Then she dismissed even that.

Once outside the room, Katalin trailed the others as they headed down the corridor. Lost in thought, she still pondered the obvious change in Ira. She remembered five nights ago talking to Dr. Merodious immediately after Ira's surgery and his telling her of the unusual gold cross Ira held tightly in his hand when being wheeled in. She also remembered walking the grounds of the hospital with Paul and praying with him by the large sycamore tree and Paul stating afterwards, "I think God is very much at work in Ira's life."

Katalin suddenly felt something like an electric charge. Her arms swarmed with goosebumps. She now suspected what it all meant! All these years she hoped and prayed it would happen to Sarah. Instead, to her shock and amazement, it may have happened to the most unlikely of souls! Though it was beyond her comprehension, she knew it wasn't beyond God's power. Improbable as it was, Ira may have had an encounter with the Lord!

Chapter 20

Snowflakes penetrated the night sky like a cloudburst of confetti, tossed and swirled about, then fell soft as pillow feathers, spreading a white blanket across the entire city. Outside Brooklyn's Bushwick Hospital the wet and cold powdery residue formed into miniature mountain peaks on the hoods and tops of cars. The barren and leafless trees surrounding the area resembled an army of cotton-cloaked sentries. While walking to their cars, everyone pulled their coats up over their ears to protect themselves from the biting cold. Paul joked that they all looked like a herd of turtles retreating into their shells.

With hurriedly said good-byes, they quickly ducked into their cars. Paul drove Katalin while Sarah was leaving with Marvin and Ruth. Marvin had turned on the ignition to his Chrysler when Ruth suddenly shrieked, "Omigosh! I left my purse in Ira's room! How could I be so forgetful?"

Marvin immediately threw his hands in the air pleading for the heavens to spare him any more absent-minded females in his life. He then drove to the front entrance where Ruth quickly jumped out, promising to return in 15 minutes after he and Sarah ducked into a nearby café for a quick cup of coffee.

When Ruth reached Ira's private room, it was dark inside except for the light streaming in from the hallway. On one side of Ira's bed, the stillness of the night was interrupted by the heart monitor beeping away with its shrill, high-pitched birdlike chirping sound. On the other side of the bed was the bag of intravenous fluid hanging loosely from a tubular silver pole, slowly seeping into Ira's veins while he slept.

Ruth's hands were shaking. She hadn't anticipated feeling so nervous. Walking toward the corner, she reached behind the wastebasket where she had carefully and purposely placed her purse. Opening it, she took out an envelope and from it removed a large gold cross and chain. Careful not to wake Ira, she gently placed the sacred object on his pillow, between his head and her daughter's teddy bear.

Something suddenly grabbed at her wrist! A cold chill rushed through her veins! Gasping out loud, she jerked her arm backwards but couldn't escape the clutches of someone's hand! Her heart racing, she looked down to see Ira wide awake and staring at her. "Ira! Let me go! I didn't mean to wake you."

Ira loosened his grip on her wrist. "You scared me, creeping up like that. What are you doing here, Ruth?" Before she could answer, he spotted the cross on the pillow. Picking it up and fingering it, his face registered disbelief. "How in the world did this get here?"

Standing by the side of the bed, Ruth closed her eyes and swallowed hard, then took a deep breath trying to regain her composure. Embarrassed, she hurriedly concocted a lame excuse and half-truth. "Ira, I've got to go. Marvin and Ruth are waiting outside in the car in the freezing cold."

Holding the chain between his thumb and index finger, Ira swung the chain back and forth like a pendulum, then looked up suspiciously at Ruth. "Ruth, did you put this here?"

"You don't recognize it?"

"Recognize it?" Ira was incredulous. "Why should I recognize it?"

"Because it belongs to you—at least that's what I was told."

"By who?"

"The hospital chaplain."

"When was this?"

"When you were in surgery. Downstairs, down the corridor from the lobby, is a small chapel. I went there to be alone, to pray for you. I couldn't imagine our losing you, Ira, thinking what it would do to the family. Precious Sarah, all the loss she suffered already...and your dear children. I don't know how any of us would have coped."

Ira gulped hard. Ruth went on. "While I was in the chapel, crying and praying, this chaplain walked in. He was there late because another family in the hospital had just lost an infant and he was attempting to comfort them. My meeting him was mere coincidence. We briefly talked. I told him who I was and why I was there.

"Well, as they say, God works in mysterious ways. Our meeting each other turned out to be even more of a coincidence. Only an hour earlier a male hospital attendant who had helped wheel your gurney into surgery had given him the cross you're now holding in your hand. The attendant gave your name to the chaplain, saying they practically needed pliers to pry the cross from your hand. He said you had lost so much blood they weren't sure you were going to survive, and the chaplain was in the process of preparing himself, if necessary, to meet with our family, also to return the cross to whomever, seeing as how it must have meant so much to you.

"So, there I was, talking with him in the chapel. I told him that we were Jewish and asked if I couldn't return the cross instead. Naturally I was worried about Marvin or Sarah's reaction."

Ira was moved by Ruth's prayerful concern for him but was suspicious of her explanation. He sensed she wasn't telling him everything. "How about your reaction, Ruth?"

"Reaction to what?"

"To why I would have a Christian cross instead of, let's say, a Jewish *mezuzah.*"

"Well, of course I was curious. I still am."

"It doesn't upset you?"

"Should it?

"It would most Jewish people. Most Jews are offended by anything relating to the crucifixion."

"I'm aware of what the cross represents, Ira...but that's between you and God. In truth, it's none of my business."

"But by returning it you've made it your business!"

"I'm sorry, maybe I shouldn't have. I just didn't want the chaplain to make a public display of it. Have you spoken of it to Sarah?"

Ira took a deep breath. Placing the cross on the pillow, he drew his hand down over his face. "Is all this really happening, Ruth?"

"Yes, Ira. You were shot. You almost died and now you're in the hospital—by the grace of God, miraculously recovering."

"That's what I keep thinking about, Ruth. The grace of God. Only problem is, what God? And no, I haven't talked with Sarah yet. I haven't had that much time to think things through or be alone with her. I also wanted to be sure I wasn't losing my mind."

"What do you mean?"

"Just feelings that I'm trying to sort out. It all happened so fast. One minute I'm at the store doing inventory, the next thing I know I'm staring at a gun pointed at my head. I remember in my mind crying out to God to somehow spare my life. Thirty-two years old and everything I ever wanted, cared for or believed in was suddenly hanging in the balance.

"What's so strange is that a week earlier, after I met Paul for the first time and Sarah and Katalin were momentarily away from the table, Paul and I got into a private discussion about God—who God is, or even if He is and now this.

"You think getting shot was God's response?"

"I think your showing up with a cross, telling me I had it in my hand when being wheeled into surgery might be?. Ruth, I don't know where the cross came from. I wasn't even aware of its existence before you came into the room. Yet after being shot, I distinctly remember lying on the floor, in the worst pain imaginable and I can usually tolerate pain real well, looking up and seeing a cross. It has to be the same one, only at the time it appeared to me to be a thousand times larger. It encompassed my entire view. Ruth, maybe the cross by itself wasn't a sign, or answer from God, but it wasn't the only thing I saw."

"What do you mean?"

"I saw another cross...and it looked to be of my own blood."

Ruth's expression bore her surprise as she seated herself in the chair next to the bed. "Ira, what are you talking about?"

"I know you're not going to believe this, but your bringing this one cross to me convinces me that the second cross may have been real and not just my imagination. When I was lying on the floor, bleeding, I looked to the side and on the floor stained in my own blood was the perfect image of another cross."

"Ira, when Marvin scrubbed the floor of the office where you were shot, it was saturated with blood. Every section of tile and every grout line. In fact, the floor was so covered with your blood he finally decided to rip it all out. Realizing the full impact of what happened to you both sickened and angered him. However, he never mentioned visualizing anything unusual. Had he, I'm sure he would have told me."

"I didn't think you would believe me. I can only imagine what Sarah will think. One thing I'm sure of though, Ruth. I'm more sure now than at any time in my life that God really does exist and He's the only reason I'm still alive."

"Ira, I didn't say I didn't believe you."

"Sure you did."

"Well, I didn't mean to imply that you were hallucinating. What I meant was that maybe what you saw was real to you only."

"How can that be?"

"Sometimes Ira, God reveals something to someone supernaturally. The prophet Daniel received visions of the future. Then there's the story of Jacob's ladder. In the New Testament many people had visions. I've heard Christians talk about Stephen who, when being stoned to death, saw the heavens opened. The Apostle Peter saw this sheet...and John . . . and Saul of Tarsus on the Road to Damascus . . . and . . ."

"Ruth! I'm Ira Katz, remember! What's all this vision stuff?"

"Maybe the cross you saw on the floor . . . well, maybe it was really real! And it was God doing it...and maybe it wasn't *your* blood you saw... but the blood of someone else who lived almost 2,000 years ago."

Ruth swallowed hard, nervously anticipating Ira's response to her unusual speculations, especially her inadvertent concluding remark.

Ira stared back at her, startled and speechless. "I can't believe I'm hearing you talk like this, Ruth. If I wasn't hearing it with my own ears and looking straight at you, I'd swear it was Katalin talking to me. Do I need to remind you, Ruth . . . you're Jewish."

"So are you. Yet you're the one who admitted, when being robbed, to ask God to make Himself real. You're the one who was desperately holding onto a cross when they brought you in. You're the one telling me you saw something that probably didn't exist to the normal person, what I'm almost certain was a vision."

"Right! but you're supposed to tell me I'm mixed up and confused."

"That's just it Ira. I don't think you are!. I think what you saw was very important and very real."

"Jesus is not for the Jews, Ruth! Any rabbi will tell you that!"

"Then why are you so troubled? Why not just dismiss what happened to you as a delusion?"

"Because . . ."

"Because? That's the type of answer I would expect out of our children."

"Because . . . I don't know. What if Jesus was, or is, who He claimed to be. What if all these thousands of years we've been wrong? But then how can He be who He claimed? What kind of Jewish messiah would allow His own people to suffer through inquisitions and genocides and every type of persecution. It doesn't make any sense."

"Ira, I really have to go before Marvin comes charging up here like a mad bull. But in answer to your question, all I can say is that anti-Semitism, hatred of the Jews, existed well before Jesus' time. So don't blame Him! In Egypt the Hebrews were slaves and Hebrew children were thrown into the Nile. The Amalekites were our enemy and so were the Philistines, the Canaanites and the Assyrians. Even Haman planned to destroy all the Jews of Persia."

"Ruth, why are you defending Christianity?"

Ruth had difficulty keeping her emotions in check and grew increasingly impassioned. Then in a torrent of emotion, "Doggone it, Ira! We started Christianity! Jesus was Jewish! He belongs to us!"

"What's gotten into you Ruth!?"

"Ira, it just makes me so angry. Initially the great controversy was whether we Jews should take Christianity to the Gentiles. Then Peter, a Jewish apostle, had a vision and was told to preach to the Gentiles. Now, 2,000 years later, if we Jews even mention or talk of Jesus in a positive manner we are ostracized or labeled as *meshumed* [traitor]. I don't dare discuss Jesus with Marvin or he flies into a rage."

"Because Jesus is an anathema to our people, Ruth."

"No, Ira, He's an enigma, not an anathema. And you just admitted He saved your life!"

Ira's eyes suddenly grew wide. "You know, it just came to me! You always liked quoting from the New Testament. I just figured it out! You're one of them aren't you!? Ruth, This amazes me! You're a Christian aren't you!? All these years I've known you and never really suspected..."

Tears began flowing from Ruth's eyes as she still strained to keep her emotions in check, speaking breathlessly. "For seven years I've wanted to tell someone! anyone! but I've been so afraid. Ira, have you ever loved someone so much you wanted to scream it out to the world? Have you ever learned something so profound it would dramatically change people's lives but circumstances didn't allow you to speak of it!

"Yes Ira, I'm a Christian and I'm proud of it! But if Marvin ever finds out, I fear I'll lose him . . . and probably all my friends as well. Ira, I beg of you! You mustn't tell anyone, not even Sarah, or it could somehow get back to Marvin."

"Ruth, what are you afraid of? Marvin would never leave you." Needing a brief respite and without asking, Ruth poured herself a glass of water from the pitcher near Ira's bedside. Then she responded.

"Ira, I know my husband. He'll tolerate gentile Christians but he has nothing but contempt for those of the Jewish faith who turn to Christianity. You remember Joel Chernoff?"

"Of course. We played together as kids. Whatever happened to him?"

"He's living in California now, where Jews tend to be more liberal. He came back from the war a highly decorated soldier but he also came back a Believer and Max, his own father, refused to speak to him. In fact, Max, had a mock funeral for his son and said as far as he was concerned, his son died in the war. It is so tragic and so sad, and now Max is very sick and he insists no one is to tell his son or even speak his son's name around him."

"I can't believe that Ruth?"

"But it is true Ira. Max was born and lived in Russia and saw awful things happen to his parents and cannot bring himself to reconcile his tortured memories with a son he thinks has betrayed his parents name.

Don't you see, it's the fear of most Jews. Somehow, should the Christians be right, then the Jews deserve to be the world's whipping boy. The world has so distorted the truth of what Jesus was all about. He was all about love and forgiveness. How Marvin would react should he discover I also am a Believer, I'm not sure. But I have no desire to find out."

Ira was listening to every word while propped up on his pillow and looking down at his feet. When Ruth was finished, he shook his head in disbelief. "The longer I live, Ruth, the more I realize how little I know of people, or even myself for that matter. Right now, if you dropped a ton of bricks on my head, I couldn't be more shocked."

Ruth felt a sense of relief and a cleansing of soul for finally having the courage to speak of her faith. Alongside those feelings was some trepidation. "Promise me, Ira . . . promise me you won't tell what I told you to anyone."

Ira turned his head towards his normally staid sister-in-law. He couldn't remember ever seeing Ruth so emotional. Her facial expression mirrored her concern over leaving herself so vulnerable.

Ira always liked Ruth but never felt any great empathy for her, thinking her too remote and self-sufficient. Now, in an effort to help him through his own crisis and confused state of mind, she had bravely poured out her soul to him, causing his perception of her to change dramatically.

Looking into her swollen eyes and noting her anxious appearance, he suddenly felt protective of her. Though not wishing to keep any more secrets from Sarah, circumstances dictated that he do just that. Extending his arm, Ira took Ruth's hand in his. "I won't tell anyone, Ruth. It will be hard not mentioning anything to Sarah, but I'll not say anything. I do feel you're over-exaggerating about Marvin though. He loves you a great deal. He wouldn't walk out on you, no matter what you believe."

"Thanks for saying that, Ira. I just don't want to take that chance. Perhaps if I had told him seven years ago, it would have shown more trust on my part and no longer an issue." Still choked with emotion, Ruth pulled her hand from Ira's grip and slowly rose from her chair. Once standing, she continued speaking. "As for telling Sarah that I'm a Christian, I can't ask you to keep it a secret forever. I wouldn't want that she should be angry with you. If you would only not tell her until your family moves to Arizona. That way there would be less chance of something being said or overheard accidentally."

"You think Sarah's some kind of blabbermouth?"

"Of course not! Sarah's one of the sweetest, most conscientious people I know. At the same time, if something did slip out that caused a rift in our marriage, knowing Sarah, she would never forgive herself. She would only blame herself. It's like asking her to carry yet another burden."

"What should I tell her about me and about the visions I had?"

"I can't answer that Ira! I wish I could. But if I'm an example of what not sharing your innermost feelings with your spouse will lead to, all this secrecy. I would think strongly about somehow telling her. Besides, she doesn't feel the same animosity towards things related to Christianity as Marvin does. Because of Katalin and of the German soldier who saved her life, she has a certain fondness for Christians. Your wife once told me that if she weren't Jewish she would definitely become a Christian. She even admitted to me once about harboring a curiosity about Jesus."

"Funny. She never told me that."

"Well, like me, she was probably afraid of how you would react."

"You mean my own wife was afraid of me?"

"It happens, Ira. You and Marvin are everything to us, though not perfect, mind you."

Ira smiled and Ruth reciprocated. "God bless you, Ira, and thanks for allowing me to share my feelings. All these years I've wanted to tell somebody of my faith in the hope they might come to know and believe as I do. Ira, the great Jewish writer, Sholem Asch?"

"Yes...what about Asch?"

"He once said, 'Every act and word of Jesus has value for all of us. Why shouldn't I, a Jew, be proud of it?' "There are other outstanding Jews who not only don't disparage of Jesus, but who wish to reclaim Him."

"Right now, Ruth, I think I'm somewhere in between."

"Go with your heart, Ira. I'll be praying for you."

When Ruth reached the doorway, Ira called out to her. "Ruth, you're much deeper than I thought you were."

Ruth turned and smiled. "I hope that's a compliment."

"I meant it as one."

After Ruth left the room Ira reached to the side of his pillow and picked up the cross. Carefully examining it, he stared up at the ceiling. "Okay God, what other surprises do you have in store for me?"

Chapter 21

Three things are necessary for the salvation of man: to know
what he ought to believe; to know what he ought to desire;
and to know what he ought to do.
— St. Thomas Aquinas (1273)

From being born, to lingering at the precipice of death, to now possibly
. . . rebirth. As the morning sun filtered through the venetian blinds
the sixth day after he almost perished, Ira sat up in bed. Tearfully, he
thanked his Maker for the gift of life.

"I don't know you, God, I really don't, but I know you know me.
Why you've allowed me to live, I don't know either. I apologize for my
rebellion and I'm sorry for all the problems I've caused people in my
life.

"I can handle the physical pain, Lord, but the pain inside, the
contention, the bitterness, the hurt, the emptiness . . . I just can't handle
anymore. And now I've even taken a life and, despite the circumstances,
I feel great remorse. I wish I could have talked to him and told him there
was another way. Why I'm alive and he isn't, I don't know. I don't know
anything anymore. I feel so helpless, so unsure what life is all about.

"One thing I do know is that I don't like what I've become. I love
being Jewish, Lord. I've always been proud to be one of the people of
The Book. Yet I'm left with questions that go unanswered, with dreams
and hopes that keep fading. Now I understand better the psalmist who
cried, 'My spirit groans.'

"I've heard Katalin speak so many times on how one ought to give
themselves to you. I struggle so to even say your name . . . and may the
rightful God forgive me if I'm wrong, but believing you, Jesus, to be that
rightful God, I'm asking you to take over my life. Help me to be a better
husband, a better father, and a better human being. I put my life and my
very soul into your hands."

Immediately after Ira's prayer, a nurse entered the room with a tray
of consommé soup, apple juice and strawberry JELL-O. It would be his

first attempt at a liquid diet. But it would be hours before Ira would re-awake from the most peaceful sleep he ever entered.

Sarah opened the door to her apartment and for the second straight day, the postman handed her bundles of mail, numerous letters and telegrams—mostly from anonymous well-wishers who had read of the shooting incident in the newspapers. Almost to a person, the missives contained expressions of sympathy and admiration.

Despite the sudden and favorable notoriety, Sarah was filled with mixed emotions. There was the inevitable comparison of how someone Jewish was regarded in American society to that of the Jew in Germany. To her thinking, it didn't make any sense. In addition, Ira's hero status— suddenly becoming a John Wayne-type figure as a result of being forced to take a life—was unsettling. Sarah was brought up to believe that every life had purpose and value. Though Ira had no choice, still in the process a human being was lost for all eternity.

Sarah worried too that her husband's newfound fame was having an undesirable effect on their son. Since their move to Arizona was now delayed, she decided to enroll David-Jacob in second grade. Already, the first two afternoons after school, there was no shortage of childhood peers anxious for David-Jacob to play with them. She observed as her son's chest swelled with pride, and she grew concerned that in conversation he gloated over his father shooting "the bad man dead through the heart."

It disturbed her enough that she eventually phoned Rabbi Kramer. Embarrassed, she apologized for not attending *shul* [synagogue] more regularly, but Rabbi Kramer was more than gracious to her. He also eased her conscience about David-Jacob's seemingly callous remarks. The wise, older rabbi assured her that her son's anger and indifference was merely a way of covering up his fear of almost having lost his father. The "bad man" to David-Jacob wasn't a real person, but his father was . . . and the boy wasn't ready yet to accept that his greatest hero was mortal. Rabbi Kramer reminded Sarah that children have their own way of coping with tragedy and she was reading her own fears into how David-Jacob was adjusting to his father's being shot and to the thief's demise.

He then used the opportunity to encourage Sarah and the family to begin attending synagogue on a more consistent basis. He reminded her that when Ira was younger he had an inquisitive mind concerning the Torah and Talmud and that many—including himself—thought that Ira would one day become a rabbi. After praying with Sarah over the phone, he invited the family to meet with him once Ira was up and able.

After talking to Rabbi Kramer, Sarah felt comforted, as if she'd just spoken with her grandfather who was long deceased. At the same time she ached inside, feeling a spiritual void. She decided that when next visiting Ira in the hospital, she would again stress the need for their starting back to Temple—if not for Ira's own benefit, then for hers and the children's. She felt encouraged by Ira's recent openness and was sure he would listen to her.

If Ira learned anything from his hospital stay, it was that regardless of his state of mind, sleep or physical condition, the only thing that would deter his nurse from taking vitals would be an executive order from President Truman. Still, he was happy she awoke him so he could ask for another dose of morphine.

Minutes later, when the nurse was completing the chart at the edge of the bed, an unexpected visitor arrived. "So, Ira, here I had been feeling sorry for you. Yet all day you get to lie in bed and ogle the pretty nurses."

The nurse turned and smiled as Ira greeted his long-time friend. "Rabbi Kramer! It's good to see you. I agree the nurses are pretty but I would change places with you in a heartbeat. Have a seat."

The rabbi seated himself in the cushioned chair next to the bed. He was wearing a skullcap over his slick bald pate and he had short, curly, snow-white sideburns. For a man of sixty, he could still pass for a youthful fifty and had a kindly face with an engaging smile. As the nurse was about to leave the room, she thanked Rabbi Kramer for his compliment, adding saucily, "By the way, Rabbi, I think you're kind of cute too."

"I'm a widower you know . . ."

"But I'm Baptist . . ."

"So you'll have a *mikva*."

Seeing the questioning look on the nurse's face, Ira explained, "It's a ritual Jewish bath—almost like a baptism, only confirming one's Jewishness."

The pleasant, middle-aged nurse laughed. "I'm sorry, Rabbi, I'm also happily married. I just like flirting with older and handsome Jewish men."

"Humph, Gentiles. Who's to understand them?"

The nurse left the room and Rabbi Kramer turned his attention back towards Ira. "So, how you feeling? I take it you're not up to boxing Joe Louis yet?"

"I'm afraid not. But each day I feel a little better. You seem to be full of spit and vinegar though. Too bad the nurse was married."

"Ira, I already had the best for thirty-seven years, Jenny, may God rest her soul. How do you compete with the memories? You don't. Eh, to get married again I need like a *loch in kop* [hole in the head]. So! not to change the subject, but everyone in *shul* has been praying for you and the family. You sure you don't want for our help? I talked to Sarah over the phone an hour ago. She says everything is fine. I want, however, that I should hear that from you."

"Thanks, Rabbi. I really can't think of anything."

With the pain medicine beginning to set in, Ira found himself relaxed and enjoying his conversation with Rabbi Kramer. As a young teen, the rabbi was Ira's spiritual mentor, the one who presided over Ira's bar mitzvah when he was thirteen. He was also very close to Ira's parents when they still lived in Brooklyn. Ira knew he could never share of his new found faith. More than ever now, and as much as he respected Rabbi Kramer, a gulf now separated them. Ira was sensitive to the fact that if the rabbi knew of his confession of faith hours earlier, he might never speak to him again. In his mind's eye, Ira imagined Rabbi Kramer ripping his shirt open, in a manner similar to rabbis of old tearing their vestments upon hearing something sacrilegious. In reality, the rabbi would likely express his anger with a verbal tongue lashing and do as Ruth feared--accuse him of being a *meshumed*.

Now Ruth's apprehensions became his own. Ira suddenly realized how much his being a Jew and a follower of Christ would be offensive to many other Jews. By making the decision he did, the remainder of his life would be spent in a delicate balancing act, trying to live in two different worlds. His immediate concern was wondering, still, how to tell Sarah.

Ira continued to stare at Rabbi Kramer who had his eyes closed and was moving his lips silently in prayer. As he finished praying, he observed Ira's eyes fixated on him. "Nu, you have something you want to ask before I go?"

"Not really. Well, in a way I do and in a way I don't. I'm not sure you can answer, and I don't mean that to be an insult."

"So who's insulted?"

"I think a lot about the man I killed . . . whether there's really a heaven or hell. I know you and my father used to discuss the Talmud a lot, talking about the 'world to come' as the Talmud describes it. I wonder, Rabbi, since I violated one of the supreme commandments in taking a life, does that prevent me from the world to come? I mean, I realize it's all argument and speculation, the Talmud being just so much conjecture on a variety of subjects."

Rabbi Kramer was mildly offended. "Speculation! Conjecture! You speak of the Talmud as if it is no more than a book of fairy tales! I might remind you that the Talmud is second only to the Hebrew scriptures in terms of its importance. The 316 debates recorded in it are a literal storehouse of Jewish religious experience and wisdom accumulated through the ages. It's a collection of interpretative opinion by the greatest Jewish minds ever. Today, traditional Jews live more by Talmudic law than by biblical law."

"Rabbi Kramer, I wasn't minimizing its importance, only that it contained so many different opinions on almost every subject. For instance, when you used to discuss the Talmud with my father, I remember the two of you arguing at great length over the subject of the 'hereafter.' You two were always at odds. If I remember correctly, didn't some in the Talmud take the position that there might not even be a hereafter or a world to come?"

Ira was indeed curious. Although his realm of faith had suddenly taken on new parameters, it was still Jewish blood that flowed through his veins. He sensed his salvation was now secure, but he wasn't knowledgeable enough about his new Christian faith to know for certain. It couldn't hurt to have the assurance of the mother religion as well. He would feel better if the Jewish idea of eternity still included him. If not, it would be all the more reason to take sanctuary in Christianity. Knowing now how much he valued life, how much more he desired the promise Christians had in *eternal life*. It would also make it a lot easier explaining to Sarah the reasons for his conversion.

Rabbi Kramer stroked his chin, contemplating his response. Then he nodded. "Do I think there's a hereafter or world to come? Of course I do. So did your papa. What we argued about is who gets to live in the next world. The Sadducees were the ones who argued against there being a hereafter—unsuccessfully, I might add. They contended that the soul became extinct when the body died and death was the final end of the human being. The Pharisees, mostly of the school of Rabbi Hillel, presented far greater evidence for there being a resurrection or world to come, often referring to the text of Isaiah to back their arguments."

Ira persisted in his questioning. "But who did the Pharisees say would be resurrected?"

"Well, there were differences of opinion, even among themselves. Some argued that only those who lived by the Torah--Genesis, Exodus, Leviticus, Numbers, Deuteronomy—and taught their children the

Torah, could be resurrected. Others took the position that only those who lived and were buried in Israel could have an afterlife.

"Then they split hairs and said as long as a Jew had walked four cubits in Israel before being buried elsewhere, it was okay. Still others maintained that righteous Gentiles and Jews could participate, but not so wicked Gentiles and Jews. Some arguments for exclusion included if a man crossed a stream behind a woman, or if a man shamed another man in public.

"There were also classes of people who weren't thought to be reputable enough, for example, teachers of children, minor officials in the synagogue, enchanters, butchers, and even certain judges. Of course, I don't agree with everything, you understand. To me, it is enough that a person loves God and obeys God that he is worthy of the world to come. Unfortunately, however, your Rabbi Kramer isn't in the Talmud."

"So from all the learned and esteemed religious leaders who so capably debated their positions, how do you decide who is right?" Ira asked.

"You decide by means of the brain God gave you. Sometimes you take from the best of all their arguments, together with your own reading of the *Tanach* [entirety of Hebrew scriptures], and you form your own opinion. Would God refuse such a person, were that person only thirsting for more knowledge of Him?"

"I understand what you're saying, but why would God make everything so confusing? Why not make everything black and white like the Ten Commandments, so that there would be no doubt about a world to come or who gets to go there? I like your answer about loving and obeying God, Rabbi. But is it you and I who decide we have loved and obeyed enough? Or is it God who decides?"

"Ira, I'm becoming *oysgematert* [exhausted] by your questions already. You make an appointment, we'll talk." Then the rabbi changed the subject. "So, do you and Sarah stay in touch still with your little *goyisheh* friend Alma . . . Heather . . . whatever her name is?"

"You mean Katalin? Sure, she's like part of the family."

"Humph, I'm surprised she hasn't converted the two of you already. A nice girl, mind you, very sweet young lady, but those are the kind that are the most dangerous. You know, Ira, what I have most of all against Christianity?"

"What's that, Rabbi?"

"We Jews do all the work, the Christians get all the gifts!" Ira smiled as the rabbi rose from the chair. "Ira, I have to go, I have another appointment. So tell your lovely wife I miss her and the family and should she even have to hit you over the head with a frying pan, you be a *mensh* [honorable person] and start coming again to *shul*."

"Rabbi, as soon as I'm able, I promise I'll be there. I don't know if Sarah told you or not, but we're planning to move to Arizona."

"She told me, but she says you are to have another operation first?"

"Probably in late December or early January. They're going to sew my colon back together. It will likely be February or March before we finally move."

"So, until then, when you go to live with the jackrabbits and coyotes, I'll expect to see you in the house of God." The rabbi winked and smiled at Ira and then left.

Ira took a deep breath. Every mention of synagogue caused him to feel tense. Sarah had always told him that two of his strongest characteristics were loyalty and integrity. Yet the longer the rabbi remained, the more Ira began feeling disloyal and deceitful. In a way, he was turning his back on Judaism, the faith that initially nourished him.

Whether it was discretion or a lack of courage that prevented him from telling Rabbi Kramer he had become a Christian, he wasn't sure. He only knew that he had passed a point of no return in his life. The Jews were a brave and unique people who, though the world regarded as strange, still Ira was proud to be numbered among them. But searching the depths of his soul for answers to the meaning of life, he kept coming up empty. Certainly God hovered among the Jews but there was a constant sense of frustration that seemed to him too evident. There was that element of constant struggle among his people that never seemed to get resolved. He saw it reflected in the faces of his friends and family. Each passing year it continued to gnaw at him. Something about the Jews and their mystical union with God was incomplete. To be the people called <u>chosen</u>, there should have been a greater feeling of contentment. As a teenager Ira had once secretly read parts of the New Testament. While not accepting its premise, that Jesus was the Jewish Messiah, Somehow this great Jewish adversary did not come across to him as this horrible malefactor. In fact he was somewhat moved by the character of Jesus and it frightened him to the point of his vowing never again to open the pages of the Christian's bible. A vow which until this day he had kept.

Sitting up in bed rehashing his conversation with Rabbi Kramer, Ira pondered what it was about the personality of Jesus that so stirred him those many years ago, so much so that it frightened him away from investigating any further. Several minutes went by while he racked his brain trying to come up with an answer. Then it was as if the blinders finally came off. When discussing with Rabbi Kramer the many theories postulated and hypothesized by esteemed men of Jewish faith and recorded in the Talmud, there was never a firm conclusion arrived at regarding salvation and the world to come. After thousands of years, the Jewish people still appeared unsure what God expected of them. In addition, even the best of them could only guess as to the who, the when, or the if, concerning their promised messiah.

And while His people argued, debated and meticulously picked apart the scriptures searching for life's hidden truths, Jesus left no room for doubt. With simplicity, brilliance and eloquence, He merely exercised His authority over scriptures.

Two stocky, plain-clothes detectives were just leaving Ira's room as Sarah entered. Both detectives respectfully acknowledged her before they left. "It was only a formality," they assured her, adding that they were glad to see Ira doing so well.

Although they were cordial, Sarah felt shy and awkward in their presence. Something about the entire shooting incident had frayed her emotions. Thus far, all her experiences with members of law enforcement in America had been favorable. Yet something about authority figures who carried weapons had suddenly revived memories of the Gestapo in Germany. Up until last Friday night she thought she had finally succeeded in escaping that part of her past. Now, instead, she had come to the realization that her past would always haunt her and she just had to be careful not to let it control her.

After laying her purse and the *Saturday Evening Post* on the chair next to Ira's bed, she subconsciously rubbed her hand across the scar on the side of her chin. Ira noticed and quickly sensed her need for an extra-strong embrace. When Sarah leaned over to hug him, he held tightly to her and could feel her hot wet tears against his cheek. "I love you so much, Ira," she said brokenly. "The only way I could sleep last night was to pretend you were in bed next to me."

"Well, if you can get the nurses to stay out of our room for a while, maybe you can crawl under the sheets with me."

Ira's remark improved Sarah's mood as she wiped away her tears. "Ira! I'll even pay them to stay out."

"Sarah, with this stupid catheter sticking out of me, and this lousy IV, I don't think it will work."

Sarah grinned wickedly, "Honey, where there's a will there's a way." She seated herself in the chair and reached her arm across so Ira could clasp her hand. For brief seconds they stared into each other's eyes.

Ira could still detect a wistfulness in Sarah's presence as she started to speak. "The nurse said Rabbi Kramer stopped by to see you. I'm glad. I had no idea he was coming by."

"You're kidding! I thought you were the reason he came."

"Not at all. At least I don't think so. The reason I phoned him this morning was to ask him about David-Jacob, how this whole incident might be affecting him."

"So you didn't put him up to twisting my arm about coming to synagogue?"

"No, although he did mention it and it certainly wouldn't hurt if we started attending again."

"Okay!"

"Okay! Like in, you mean you'd like to?"

"Sure."

"Ira, that's wonderful! It would mean so much to me. Do you mind if we also enroll David-Jacob in Hebrew School?"

"Whatever you want."

Ira's being so obliging aroused Sarah's suspicions. "Ira, I was hoping you might agree with me but I thought it only wishful thinking on my part."

"Why do you say that?"

"Well, given your attitude of late on religion in general. Your feelings about God. But maybe that's all changed now? Anyway, I desperately feel the need to be involved in synagogue and with our faith again. I'm just surprised by your willingness."

Ira was confused as to how to respond. She had perceived him right but now everything had changed, except Sarah wasn't aware of just how much change had really occurred. Now as a result of his own desire to have a closer relationship with God, he was more acutely aware of Sarah's spiritual needs. His being shot had dramatically changed both their priorities. But how to tell Sarah he was going down a different spiritual path than her—without feeling he had somehow betrayed her—was the problem.

He was only half listening as Sarah began speaking about Joshua-Caleb. Going back to synagogue didn't pose a problem. While there he could still silently worship God in his own way. Besides, he knew he would be uncomfortable worshipping in a church environment—at least for now. The dilemma facing Ira was that he couldn't be dishonest by pretending to practice Judaism when he believed in his heart that Judaism stopped short of accepting its true Messiah. Already, since this morning's prayer of faith and submission, he was beginning to feel a tremendous release, a sense of peace in knowing that he no longer had to carry all of life's burdens on his own shoulders. The peace in knowing that all the sins of his life were totally forgiven and he could finally put his tortured past behind him. If nothing else, Ira had remembered those assurances from glancing at the New Testament sixteen years ago. Also, he had long been listening to Katalin when Katalin didn't think he was.

Ira knew now that he didn't ever want to go back to living and feeling as he did before, yet he felt as if a sword hung over him—a sword that came between his truce with God and his deep love for Sarah. He didn't know how to reconcile the two. He wished fervently that Ruth was there to help him. Then he remembered her telling him that she would be praying for him.

Ira took a deep breath while considering how to proceed. Meanwhile, an irritated Sarah stopped speaking when she realized her husband wasn't paying her any attention. Engrossed in his own thoughts, he didn't notice she had stopped. Instead he said, "Sarah, can you get me my robe and slippers. I feel like walking."

Sarah complied and helped Ira out of bed. Once out in the hallway, he put one arm around Sarah's shoulder for support and used the other to push the IV pole forward. He then decided to tell his wife what had happened, starting at the beginning.

"Sarah," Ira spoke cautiously, "a long time ago, when I was still in my teens, I read a particular book about a certain individual. The protagonist of this book said things that stirred my imagination. No matter how much I tried to put this character, and the things attributed to him, out of my mind, I never did completely. Even the theme of this book, which I found difficult to comprehend, still lingered somewhat in my mind.

"I hope you're not talking about Karl Marx, because I despise communism," Sarah interrupted. Ira stopped pushing the IV pole, gently holding on to it for support as he drew back his arm from around Sarah's shoulder. Standing inches away from her face he nervously bit his lip and looked his wife straight in the eye. "No, Sarah, maybe it would have been easier to tell you if it was Karl Marx."

"Ira, what's the big mystery?"

"Sarah, the protagonist of this book—the hero if you will—was a Nazarene. The book was the New Testament."

Sarah's mouth immediately dropped open as she lifted her eyebrows and turned her head away. When she looked back at Ira, her expression was one of incredulity. "Ira! I love you to death but I don't know how many more surprises I can take from you!"

"Well, maybe we should sit down, Sarah. Because the finish to this story began last Friday when I had a gun pointed at my head and I was praying for my life."

Ira and Sarah walked to the opposite end of the corridor where they found an empty waiting room. Once seated, Ira spent the better part of the next hour going over in detail all that had happened to him. He began by filling in the remaining gaps and of the mysterious gold cross he had discovered on his pillow only last night—possibly the same gold cross he witnessed days earlier after being shot. He deftly sidestepped any mention of Ruth. Without sounding apologetic, he then told Sarah of how in the morning he awoke from a troubled night's sleep and asked Jesus to take over his life. He also told her of his vision, which as he expected, Sarah immediately said was a hallucination.

Sarah sat numb and expressionless, trying to absorb it all. Then Ira concluded, "In a way," because of the genocide in Europe, and having no one I could blame, I, in large part blamed Christians. I even blamed the Katalin's of the world and wanted no part of them. I allowed my anger towards God to affect me to the point I had become a sort of modern-day Jonah. Whenever God was even mentioned, I just wanted to avoid the subject entirely. I only desired to keep running."

"How were you able to keep me so much in the dark?" Sarah interrupted.

Ira shrugged his shoulders. "It was just a good acting job," he admitted. "I felt too proud and protective. I just wanted to keep you in a pumpkin shell . . . and keep you there very well."

Ira then told her that his occasional flare-ups with Katalin was the threat of what her religion represented to him. Ira told Sarah, "It did not matter if what I had convinced myself to be true, was true. What mattered was finding someone to get even with. Since liberating the camp at Ohrdruf, and knowing I couldn't fight God, I could still go after some of His people." Katalin became very convenient. Ira went on to explain, "Judaism always posed more questions for me than it provided answers." He still professed his love for being Jewish, adamantly maintaining that regardless of what anyone might say, he would always be a Jew. "Besides," he stated, "anyone born of a Jewish mother is considered a Jew, period!"

Ira praised Judaism as an honest attempt at discerning the will and true nature of God. Then six days ago," Ira told Sarah, "I just cried out to any god who would hear my plea for life. All my wanting to live was because of you and the children. And I believe with all my heart that Jesus was the one who left His signature. I am absolutely convinced of that! My regret now is never having shared these feelings with you. I was so wrong. That is why I am trying to be as open and honest as I possibly can now.

"Ira, I never even had an inkling."

"I'm sorry, Sarah," Ira apologized. "It's only recently that I've been able to open up. I don't know what else to say except how much I love you."

Sarah rose to her feet, turned her back to Ira, and walked a short distance away. Anxiously watching her, Ira feared that what he had shared could cause irreparable harm to their marriage. Dismayed, he couldn't remember a moment when he felt a greater tenderness for her. He knew that, if asked, he would willingly die for her. The one thing he knew he couldn't do was renounce his declaration of faith and he fervently hoped she wouldn't ask that of him.

Ira's hands were folded in his lap when Sarah turned to face him. He was puzzled by her blank look. In a monotone voice, tinged with sarcasm, she threw her first dart. "So, do you plan to go to church now?"

"No, I wouldn't be comfortable in a church setting, Sarah, at least not now. In fact, I was thinking that going to synagogue was a good idea although, admittedly, I would be listening to everything from a different perspective. More than likely I'd be listening to see how God was laying the foundation for the New Testament. I won't lie to you though, Sarah. It's been said that the heart will eventually reject what the mind won't accept. Right now I have a real hunger to learn more about Christianity. I want to know more about the person of Jesus. You'll likely see me reading a lot of Christian material."

"I see, and do you expect me to start believing like you do? Because I won't! Not now, maybe not ever!"

"I understand that, Sarah. I'm not asking anything of you except that you give me the chance to show how much I still love and need you. Sarah, I just want to be a better person all the way around. A better husband to you. A better father to our children. I mean that from the depths of my heart."

The corner of Sarah's lip curled upward and she bit down, as if still trying to figure Ira out. "Well, I've never really had much complaint with you in the husband and father department. What I have complained about is that you be more open and honest with me about your feelings. Now that you have, I can't very well fault you for doing what I hoped you would. What's ironic is, now I almost wish you weren't so open and honest. Katalin always warned me, 'Be careful what you pray for because God might answer your prayers.' So, what now, Ira?"

"Don't stop loving me . . ."

"Ira, if tomorrow you decided to become a giraffe, I wouldn't stop loving you."

Feeling a sense of relief, Ira cracked a smile. "Even if I became a Christian giraffe?"

"Well, I'll admit, becoming a Christian is one thing. Becoming a Christian giraffe is an entirely different matter. I think you'd be pushing your luck. Ira, on a more serious note I'll always love you, no matter what. I can't ask you not to be true to your beliefs. Even being your wife, I don't have that right. I'll simply have to adjust. You'll have to be patient with me though. Give me time, and please don't try to change what I believe. I'm sure from time to time, out of curiosity, I'll ask you questions.

"I have nothing against Christianity," Sarah weighed her words carefully. "You should know that through my friendship with Katalin. But I wasn't prepared for my Jewish husband becoming a Christian. I'll say this, however, given the choice of your being an atheist or being a Christian, I'd prefer the latter. God is very important to me, Ira, and I want Him to be important to you, even though we might disagree on just who God is." She paused, then asked, "You really don't mind if we start DeeJay in Hebrew School?"

"No, I think it would be good for him to learn more about ethics, faith and morality."

"What do we tell him about you?"

"Nothing now. I don't think he would understand anyway."

"I agree. But do you think someday you might end up choosing to attend a church rather than a synagogue?"

"Maybe . . . someday. I don't have all the answers right now, Sarah."

"Ira, we need to be careful about who we tell. Marvin would have a fit. I doubt also that Ruth would understand."

As soon as Ruth's name was mentioned, Ira shuddered to think how Sarah would react if he told her that Ruth had been a Christian all along. "Sarah," he answered, "nobody needs to know anything. Of course, anything I tell you, I can automatically assume Katalin will know."

Sarah laughed. "And if Katalin knows, Paul is now likely to find out. But that should be the extent of it."

Ira nodded in agreement. "And Sarah?"

"What?"

"I have to confess, I have one more secret."

A look of dread crossed Sarah's face. "What . . . what? Ira, don't do this to me!"

"Sorry Sarah, but lately I've had this incredible desire to kiss you."

A relieved Sarah broke into a broad smile. "Ira, you big dumb giraffe. I hope you're not all talk and no action."

With a gleam in his eye, Ira managed, with the IV pole as a crutch, to rise to his feet. Moments later, two nurses walked by the waiting room and caught the two in a loving embrace. Both nurses started giggling. One of them commented to the other, "Must be newlyweds."

"Gosh, I hope not," the second nurse responded. "What a horrible place to have to spend a honeymoon."

Chapter 22

Thanksgiving Day was a joyous occasion for the gathering at Marvin and Ruth's house in Jamaica Heights. All who were there felt they had much to be thankful for. The celebration included both Katz families, Elsa and Sam Rosen, Paul and Katalin.

Marvin said the blessing over the meal and Paul, who had endeared himself to the Katz's since the shooting, concluded with a non-sectarian prayer of his own. In the middle of his prayer, when giving thanks for Ira's remarkable recovery, Paul's voice momentarily broke. There was hardly a dry eye. After much sniffling it caused the somewhat less sentimental Marvin to toss his arms in the air and cry out, "Enough already with the tears. Ira might think somebody actually loves him."

Baby Joshua-Caleb awaited Marvin's arms before he decided to regurgitate his baby peas and carrots. David-Jacob—who played with his cousin Rachel in the back yard—-became the subject of conversation at evening's end when it was realized he had left the house intact. This prompted Marvin to exult, "*Mazeltov!* God is still in his heaven and performing miracles!"

The surprising news of the evening came when Marvin announced during dinner that he had purchased land in Jamaica Heights to immediately begin construction on a new store. When completed, he would close the downtown store.

Later that evening, as Ira helped Ruth clear the table, the two had a brief time to discreetly compare notes on their now-common faith in Christianity. They were both acutely aware of the delicate situation their beliefs had placed them in and it caused Ruth's wry sense of humor to come to the fore.

"Just think, Ira, Marvin doesn't know that either of us are Christians nor do the Rosens. Only Paul, Katalin and Sarah know that you are. Only you know that I am. Sarah doesn't know that I know that you are because she doesn't want to tell me for fear I might tell Marvin, not realizing I am also a Christian.

"Think what havoc we can wreak," she laughed. "We'll hand Marvin a note telling him that we are both Christians and then we run out the door and down the street as fast as we can."

Ira chortled over her suggestion while scratching his head. "Ruth, I don't know about you, but in my condition I couldn't run fast enough, and I'm not quite ready for my angel wings just yet."

Katalin had a special reason to be thankful this Thanksgiving season. Her feature series on local Holocaust survivors had been published and was well received. Readers of the *Daily Eagle* as well as her peers at the newspaper gave her plaudits. She remained calm on the outside, but inwardly she was delirious with joy. Becoming a journalist and seeing her name in print was her long-held dream.

Most gratifying was that she was able to justify Neil Simmon's faith in her. Equally satisfying was that in Part One of the four-part series she was able to pay tribute to her and Sarah's parents and the legacy of love they left behind. Although a story of triumph over tragedy and a will to survive, the account of their own escape and making it to America's shores was more a testimony to the indomitable faith and courage of others.

She also mentioned Sarah's German soldier, but only in a general sense, referring to him in her article as the Corporal. His heroic actions would hopefully present another side of the German people.

In the course of her interviews with camp survivors she detected a commonly held and blanket hatred for all Germans. One of the messages she wanted to get across was that not all Germans or people who lived in Germany were to blame for what occurred—at the same time, not making excuses for Hitler and those who subscribed to his contemptuous beliefs. She wrote of Hitler's legions, describing them as "Human beings devoid of conscience," adding that, "Nuremberg judged them, but only God could properly sentence them. Therefore, those of us who suffered loss need to remember but not dwell on our tragedy—which serves not to the benefit of man or the will of God. Remaining confident, in addition to Nuremberg, the guilty faces ultimate adjudication in God's chambers."

She was in her element. At long last, she felt that the pieces to the puzzle of her life were coming together. Not only was her desire to become a journalist and writer now a reality, but her relationship with Paul was continuing to grow stronger. She could never remember feeling as passionately about any other man.

Two weeks into December, with the church pageant over, Paul had three days off and he and Katalin spent the first of those days together buying presents, along with a four-foot Christmas tree for Katalin's apartment. They then spent the evening baking cookies and consuming them, decorating the tree and kissing under the mistletoe.

As a special treat on the second day, Paul took Katalin to Lundy's stucco moorish grotto in Sheepshead Bay where, along with hundreds of other patrons, they downed an oceanful of clams and bluefish. At night they went to see "Red River," starring John Wayne and the new and handsome matinee idol, Montgomery Clift.

The third day, Paul took Katalin to the Peter Luger Steak House near the Williamsburg Bridge, a place well known for its sawdust floors and giant-sized steaks. Later that evening they strolled the beach barefooted at Coney Island and kissed under the boardwalk.

Katalin knew she was falling in love. At first she questioned herself, wondering whether it was just her growing dependence on Paul for her own happiness that was really motivating her feelings. *Was she really in love*, she wondered, *or just loving Paul's company?* Then one night she had a frightening dream that the war was still going on and Paul was sent to Guadalcanal where his own brother was killed. Then she, too, received that dreaded telegram from the war department, "We regret to inform you . . ."

The dream was so real and haunting that it disturbed Katalin deeply. In revealing her dream over the phone to Sarah, she started to cry and Sarah had to sharply remind her that it was only a dream. At the same time, Sarah told Katalin of reading about a psychologist's theory that sometimes a person's worst fears manifest themselves in dreams, fears that otherwise might be too painful to deal with during waking moments.

Katalin didn't tell Paul of her dream, worrying that he might think her insecure or unstable. However, with more time on her hands, she had more occasion to think about her past. For several years now she had been so busy she almost forgot she had a past. It seemed her growing up years were just a story she got used to telling but that didn't really happen. Now with Christmas just two weeks away, the stark reality was that her story was very real: her family was dead and her relatives were also, or at the very least trapped in communist Hungary, probably never to be heard from again.

Other than the Katz's, Paul had now become the only human source of real happiness in her life. Jesus was her anchor but her desire for a mate often consumed her thoughts. Even God the Father, when creating the foundations of earth and life, knew the value of family and friends. In every facet of the creation, God looked upon His creation

and said, "It is good." Only in His creation of man and seeing man alone
did He say, "It is <u>not</u> good."

Two days before Christmas Katalin was off work and busily
cleaning her apartment when Paul called. Although they were supposed
to get together in the evening, he wanted to come over immediately and
introduce her to a friend who asked to meet her. The unnamed friend
was bringing with him a special gift to put under their jointly-purchased
Christmas tree.

Katalin spruced up her apartment, took a quick shower and
dressed to await Paul and whoever it was he was bringing by. She tried
to think of all his companions and could only come up with those at
church. Then it occurred to her that there was one person that Paul was
perhaps closest to whom she had not yet met—his Jewish friend from
Queens with whom he served in the Navy and who was soon to become
a rabbi.

Within the hour Katalin learned she had guessed right. Paul arrived
and introduced her to Sam Bender, a ruddy-faced, red-haired, stocky
man with Popeye-like forearms and biceps. He looked to be about
thirty.

Attempting to shake Katalin's hand, Sam Bender had to extend his
arm around a large gift-wrapped package he was carrying. "Sam, let me
take that from you, then we can greet properly." Katalin took the bulky
box and placed it underneath the Christmas tree. Returning to again
greet Paul's friend and thank him for the gift, Katalin gave him a brief
hug.

Immediately taken by her, Sam acknowledged her graciousness
with the words, "'She was a phantom of delight when first she gleamed
upon my sight.'"

Katalin blushed. "I'm flattered, Sam. I believe you're quoting
William Wordsworth."

"I am, Katalin, and now I'm even more impressed. How is it that
you know Wordsworth?"

"I love poetry, although I'm afraid I don't write it very well. I enjoy
Donne, Milton, Longfellow, Shelley, Emily Dickenson—almost all good
poets. I also appreciate men who memorize and recite verse. It's a very
attractive quality."

Standing nearby, paying scant attention to their conversation,
Paul bit into an apple he lifted from a fruit bowl. Sam interrupted his
talk with Katalin and turned to give Paul a hard stare. "Paul, you goofy
hillbilly yutz! How is it that you end up with such a refined and beautiful

young lady? Especially when all you can recite are Mother Goose nursery rhymes, and the only song you know is 'Froggie Went a Courtin'?"

Paul was unfazed by Sam's facetious remarks, instead breaking into a wide grin. Feeling a sense of duty and loyalty, Katalin walked to Paul's side and whispered into his ear. Then she and Paul started snapping their fingers and broke into song:

"Froggie went a courtin' and he did ride, A hum a hum
Froggie went a courtin' and he did ride, A sword and
pistol by his side, A hum a hum . . .
"He rode up to Miss Mousie's door, A hum a hum
He rode up to Miss Mousie's door, Where he had often
been before, A hum a hum . . ."

Sam was amused and said, "Hey, if we're going to have a hootenanny, I'm joining in." Soon he was also clapping his hands to the rhythm and joining in:

"He took Miss Mousie on his knee, A hum a hum
He took Miss Mousie on his knee, And said, 'Miss
Mousie will you marry me?' A hum a hum . . .
"'Without my Uncle Rat's consent, A hum a hum
Without my Uncle Rat's consent, I would not marry
the President', A hum a hum

On the next verse, Paul took Katalin by the hand, twirling her about. Then they both started stomping the floor and kicking up their heels as Sam continued clapping to their three-person jamboree. By the seventh verse, Paul could no longer keep up with the boundless energy exhibited by his partner and gently offered Katalin's hand to Sam. He then clapped and sang through the last verse he could remember:

"Then Uncle Rat laughed and shook his sides, A hum a hum
Then Uncle Rat laughed and shook his sides,
To think his niece would be a bride, A hum a hum"

At the mention of the word "bride," and for a brief moment, Paul and Katalin's eyes linked in a magnetic trance. Exhilarated but winded, the three congratulated one another and plopped down on the sofa with Katalin sitting in between. The first to catch her breath, she left to prepare corned beef on rye sandwiches for the two men. Minutes later, Paul and Sam joined her in the kitchen where they sat at the table and Paul said grace.

Katalin had several questions she wanted to ask Sam, questions that related to his long-time friendship with Paul and that would provide her a keener insight into the man she now loved. Somewhere in her past she heard that a man could best be described by the company he keeps. Sam was obviously that company.

"Sam," she said, "I just want to tell you and Paul that dancing with the two of you was one of the more delightful and enjoyable experiences I've had in recent memory. But I'm dying of curiosity. How is it that the two of you—both grown men—have memorized verses to, of all songs, 'Froggie Went a Courtin'?'"

After some hesitation, Sam glanced at Paul, then replied, "Well, pal, I don't know why you kept it such a big secret but, as John Donne wrote in his poem of 'Meditation', 'And therefore never send to know for whom the bell tolls; It tolls for thee'."

Paul nodded, then said to Katalin, "Sam's right. I've probably only made it a big deal by not telling you."

Katalin was confused. "Telling me what?"

"Well, we learned to sing all the verses to 'Froggie Went a Courtin' as part of our initiation ceremony after graduation from military training."

Katalin grinned. "So why is that so unusual? I think it's cute when men do silly things like that."

"Well, some of us were cute. Sam was always ugly, but out of my good graces I decided to sing with him anyway."

Sam leaned back in his sofa seat. "Good thing you did sing with me so everyone wouldn't notice that your voice hadn't broken yet."

Katalin shook her head over their adolescent behavior. Out of the corner of her eye she saw Paul looking in her direction with a contemplative stare. Then he sighed and went over to the refrigerator. "Do you mind, Katalin?" He took out a Coca-Cola. "I'm dying of thirst."

"Not at all. There's a bottle opener in the drawer." After snapping off the cap, Paul took a large swig then casually leaned against the counter, holding the bottle at waist level.

"Katalin, Sam and I weren't talking about graduation from Officer Candidate School. In fact, we only knew each other casually at the time and we weren't exactly friends. In OCS we had some personality clashes. It was after we graduated from OCS and both were stationed aboard the Wasp in December of 1942 that we got to know each other better and became good friends. We both were bored in our assignments."

Paul nodded towards Sam, who took up the story. "I was a supply officer, Katalin. It was very tedious and mind-numbing duty. All I did all day long was receive requests for provisions and general stock material. Mostly, I listened to complaints, and all the while a war was going on."

"I see." Katalin looked back at Paul. "Paul, didn't you tell me you were in Personnel?"

"Yes."

"And I take it you're going to tell me that you too were bored with what you were doing?"

"Exactly."

"Well, I would think that most soldiers or sailors would be happy to be out of harm's way, though something tells me that wasn't the case with the both of you. So what's the big secret you two are about to tell me?"

"That we volunteered and were accepted into UDT—underwater demolition. We became Frogmen, hence our 'Froggie Went a Courtin' initiation song. Of course, we had to go through some rigorous training first, most of it at a California beach, not too far from Coronado."

"You're kidding!?" Katalin was genuinely surprised. "Why that type of duty is practically suicide! I'm surprised you never told me about this. "

'Yes, it was dangerous, but we were well trained. And there was little difference between us and combat soldiers. What we did was to spearhead amphibious landings, clearing the way for the Marines storming the beaches.

"Remember, my brother who was killed was a Marine. We never knew beforehand what our assignment would be, but whenever I personally was out there doing my job, I couldn't help thinking of my brother. A lot of times it kept me from being scared. I felt as if Thomas were somehow smiling down on me for helping his fellow Marines. I guess, in a sense, it was a way of keeping his memory alive.

"I didn't tell you about what we did because much of it was classified—and still is. I wasn't sure initially just how far our relationship would go. I didn't know if it was necessary to tell you until we got to know each other better. I'm still reluctant to share my story with our congregation, although I've told Pastor Frey. I don't want my service background to detract from the message of preaching Jesus Christ. I don't want people to be curious about me, but rather be curious about who Jesus is."

Katalin nodded. "I'm not mad at you, Paul. I understand. It just took me by surprise because I thought I knew you so well. I'm so naive still. If I've learned anything in this life, it should be that nobody is ever who they appear to be. It's just so disconcerting."

Sitting next to her, Sam reached over and gently squeezed Katalin's hand. "Katalin, it would be a pretty boring world if you could figure everyone and everything out. If God didn't allow a little mystery into our lives now and then, life itself would be dull. Why, there would be no such thing as a mystery novel. There would be no great discovery in science. The wonder of God might cease to amaze us if He were to tell us everything about himself. For that reason, I think even in heaven— although my concept of heaven differs from the two of you—I think, even then, God won't reveal everything to us.

"Think as a child, Katalin, the wonder of nature, the miracle of the tiny ant and how it labors daily, the spirit that seems to flow in a river stream and how it refreshes and continually nourishes the soul. The incredible mysteries that lie beneath the oceans and in the heavens, we explore to stretch our minds, but mostly I think we explore to find God.

"Perhaps even war, Katalin. One of the greatest mysteries is why a 'good' God would allow wars to go on ad infinitum? But maybe He allows war so we will yearn for the peace that can only be found in Him. As for man, he is at best a mystery, in constant search of himself, probably best left undiscovered."

Whatever questions or doubts Katalin had about Sam were resolved in his soliloquy. Turning her head and looking at him admiringly, she said, "Sam, when I was little, my father would invite his learned Jewish friends to our house for great discussions on philosophy. I was always warmed to the heart by their wonderful compassion for life and their desire for knowledge. You're no different, Sam. You'll make a wonderful rabbi because, like the others, you have the heart of a poet."

Sam gave Katalin a kiss on her forehead and stood up. "I've got to go. Paul, I'll take the subway. I don't want you should have to drive me back." Paul's protestations were to no avail.

As they reached the door, he turned to Katalin. "Two things, little princess."

Katalin interrupted, "I am five feet, two inches, Sam. I am not that small."

Out of the corner of his eye, Sam could see Paul grinning at him. "My apologies, young lady, the lovely woman who has stolen the heart of my best friend."

"C'mon Sam, you're making me blush."

Sam laughed. "I wanted you to know, Katalin, that the present I brought in was entirely Paul's idea. I was only asked to help acquire it for you and I felt privileged to do so. I think you'll find it to be very special and you should open it last."

"I shall, Sam. Whatever it is I know I shall treasure it, and thank you."

"One more thing, Katalin. I wasn't sure exactly how to bring this up but I read in the *Daily Eagle* the story of your parents and of their remarkable courage. A committee is being formed in Israel that wishes one day to pay homage to those righteous gentiles who risked—and often times lost—their lives defending the Jewish people. I would like to make your parents known to them. Perhaps when we meet again we can talk about it."

Katalin was deeply moved. Choked up, she replied, "Sam, I can think of no greater Christmas present than what you've just given me.

I hope we get to see you a lot more."

"Well, with an invitation like that I won't refuse. After all, 'Think where man's glory most begins and ends, and say my glory was I had such friends.'"

Katalin strained her mind trying to come up with the name of the poet. "I'm afraid I don't know that one, Sam."

Sam smiled triumphantly and turned to shake hands with Paul who was once again biting into an apple. "See you after the holidays, friend."

"For sure, Sam. Oh, and Sam . . ."

"Yeah?"

"Yeats! 'The Municipal Gallery Revisited.' That's the writer and poem you just quoted from. Katalin, I'm going to fix me another corned beef sandwich, do you mind?"

Katalin was almost too startled to respond. "Why no, uh-uh, help yourself."

Paul left for the kitchen while Katalin and Sam stared blankly at each other, scratching their heads. Both wondering simultaneously, "How in the world did Paul know that?"

Chapter 23

The following day a blizzard covered the city, snarling traffic and leaving the subway as the only means of transportation. To Katalin, the several inches of snow deposited on the sidewalks and streets only added to the uniqueness and wonder of the Christmas season. It was the season of celebration of her Savior's birth, a time of wonder and expectant joy, a time when people paused—if only briefly—to reflect on the miracle of life itself and the one Individual who raised humanity to a higher level and made the beggar as important as the king. It was the season in which people—regardless of circumstance—dared to hope.

Every time Katalin passed a Salvation Army bellringer, she felt compelled to give. Earlier in the month, when shopping with Sarah, Sarah had to restrain her from depositing any more money in the kettles.

"Well Sarah, the poor need the money worse than we do," she insisted, to which Sarah responded, "If I spend another day walking the city with you, *we* will be the poor. A day should go by when you don't feel like you have to feed and clothe the world. Ten times already today I've put money in these kettles because of you. And mind you, not one bell-ringer has wished me Happy Hanukkah."

"Well, that's because they don't know you're Jewish."

"God forbid they should know I'm Jewish, giving to Christians."

"That's because you're a warm-hearted person, Sarah."

"No, it's because whenever I'm with you, you make me *farblondjet* [mixed up]."

During the season's wintry nights an extravagance of flashing neon lights competed with each other to lure holiday shoppers inside merchants' stores. Numerous radios and record players hooked up to outside speakers spilled forth the mellow voices of Bing Crosby, Nat King Cole and others to put people in a cheery Christmas buying mood.

Everyone's white Christmas had already come true. Sales of "warm woolen mittens" were on the increase and it wasn't a stretch of the imagination to envision "roasting chestnuts by an open fire" or riding in one of Central Park's "one-horse open sleighs."

Most surprising to Katalin were this year's number of Santas, either inside stores, standing in front of stores or on the many street corners by bell-ringer's kettles. With the boom economy of 1949, Christmas was being marshalled and merchandised as never before and the rotund, red and white costumed General Santa was every merchant's field commander.

However, the jolly saint had caused Katalin some apprehension. She wondered how many children, upon discovering their Christmas icon was less fact than fiction, would apply logic and some skepticism to whether Jesus Christ was also a figment of man's imagination. At the same time, Katalin had a sense of her own hypocrisy. The spirit of what Santa Claus represented, the squeals of joyous laughter coming from the mouths of children when seeing or talking to Santa had brightened her spirits as well.

Saturday, Christmas Eve day, Paul called Katalin to make certain she was still coming to the six o'clock service. Several choir members had already called the church, saying they had miserable colds and would be unable to sing. Having felt guilty for not participating in the Christmas pageant, Katalin was only too happy to substitute in the choir.

She agreed to meet Paul at four-thirty at the last subway stop closest to church. From there they would trudge together through snow the five blocks to church. Paul joked that he would bring with him an extra pair of skis. After the singing of carols, a brief sermon by Pastor Frey and communion led by Paul, they would again brave the elements to get to Ira and Sarah's apartment at a decent hour for leftover turkey and freshly baked cherry pie.

The singing of Christmas carols was moving and inspiring. Half the evening service was dedicated to celebrating through song the King of Glory and His uniquely humble entrance into the world. Katalin's spirit came alive. The last carol, "Silent Night," evoked strong memories as she remembered singing it as a duet with her mother at a long-ago church service.

Now, at the song's inception, all the lights were turned off and the first person in each pew was given a lit candle. That person then proceeded to light the candle of the next person and so on down the aisle.

A deep sense of reverence and holiness permeated the congregation. Both Paul and Katalin felt the overwhelming presence of the Holy Spirit in a way they never experienced in the church before.

Pastor Frey's short message was a gentle reminder that the Christ Child worshipped at Christmas didn't come into the world to remain a child. He grew into a man unlike any the world has ever seen. He was crucified, buried and resurrected and now ruled over heaven and earth . . . but not as a babe in the manger.

Katalin was impressed by the gentle and fatherly manner in which Pastor Frey spoke to the congregation. He cautioned the worshippers not to think of Jesus as a form of holy Santa Claus, reminding them that Jesus didn't come to give *presents*, but rather to give His *presence*.

In his black robe, Paul led the communion service and Katalin's heart nearly burst with pride. Nothing so impressed her as a man who wasn't afraid to be tender, yet fought the spiritual battle with the heart of a lion. In the relatively short time she had gotten to know Paul and fall in love with him, she knew he was that type of man.

Back at Ira and Sarah's apartment, the second annual Christmas Eve Scrabble War began. Ira and Katalin faced each other across a folding Samsonite table, sandwiches and Cokes by their sides. A half-hour time limit was in force. If the game wasn't over at precisely eight thirty-eight, whoever was ahead would be declared the winner.

Meanwhile, Paul and Sarah sat on a nearby sofa discussing Ira's pending surgery in mid-January. Sarah had her hand on Joshua-Caleb's bassinet and was gently rocking it. Her infant was gurgling loudly, while noisily shaking a new rattle given to him by Paul and Katalin.

The pair also brought other gifts to celebrate the occasion and their close friendship with the Katz's. Ira was given three paperback western novels written by his favorite author, Zane Grey. Sarah received a pair of patent leather gloves, along with an Expert Dell Crossword Puzzle book and a box of chocolates; David-Jacob, twenty-five penny bubble gum cards and a new Brooklyn Dodger baseball cap.

The Scrabble contest moved along at a steady pace, and Paul and Sarah periodically rose from the sofa to check on the score. With only ten minutes left, a pajama-clad David-Jacob, busily working a large wad of bubble gum in his mouth, came out of his room and stood next to his father. "Are you winning, Daddy?"

Ira placed his hand gently on his son's shoulder and took a deep sigh. "Afraid not, Tiger. In fact, your Aunt Katalin is making Hungarian goulash out of me. She hasn't won yet, but I am down some fifty-one points with very few tiles left."

Katalin smiled at her surrogate nephew. Then, noticing a sly, devilish grin creep up his face as he edged towards her side of the table, she immediately suspected he was about to try and divert her attention from the game.

"Hi, Aunt Katalin."

"Hi David-'shmakob'! How many pieces of bubble gum do you have in your mouth?"

"Four, no five! I can probably chew eight or nine at a time if I want to."

"I'm sure you could, but I don't know if your teeth would be very happy."

"Nor his mom!" Sarah called from the couch, adding, "DeeJay, leave Katalin and your dad alone. They're playing a very important game."

"I know, and Dad is losing."

"Well honey, he can manage to do that all by himself and without your help. When they're through, we're all going to have some cherry pie. So let them finish."

"I will in a minute, Mom, but I need to ask Aunt Katalin a question first."

"Okay, and then stop bothering her."

Katalin placed another group of tiles on the board for Ira to add up, then she turned her attention to her little friend. "Do you want to ask me a question, sweetheart?"

"Uh-huh, do you and Pastor Paul smooch a lot?"

"Why do you ask that?"

"Because, I just want to know."

"DeeJay, Pastor Paul is an excellent smoocher and he has cute dimples, just like you. In fact, why don't you come closer. I haven't had a smooch from my David-Jacob in a long time."

"Yuk, No! Oops! My gum!" A large chaw of bubble gum spewed from his mouth onto the game board, sticking to a couple of tiles. David-Jacob hastily grabbed back the wad of gum, plucking from it the wooden tiles and shoving the sticky substance back in his mouth.

Ira mildly admonished him and sent him to the kitchen for a wet rag. When he returned with the rag and gave it to Katalin to wipe the Scrabble board, he spoke again. "Aunt Katalin, since you and Pastor Paul like smooching so much, does that mean that the two of you are getting married?"

An uneasy Katalin nervously looked in Paul's direction. He had a bemused look and his face appeared redder than normal.

"Well?" David-Jacob persisted.

Katalin chose her words carefully. "DeeJay, we both plan on getting married someday."

Sarah attempted to lessen Paul and Katalin's discomfort by telling her son to come with her to check on the cherry pie in the oven. She walked past him on the way to the kitchen but he didn't immediately follow her. Instead, he walked over to Paul and tugged on his sleeve. "Pastor Paul, are you going to marry Aunt Katalin?"

"Um-m-m, we . . . ah . . . we haven't discussed anything, but we'll be sure and let you know . . . if and when we do . . . decide to discuss . . . if we do . . ." He rolled his eyes at Katalin. "I feel about as awkward as a blind bear in a bramble patch. Help me, Katalin."

Before Sarah could quiet her son or Katalin could sneak up behind him, David-Jacob verbally heaped on the molasses to an already uncomfortable subject matter.

"You hafta marry her, Pastor Paul, 'cause you know why?"

"No, I don't. Why?"

"'Cause if you don't, she's gonna become one of those 'spinister' ladies that never marries and she won't be able to have babies." Without giving the stunned and embarrassed Katalin a chance to speak, David-Jacob continued.

"See Pastor Paul, Katalin said she doesn't care if nobody marries her 'cause she's going to buy herself some squirrels and put 'em in cages and stuff and also rabbit houses. She's going to live in the woods by herself with a stupid lamb and when she's an old lady she's going to buy a little orphan girl and pretend she's hers. But if you marry her, then maybe she won't hafta do all that stuff and both of you can maybe have boy babies instead of dumb ol' girls." Katalin was aghast!

"David-Jacob Katz! I am shocked that you would believe a silly poem that I recited to you months ago. In fact, you know that none of what you've just told Pastor Paul is true about me, don't you!"

David-Jacob put his hand over his mouth and began giggling. Katalin glared at him. "Why you little rascal you! Come here! I'm going to get even with you and kiss you a thousand times all over your face you little stinker!"

Katalin lunged at David-Jacob and was able to grab an arm before he broke free and, while hysterically laughing, he made a beeline towards his dad. The last half-minute, Ira had ignored the goings on, deeply engrossed in trying to find placement on the Scrabble board for his seven letter word and fifty bonus points.

Just as he found it, his face lighting up, his son tripped and went zooming across the top of the flimsy card table. The table collapsed, scattering the wooden tiles in a dozen different directions. Ira felt ridiculous, seated in his chair with no table in front, holding aloft a rack of tile squares with no Scrabble board to place them on.

As David-Jacob jumped back to his feet unhurt, his mother—eyes towards heaven—muttered to herself, "God of Abraham, Isaac and Jacob. I know there is a special reason why you blessed me with this child, but for the life of me, right now I can't remember what that reason was."

Seeing David-Jacob looking so downcast and pathetic, no one had the heart to lecture or upbraid him. He then obeyed his mother's instructions to leave the room and wait in the kitchen for cherry pie.

Paul noticed Ira with his eyes glazed, staring into space and still holding the tile rack. "Ira, what are you doing? You look like you've just lost your best friend."

"Worse Paul, look at these letters." Everyone crowded around Ira and peeked at the seven small square tiles sequenced to each other on the rack. The letters spelled the word "s-a-m-e-k-h-s", causing eyebrows to be raised.

"Ira, that's not a word," Katalin insisted. "And not only that, I was almost sixty points ahead. Face it, you lost."

Ira was adamant. "Uh-uh!, *samekhs* is the plural form of the fifteenth letter of the Hebrew alphabet. I was about to place it on the board, on a double word score no less, and it was going to be worth ninety-two points. Katalin, you were seconds away from ignominious defeat."

Once the Scrabble tiles were picked up from the floor, the ravenous appetites of the four adults and one soon to be seven-year-old made quick work of the hot cherry pie. A more sedate David-Jacob then gave apologetic hugs to everyone and proceeded to bed. Since Pastor Frey's visiting brother-in-law was preaching the Christmas sermon the next morning, Paul and Katalin were able to relax, conversing with Ira and Sarah until the late evening hours.

During their conversation, Sarah said that the doctors were optimistic about the re-suturing of Ira's colon on January 15th. The family then hoped to move to Arizona by mid-March. They desperately wanted to get David-Jacob started in school, making friends, and get the store going as soon as possible.

"Why do you want to live in a state notorious for its killer summer heat?" Paul asked Ira.

Ira related how that, since a boy, he had loved the old West. He was fascinated by its lore, its heritage and the mystique surrounding its old ghost towns. Arizona had its wilderness areas, its distinct rugged mountains and wild animals that were still roaming the desert. To him, it was a section of the country where one could find solitude, where the blaring of car horns was replaced by the wailing of coyotes.

Listening to Ira, Sarah realized she never truly understood her husband's long-seated passion for wanting to move to Arizona. She thought it was his one-time war buddy, already living there, who had first stirred his interest. Until recently, Ira wasn't always that forthright but, before her very eyes, his personality was transforming. She loved the old Ira, but the new and improved version was even more exciting.

Then Paul shared his vision of the future. He also desired to move west, but to California. In five years he wanted to pioneer his own church in San Diego. He shared how when he was in California going through his UDT training, he fell in love with the port city. He loved its weather, its scenery and its many pristine beaches. One of his sisters was also planning to move there.

Upon hearing that San Diego was only a seven to eight hour drive to Phoenix, Katalin and Sarah's ears perked up. Both were on the same wave length, " . . . marry this guy and we might still end up spending our vacations together!" The night of conversation, companionship and shared expectations ended at one o'clock in the morning. During the entire evening, not one word had been mentioned concerning Ira's conversion to Christianity. It was still too sensitive a subject. However, everyone was aware that he was pouring over the Bible daily and memorizing scripture verses. He had also nearly finished a book on apologetics Paul had given him two weeks ago, Frank Morison's, "Who Moved the Stone?"

When saying their goodbyes, Ira offered his gratitude to Paul and Katalin for helping him find a peace he had never known before. He wished them the merriest of Christmases and then, with a catch in his voice, he expressed how he valued their friendships. He concluded by telling Katalin she was doomed to lose to him the next time at Scrabble.

Christmas morning was one of those mornings when Paul and Katalin wished they could stay in church and sing praises to God forever. After the service was over, they stood on the snow-swept landing outside the narthex, exchanging handshakes and hugs with everyone they knew. The weather was biting cold and every time they spoke, vapors of fog whisked through the air. Still, Paul and Katalin felt gloriously alive, their faces radiating the light of love they felt for each other. Those who knew them well grabbed Katalin's hand, inspecting it for an engagement ring that wasn't there. Though it caused the two embarrassment, they were both delighted that people in the church appeared to approve of their relationship.

Afterwards, Paul momentarily left to change clothes at his cottage a block away from the church, before they headed to Katalin's apartment where Katalin prepared hot cocoa and toast to tide them over until they were through opening Christmas presents.

She changed into levis, sweatshirt and sneakers, and soon they were sitting cross-legged in front of the tree, separating their individual presents. Paul had gifts from family and friends from South Dakota, three from Katalin and a couple from Ira and Sarah. Others were from Pastor Frey and church parishioners.

Katalin's presents were mostly from Paul and the members of the Katz family, including David-Jacob and Marvin and Ruth. She also received presents from her two friends at church and a teenage neighbor girl she had recently befriended. The Rosens also sent a present.

She and Paul thought it unusual that most of her Christmas presents were given her by Jewish people. In fact, the most intriguing and unexpected gift given her was by a Jewish person she had only first met two days before, Sam Bender. Although Paul's best friend indicated that the present he brought her was primarily Paul's idea, Katalin was impressed that he, a stranger, participated in its giving. It made the mysterious gift that much more special. She decided to heed Sam's request and open it last.

Some two hours later, after unwrapping and exulting over each gift, interrupted by occasional paper and ribbon tossing, eating ham on rye sandwiches and shoving down chocolates from the box of Whitman Samplers David-Jacob had sent, Paul drew his and Sam's present from underneath the tree and placed it in front of Katalin.

Katalin leaned over and gave Paul a kiss on the cheek. "Whatever it is, Paul, I know I'm going to love it. In the last couple days I must have picked it up and shaken it a dozen times trying to figure out what it is."

"What do you think it is?"

"Well, it's heavy. Feels like it might be books of some kind."

Paul's voice grew serious as he said, "I hope in some way the present you're about to open will let you know just how much I think about you."

Katalin smiled. "Oh dear, now I'm getting nervous."

Paul and Katalin moved to the sofa with the remaining gift, and Paul anxiously waited for Katalin to remove the wrappings. He mentally prepared himself for what it would mean to her emotionally.

Once the wrapping was removed and the inside box exposed, Katalin carefully opened the box lid. Immediately she was taken aback as she saw the musical jewelry box inside. The longer she looked at it, the more mesmerized by it she became. The smoothly lacquered box was crafted in various shades of mahogany wood with a raised section of inlaid enamel centered on top. Displayed on the enamel in an effusive panoply of colors was a carnival scene depicting two young folk dancers in the Hungarian national costume of red, white and green. The picturesque background contained a merry-go-round and a calliope with smiling children holding aloft various colored balloons.

Tears welled up in Katalin's eyes and fell freely down her cheeks as she lifted the lid of the ornately designed jewelry box and the cylinder began playing "The Beautiful Blue Danube Waltz". The familiar and melancholy music stirred memories of a once happy time so very long ago.

Holding the gift in her lap, she turned to Paul with a look of astonishment. "How could you possibly know—or Sam for that matter—to conspire to buy this for me? I never once mentioned it in conversation. This is more than mere coincidence. It has to be!"

"What do you mean?"

"Paul, when I was a little girl living in Debrecen, Hungary, my Aunt Julia and Uncle Jozsef—my father's brother who lived near us—owned an exact replica of this jewelry box. They received it as a wedding gift from my parents in 1923. Whenever we went to their farm, they allowed my little brother Stephen and me to listen to it. It was painful hearing it after Stephen died. How in the world could you and Sam . . . no, I take it all back, you couldn't have known. But I'm still amazed."

Katalin suddenly felt lightheaded. "Oh dear, I think I'm feeling faint. Can you take the music box from me so I don't drop it."

Paul gently took the box from Katalin's lap and placed it between them on the sofa. "Are you okay, Katalin? Can I get you some water?"

"I'll be fine. I just need a minute to catch my breath."

Katalin breathed in and out several times as Paul handed her a handkerchief. She gratefully accepted it and began dabbing her eyes. Regaining her composure she again turned towards Paul who was looking at her with love in his eyes. This time Katalin was more insistent. " Paul, I demand to know how the two of you came to buy this for me, you in particular. Obviously Sam's right, this had to be your idea. Sarah couldn't have told you about it because I don't remember ever mentioning it to her. Please tell me."

"You need to open the music box again, Katalin. There's an envelope inside."

"There is?" Surprised, Katalin opened the music box a second time, again eliciting the haunting notes of the waltz. Her eyes opened wide with surprise as she withdrew a long brown envelope and she gasped as she saw the strange scribbling on the envelope in a foreign language—a language she was distinctly familiar with. Written across the envelope, in the Finno-Ugric language of the Hungarian people, were the words, "Katalin! Our precious doll child! Praise be to God!" Katalin shrieked and her hands trembled.

Paul, having already seen the envelope, was nonetheless curious about the writing. "What does it say, Katalin?"

"Our precious doll child! Praise be to God!" Katalin's lips quivered. "'Doll Child' is the pet name that only my aunt and uncle called me when I was a little girl. Paul! This is *their* music box, isn't it? And they're still alive?"

Paul nodded with a smile. "Very much so."

"But how!? Where . . . what . . .?"

"I'll tell you, but first let me say that Sam was being very modest. He had everything to do with getting the letter and music box. Trying to locate your relatives in Hungary was my idea but he took it and ran with it. He's the one who made the contacts."

"Why?"

"He's my best friend. That makes you also a best friend. And Sam is a Jew, who knows the heartbreak of losing family members. He said it was something he wanted to do to help restore some sanity in the world. Some of our friends in the UDT are now in Naval Intelligence and the CIA. I can't elaborate but Sam had a couple of favors coming. The United States has operatives everywhere in the world, including communist Hungary. That's all I can tell you. In fact, that's all Sam would tell me."

"Then I promise, that's all I'll ever ask." Katalin held the envelope in front of her and nervously fingered it, struggling to hold back her tears. Carefully ripping open the envelope she drew out a letter.

A small flat item, wrapped in newspaper, fell out of the envelope. Paul picked it up from the floor and held it in his hand while Katalin unfolded the letter. Looking at the paper, Paul said, almost apologetically, "Uh-oh, I forgot that the letter would be written in Hungarian."

Katalin reassuringly patted him on the knee, her hands shaking in anticipation. "It's okay, Paul, I believe I remember enough to still translate it."

"Our Dearest Katalin,"she began to read in a trembling voice." As I write this letter, it is two-thirty in the morning. Only a half hour ago we were all sleeping and someone knocked on the door of our farmhouse. We felt great fear, thinking it was the AVO and we had done something wrong. ['AVO is 'Allam-Vedelmi-Hatosag, the State Security,' Katalin explained to Paul.] "A strange man, who is now in the house with us, was at the door. He asks if this is the residence of Ferenc and Julia Zichy. Ferenc says, 'Yes, what have we done?' The man then says, 'It is nothing you have done. I only have good news to bring you.' He does not give his name, but we invite him in anyway. Since the AVO confiscated our farm three years ago, only allowing us to work it for bare subsistence, we will risk anything these days for good news. So we all sit around the table and the stranger takes out a picture and hands it to us. He then asks, 'Do you know this young lady?'"

Katalin looked questioningly at Paul, who explained, "I gave Sam a picture of you that was taken at the church picnic."

"Oh," Katalin nodded, and then continued:

"I look and I look, then I give to Ferenc and we look at each other thinking the beautiful happy lady in the picture reminds us of our precious little niece who the Nazis killed thirteen years ago. I tell this to the stranger with no name. He then asks, 'Your niece, her name was Katalin? Or should I say, is Katalin?' and he smiles big. And then we know, it is you! And we scream your name so loud that I fear everyone who lives nearby will hear us.

"I ask the stranger how it is possible that you are still alive? He only knows that you now live in a place called Brooklyn in New York and that you go to school there and are even now a writer.

"Now as I write this letter I pray that I might do so through my many tears. I am told by the stranger that I have but little time to finish, so I will tell you quickly of the family. Ferenc and I are in reasonable health now that we are grandparents in our mid-50s. Your cousin Gusti is married now with two children, a boy and girl—Andris 4 and Andrea 2, living in Budapest. Our other son, your cousin Zoltan, lives nearby. He too is married and helps us work the farm. They have two girls, Anna 2 and Kati 4 months. Your grandfather Lajos, who loved to rock you on his knee, went to live with Jesus six years ago. Grandmother Alona is in weakened health due to a stroke. She is invalid, but lives with us and is happy. When she wakes, we will tell her of the good news.

"Katalin, dear precious child of God! How we mourned when we heard thirteen years ago of your family being killed. But we knew nothing of what happened. Only we were told that the Nazis came to your father's church and burned it to the ground, and that shots were heard before the fire. We pray even now that your parents didn't suffer greatly. They were very brave people and I believe the Nazis feared them. Always the devil is afraid of those who do not fear him. We assumed the worst about you—that you were captured and taken to the camps or else shot.

"How is it you escaped? They say you too were inside the church when the Nazis came. The stranger who wishes me now to hurry with this letter also now tells me that it might take a while but they (whoever is they) will try to get a letter back to us. I will insist to the stranger that he take with him the music box that you so loved as a child. It is important that you have something of your parents to remember them. Their gift to us is now our gift to you.

"Also, I send pictures . . ."

Katalin gasped, "Pictures! Where! I didn't . . ."

"I think I've got them, Katalin. They fell out of the envelope when you took out the letter." Katalin's body trembled as she struggled to finish the letter.

". . . I am sorry dear child that I only send two pictures, but we only have three of your family. One, however, I send is of your family together and has also your beautiful little brother before Jesus took him home much too soon for all of us who grieved.

"Katalin, I cannot believe I am writing to you! Dear one! Write us soon a long letter and tell us all that has happened to you. Though many miles separate us and we cannot see to touch and embrace you, we embrace you forever in our hearts.

"May God's mercy always be with you, our much beloved Katalin."

"Your Aunt Julia"

Katalin turned to look at Paul, her eyes swimming in tears. He gave her shoulder a tight squeeze and smiled. "The letter even brought tears to my eyes, Katalin. I don't know how you made it through. Are you okay?"

"Barely . . ."

Paul then handed her the photographs and Katalin cautiously removed the newspaper wrapping. The first picture was of a youthful and happy couple. "This is my parents on their wedding day," Katalin spoke brokenly. Then the tears fell even more as she looked at the second picture. "And this was taken around 1930 when I was about seven and my little brother Stephen was five. Later that year he would die of pneumonia.

Paul took the picture. The two children were standing in front of their parents who had a hand resting freely on each of their shoulders. Katalin's father was looking very relaxed; her mother had one arm around her husband's waist and was happily smiling.

"I remember my mother as always having a praise song on her lips," Katalin told Paul. "She loved people immensely and even when working hard, she assisted my father in church. No hardship was too much for her to endure. In her presence there was always peace."

Only now did Katalin realize how much of a source of strength her mother really was to the family. She so missed their intimate talks together. Her little brother she remembered as her special little playmate. *How wonderful if he were still alive*, she thought. *Right now we could be sharing childhood memories together.*

Katalin pressed the photographs to her heart and closed her eyes as tears rolled down her cheeks. Then she handed them to Paul. "Your father was very distinguished looking," he told her. "And seeing your mother, it's obvious where you got your beauty. I can also tell from the picture—and your smiles—that you and your little brother were two very happy children."

"We were extremely happy children." Katalin took the pictures back from Paul and placed them in the music box.

"You know, Katalin, I wasn't counting on the music box. I hope the memory of it and the music doesn't make you always sad."

Katalin turned to face Paul, lovingly running the back of her fingers down his face. "Paul, you know as I do that there can't be healing until first there is mourning. Even seeing the photographs, remembering again what my family looked like, realizing how much I miss them, I can't think of a greater Christmas present. Sure, the music box makes me sad, but I'll get over it. The letter, the music box, the photographs, all remind me of a time that can never be recovered. But they also remind me that I had those times. Don't you see?"

"I think so."

"Paul, in Hungary there are many gypsy musicians. It is said that the most skilled gypsy musicians can make a person remember their fondest memories. In time, the music box will become my skilled gypsy musician. And I have you and Sam to thank for it."

"I had to find some way to prove my love to you," Paul said gently. "That's what I explained to Sam. Probably, with few exceptions, every man you've ever met has told you he's loved you. I didn't want to be just any man, Katalin. I care about the real you! Not just the pretty outside, but the suffering, weeping girl inside.

"How you've made it this far in life without completely falling apart, I'll never know. Katalin, just losing my brother was traumatic for me. You had lost everyone close to you and still you kept going, giving part of yourself to everyone you met along the way. It's time the world gave something back to you.

"I've been afraid to tell you how much I love you, but no longer. I've loved you from the very beginning, from the first time I met you in Pastor Frey's office when you came in to interview me, and I knew it for certain after the church picnic. But I believe love involves doing and showing, not just saying."

"I love you too, Paul! With all my heart! And I've wanted so long to tell you that!" Katalin threw her arms around Paul's neck and they clung to each other in a deep embrace.

Finally she broke away. "I think we had better go outside and build a snowman."

Paul took a deep breath. "Reluctantly, I have to agree. But before we build the world's finest looking snowman, I promised my parents I would call them today. My sisters are also at the house. If I can use your phone, I'll pay you back."

Katalin turned around to face him. "Sure . . ."

"I also promised them that they would get to talk to you."

"Oh Paul, I don't know them. I'd be much too scared."

"There's no reason to be scared, Katalin. Through my letters, they've already come to know you and love you as I do. Also," he added, "tonight Pastor Frey and his family would like us to come for Christmas dinner. I didn't commit us. I told them I would ask you."

"I suppose, sure, if that's what you want to do. I'd enjoy having dinner with them."

"Katalin, if nothing else, you just need to know how much you're loved. No one can ever replace your family but you mean a lot to an awful lot of people. And right now you're the most important person in my life."

Katalin was moved by Paul's words. "Thank you, Paul. I wonder if your brother Thomas and my family have met yet in heaven?"

"Well, heaven is a big place, but it's entirely possible."

"I think they have. And I think they're all hoping we make your phone call home, and build our snowman before I start planting kisses all over your face."

"In that case," Paul laughed, "someone should tell them to mind their own business.

The next day Katalin worked at constructing a letter to send to her Aunt Julia in Hungary. Her primary problem was where to start and where to end. She must be careful what she wrote, however, in case it fell into the wrong hands. After completing a dozen pages, she felt her story was only half told. She had earlier decided against sending her own byline newspaper article, thinking it too impersonal and self-serving. Paul assured her that Sam would manage to get the letter translated into Hungarian before her aunt received it.

Chapter 24

A week later Paul made a date with Katalin for dinner at Sandor's, a Hungarian restaurant that Katalin favored. He picked her up at five and drove to the church. "The dinner reservations are at 6:30," he told her, "but I have some important business at the church first."

Katalin was surprised when they reached the church; there were no cars in the parking lot. What was Paul's important business, she wondered. But inside, she could hear no voices and the sanctuary was dark and empty.

"Paul, what's going on? Why are all the lights off?"

"Come on in and I'll tell you," Paul said mysteriously.

Mystified Katalin followed him into the church, where he switched on the sanctuary lights and proceeded to the front. Paul stepped up to the platform, took some matches from the pulpit and lit the candles of the two standing candelabras. Katalin curiously stood watching him.

"They're gorgeous, Paul. The candles really light up the sanctuary."

"Yes they do, don't they," Paul agreed. "I love the church! Although I know the church refers to God's people, one still can't help but feel that even the building is blessed."

Paul stepped down to Katalin's side and took her hand. "Would you come up on the platform with me, Katalin?'

When she looked quizzical, he grinned somewhat self-consciously, "Humor me, Katalin?"

"Okay," she said and allowed him to lead her to a place before the lighted candles. Then Paul knelt down before her and spoke softly but clearly, "Katalin Zichy, I love you with all my heart and want to spend the rest of my life with you, taking care of you and doing my best to make you happy. Will you marry me, Katalin?"

For a moment Katalin was speechless, then she said breathlessly, "Yes! Yes, you know I will, Paul."

Standing to his feet, Paul reached into his jacket pocket and took out a blue velvet case and pressed it into her hands. "As a token of my love I want to give you this."

In dazed wonder, she opened the case and viewing the diamond solitaire engagement ring, Katalin's face flooded with tears. She shakily managed to slip the ring on her finger and looked at Paul. "It's so beautiful! I don't deserve it and I don't deserve you!"

"You're wrong, Katalin. You deserve so much more!" Paul wrapped Katalin in his arms and when tears continued to run down her face, he took a handkerchief from his pocket and gently swabbed them away. They held tightly to each other, neither saying a word or needing to.

Finally Katalin drew away. "This is the most beautiful moment of my life. How did you ever come up with the idea of proposing in church?".

"Marriage is a sacred thing in God's eyes," Paul said softly. "I want ours to always be a sacred union."

The two of them blew out the candles and started down the aisle, with Paul's arm about her waist. Suddenly Katalin giggled.

"Paul?"

"What, Katalin?"

"I hope I'm not being unromantic, but I'm hungry!"

"Well, let's go meet everybody!"

Katalin stepped back from Paul's arms. "Everybody?"

"Katalin, everyone we know, knew I was proposing to you tonight."

"Huh?"

"Well, Ira and Sarah have known about it for a couple days. Then Sarah suggested that they meet us afterwards and we could all celebrate together. I didn't know how to say no to her and she was so convinced that you would accept my proposal of marriage that she was really an encouragement to me. Anyway, she called me this morning and confirmed the reservations. She also said she had told Marvin and Ruth, and then Marvin being Marvin decided to invite himself and Ruth to the celebration.

"Last, but not least, with all the other important people in our lives wanting to be part of this, I thought it only proper that I invite Sam Bender. He may or may not be bringing a friend. So we're going to be having dinner tonight with half of Brooklyn. I hope you don't mind."

"I don't. I'm glad they're all going to be there. But—Paul, what if I hadn't been ready yet to get married? What would you have done?"

"I had a one way ticket on an ocean liner leaving tonight for Madagascar."

Katalin laughed. "I'd have come after you. I hope one day our children are as funny as you. And speaking of children. . . You do want children, don't you?"

Chapter 25

Marvin and Ruth called earlier and said they wanted to treat at Gage
& Tollners. They would celebrate Marvin's transfer of money into an
Arizona bank whereupon they would all get rich after Ira purchasing real
estate in America's baby state. Besides, Marvin declared, 'my younger
brother has lost so much weight since the shooting he could now play
the scarecrow in the Wizard of Oz', suggesting that it was time to start
fattening his younger brother up again.

The Rosen's had arrived at the apartment to watch over DeeJay
and Joshua-Caleb. Ira walked into the living room where Sarah looked
admiringly at her husband who was slapping at his face, dabbing on
the very popular and newest of men's fragrance, English Leather. The
two of them kissed their children goodbye. Turning and smiling to the
Rosens, they whispered them thanks and good luck. A minute later they
were anxiously waiting outside at the sidewalk's edge for Marvin to pick
them up. An afternoon conversation with a stranger then popped into
Ira's mind.

"Sarah, did I tell you I got a phone call from an older gentleman
today? Paul had told him to call me, since he also was a Hebrew-
Christian"

Sarah noticing a nick on Ira's chin, licked her index finger and
lightly touched the area. "No, you need to be more careful when you
shave. So, tell me. But first, how do I look?"

"Like you always do...beautiful as ever. Why do I have to keep
telling you that?"

"Because Ira...when men stop telling their wife that, maybe at
least the wife still knows the husband is paying attention. Women
aren't always as confident as men. So what did this person and you talk
about?"

"He told me I am not the only Jewish person in town who believes
in Jesus. Remember my telling you the other day that I thought I might
be. Oh another thing, he said to try and use Jesus's Hebrew name,
Yeshua, when talking to other Jewish people about how I believe.

Yeshua is less offensive to Jewish non-believers, he said. Reason being, and I kind of agree, because we all know how many of our people have been persecuted in the name of Jesus, or Christ, like when others have called us Christ killers.

"He also told me that he is part of a small group of maybe seven people, two of them women, who are also Jewish Believers and who meet once a month at someone's home. They someday hope, when their group gets a little larger, to have an actual building where people like themselves, who are not always comfortable in a church setting, can meet. It will be a place where they can also still observe some of the Jewish feasts and holidays, even though they believe in Yeshua, but where they can worship Yeshua in a more Jewish surrounding. It is a way of still maintaining their Jewish identity while worshipping their messiah. He would like us to come to the meeting. I told him we are moving to Arizona in another month and that you are not a Believer and he said, both of you come anyway, even for one meeting. He said we would enjoy the food and the hospitality. So, how would you feel about going?"

"What did you tell him Ira? Because I don't feel I would belong."

Ira rested his palms on Sarah's shoulders and stared her between the eyes, then as was often his custom, deftly lifted her chin with his index finger so she couldn't help but look directly into his eyes. 'I go nowhere without you. We are one flesh, you and me. So far you have been very supportive of my reading the bible but I need also, as Paul said, to be with other "like-minded" Believers. I have so many questions still and I want to learn. I will never try to convert you. You know I never have. By the way, the gentleman I talked to also said they never use the word converted, like I just did. To do so gives the impression one is abandoning his Jewish-ness for something else, when in fact, as Believers, one often feels even more Jewish by "returning" to the messiah one previously did not recognize. He calls it, or rather calls himself, being "Completed." This way people understand that those like us are always proud still to be Jewish. I like that way of explaining things."

Sarah smiled ...

"Ira...I am more fortunate than most Jewish people. I have seen up close the very worst of mankind but I have also been blessed as few others, to have known Christians, like Katalin, and certainly knowing, however briefly, a very brave young German corporal, who risked his very life for me and who undoubtedly was a Christian. I have also read of other wonderful Christian people who risked their lives for our people. So, if you desire that I attend the meeting with you, even though I have my reservations, then I will do so and without complaint. Besides, I like the change in you. I like seeing you be happy again, being passionate about God, and I appreciate that you have not tried to change my mind about how I believe. But all this change in you is still difficult for me to get used to. Of course, I will admit, not as difficult as I first thought."

"It might not be so unusual as you think that Jews can believe in Jes..I mean believe in Yeshua. This man told me that Felix Mendolssohn, the great composer, was a Hebrew-Christian. Queen Victoria's Prime Minister, Benjamin Disraeli was. He also said there were many great Jewish men of science and literature who were Jewish Believers. He said there is a man named Rachmiel Frydland, who also survived the holocaust, while losing most of his family, yet is now one of the more recognized leaders in the small but growing Hebrew-Christian community. He said, that this Frydland offered that while it is impossible to know the numbers today of Jews who do believe in Yeshua, but he estimates there may be as many as 35,000-40,000 in the world. I told him my prayer is that one day, before the Lord calls me home, there would be hundreds of thousands like us."

"You're dreaming, Ira. That will never happen. But...hope you should always have, so don't pay attention to me. Meanwhile, where are Marvin and Ruth? We have a 7:00 reservation."

"Okay...but one more thing."

"One more thing. I am afraid to ask already. One more thing... what?"

"I do need to tell Marvin.'

"Tell Marvin what!?"

"Tell him about how I believe...of course.."

"Ira...do you have a temperature!? Do you realize by your telling Marvin, how he would react!?"

"Yes, but it is not possible for me to keep secrets any longer and I sense the Lord telling me to do this. I don't want to keep this from Marvin and him find out later and be angry that I was keeping secrets from him still. He has already taken me to task for not telling him about our moving to Arizona or about what happened in the war. I just can't do that anymore."

"Ira, when you make your mind up about something I know how difficult it is to change it. But please! Think hard! This is a sensitive area for Jews and should you tell Marvin, be very, very cautious about *how* you tell him and *when* you tell him.

"Think about before and how you felt about Katalin and the trouble it caused you. I can deal with it because of the reasons I have told you. But I fear Marvin can get very emotional over telling him such things. So promise me! Be very careful!"

"I Promise."

Marvin's car squealed up to the curb. Soon, the four were headed to Gage & Tollners. Ira was seated in the back seat with Sarah for the fifteen minute ride. While the others were engaged in small talk, Ira allowed his mind to drift and center on all the other events going on in the world. Events that in the past he knew would have frustrated him, but no longer.

If the beginning of any New Year had brought with it the renewed hope and promise for peace and tranquility, how much more, Ira thought, the hope and promise of a new decade. Yet it was only the second month of the beginning of the 1950's and already there was a new problem confronting the world. Russia now had the bomb and like Germany before it, was desiring of flexing her muscles. It made Ira more convinced than ever that the Book of Ecclesiastes had it right. *"There is nothing new under the sun."* The old adage was true, 'The more things changed, the more they stayed the same.' Only, instead of Germany, now it was the Soviet Union.

Still, no matter how unstable or fragile the world was, he was learning to give his worries and concerns to God. Whereas before he felt he was always in battle, always contending against someone or something, if only in his own mind, he was now able to find a certain inner peace. It was reassuring to know that what happened in the world was largely God's battle and not his. He could only do as God instructed him.

Through his diligent reading of the New Testament he was confident that the only peace that could be found in this world could only come from within. Ira accepted that the world's struggle against constant chaos was not always what it appeared to be. It was only symptomatic of a greater struggle going on since Adam and was of a spiritual nature. Ira's favorite verse and one that he recently memorized was found in Philippians 4:6-7, "Do not be anxious about anything, but in everything, by prayer and petition, with thanksgiving, present your requests to God. And the *peace of God*, which transcends all understanding, will guard your hearts and your minds in Christ Jesus."

Ira knew it was true what certain historians wrote. "Peace was merely a time between wars." Understanding that elemental truth, Ira felt more obliged to invest himself in the scriptures, receiving from their reading a solace he had never quite known before.

Ira thought about those who had become conquerors and sought conquests, the Alexander's of the world, the flamboyant conqueror who in the end tasted glory for but a few short years only to die just a month before his 34th birthday and then only for all his spoils to be divided up four ways. There were others who had Alexander's insatiable desire for power and fame. Those who coveted and made images to themselves, having great monuments constructed in their likeness as if posterity would bestow upon them some sort of divinity. In similar manner, were the Pharaohs, who desired to be buried with certain artifacts they could take into the next world, there were those leaders who had convinced themselves that becoming peers of one or more of the false gods that they themselves worshipped, they too could become immortal in the next life.

But at a particular point in history, the world was rocked and turned upside-down, when appeared on the scene an itinerant Galilean preacher whose words were not those of a conqueror, nor of one seeking any images to himself but offering instead to teach humility by role-modeling His servant-hood to humanity. It appeared Jesus did everything the reverse of man. Where man boasted, He chose to be humble. Where man cried revenge, He said to turn the other cheek. Where man said to hate those who despise you, He said, love your enemies. 'Anyone,' He said, 'can love a friend.' Where man gloated over his own good fortune, Jesus reminded all, that in His kingdom, "the first shall be last and the last first." With words devoid of sanctimony, he deferred tribute, never attempting to draw attention to Himself. When people lauded Him, He was gracious and told them instead to pay homage to his Father who sent Him. He was Lord but he never lorded over anyone, he only handed out invitations. He flew under the radar, yet in so doing he destroyed conventional thinking to such a great extent He couldn't help but get noticed. There was never a man like Him nor would there ever be again. Napoleon stated that he tried in vain to find the similar to him. The irreligious, Albert Einstein admitted to being enthralled by him. And when Jesus took on the role of man, He subjected Himself to man's mortality and never asked of His creation anything He Himself was not willing to endure, even when it meant wrongful persecution and suffering the Cross. As one writer, Dorothy Sayers, put it, "He was born in poverty and died in disgrace and thought it all worth while."

Ira remembered a couple months earlier, when he was at the precipice of eternity and peering into the abyss in unutterable fear, realizing his life might soon end. He remembered how quickly his atheism faded. Crying out to the God he deserted, only to discover that God had never deserted him. Then, in somewhat strange and unusual circumstance, Yeshua had left Ira his calling card in the form of a cross on the floor and an ornate cross that somehow dangled in mid-air and encompassed all of his then fading vision.

Later, and just as astonishing, he was to discover that same ornate, descriptive cross on his bedside pillow, delivered in clandestine manner by the most unsuspecting person of all, his very own, very active in the Jewish community, very Jewish sister-in-law Ruth, who had quietly and cryptically been a Christian all along. It was all still so surreal. As a consequence, Ira finally came to the conclusion that he now had acquired an indebtedness. An indebtedness to share what the Lord had done for him regardless of circumstance and regardless of consequence. He had to share with others and the first on his list of people to share his testimony with was his brother. Ira concluded that if Marvin didn't hear it from him, he might never be willing to hear the message of salvation from anyone else. He might never be vulnerable enough to learn of the saving grace of their, not *'when the Messiah comes,'* Deliverer, but their *'already having been here,'* Jewish Messiah. Ira knew he had to be the one to tell Marvin because even his own wife, Ruth, was fearful of doing so. Somehow, tonight, if at all possible and over Sarah's objections and concerns, Ira would tell Marvin he had become a follower of Yeshua and in the hope that Marvin also would see the light. To not do so would always weigh on his conscience.

Half way through dinner Ruth smiled obliquely at Ira, "Ira, you seem preoccupied. You feel okay."

Ira cautiously returned her smile. "I feel great, Ruth. Thank you, and you, too Marvin for treating us. And Marvin, you are a really good brother to me in so many ways."

"Eh..since father passed away and mother lives in Key West playing Canasta all day, someone has to take care of you. That's in the Talmud of Marvin you know." Also, since I made the money transfer today for the land I wish you to buy. I want only that you always tell me exactly what is on your mind whether you think we are buying the right piece of land or not. No more secrets like before."

"I agree, no more secrets, and someday I would like to read 'Marvin's Talmud'. Your always being such an intelligent man, such a good Jew and one I know who God looks down upon favorably. It is also the reason why I need to share something with you."

"So why are you saying all these good things about me? I already said we are paying for the meal tonight." Ruth forced a laugh and looked over to Sarah who was gritting her teeth and staring into her dinner plate. It became obvious to both women what Ira was up to.

"So what is it you want to share?" Ira looked over at Ruth and immediately recognized her uneasiness, watching her lips silently forming the words, *no!...no!...no!* Suddenly Ira hesitated, wondering if indeed, he had picked the right time

"Nevermind, it is nothing of consequence and something we can talk about another day."

Marvin looked questioningly at his younger brother. "What!?...no never mind. You have something to say, then say it. This is what I was talking about. First you don't tell me about wanting to move to Arizona, or about your time in the war. We are brothers, no more secrets." Ira's mind still racing, he now felt trapped. He concluded he had no choice but to go forward with his original intention.

'When I was shot...er...when I was first gun-butted about the back of the head, I knew...knew that it might be all over for me. I told you I had also, since the war, become an atheist, remember?" Ira nervously bit his lip stalling for time, hoping something would happen so he would not have to continue. But nothing did as sweat formed on his brow. He had no idea it would be this difficult.

"Yes...nu! So get to it. What is it you are trying to tell me."

"No really Marvin...some other time I will talk about it with you." Ira looked over to see Ruth breathe a deep sigh of relief but her sigh would be only temporary.

"No...you will talk to me now about what you want to tell me. I just transferred one-hundred-thousand dollars to a bank in Arizona called Valley National, so when you and Sarah get there you can buy all the land you can for us north of some street called Camel's Road"

Ira corrected, "Camelback Road, that is where we might also put our store."

Marvin jumped back in. "Okay, Camelback Road. So I don't want ever there should be anything we can't talk about like before. Like also your previous problems with Katalin and again, what happened to you in Germany. I trust you and so you can trust me. So no more secrets! So whatever it is you want to tell me, tell me already!"

Ira felt cornered and could barely get the words out of his mouth.

"Marvin...I...um...had...um...when, I was attacked, I had a very, very powerful religious experience.' (Clearing his throat), "One that has made me view life differently.' There was dead silence. Then Marvin spoke.

"Good! Religious experiences are good and my brother the atheist needed one. So you are going to become more Orthodox and study Torah, more Talmud, Mishnah. Maybe even become a teacher one day. All that is good and it will be good for your children!"

"Well...Marvin...not exactly."

"What do you mean,'not exactly' you going to study the *Upanishads* and become a Hindu!? What do you mean, 'not exactly?'" The women were now staring straight across at each other, then both cast their eyes heavenward, as if the sky was about to fall.

"Well...Marvin...you might just wish that was what I was going to tell you. I mean, that I really was thinking of becoming Hindu, I mean...er...or Buddhist. Because the real truth is that I, not once, but twice, during my cry to God, received, visions of a Cross. So I have been studying, not the *Upanishads,* but the New Testament, even though I know the Talmud says for we Jews not to do that. But, um...I have been studying the gospels, in fact, with great zeal and...."

Marvin first pursed his lips, then spit a piece of steak out on his plate as his eyes grew wide and he leaned forward from the booth in which he was seated. Inching his face ever closer to Ira. His growing look of incredulity concerned Ira.

Ira rolled his tongue about his top dry lip, genuinely frightened and intimidated by his older brother's sudden change in countenance and wondering once again if he should continue, but knowing he had to conclude. In a halting and monotone voice "...and...I...have... known... a

...great peace since my experience...and...and recovery...and I wanted also that you should...should...know...you know...that"

Marvin waved his index finger menacingly, just inches from Ira's face and stopped him in mid-sentence.

"No!...My brother I don't know anything of the kind except that you hallucinated! Furthermore that you should have told someone, told the doctors or a psychiatrist, someone! Anyone! That you had these peculiar visions and they could have put them out of your insane mind immediately. Maybe even put you in Bellevue instead so that not one, but several head doctors could have examined you! Don't you agree!?"

"Marvin, I wasn't imagining. I'm being serious."

"So am I. Maybe you ate a poisoned mushroom before you got shot? Look, you want to become a Buddhist...a Hindu Swami or whatever they are called, you want to grow a tail even and become a donkey even, you can become a donkey. I don't care! A believer in Jesus though, you don't become. So forget about any crosses! Remember Norman Nussbaum...

this friend I had in high school. He thought it might even be fun to be a four legged creature for a day even if it meant being a donkey. So it is entirely possible Ira that you might think about wanting to become a donkey. And still Norman Nussbaum, he eventually became a lawyer, so, a donkey, a lawyer, what's the difference! (with each passing word, the pitch in Marvin's voice appeared to rise another decibel) But I also once had a vision! Did you know that Ira!?" Ira knew now and for a certainty, that his entire attempt at witnessing to his brother had been a complete disaster and at the very least, he had chosen the wrong time to witness to him. Now the problem was how to extricate himself from his brother's facetiousness and outright derision for what he previously was attempting to tell him.

"No..I ah..wasn't aware that you once had visions? What of?"

"You don't remember?"

"No..remember what Marvin?"

"Mermaids! Ira! Mermaids! " Marvin screamed! loud enough for everyone sitting close by to hear. An elderly man in the booth next to them suddenly rose half way up, straining and peering about the restaurant thinking someone had spotted mermaids.

"Mermaids!??" Ira's mouth was agape. Ruth and Sarah, embarrassed by Marvin's shouting, had perplexed looks?" What on earth!?

"When was this? What mermaids!? You had visions of mermaids!?... and Marvin, you don't have to yell. I'm not deaf."

"When we were at the Catskills, Ira! you don't remember, when I was a teenager and I fell into the lake and almost drowned and Mindy Parker had to give me mouth to mouth resuscitation. You remember Mindy Parker! (With his palms Marvin shaped the outline of an hourglass) Marilyn Monroe should have looked so good. All the time after that I had visions of Mindy Parker rescuing me and in my dreams and visions she had become a bonafide mermaid."

"That's ridiculous!...and why are you telling me this Marvin!?" Ira was mystified but continued listening intently as Marvin now had about him a strange and glassy-eyed look.

"Ridiculous! Ha! What you just told me is what is ridiculous! Next you will tell me you had visions of sugar plum fairies. Because Ira, as crazy as I was thinking, ridiculous as you call it, having almost drowned, then having these crazy visions about Mindy Parker and really thinking she was this real live, gorgeous mermaid, you didn't see me!"

Marvin wildly gesticulated using his arms "Me! Marvin Katz! good Jewish boy! jumping back into the lake and wanting to grow fins and gills so I could become Mindy Parker's fish lover did you!? Of course not! Why not!?…because I knew that one day, instead of a sea creature, I wanted to grow up and be a mensh!, an honorable and upright human being, not a crazy person and talking like you're talking now. That way, everyone could be proud of me. Up to two minutes ago you were also a mensh, then you tell me about your hallucination! vision! whatever? and now I am not so sure. But, if you forget this fantasy, who knows, maybe you can again be normal!"

Ira reflected once more, *this was really a bad idea.*

"I'm sorry Marvin. Obviously this is not something you wish to hear from me. But you asked me not to keep secrets from you and I thought, well that…that is why I thought that you should know."

"Ira…let me tell you something. Sometimes in our moments of desperation we think we hear or see things that really are not real. My seeing mermaids and thinking for example that Mindy Parker might really be one. And sometimes, maybe sometimes, we have secrets that maybe shouldn't be told. So maybe I was wrong Ira, about what I told you about keeping secrets. Especially since, in the first place, the secret you just told me is one I don't want to hear. And in the second place, I am not so thrilled you told me about it in the first place!" Ira saw the opportunity to end the discussion.

"Marvin…I have always known you to be a very wise man and maybe you have a point and I agree that maybe there are things that are best not talked about until another time." Marvin loudly shot back…

'Or maybe even never Ira! Did you ever think about that!?"

'Right…maybe never. And since you think I was just hallucinating, we will leave it there. Meanwhile, I know there are times when I know I don't always say the right things at the right time and because I have so much love and respect for you, maybe you are right and I will never speak to you of this again."

Marvin grinned sarcastically "Good! Now when you get to Arizona, the first thing you do is you go see a crazy doctor to rid yourself of visions of crosses and maybe even Tweedly-Dee and Tweedly-Dum. This way Sarah, your lovely wife does not have to worry about you like I am worried now. Meanwhile, I will be here in New York so I shouldn't have to worry so much anymore as she does. But unfortunately, she is forced to live with you. Now that this discussion has ended, I think we should all order dessert." Marvin picked up the menu and angrily buried his face in it.

The rest of the evening was contrived conversation but mostly silence. All four desperately wanting the evening to end quickly.

Once back at their apartment and in bed, Ira turned to Sarah. "Whew! I guess I still have a lot to learn" At first, Sarah was going to remind her husband about her warning earlier in the evening. But then recounting Marvin's reaction, recollecting Marvin's suggestion about how Ira should consider his becoming a donkey and the pained look about Marvin's face, she broke out in unstoppable laughter. Ira soon burst into laughter as well, then rolled over and fell across Sarah and into her arms where he soon fell asleep. As Sarah gently stroked the back of his head, her eyes misted. It was the first time Sarah had heard Ira laugh this hard in five years.

Chapter 26

March 17, 1950

"All aboard! Southwestern Limited . . . destination, points west!" the conductor shouted. Included in his list of cities was Phoenix, Arizona. For Sarah and Katalin it was all coming to a grand climax. A major chapter in each of their lives was about to end.

Prodigious Grand Central Terminal, described by one writer as "one of the grandest spaces the early twentieth century ever enclosed" was the site of departure for Ira, Sarah and their children. Opened in 1913, the world famous terminal now handled an estimated 550 trains a day. Today, March 17 and Saint Patrick's Day, to friends and family of the Katz's, 549 of those estimated trains would become irrelevant.
Marvin, Ruth and daughter Rachel, along with Paul and Katalin, had come to bid them farewell.

Watching his brother's suitcases being loaded on the train, Marvin grew quiet. He embraced Ira and freely shared how much he would miss him.

Marvin realized that it was not only his brother's companionship he would miss but that of his family. He sensed it most strongly three nights before when he told Ruth, "If Ira decided to stay and not move out to the *meshuggeneh* [crazy] desert, I would even let David-Jacob come to our house once a week and break a door hinge . . . maybe even a cheap vase. Surprisingly, he mentioned nothing about Ira's attempt to proselytize him. It seemed to no longer matter.

Ruth Katz was standing near Sarah and Katalin, taking charge of Joshua-Caleb until it was time for everyone to get on the train. She was both holding him in her hands and intermittently putting him down on his feet, watching him as he would toddle a few steps before invariably falling to his knees. He always seemed to fall near a strange piece of debris which he would attempt to put in his mouth. Ruth was brushing back tears from her eyes but was otherwise keeping a brave face.

Paul felt more awkward than the others. He too would miss Ira and Sarah but not to the extent of the rest. He felt his job was primarily to give moral support to Katalin, frequently putting his arms around her shoulders and squeezing her tightly.

When Ira wasn't talking to Marvin alone, he stood close by Sarah trying to offer her any strength he could. He agreed when Marvin described Sarah and Katalin as "emotional wrecks." The two had used up so much facial tissue it prompted Marvin to remark, "God forbid this train should be delayed an hour. I promise you, the first thing I'll do is call my broker and tell him to buy stock in Kleenex."

Seven-year-old David-Jacob had earlier done a disappearing act in the massive concourse but, before he was missed he had found his own way back. Using his own money, he had gone to purchase three giant size Hershey bars which he handed out to each of the three women. "Whenever I see Mommy crying, Daddy buys her candy and makes her feel all better," was his explanation.

Ten minutes later, upon seeing the women all crying again, a frustrated David-Jacob tugged on his father's shirtsleeve. "Bad idea, Daddy. A hundred candy bars wouldn't stop *them* from crying."

"Last call!" the conductor shouted as the locomotive began making *shooshing* sounds. Soon the family was aboard the Southwestern Limited, sitting next to one of the windows, waving and blowing kisses goodbye. Minutes later, the train pulled out of the station and part of everyone's world was a lot sadder.

The four adults and Rachel stood by the tracks a while longer, trying to console one another. Sarah would be coming back the end of May, bringing the children, and staying with Marvin and Ruth until after the wedding on June 16th. She would be Katalin's matron of honor and David-Jacob would be the ring-bearer.

Katalin shared with Marvin and Ruth that she and Paul would also likely move to the west coast in the not-too-distant future. Once they did, it would make seeing Ira, Sarah and the family a lot easier. But it wasn't the same and they all knew it. Nothing was going to ease the pain of this day except time.

Finally Marvin grew impatient, stating he had enough "crying in his beer" and jingled his car keys at Ruth. "King Kong beckons," an irritated Ruth said to Paul and Katalin. "We love you two. Keep in touch."

Walking out of the train station, Katalin sniffled, trying in vain to hold back her tears.

Paul smiled sympathetically. "I'm sorry, Katalin. I wish there was something I could do or say."

Katalin smiled bravely. "There is, Paul! I'm going to need a lot of love and a lot of attention from now on."

"Well, that's what I'm here for!"

Katalin threw her arms around him. "Yes," she said, her spirits lifting in anticipation of the days to come. "And God sent you just in time.

AUTHOR'S NOTE

A recent article in a messianic newspaper out of Israel, Jerusalem News and World Report, placed the estimated figure of Jewish Believers around the world at somewhere over 350,000. The number of messianic synagogues in the United States has now swelled to over 400.

If you wish to contact Ron, you may write him at:

Ron Benjamin
7850 N. Silverbell #114
PMB 154
Tucson, Arizona 85743